A SCI-FI BRIDGE ORIGINAL ANTHOLOGY

BRIDGE

ACROSS THE STARS

Edited by
Chris Pourteau and Rhett C. Bruno

Presented by

For Those Who, Today, Dream of Tomorrow

CONTENTS

FOREWORD TO THE COLLECTION

by Kevin J. Anderson

WHEN I WAS A KID, THE UNIVERSE OPENED UP FOR ME WITH thought-provoking and imaginative space adventures about colonies on other planets, alien intelligences, time travel, and mind-bending scientific inventions.

My real world was nowhere near as exciting. In fact, it was quite mundane, and I think I was the only dreamer for miles around. As a boy I lived in a speck-on-the-map small town in southeastern Wisconsin, not the sort of place that would inspire big thinking and lots of creativity. Sure, it was a charming laid-back environment straight out of a Norman Rockwell painting, with red barns and cornfields, where nobody locked their doors and where all of the neighbors were related to me somehow. Franksville, Wisconsin, was a place with absolutely no imagination, and no excitement.

Anyone who longed for adventure beyond the stars had to travel vicariously.

And that's where the library came in, with its science fiction section, which comprised the top half of one tall set of metal bookshelves. At the time, reading four entire shelves of books—each book sporting a little rocketship logo surrounded by an atom symbol—seemed a daunting task. Like the characters I watched on *Star Trek* (which my young imagination didn't think was nearly as good as *Lost in Space*, because it had more monsters), I decided to embark on a five-year mission "to boldly go where no man has gone before." Or at least where no kid in my town had gone before. I wanted to read *all* the science fiction, every book in the world (and surely my library had them all on that one set of shelves). Poul Anderson, Isaac Asimov, Ray Bradbury, Arthur C. Clarke—yes, I started at the beginning of the alphabet.

But even that was too slow a delivery system. I needed <u>more</u> science fiction. And faster.

I discovered that the way to get the most science fiction ideas delivered like a triple espresso was to read big SF anthologies. My small-town library had every volume of Nebula Award winners and an entire set of the Orbit anthology series edited by Damon Knight. But a lot of those stories were too artsy and esoteric for my 12-year-old tastes. I didn't know anything about the New Wave movement or experimental writing; I just wanted great stories. I was in the Age of Wonder.

Then I discovered the story collections of Ray Bradbury and Isaac Asimov. Asimov would take an idea and run with it. Bradbury blew my mind in collection after collection, *The Golden Apples of the Sun, The Illustrated Man, R Is for Rocket, S Is for Space, The Martian Chronicles.* Best of all, I discovered several giant SF anthologies edited by Groff Conklin: *A Treasury of Science Fiction, The Big Book of Science Fiction, Great Short Novels of Science Fiction.* These were massive tomes chock-full of adventures taken from the pages of the best pulp magazines—*Amazing Stories, Astounding Science Fiction, Thrilling Wonder Stories*—the true breeding ground of the genre.

During the summer when I was reading those anthologies, I might have slept in small-town Wisconsin, but my mind really lived in the wildest frontiers of space and time. That's when I really fell in love with short stories.

And it wouldn't do just to read them. I decided to start writing stories of my own and sending them to magazines. I began to get those published, nearly 150 of them so far.

Even though some of the magazines are still around, today's true breeding ground for the best short SF stories is in anthologies. And the most fertile land for new anthologies comes out of the indie presses. Some anthologies are assembled along traditional lines, such as those from my own WordFire Press, but others are more of a co-op venture with ambitious indie writers and publishers throwing a party with their imagination. *Bridge Across the Stars* is one such book.

Here, you'll find a wide selection of big SF stories, big ideas and big adventures written by well-established veterans such as Maya K. Bohnhoff and Will McIntosh to extremely successful Indie authors such as Lindsay Buroker, David VanDyke, Jason Anspach, Daniel Arenson, and Patty Jansen. You'll read great tales by emerging talents like Rhett C. Bruno, Craig Martelle, Chris Pourteau, Ann Christy, Chris Dietzel, David Bruns, Steve Beaulieu, Josi Russell, Lucas Bale, and Felix R. Savage. Turn your imaginations loose.

To find these great stories, you don't have to do your searching like I did. You have the stories right here in your hands. (But wouldn't it be cool if someone actually discovered this collection on a shelf in the science fiction section of a tiny, small-town library?)

Oh, one other thing about all those big anthologies that I read as a kid. I remember many of them had Forewords, where the editor talked about the stories themselves and his process in choosing them.

I never read the Forewords. I just dove right into the stories.

So what are you reading this for? Turn the page and get started on the real fiction!

ABOUT KEVIN J. ANDERSON

Kevin J. Anderson has published more than 140 books, 56 of which have been national or international bestsellers. He has written numerous novels in the Star Wars, X-Files, and Dune universes, as well as unique steampunk fantasy novels Clockwork Angels and Clockwork Lives, written with legendary rock drummer Neil Peart, based on the concept album by the band Rush. His original works include the Saga of Seven Suns series, the Terra Incognita fantasy trilogy, the Saga of Shadows trilogy, and his humorous horror series featuring Dan Shamble, Zombie PI. He has edited numerous anthologies, written comics and games, and the lyrics to two rock CDs. Anderson and his wife Rebecca Moesta are the publishers of WordFire Press: http://wordfirepress.com.

AS THE SPARKS FLY UPWARD

by David VanDyke

Yet mankind is born unto trouble, as the sparks fly upward.
Job 5:7

FIRST LIEUTENANT JOSEPH "BULL" BEN TAUROS, EARTHFLEET Marines, jerked upright in his bunk as the assault carrier *Melita's* General Quarters alarm shrieked. In droll counterpoint, its recorded voice calmly called all hands to battle stations. Adrenaline warred with sleep as Bull rolled to his feet and pulled on his combat underlayers with well-drilled motions. The smart cloth resisted shrapnel, spread heat, wicked sweat, compressed injuries and more, all in service to the battlesuits that kept every Fleet Marine alive.

As he dressed, Bull waited for more detail to come over the PA. Were they under sudden attack by Meme Empire ships? Was the carrier reacting to flash orders that would send her boosting for a rendezvous in battle? Or was it a no-notice drill?

It didn't matter. His actions were the same.

At least they were until the lights went out. A shock took his feet out from under him, and he found himself falling gently to the floor, a sure sign the gravplating had defaulted to emergency backup.

And a sure sign of severe damage to the ship.

Accessing his cybernetic chipset, Bull extended his optical implant's range up and down until the combination of UV and infrared gave him limited sight. He completed donning his equipment, keying his internal comlink as he did, hoping someone was up.

"I'm here, Bull," he heard his company first sergeant, Jill "Reaper" Repeth, reply, "but I can't reach the bridge. Aux-conn says the task force got jumped and the other ships have their hands full, so we're on our own."

"On my way to the armory," Bull said. He'd feel a lot better in a battlesuit.

"Meet you there."

In the passageways, dim emergency lighting gave plenty of illumination to his implanted eye. He smelled the telltale tang of combustion mixed with fire-suppression chemicals. Swabbies in damage control gear hurried past, using handholds or magnetic boots to assist their movements.

Bull did the same, and had almost reached the armory when his field of view shredded. Instinctively lifting his arms and squeezing his eyes shut, he felt a roaring wall of debris fling him backward, and he took a blow to the head.

A long moment later, he shook free of a half-ton of wreckage that would have pinned him if the gravplating had been operating at full. As it was, a strong, steady push left him standing free in a section of passageway, bruised and foggy-headed, but otherwise uninjured.

"Reaper?"

No answer.

He ran through channels. "Any station? Anyone?"

Nothing.

Dammit. Maybe it's my comms, or maybe there's nobody to reach.

A quick examination showed the corridor ahead to be hopeless. Something had punched deep into the ship, probably a hypervelocity penetrator, or *hyper*. The non-explosive living bullets were favorites of the alien Meme and their slave races—cheap, semi-smart, easy to gestate from local materials.

Bull tried to access the shipnet, but got no connection. He turned away and tried to find a route around to the armory. All the Marines' equipment was stored near the hull for maximum accessibility and proximity to the assault sleds—but not for easy damage control. Vital ship's systems occupied the prime real estate near the center of the wheel-shaped vessel.

And that protection didn't seem to have saved the ship. He could only hope the EarthFleet crew had control, and that the task force's combat vessels—missile frigates, destroyers, beam cruisers, and the fearsome, wedge-shaped armored battleship *Tokyo*—would be in better shape and come to *Melita*'s rescue.

Bull's inner ear alerted him to a drop in pressure, and he grabbed a breathing rig from an emergency cabinet and pulled it on. The lightweight, clear nanoplastic helmet mated to his skinsuit, creating a short-term spacesuit, while its two small air tanks on a back harness gave him a couple of hours of oxygen.

A tinny sound rattled through the passageway, and it took him a moment to realize he was hearing weapons fire—and the cries of the injured—muffled by the low pressure. Adrenaline flooded his system, and he instinctively enabled full cybernetic combat mode.

Combat? What the hell were people doing shooting? And Bull without a weapon. Or at least, a firearm. By the usual definitions, he *was* a weapon, if he could get close enough.

Swarming forward through the detritus of damage, he scanned for movement. As he rounded a corner, he saw a suited crewman backing up and intermittently discharging his fire extinguisher, creating a cloud of condensation.

The cloud fractured and split, showing lines of weapons fire reaching for the crewman. In response, the man clicked the tank to continuous blast and chucked it in the direction of his attacker, and then turned to run—or swim—away. He lifted his hands, startled upon encountering Bull.

"Who's shooting?" Bull barked, grabbing the man. His suit nametag read *Calvin.* "Spacer Calvin, report!"

"Sir, sir—it's one of us. She just started shooting!" Calvin struggled to get past Bull. "It must be a Meme infiltrator!"

Bull shook the man. "Focus, spacer! I need to get to the armory. Where's the nearest maintenance crawlway?"

Calvin pointed upward and back the way Bull had come. "There."

Bull hustled around the corner, dragging the crewman with him as projectiles *spanged* off the crysteel bulkheads. He spotted the hatch in the overhead, one of many maintenance access panels he normally paid no attention to.

"Hell," he said. "I can't get through there." At more than two meters tall and one hundred fifty kilos, Bull was the biggest man on the ship—a ship not designed for people his size. "You go. Try to reach the armory. Get weapons and ammo, and then come find me or any other Marines."

The man nodded and undogged the panel. In a moment, he'd vanished into the guts of the damaged ship, closing the hatch. Bull wondered whether the frightened man would do his job, or simply hide.

No matter. Bull crouched at the corner, readying himself. His enhanced hearing detected unhurried footsteps advancing toward him.

When the sound reached one meter's range, Bull surged upward and around the corner, reaching for the firearm he expected the infiltrator to hold. His textbook attack found a pulse rifle exactly where he anticipated. His right hand closed on it, wrenching it away while his left hand blurred, its edge slamming into the wielder's neck just below the jaw.

It takes a lot to break a human neck, and Bull had put more speed than power into the blow, so the target merely slumped slowly toward the deck. Bull had already thought of several reasons not to kill, beginning with his need for information and ending in the possibility that he—no, *she,* he saw—was just an ordinary woman, influenced by Meme biotech. Mind control, in other words, and it might be reversible.

Bull shuddered with the same visceral horror most humans felt when contemplating the amoeba-like Meme, their Blends, and their slave races. Better to die than be brainwashed and lose what made him human.

Fortunately, if given time, such a reprogrammed person could be cleansed of alien influence. So, Bull snagged the unconscious shooter and pulled her through the nearest door into a cramped enlisted quarters.

When he placed her on a bunk, he saw a fresh-faced, sweet young thing looking barely out of her teens. Then again, with the Eden Plague, everyone tended to look young.

Eight beds lined the small room, folded out from the side walls with a narrow passage between. No crew were present. They'd all be at their stations.

Bull had just strapped his prisoner tightly into the bunk using the acceleration webbing when another crash ripped through the ship's structure. Bull felt the shock in his bones. While he'd never experienced a ship die around him, in that moment he thought *Melita* might have taken a mortal wound ... and he still couldn't reach anyone on his comm implant.

Yet, the assault carrier was in open space. The crew would fight to save her, as would her sister ships. Right now, Bull had a different problem.

Klaxons rang again for a moment, and then died, leaving only an eerie silence. After a moment, Bull detected a faint hissing, and then a scraping *creak* as the compartment sealed itself. His inner ear adjusted, this time to slightly increased pressure. The telltale on the rig he wore showed just over one-half standard atmosphere, enough to breathe.

If the cabin had sealed itself, that meant no ventilation. He had the air in the tank, and his prisoner had whatever was in the room.

Bull was sorely tempted to force open the door and go back out, but there was no way to know what he'd find—and doing so might condemn the woman on the bunk to death. That was always an option, but for now, he needed information.

The crewwoman's standard coverall nametag read "Wang," though she looked more Caucasian than Chinese. An unusual case, or an alien mistake? Bull could imagine a cursory Meme study showing Wang to be the most common human surname on Earth, but mismatching ethnicities when they rewrote the woman's memories.

Bull searched the bunk storage drawers until he found a water bottle. After making sure it did actually contain water, he squirted a stream into Wang's face. The woman came to, lifting her head to stare fixedly at Bull.

"Why am I restrained?" she asked.

Bull gazed back without speaking. He found the woman's reaction interesting. He would have expected sputtering, cursing, protests, maybe spacers' jargon. Instead, this clinical attitude. He sat on the bunk opposite her.

"Have you captured me?"

Slowly, Bull nodded.

The woman laid her head down and stared upward at the bottom of the bunk above her. "I failed."

"Guess so." Bull sat back. So, Wang seemed to know she was an enemy. "What exactly was your mission?"

"I don't know."

"You tried to kill people. You may have succeeded. You were shooting up the passageways."

"I…"

Bull waited for long seconds. When it became apparent his captive wasn't going to answer further, he said, "Who are you?"

"Security Technician Third Class Jennifer Wang."

"When did you come aboard ship?"

"Sixteen days ago, at Triton."

"Before that?"

"I may not say."

"You *may* not. You mean, you're not allowed to?"

"Correct."

"By who?"

"By *whom*. Objective case, English language."

A chill went through Bull. He leaned forward and gripped his weapon tighter. The fresh face of youth, the odd mixture of knowledge and social naiveté… "You're a Pureling."

The woman turned her head away. "I don't know that word."

Bull forced himself to relax and chuckled grimly. "That damn near proves it. Every real human knows that word. It means you're a vat-grown clone, programmed with fake memories and infiltrated into EarthFleet."

"That would seem to make sense."

"And now you're my prisoner. I should kill you."

"I would prefer not to die."

Bull sat back. "Interesting. Why haven't you killed yourself?"

"Because I would prefer not to die."

"You said that. What I mean is, why are you being allowed to refuse? Purelings are compelled to kill themselves when captured, usually by using programmed biofeedback techniques to stop their hearts."

"I know nothing of that."

"What *do* you know?"

Wang wormed her right hand out through the netting, enough to free it from fingertips to elbow. She turned its palm to Bull. "I know I got this scar when a dog bit me as a child."

"As a child where? And when?"

"I don't know."

Bull leaned forward. "And I don't see a scar. Do you?"

The woman turned her hand. "No. But I feel it. I don't understand."

"The Eden Plague would heal all your scars—especially if it were years ago."

"It *is* strange."

"You're a Pureling. It must be a random scrap of memory. Something cut and pasted from the mind of a real human."

"I *am* a real human."

"I beg to differ, Pinocchio." Bull sighed, and tried his comms again. He hefted the pulse gun. "I should kill you."

"I prefer—"

"Yeah, I get it. That's the only reason you're not dead."

"You respect my preferences?"

"I don't murder prisoners of war."

"Why not?"

"My own moral code. It's not about you."

"Then I am human. You would murder an alien."

"I wouldn't *murder* anyone. I would kill you if I had to … but you're sentient." Bull remembered a Blend, an insectoid called Maydar, who had died trying to defect to EarthFleet.

"It is immoral to kill sentients?"

"It's immoral to *murder* them."

"What is the difference?"

Bull rubbed his neck and grimaced. He'd pulled a muscle, and sitting here didn't help. "Self-defense. If you try to kill me, I'm free to kill you."

"Then you may kill me now, though I do not prefer it. I tried to kill you."

"Yeah, no ... you don't understand. Now that you're helpless, I won't kill you. It would be murder."

"So murder is killing the helpless."

"Yes."

"What is the opposite of murder?"

"Ah ... saving, I guess. Rescuing. Giving your life so others can live. That's real humanity."

"Dying in place of another person is human?"

Bull nodded. "I'd say that's the ultimate expression of humanity."

"But that means killing makes one inhuman. Yet humans kill each other. This makes no sense."

"Ben zonah, you're like a child. Look, it's not always black and white, and I'm not the right guy to explain it." Bull sighed, running his eyes over her face. So young, so sweet ... but she'd been shooting people. At people, anyway. "You say you want to live. You say you're human. Humans shouldn't murder other humans."

"Humans have routinely murdered other humans for many millennia."

"Mostly we quit that when you aliens showed up."

"I am not alien."

"Well, you're not a woman."

"I am a human woman. I've seen you around the ship. I have feelings for you."

"For me?" Bull laughed. "You don't know me."

"The feelings are real."

Bull thought about his first crush, at the age of twelve, and the overwhelming ache of it. If Jennifer Wang were a Pureling, only recently decanted from a Meme cloning pod and programmed to mimic humanity, she'd never have experienced such intense emotions—until her adult hormones recognized a suitable male.

"Very flattering, but that only proves you're a sexual animal. It doesn't mean you're human."

"I want to be human. I could not abort my compulsion to attack the crew, but I resisted. I fired, but I hit no one. Do you really think I could not have killed crewman Calvin?"

"Maybe not. So you claim you tried not to kill them?"

"It did not seem right. As you say, I did not wish to murder, so I am human. I *am.*"

Bull shook his head ruefully. "Maybe you are. Mankind is born to trouble…"

Wang's lips curled in a wistful smile. "…as the sparks fly upward."

Bull's eyes narrowed. "Where did you hear that saying?"

"I do not know. Perhaps it is another piece of implanted memory. What does it mean?"

"It means, just as surely as the sparks rise from a fire, people will cause themselves problems."

"Not if they submit themselves to the Meme."

Bull snorted, half a laugh. "You think the Meme have no problems?"

"Only from those who resist."

"And resistance is futile, huh? Screw that."

"I do not understand."

"I'd rather have human problems than alien solutions."

Jennifer chewed on that one for a while. "So the saying counsels acceptance of trouble."

"That's one way to understand it. The saying is from Proverbs, a book of my people, written by King Solomon, said to be the wisest man who ever lived."

Her forehead furrowed in thought. "So it must have a deeper meaning."

"I was taught it's a caution against believing you can completely control a situation, and against the illusion of perfectibility."

"The Meme seek perfection."

"The Meme seek dominance, control, and stability. Not the same thing at all."

Wang folded her freed hand into her trapped one. "So to have problems is to be human."

"Yeah."

"That proves it, then. I must be human." Jennifer smiled and glanced down at her bindings. "I seem to have problems."

Bull felt a laugh bubble up in his throat. "You sure do, Miss Wang." He sobered. "We both do. We're stuck in a room with limited air, and I can't get ahold of anyone." Bull tried his comms again, to no avail. "If I force the door open, you'll die. I have only about eighty minutes of air left myself. I could start banging on the walls with metal, but I have no idea if that would attract friendlies or enemies. Protocol in this situation is to stand by and let search-and-rescue find us."

"Then our way ahead seems clear. We wait."

"For now." At some point, Bull would have to force open the door and try to find more air tanks, but he wasn't yet at that desperate point. Doing so would kill Wang.

For long minutes he tried to think his way through the problem, tried to come up with a way to keep Jennifer alive while he sallied forth. He began methodically going through all the storage compartments in the room, hoping for inspiration.

Most of what he found consisted of the personal possessions of the crew who bunked there. They'd taken their suits and breathing rigs when the alarm had sounded. He'd hoped to be able to MacGyver some clever solution out of available parts, but there simply wasn't anything of use for breathing.

Jennifer Wang watched him as he searched, but said nothing.

After he sat and thought some more, one option occurred to him. If he kept the nearly empty first tank on his breathing rig, now down to about ten minutes, and detached the second, full tank, he could give it to Jennifer before forcing his way out. The Pureling could release the air after Bull left and sealed the door. It would be wasteful and inefficient, but it would give Bull about ten minutes outside, ten minutes to find more air.

As he watched condensation running down the door and felt the cooling temperature in the room, he realized air wasn't their only problem. The damaged ship's heat was leaching away. And, the longer he waited, the more he used up the air supply in the short tank. The rig was simple, and didn't allow him to transfer air from one tank to another. It had two bottles to allow one to remain in place while the other was swapped out.

Bull stood. "Okay, Miss Wang, you say you don't want to die."

"That is correct."

"Have you given up on trying to kill people?"

"I will not murder anyone. I am human."

"Good." Bull released the netting and motioned Jennifer out of the bunk. She took his hand and held onto it as a child or a lover might, until he peeled it away self-consciously. Any feelings she had for him—or he had for her, if he didn't guard against them—were irrelevant right now.

Even if her body was adult, her mind and emotions seemed those of a bare adolescent.

He turned his body mostly away from the Pureling, but gripped his pulse rifle tight and kept his senses alert, watching over his shoulder for treachery. "One of those air bottles will show full. Take it off the rig. When I leave the room, I'll dog the door tight. Open the tank and you'll have air. I'll try to find more oxygen and contact rescue. You just sit tight."

"I prefer to stand."

"Then stand over there, out of the way." Bull pointed to the back wall. "Don't hold your breath. It will rush out when the pressure drops. Just remain calm and open your bottle when the door shuts. Ready?"

Jennifer hefted the bottle, hand on the valve. "I am ready."

"Here I go." Bull rotated the dogging handle and set himself, pulling slowly but inexorably against the air pressure, exerting his entire cybernetic strength. There came a prolonged rushing sound, and he felt the air depart the room at the crack between the door and the jamb.

As soon as possible, he opened the door and slipped through, pulling it shut behind him and dogging it. His smart suit constricted and the clear flexible plastic of his breathing rig inflated tight against the vacuum. Inside the room, Jennifer should be refilling the space with air, air for perhaps an hour at most ... probably less.

Now it was up to him.

Turning, he switched on his rig's headlamp and surveyed the cold wreckage around him. To the left, debris filled the passageway. To the right it looked clearer, so he headed that direction. Bull picked his way carefully through, alert for attackers, and also for sharp edges that might cut his suit.

Light flickered ahead in the airless silence. He rounded a corner to see the backs of two suited crew, firing weapons away from him. Another lay unmoving on the deck, sliced open by laser fire.

Bull debated for just a moment. What if these were Purelings rather than real crew? How could he tell? This was always the problem with Meme infiltration.

The suits decided it. Jennifer Wang hadn't been in a pressure suit, probably because when her programming tripped, she was supposed to do as much damage as possible, as fast as possible, and then be killed. Putting on a suit would waste precious time, and suits were clumsy.

But with the ship wrecked and the passageways in vacuum, who were the enemy the crew were fighting?

Have to play the odds, Bull told himself. He moved forward to the corner and stood above the defenders, who crouched below. His height allowed him to take a half-covered position above them. He leaned out slightly for just long enough to let his optical implant grab an image of what was beyond, and then pulled back as he examined it.

He saw a maintenance bot—really a telefactor no doubt controlled by a Pureling tech nearby—wielding a heavy cutting laser. A moment later it flashed green and one of the crew jerked back, his exposed arm holed.

The laser would need a few seconds to recharge. Bull immediately leaned out with his pulse rifle. Cyber-optics connected to his hardwired nerves allowed him near-perfect accuracy with his weapon, and he laid his aim point on the bot's communications node. A burst blew it apart, and the robot froze, now offline.

Bull rushed forward and wrenched the laser off the thing's arm, detaching it from its power pack just in case. He then returned to help the crew.

The uninjured one, a woman, was treating the other crewman with the wounded arm. Bull tried his comm, but still couldn't raise anyone. He put his head against the uninjured woman's helmet to transmit his voice. "What do you know?" he yelled. "Report!"

Her reply was tinny as she shouted back. "Sir, we were winning until those hypers slammed into us. Then all hell broke loose, and we ran into that bot, so I have no idea."

Bull clapped her shoulder. "Let's get this man to the infirmary. You carry him, I'll lead." The low gravity would make pulling the wounded man along easy. He didn't wait for her reply, but made his way past the broken bot and down the passage.

He came to a ladder leading upward, toward the infirmary. He climbed it effortlessly. The hatch at the top was closed, of course, dogged automatically as separate sections were sealed against breaches.

The mechanism would allow it to swing either way, out or in. Letting it swing out, toward himself, would make opening it easy, but closing it very difficult if the other side were under pressure—and vice versa. He decided to push it inward.

Once he undogged it, he used the manual operation lever and his strength to force it away from him slightly. A hiss of air proved the other side to be pressurized. He slung his weapon and turned to wave at the crewwoman, signaling her to pass the injured man to him.

With one hand grasping the injured man, he placed the other on the lever and gave it a powerful push. The door opened with a rush of air toward him, and Bull launched the man upward through it, then reached down to grab the woman. She was already moving. All he had to do was push her against the airflow and then follow her through. Once inside, he let the hatch slam shut and dogged it again.

The barrel of a pulse rifle greeted him, held by a battlesuited Marine, and he spread his hands. "Lieutenant ben Tauros," he bellowed through the muffling layer of the breathing rig.

The rifle was already dropping to show Gunnery Sergeant Kang's insignia and name behind it. "Good to see you, sir," the NCO said through his open faceplate. "We have most of the ship secure from the attackers, but she's in bad shape."

The crewwoman towed her comrade past the two Marines, toward the infirmary. Bull let her go. She didn't need his assistance anymore, and he had his own job to do. "Can I get to the armory? I feel naked without a battlesuit."

Gunny Kang shook his head. "Doubtful. Reaper and I and a handful of Marines barely got our suits on when the ship got hit. One of the other armories might be intact, but I doubt any suits will fit you, sir."

"Right." Battlesuits were customized to their wearers, but the spares could theoretically be operated by anyone— anyone that could fit in them, that was. He wished he had the luxury of a spare in his size, but war materiel was always in short supply, even for frontline Fleet Marines. "You got comms? I can't seem to raise anyone."

Kang slapped his helmet. "Yes, sir. Ultra-wideband is functional, but the HUD system's having trouble updating and passing data with all this damage. Reaper's got a scratch squad finishing off the last resistance."

"Captain Morehead?"

"No contact, sir. Might be KIA."

"Bridge? Aux-conn?"

"Aux-conn is coordinating."

"Fleet SITREP?"

"Winning the engagement, though with severe casualties. Some kind of stealth ambush, but no details. My gut tells me if we get through the next hour, we'll be okay."

"The next hour…" Bull checked his chrono. Twenty minutes since he'd left Jennifer Wang stuck in the bunkroom. The Pureling should be all right, but it was remarkable that Bull hadn't run out of air yet. He was sure he'd only had about ten minutes.

He unsealed his clear flexible helmet, taking a deep breath of ship's air. It smelled of metal and burnt plastic, but it refreshed him anyway. He then shrugged out of the harness that held the air supply on his back. "I need a couple of full bottles. This one's gotta be empty…"

Bull trailed off in confusion as he looked at the air tank's gauge. Forty minutes of air remained. That was impossible. Unless… He felt the color drain from his face and fear seize him. "Oh, *shit!*"

"What, sir?"

"Get a breathing rig or a spare suit and two extra bottles, now! And follow me!" Bull pulled the rig back on and sealed it.

Kang scrambled to find the gear while Bull readied the hatch for opening. When Kang came back with a sack, Bull popped the seal and yanked the hatch open, waving for Kang to go through first. That allowed the armored Marine to take point security and left Bull free to shut and dog the hatch. Then he took the sack from Kang.

Using standard combat hand signals, Bull directed Kang toward the bunkroom. They didn't encounter any resistance, and soon reached the door. Bull opened the sack and took out a breathing rig, checking to make sure it could be activated with the flip of a switch. He then undogged the door, slamming his shoulder into it to pop it open, knowing as soon as he did, all the air in the room would vanish and he'd have to help get the rig onto Jennifer so she could breathe.

The door flew open and far less air than Bull hoped rushed out … as little air as he feared. Jennifer lay in one bunk, eyes closed and a faint smile on her face, the empty air bottle she'd taken from Bull's rig clutched to her chest.

The bottle that should have contained an hour's air when she took it.

But Bull's bottle still showed forty minutes left.

Which meant that Jennifer had deliberately taken the near-empty one, and when she'd opened it after Bull left, she'd had no more than ten minutes to breathe, if that.

Why the hell had she done it?

Jennifer wasn't breathing, and her face was pale and bluish. Bull fitted the rig onto the woman, activated it and began an awkward CPR sequence. "Give her a battle-stim!" Bull barked, forgetting that no sound carried in vacuum. He showed Kang the hand signal for medical assistance and mimed injection with one hand, the other continuing the chest compressions.

Kang popped open his drug module and injected the motionless woman with a battle-stim, and then shut the door and cracked the valve on an air tank. Air flooded the room and Bull's ears popped, and for another ten minutes he worked on Jennifer. "Come on. Come on!" he recited, over and over.

But it was clearly too late. There was no sign of life. Even the Eden Plague couldn't overcome total lack of oxygen and cell death.

Bull sat back and wept, gasping.

Kang turned away.

Bull shook his head awkwardly to clear his eyes, and then peeled open his helmet to wipe them with the back of his hand. "Dammit. Why did she do it?"

Kang's harsh voice was uncharacteristically gentle. "Do what, sir?"

Bull waved vaguely, as if at flies. "Against my orders, she took the empty bottle. She left me with all the air."

Kang sketched a salute. "Then she was a hero, sir. She sacrificed her life for you. She was EarthFleet."

"She wasn't EarthFleet."

"Sir?"

"She was a Pureling." Bull reached over to close her eyes.

Kang didn't reply for a long moment. "I don't understand."

Bull picked up Jennifer's air bottle and turned it until he could see something written on it in large block letters. She must have found a marker. "I don't understand either, but she did. Better than most, I think."

He handed the bottle to Kang, who read the words aloud.

"I am human."

ABOUT DAVID VANDYKE

If you enjoyed this Plague Wars/Stellar Conquest short story, check out the full series at http://www.davidvandykeauthor.com/plague-wars-series, or connect with him on Facebook at https://www.facebook.com/AuthorDavidVanDyke.

David VanDyke is a Hugo Award and Dragon Award finalist and bestselling author of the Plague Wars, Stellar Conquest, and Galactic Liberation Sci-Fi adventure series, which have sold more than 300,000 copies to date. He is co-author of BV Larson's million-selling Star Force Series, Books 10, 11 and 12. He's a retired U.S. military officer, veteran of two branches of the armed forces, and has served in several combat zones. He lives with his wife and dogs near Tucson, Arizona.

PEACE FORCE

by Ann Christy

One

"How long?" The old woman says when she finally lifts into consciousness.

"A long time. Take it slow."

The old woman looks up at the person and sees a caring face. She's too blurry to make out details, but the old woman's vision will clear. It always does.

"How long?" she repeats, her voice a creaking rasp.

"Two hundred-thirty years, Director Swanson," the sweet-faced, younger woman answers.

Her arm tingles when she lifts it to her forehead. Soon the tingles will become pain, but that too will pass. "So long."

"Let me help you," the younger woman says, slipping an arm around the Director to take her weight.

The helper is stronger than she looks. There's not a hint of effort as she lifts her charge into a sitting position. Director Swanson tries to look around the room as she rises free from the cryo-couch's sides, but the blur prevents her seeing more than a room with too much white in it. A hospital room? It's certainly not the room she went to sleep in. A lumpy bit of gray moves along a distant wall.

"Who are you?" she asks the human-shaped lump.

"Director Swanson, I'm Facilitator Gray."

The director chuckles at the appropriate name; a gray swath is someone named Gray. How funny.

"Come closer so I can see you. And don't call me that or else I'll feel old. Just call me Swanson. I like that better."

The form approaches, resolving into another woman, though one of such angular slenderness that she barely registers as that gender. "As you wish," Gray says, inclining her head.

The pain begins and Swanson tries to hide a grimace. It's always like this. Numbness replaced by tingling replaced by a searing pain. It shoots down each limb like lightning. But after the pain passes she will feel herself again, so it's not worth acknowledging. Everyone must deal with pain sometimes.

"Healer Four-Alpha, is there something wrong with her?" Gray asks.

Swanson eyes the Facilitator. Gray's voice is strangely without compassion or emotion, as if Swanson were a machine with a glitch rather than a human waking from a too-long cryo-sleep. And that name. Who calls another person Four-Alpha? More changes?

The Healer leans down to look at Swanson's face. Unlike Gray, her expression is exactly what one would expect from a good nurse. She smiles and attaches a small patch to the back of Swanson's thin-skinned hand, then looks at a display next to the cryo-couch.

"No, Facilitator Gray. This is entirely normal for such a waking. She's in pain, but it will pass. She's awakened seventeen times before, however, and each will be more difficult than the last."

The Facilitator nods, satisfied, then stands still to wait.

Swanson has been asleep a long time, but all this is very strange and not what she expected. The Facilitator Class was designed to be efficient and less emotionally driven, but this one seems almost *too* cool. "What's wrong with you? You're a very odd duck," she says.

A flash of confusion crosses the angular face, which is actually a relief. At least Swanson can be sure Gray is human. Well, she can be *almost* sure. That certainty evaporates when the Facilitator answers her.

"I'm not a duck. I'm a Facilitator."

With a snort, Swanson holds out her hand for the Healer. "Help me up. I need to stab that thing to be sure it bleeds. Got anything sharp?"

Even Gray looks alarmed at those words. The Healer merely pushes the medical cart a little further away from Swanson with her foot. It's done very discreetly, but Swanson laughs anyway.

"Why would you want to make sure I bleed?" Gray asks.

"Because I want to deal with a human and you're like a ghoul, maybe a robot or something."

"I'm human. I assure you. There's no need to stab me."

The delivery is so deadpan that Swanson can only shake her head. "Whatever." Now that she's standing, she finally notices that hers is the only cryo-couch in the room. "Where are the others?" she asks.

The Healer still grips her hand and places her other hand securely on Swanson's back to help her take her first steps in over two centuries. Swanson watches the Healer carefully as she answers. "Gone. The Humanity Directors made their final decisions. Of your group, the Peace Force

Directors, you are the last. Director Glenn went into the virtual world and Director Taylor died during his last revival."

This is surprising news, and also sobering. Swanson realizes she is now alone, the sole decision maker left in the entire human race. Her body seems to come alive with adrenaline. She hadn't expected to be the last. Surely, out of the eight Director types, the Humanity Directors would have been last. Shouldn't they be tweaking these final humans until the last moment? Glancing at Gray, Swanson can't help but wonder if the Humanity Directors hadn't tweaked too much.

Gray is still watching her with complete calm, an unsettling lack of interest in her halting steps or the old body in front of her. Swanson asks, "Why did you let Glenn go into the Virtual?"

"I did not," Gray says without missing a beat. "That was my predecessor. The reason was logical, however. Director Glenn would not have survived another cryo-sleep."

Quite suddenly, everything comes together. Swanson's DNA imprint was chosen for this job because she would be smart and quick. And she was, usually seeing all the angles before anyone else at the table. This moment was no exception.

"Ah, I see," she says, then glances at the Healer still preventing her from keeling over on wasted limbs. No matter how brilliant the cryo-sleep technology, there was always some residual effect and the length of sleep she'd just endured had never been intended.

The Healer lacks subtlety, but at least she seems to care, thought Swanson. "Facilitator, this is not seemly."

Gray answers in that same deadpan manner. "The truth is always correct."

With a roll of her eyes, Swanson eases her hand from the Healer's and faces Gray, standing as straight as she's able to. "Well, you're at least true to your design. Let me be sure

I understand. You waited so long to wake me because you believe I will not be able to sleep again. Is this correct?"

"Yes."

"And that means you need a decision maker. A *final* decision. Correct?"

"Yes, Swanson. This is correct. Or we will need your authorization to create another Director if a decision is not yet deemed wise."

A ghost of a smile touches Swanson's lips. All these centuries and now, it's time. Finally. "That means we're finally done. At last. Let's make some decisions then, shall we?"

Two

Swanson feels good, or at least as good as someone of her normal biological age should feel. The effects of her long cryo-sleep have either worn off or been pushed away by good medicine and excellent care. The Healers are marvelous. She sips a cup of hot tea as she reads yet another of the reports that have piled up during her latest, long absence.

The room around her feels empty, and it's distracting. The Director's Conference Hall was meant to hold all the Directors from all eight lines while they worked. Each line was tasked with decisions in one area. The Humanity Directors worked on putting the last biological humans into the virtual worlds, then with tweaking the Facilitators and Healers—well, their Loaded Strands—so they would have humans perfectly suited to tending the virtual worlds. The Nature Directors repaired the planet and repopulated it with animals either recreated from historical samples or bred from existing members. The Infrastructure Directors, the Space Directors … and all the rest … had their tasks. So many generations of them had been born, learned their trade, then faded for the next in their line.

Only when their Final Decision was made, and their tasks confirmed complete, could they join the other Directors in the Virtual and have no more Directors in that line decanted to continue the work.

It was strange to be the last. Swanson had never expected it, so she hadn't prepared herself for this feeling. Shaking her head to get rid of the strange sense of isolation, she returns to the report in front of her.

It's yet another of the bad ones. Making a face at the horrific details collected from the quantum buoys, she sips again, but this time, there is a bitter aftertaste. It isn't from the tea really, but rather from the evil transmitted back to Earth with such ease. The ones who created the Seed ships had much to answer for. And they would have answered, had they still been alive. Perhaps it's good that the virtual worlds came into being long after those responsible for the atrocities born from those first colony ships had passed into history.

Her eyes flick to the side. Facilitator Gray is sitting with unnatural stillness at the table to her left. At least Gray's no longer staring at her. With a snort of disgust, Swanson lowers the tablet and says, "You really will sit there all day, won't you?"

Gray meets her gaze with perfect equanimity. "Of course. It's my duty."

The label on the report Swanson's just read tells her it's number thirteen out of sixty-four. She narrows her eyes at the tablet, then asks, "And all of those reports are bad? All aberrant?"

Tilting her head the tiniest bit, Gray says, "Most of them. But we don't receive all reports anymore. Decay or breakage has cut some of the buoy communications."

Her teacup rattles a little in the saucer as Swanson sets it down. The shakes are still there. "But this last one here was a report from a planet in progress. They hadn't even gotten the world habitable yet. They have some sort of slave situation, yet they've barely begun their work. How could things go so wrong so quickly?"

Gray's shrug is awkward, as if she were unaccustomed to such gestures. "We're not sure, and there's no way to find out. The Seed ships were entirely divorced from our data streams prior to launch to protect their integrity. Nothing of their design or specific protocols was left on Earth—to prevent us from interfering in the future. Unfortunately, that also means we can't correct our errors. There is…"

Swanson waits for Gray to continue, but she doesn't, merely looking uncomfortable in her seat. "Well, what is it?"

"It is possible that one line of the ships has been corrupted from the beginning."

"One line? Explain."

When Gray begins to speak again, Swanson can see that stating facts eases Gray, makes her more comfortable. It's hard not to wonder if perhaps they hadn't gone too far in designing the Facilitator class. Perhaps they should have left more people skills in place.

"Director, as you know, there were two Seed ships initially. Each would go to a different planet already determined to be a good candidate, confirm that data, and then replicate themselves using locally sourced materials. Then they launched their replicated ship toward the next candidate—which was determined during the replication phase—and only then begin the terraforming process. All the while, they expanded themselves into their final state, complete with all the facilities required for the long terraforming process. Only when all that initial work was done did they decant the first wave of Loaded Strands—the scientists and engineers—to confirm and guide the work planetside. You know all this?"

Waving her hand for Gray to get to the point, she answers, "Yes, of course."

"Well, the number designation for each ship is coded so no one on Earth would ever know exactly where the ships are located or which ship line they were created from. Again, it was done to prevent interference by Earth at some future date. The numbering system almost seems random."

Understanding now where Gray is heading, Swanson says, "But it's *not* truly random."

A hint of a smile lifts Gray's angular features. "No. We deciphered the code. In most cases, the corruptions appear to be from the line of the first Seed ship. There are two—both probably caused by planetary disasters after colonization—that we link to the second ship, but none during development. The slavery issue you just read about takes place on approximately half the ships in the first Seed line. This cannot be coincidence. It is likely a shared flaw in the code across that first line of ships."

Swanson takes up her teacup again and sips, considering all the ramifications. "Well, that does make the initial tracking easier in some ways. If our Peace Forces can catch up to the ships of the second line, then they can wipe out the problem once and for all."

Gray gives another of those noncommittal nods.

"What?"

"We believe that the original plan may be somewhat shortsighted."

Again, the teacup clatters into the dish, but this time, it is the pricking of her pride that shakes her fingers. "How so? You do realize we've been planning this since before I was even born. Before my mentor or even his mentor was born. Thousands of years of cryo-sleeping Directors have planned this down to the nanite."

"Director—" At her glare, Gray corrects herself. "Swanson, I don't mean to counter any plans, because the plans are perfection. It is only the additional information that calls for some alterations. I did note the two aberrant systems.

In each case their social constructs changed in unacceptable ways after planetary disaster. Please observe."

With that, Gray waves and a display lights up centered over the big table. "This is what we were able to reconstruct from the data we received from the quantum buoys. The stream was somewhat corrupted."

On the display, a small girl no more than a handful of years old is strapped to a T-brace, every part of her that can move secured by wide, dark straps. The brace is tilted a little and without any preamble, a man wearing a hood and little more than a loincloth steps up and swings an axe. First one arm and then the other are severed under the power of two quick blows. Very quickly, another man comes forward and slaps handfuls of black goo onto the girl's bleeding stumps, then sets them alight with a torch.

While Swanson's hand comes up to cover her mouth at the horror, the girl barely moves. When she is lifted from the brace and turned around, Swanson sees that her mouth is gagged and her eyes closed, but the little girl's chest hitches with uneven breaths.

"Turn it off! Turn it off! How dare you show me this monstrosity!"

The display disappears with another wave of Gray's hand, but she seems entirely unaffected by the horrors they have both just witnessed. Wisely, the Facilitator says nothing and waits for the older woman.

Regaining her composure by reminding herself that this happened long ago and far away, Swanson swallows down the bile that has risen in her throat. "And the other? I don't wish to see it—only tell me."

"It is the opposite of this, but equally brutal. All save three percent of males are killed at birth. The rest are kept for breeding."

This is terrible. Too terrible. Swanson slides an elbow onto the table so that she can rest her forehead in her hand.

Her head has suddenly become so very heavy. She understands what Gray is saying even without saying it. Still, she must have it confirmed.

"And you're sure these atrocities happened after planetary disasters?"

"That is correct. In both instances. The one from the video is from a planet that had the terraforming process well underway and nearly five thousand Strands on the planet. No Loaded Strands, of course, since they maintain memories of their original life on Earth. Only Strands that started as infants without memories can become colonists. Previous reports indicated all was well and breeding was proceeding on the surface. An asteroid impact soured their land and within a few years, the beginnings of this system were evident. That girl was to be a Voice; a female who can speak. Most females are Hands, which means they work, but have their vocal cords removed."

Anger courses through Swanson's stiffening limbs. It is this kind of brutality on Earth that made humans create the Seed ships in the first place. The ships were meant to give them a chance to develop without strife or war, without struggle, on new worlds untainted by humanity's savage history. They were meant to make us better, to help us evolve as a species.

That has clearly not happened.

"Well, then, I know the first place the Peace Force should go," she says through gritted teeth.

Gray sighs a little, a strangely human gesture from someone almost entirely divorced from emotion. "While we have made strides in understanding the numbering of the Seed ships, we will not experience those same successes with the planets. Their numbering is truly random. Only the Seed ships know those locations so they know which planets have already been taken. We do not and will never know where that planet is."

Squeezing her eyes shut at the memory of that footage, Swanson says, "But the advances in sensors on the new ships…"

"Yes, they will help. Eventually, the Peace Force will find them."

"Eventually," Swanson sighs.

Three

The horrors of a few days before are almost forgotten as she flies over the land. Looking down at the plain, Swanson can't help the smile that transforms her face. The Earth has become perfection. Beauty at its highest point.

"All is going well?" she asks Gray, who sits next to her in the small airship as it hovers over the only place in the world left for normal humans … except they're not humans anymore. Rather, they are now digital humans inside a digital universe.

"Perfectly," Gray answers, eyeing the structures in the center of the plain with cool eyes.

With a scowl, Swanson turns to the Facilitator. "Details, please."

"As you wish, Dir … Swanson. The virtual worlds have had no problems. Currently, there are nineteen inhabited planets … virtual ones, of course. Expansion has been limited and sufficient barriers are in place to maintain the challenge. There are three hundred conflicts ranging from open war to small, localized skirmishes. At the moment, there are two pandemics and six limited epidemics. On Earth Prime, there is a political battle consuming the populace."

Swanson raises an eyebrow at that. "Really? Political battle?"

Gray nods. "Yes. Ennui was setting in at some locations, so we switched out candidates and put a highly unstable leader in place. We are seeing a significant uptick in cohesion in individual human data-prints. As you know, ennui or too much peace brings degradation of the system and cause individual human data-prints to fragment."

Her lips twist at that news. Swanson, like all the Directors before her, must remain biological, only going into the Virtual at the end of her physical existence. Most humans are born only as digital forms in the virtual worlds. They never suffer the indignities she suffers now as an old woman. Not truly. While they age or get sick, and eventually die inside the Virtual, even those things are made less awful than they are in the real world. Suffering is attenuated.

The only truly natural humans remaining are the Director class. They are decanted from unaltered Strands as babies and learn their duties at the knees of the previous Directors. It is only now, as the project nears its end, that no new Directors are decanted.

Soon, there will be only altered Strands left in biological form, DNA imprints altered so much that they serve only the purpose they were made for. Facilitators to protect the facility that houses all the billions of humans in their electronic forms and a few Healers to tend the Facilitators and oversee decanting new Facilitators. That's all. The rest will enjoy the Virtual, which contains worlds without limit.

Heaven. Yet also hell sometimes, it seems.

The Director can barely wait to join the rest of her kind. Soon.

An irregularity in the perfectly concentric circles surrounding the black dome catches her eye. Swanson points to it. "What happened there?"

"A minor problem that will be corrected soon. Giant sloths upset one of the power receivers. It happens sometimes. We have more than sufficient power. They would have to upset a great many receivers before we had problems."

"Does this happen often?"

Gray inclines her head a little, then says, "Often enough. Do you see there? The tiny spot of white? No, just there."

"Oh, yes, I see what you mean. What is it?"

"Wolves got to that one."

"Wolves?"

"Yes. And over there, the small patch of brown at the perimeter?"

"Yes. It looks like freshly turned earth."

Gray nods. "Exactly so. Some burrowing animal gnawed through the subterranean lines there. We're not sure what species, since the animal was gone before we got there."

Swanson's brows draw together, another of those tickling sensations crawling up her back. "Do you mean it simply gnawed through the lines and then went away. Just like that? Before you could get there?"

There's no hint of any underlying uncertainty in Gray, only the matter-of-factness built into her genetic code. "Yes, just so."

"And you don't find that odd?"

Gray's eyes are without emotion or concern, and that concerns Swanson. "No. They are animals. We cannot know their motivations."

Looking back upon the perfection that is all of humanity, a single black dome housing an entire galaxy within the databank of one computer, Swanson is struck by a memory. It's an old one, from when she was young and learning to be a Director from her mentor. Director Tyrell had already been old then, but he'd laughed with abandon and was always kind to her. He'd once said that the world had not forgiven humanity its trespasses. He'd said that even though we took very little from the world now, it would someday shake humans off like a dog shakes off fleas.

At the time, she'd merely laughed at the notion of the Earth having a long memory. Glancing at that spot of freshly turned earth and wondering if the animals had expressed the planet's frustrations through their actions, she wishes she hadn't laughed then. She wonders what else the Earth might choose to exact its revenge upon.

"Gray, do the Facilitators still maintain a data backup for us?"

Gray nods. "Of course."

Swanson turns away from the plain and toward Gray's seat. "You should consider moving it to the moon."

The Facilitator waves and the little airship darts back in the direction of the Director's hall. "That seems a misuse of resources. We're quite fine here, Director. And that final decision was made a long time ago by the Humanity Director. We can't change it now."

Expelling a short, bitter sounding breath, Swanson leans back in the comfortable seat and closes her eyes. Gray can't understand. Perhaps that's better in the long run. Someday, perhaps someday soon, the flea that is humanity will be shaken off. The Earth has a long memory, after all, it seems.

Living forever in the virtual worlds never did sound all that appealing to Swanson. As long as the Peace Force is completed and sent on their way, she'll be satisfied. Anything beyond that is extra.

Four

"Swanson, are you alright? Do you need assistance?" Gray asks.

They've just docked with the Peace Force ship in orbit, and the trip up was far more difficult than Swanson remembered it being. Of course, the last time she was up here was about three hundred years ago, when the ships weren't nearly this big or imposing. Time is playing havoc with her.

Pushing Gray's hand away, Swanson levers herself up from the couch and flings the straps back. There's a jarring clatter of metal on metal. "I'm perfectly fine, thank you."

Gray stands still as always, waiting for Swanson to tidy her clothes and regain her steadiness. Swanson again feels that urge to stab Gray and see if she's truly organic. Instead, she takes a deep breath to push away the annoyance and smooths back her short, gray hair.

"Lead on."

Swanson read all the briefs and even watched some of the videos prepared for her, but seeing the giant vessel with her own eyes is another thing altogether. The ships are so large, so incredibly present. As they'd approached the landing bay, it was all she could do not to jump from her couch and run to the window, craning her neck to see it all at once.

When they get through the airlock and are met by the ship's Captain and the commander of the troops for this vessel, the shock is intensified. It's one thing to read the averages of height and weight of this time's personnel, it's another thing to meet them in person.

The Captain is personable and what the Director would call average. Nothing too extraordinary about her, but then again, the Captain will never fight a battle with her body. She'll fight using the ship if it comes to that.

The troop commander—the General—is another matter entirely. She's a monster. Towering over the Director by a foot or more, she must weigh nearly twice what Swanson weighs, maybe more. Her muscles are ridiculous, and her mouth and lips are covered in scars.

While touring the ship, Swanson grows ever more unsettled. Given the hardiness of the X chromosome and the ability to alter it more significantly without causing failure, it's no wonder that they finally settled on an all-female crew, but it's still strange to see it. Directors are always male, then female, then male again … and so on down the lines. In real life, altered humans are almost always female. It makes Swanson feel like the odd one out in a way. What is she compared to these competent people?

And after seeing that video of the horrific planet and that little girl, she has to wonder if they're creating the beginning of such a thing all over again, right here and now.

Swanson is jerked from her musings by the General's shout. "Hey you, Douchebag! Did you sandpaper those boots or are you just a lazy twat?"

Shaking her head at the archaic insults, Swanson looks at the trooper receiving them. She's huge, like the General, and squatting in a clear area in front of an opening with a sign above it that reads *Suit Preparation*. The woman laughs, then salutes and shouts back, "I am a lazy twat, sir! I will correct that immediately!"

The Captain nudges the General and grins. "She's the one doing the suit demo?"

Nodding, the General shouts to the trooper, "No, you won't. You'll do the demo, then you'll correct yourself. But you better make me proud in there!"

Standing taller and straighter, the trooper's smile is replaced with stony determination, and even Swanson can see the pride there. "I will make you proud, sir!"

The tour is long, though it might have been shorter had Swanson not been so old and frail. Many of the troopers, technicians, and administrators give her side-eyed glances. They've probably never seen an old person before, so she doesn't take it personally.

They take a break—again, mostly for her—in the General's conference room. Supposedly meant to give her time to ask questions and make decisions, Swanson decides its true purpose is likely to make sure she doesn't keel over before achieving her purpose. The food is good, if somewhat uniform in texture and shape. The tea, on the other hand, is excellent.

"Well, Director Swanson, what do you think of our little crew?" the General asks. Her surname is Bravo, because she is the overall leader of the troops stationed onboard the second ship, but Swanson can't bring herself to use it. It sounds silly.

Putting down her fork, she says, "I'm amazed. The additional generations requested during my last visit seem to have paid off. They are ideal forms. And everyone is stable? All the Strands can be replicated reliably?"

With a pleased nod, the General says, "Absolutely consistent. Though if you want to talk details, I'll need to get an Administrator in here. As you know, I'm a Military Class Strand myself."

"Of course, of course. No need for that. I've already had a long video conference with Administrator Alpha, from ship … *umm* … Alpha. I merely wanted your impressions as their leader."

"Oh, well then. You have a yes vote from me. My troopers are the best there ever was. Loyal, strong, smart. You just can't beat them."

With a small smile, Swanson says, "Let's hope so."

Both the General and the Captain laugh at that, big laughs that bounce off the walls in the spartanly furnished room. Before they can continue, the door slides open and the trim form of an Administrator enters.

She smiles brightly, looks at Swanson and says, "I'm Administrator Bravo, and I thought I'd pop in while there was a break to see if you had any questions."

Swanson gives Gray the eye, and the younger woman wisely doesn't look back at her. She must have called the Administrator, knowing Swanson's questions would stray beyond the boundaries of the expertise already present in the room.

Rather than say anything unpleasant, Swanson waves toward an empty chair. "By all means, join us."

After pouring her own cup of tea and complimenting the Captain on her brew, she sets down her cup primly and says, "I understand there was some confusion over language."

Ah, so that's it. Gray must have called after Swanson asked too many times about the name-calling she'd witnessed. Well, she did want answers for that, so perhaps this was a good interruption.

"Yes, thank you for coming, Administrator. I did have a question or two. I didn't understand some of the words being used, so I looked them up." She paused, pointing to her ear and the little computer there. "They seem to be ancient pejoratives, nasty words. I still don't entirely understand *douchebag*, but the rest have clear definitions. Can you explain? This wasn't the case during my last visit."

The Administrator practically wiggles in her seat, obviously eager to share. They were designed to build consensus, reason out problems creatively, and work well with others. While that was probably more exciting than being a Facilitator, they usually only dealt with others exactly like them, so how exciting could it be? An outsider must be a huge event for them, Swanson thinks.

"I *can* shed light on that!" she exclaims. "During the simulation runs for various conflicts, we noted that in every case the troops developed words that separated themselves from their foes. Essentially, they found a way to identify those they would fight as *other* … other than themselves, that is. Research was problematic, but we eventually identified the source."

Still unclear where name-calling came into this, Swanson prompts, "And?"

"Oh, of course. I keep forgetting you're not linked to us. Well, once the Identity Act was passed on Earth a long time ago, pejoratives were censored from all historical media, but we were able to access pure scans of old documents.

It turns out that in all conflict in which the two foes are not personally known to each other, there is a requirement in the human psyche to identify a way in which the person is "other" than themselves. Otherwise, they can't fight. It's present in all armies in history. Most of the time it was based on appearance or ethnicity or religion or some easily identifiable trait. Far back in history, humans were once divided by geography, and appearances were fairly distinct in each region. Religious devotees wore specific clothing or hair or other identifiers to distinguish them. In short, all conflicts involved demeaning or otherwise diminishing the humanity of a foe sufficiently to make killing an acceptable act."

Stunned, Swanson tries to imagine the reality described by the Administrator, but can't. "Is this true?"

With a rather inappropriate smile, the Administrator says, "Very true. We've peeked into the virtual worlds to verify our hypothesis, and even there, where pejoratives are frowned upon, it is present. In one case, there is an ongoing fifty-year conflict between two groups of people based entirely upon the wearing of red or blue clothing."

"No, that can't be true."

"Oh, I assure you, it's true. Many of those in conflict are related to each other by blood, yet the wearing of the opposing color means automatic hate and conflict. It's quite shocking."

Suspicious, Swanson asks, "And you didn't tweak the system to achieve this, did you?"

Her hand flutters toward her chest. The Administrator's astonishment is quite real. "No. Only the Facilitators can do that, and we would never request such a thing!"

As difficult as it is to believe such a thing can happen naturally, Swanson believes Bravo's denials. Administrators weren't designed to be so deceiving. "Fine, but again, how does this relate to name-calling?"

"Well, such names were being generated by our troops in simulations. The problem was that it created negative feelings that carried over into real life after battle. Appearance-based problems, primarily. We were seeing divisions begin. So, we scoured all resources to find pejoratives that could be applied to any enemy that had no correlation back on the ship. We found several. *Douchebag*, *asshole*, and *twat* were the final winners. You see, those can be applied to anyone, regardless of appearance or anything else."

"But they're using them here. I myself witnessed the General using two of them toward a trooper."

With another brilliant smile, the Administrator nods and says, "Yes! You see, by using them universally here, we diminish their power toward peers, yet they maintain power when used seriously toward a foe. It's perfect!"

Swanson can only shake her head. It's out of her wheelhouse, and the Administrators are built to find solutions like this, so accepting the practice seems wise. "Well, if you say so."

The General glances toward the wall-screen and says, "We're running a bit behind. The suit demo is next. Would you like to see it, Director?"

The truth is that Swanson is bone-tired and wants nothing more than a nap, but it's equally true that decisions need to be made before she falls over. Time is of the essence. Pushing herself up from her chair takes effort, but she thinks she hides it well enough. "There's no time like the present."

Five

The large woman seems overjoyed to be in her suit. Her transparent faceplate reveals the big smile on her face even with her toggle bar in the way. The bar also explains the scars she'd seen on all Soldier Class personnel. Given that only her head has much in the way of movement inside the large combat suit, her mouth hitting the toggle bar during combat seems inevitable. Why didn't they pad them?

The woman—named Tango-Mike-X-Ray—stomps her way into the center of the test range and slaps a metal fist against her chest. "The soldier is the suit! The suit is the soldier!"

When the General raises her hand to acknowledge the salutation, Tango sets to work. It's impressive, of that there's no doubt. With every twitch of her limbs, weapons rise or lower on her suit. Her array of weaponry impressive, her rate of fire is almost too rapid to comprehend. The metal suit makes the already large human seem monstrous. And her face is radiant as she fires at targets around the huge space. Her expression can only be defined as joy. Pure, unadulterated joy.

As the demonstration ends, the General says, "Tango, go hit the flight deck and get ready for the ball demo."

With another salute, Tango leaves the range and the General turns to Swanson. "We have a surprise for you, Director Swanson. I wasn't sure we'd get clearance for the display, but we managed to secure the flight path. Would you care to see a battle ball?"

Her eyebrows rising, Swanson smiles. This is one thing she'd very much like to see. Hearing about them over the centuries between sleeps was one thing, but witnessing one in action is an unexpected bonus.

"That would be delightful."

The trek to the flight deck is a long one, but the others keep their steps short for her. Even so, Swanson can feel her heart beating in her ears with squishy, unhealthy thuds long before they arrive. Inside the control room and separated from the troopers arrayed below on the deck, Swanson focuses on breathing deeply and lowering her heart rate while the final launch preparations are made.

At long last, the final "green" is relayed, and the Captain presses a button with a shout, "Launch the ball!"

The floor of the flight deck begins to lower, and in that growing gap is the darkness of space, barely lit by a glow from the planet below. The gap widens until the curve of the Earth—such a perfect pearl of green and blue and white—is visible. Swanson sucks in a breath at the beauty of it.

Once the gap ceases widening and the flight deck jerks against the stops, the thousand troopers arrayed with such precision on the deck begin to rise. Tiny swirls of dust on the decks behind them show their propulsion units engaging. As one, they move out of the gap, a troop of metal angels in flight.

"The screen will show you close-ups, if you like," the Captain says.

Swanson watches as the soldiers begin to join together and the battle ball quickly forms, each suit connecting to another in concentric layers. The last layer of suits rotates so the soldiers face outward, all their weapons and sensors shifting positions so they can protect the integrity of the ball.

"Aren't they quite vulnerable during such a maneuver? Particularly when landing on a planet?" she asks.

The Captain gives her a little smile and says, "That's where we come in. The ships are capable of orbital bombardment, of course, but they also provide covering fire for the balls. We'll use short-range tracers for this, but you'll be able to see how it works even so. Of course, the General is always in charge of her troops, I'm only responsible for the ship. We coordinate this type of activity beforehand." With that, she gives commands and the show commences.

The battle ball begins to spin as it races toward the planet, and bright tracer fire illuminates the darkness around them. It's beautiful.

The General's face reflects the splendor. Her face smooths, her eyes brighten. Clearing her throat, she says, "We won't land, so this will be a short trip. As per protocol, none of my troopers touch Earth soil. Of course, this isn't our first choice for corrections operations on the Seed planets. We have the full range of options, from diplomacy using Administrators, to selective corrections using more tactical means. This, however, is what we're truly capable of should the need arise. You see the methodology at work? We've incorporated all past directives, and I think we've done well."

Swanson does see, and even more, she knows this last, long sleep was worth it. Technically, the Peace Force was ready two sleeps ago—which was almost four-hundred years ago in chronological time—but these additional generations of troopers have honed the Peace Force into a finely tuned machine.

They are perfect. It is time.

Swanson looks up at the General and does something no one has done for centuries. She holds out her hand. At first confused, the General's eyes lose focus as she listens to her computer, then she smiles and holds out her own giant paw.

They shake and Swanson says, "You've done extraordinary work, and I'm proud to have met you. You will do good things, General. You will correct many wrongs. You have my full confidence."

The General understands her meaning and takes a deep breath, eyes alight. "We will not fail you."

Six

"Swanson, I have no wish to cause you discomfort, but I'm urgently needed on the surface at Director's Hall," Gray says with an uncharacteristic amount of expression. One might almost call it emotion … and not a good one.

"What's wrong?" she asks, quickening her pace toward the tiny ship.

Gray's brows draw together ever so slightly, another sign of unease that the Director cannot ignore. "I'm not certain, Swanson, but there is an irregularity in the perimeter at the Hall. Several Healers and two Facilitators are missing and cannot be located."

"Can't be located? How is that possible?" she asks, now rushing despite the thudding in her ears.

Gray only shakes her head and that, more than anything, tells the Director that she needs to hurry and complete her business. An image rises unbidden in her mind of the freshly turned earth near the power receivers on that plain where humanity lives in digital splendor. Immediately, her mentor and his booming laugh resounds in her ears.

A dog with one last flea to shake off.

Once inside the ship, they barely strap in before the launch. Gray is silent for the most part, listening intently to her computer and silently mouthing words in response. Swanson sees for herself what the irregularity is as they approach the landing pad. A part of the wall that surrounds Director's Hall—which is more like a park with buildings near the center—has collapsed into a large hole. The word sinkhole comes to mind, but Swanson knows it's no natural hole.

Or maybe it is. Animals are a part of nature.

When they arrive, there are two additional Facilitators waiting for them, each wearing the same grave expression now etched into Gray's face. They immediately arrange themselves to either side of Swanson as she exits, almost like guards.

Turning to Gray, who appears ready to bolt, she asks, "What's wrong?"

For the first time, Gray appears hesitant to answer. "Director, we have not located the missing personnel, but…"

"But?"

"We have found traces of blood belonging to two of the personnel near the collapsed wall. DNA confirms it."

Swanson closes her eyes for a moment, letting it all wash over her. For thousands of years, the various lines of Directors have made decisions. But each line had a different set of responsibilities, and her line was not in charge of humanity on Earth. That was the purview of a different line of Directors, a line that no longer existed. Once the human situation on Earth had been solved to their satisfaction, their line ended. That same end came for the Director line that handled the repopulation of Earth's animal species. As it did for the line that handled the dismantling of human debris left behind.

And it would be the same for her, the last in the line of Peace Force Directors. The last Directors the Earth would ever produce. The very last decision maker there would ever be.

Perhaps those other lines should not have considered their work complete after all.

Gray seems impatient when Swanson opens her eyes again. Her arms are tense and her feet ready to move. Ignoring that, Swanson asks, "How do you keep animals away from the Dome and the Hall?"

Gray appears confused for a moment, then shakes her head. "Animals too interested in our facilities are terminated, of course. We sweep the area outside the walls almost daily."

Looking down at her wrinkled hands, Swanson considers her next question carefully. "So, what you're saying is that the only interaction that anything living on this planet has had with humanity is to be killed by humans?"

With an almost-shrug, Gray answers. "Of course. Why would we interact?"

"Do you kill them all? Every single one that you see?"

Gray shakes her head, "No, of course not. If they go away, then we don't. We kill all that come near and don't run. We do the same at the Dome."

"So, any building or object that is built by humans means fear or death to all animals? Nothing else?"

Gray is incredulous at Swanson's questioning. "That's the point. They should fear us and our facilities. They will stay away. This is ours, not theirs."

Looking around at the sterile walkway leading to the equally sterile Director's Hall, Swanson feels as if she's truly seeing it for the first time. Perhaps the last time as well.

Gray doesn't understand, and she can't be *made* to understand, Swanson sees. For thousands of years there have been only Directors, Facilitators, and Healers. They have been the quiet remnants of humanity, leaving the world beyond their small facilities to bloom again. What Gray can't seem to understand is that they've made themselves the enemy of every living thing on the planet. Animals might not talk, but they have instincts. Like kill or be killed.

In trying to move on to the next stage of evolution, humans have made yet another grave error. There will be no next stage after this one.

To the other two Facilitators, she says, "We're going to the Decision Room." Gray is left open-mouthed in the hallway as Swanson leads the way.

The thudding in her ears grows painful as they walk the halls, and a tingling begins in her fingertips. *How appropriate that my body should fail me now*, Swanson thinks with a grim smile.

The Decision Room is spare but appropriately designed. The octagonal structure represents the eight lines of Directors. All but one of those walls is now dark. On the remaining wall glows the never-fading symbol of the Peace Force. Swanson examines it again, savoring this moment, because she knows—it's the last moment for humanity on this planet.

The symbol shows two planets, one below the other. On top is the Earth and below, a planet shaded in darkness, in the shadow of Earth. Between them stretches a hand encased in a gauntlet and carrying a sword. It is only now that she realizes it looks less like peace and more like the Earth sending someone to skewer another planet. She hopes it won't turn out that way in the end, despite the recordings Gray showed her.

They've made so many mistakes. She wishes with all her being that, in making her decision, this will be the one time that humans make the right call. She hopes she is one Director who makes her final decision wisely. Then at least the humans that have spread amongst the stars will have a chance to avoid extinction, if only they can rein in their own barbarism. Here on Earth ... well ... it's too late for us, she thinks. But for those out there amongst the stars? Maybe.

Swanson places her trembling hand on the Decision Key.

"Peace Force Director. Welcome. What do you require?"

"I'd like to ask a question."

"Proceed Director."

"If I believe that another line of Directors has made an error, can you decant new Directors for that line and reopen their decision matrix?"

Though she half-expects the answer, she still sighs when the computer confirms her fears. "No. The Directors are the final decision makers. They cannot be gainsaid. Once the final decision is made, it cannot be undone."

Swanson looks back at the two facilitators at the entrance. They seem so incredibly uninterested in the question she just asked. They're not even asking themselves why she would ask such a question. They weren't designed to, of course.

Again and again, humanity makes such bad decisions. *Even when we try to do right, we do it wrong,* she muses. She examines her mind for the truth. Is she making the right decision now? Is the Peace Force ready? The image of that planet and the mutilated little girl who would become a Voice on a planet far away flits through her mind. It's a painful image.

Even at this moment, there are Seed ships replicating, orbiting new worlds that will come to life under their long care. There are new crews being decanted in a line of flawed ships. Right now, they are eager to do good, to create yet another chance for humanity to live and grow without strife … and like the others, they will have those hopes dashed. Chaos and evil will ensue. It seems programmed in to the very DNA of humanity. And yet, she still has hope.

Director Swanson knows she can't save humans on Earth. Those decisions have been made. Their consequences are already evident as the Earth shakes the fleas of humanity from her back. She can save the others … maybe. It's worth the risk.

"I'm ready," she says, looking up again at that beautiful and contradictory Peace Force symbol on the wall.

"Do you wish to make a final decision?"

"Yes," she says, her voice barely above a whisper.

"What is your decision?"

Squeezing her eyes shut and taking one last, deep breath, she gathers her courage. Mustering up some final bit of energy, she says in a voice both loud and clear, "Launch the Peace Force!"

Her death comes so quickly, she never feels it.

Epilogue

Swanson wakes to applause. Her first thought is that she feels wonderful and when she lifts her hand, her second is that she's young again. Sitting up on the couch, she's faced with a crowd of vibrant, healthy people, all of them smiling and laughing.

"I'm here!" she gasps.

A man she would recognize anywhere steps out of the crowd. No longer old and lined with age, he's still got that booming laugh she knows so well. "You are! Congratulations! Welcome to Eternicity. The Final Director has finally joined us. Our labors are at an end!"

She takes an experimental breath and feels the air coursing through clear lungs undamaged by repeated cryo-sleeps over a thousand years of time. Her hands feel her face and find no lines or wrinkles. It's true. She's in the partition, the one part of the Virtual that Directors can inhabit. Unlike the rest of the virtual worlds, the inhabitants of this world were once physical and understand they are no longer living flesh. That means they can't live with the others, but it also means their world is endless and boundless, without death or aging or restriction. An Eternal City—Eternicity.

Then she remembers. The wall. The burrows at the receivers. The decision made long ago by some Director that moving data backups to the moon would not be a good use of resources.

Director Tyrell grabs her hand to help her from the couch and claps her on the back. His face is wreathed in smiles and without a care. Should she tell them what's coming? It may not be today. It may not be a thousand years from now.

But it will come. Their virtual world will end. The battle just beginning in the physical world on Earth will someday end it for them.

Should she tell them time is no longer endless?

Dog. Flea. Shake.

Considering Tyrell's face and the happy faces around her, she decides they have all carried enough burdens. Those who erred cannot go back and undo their actions. It is done. Telling them what she knows will only mar their time here. It would be cruel.

And really, is their future end a bad thing? Perhaps it's time for Earth to be rid of humans … in every form. Maybe a new, more deserving species will arise in time. And maybe those humans who've seeded the stars will at last find the better angels of their nature.

Yes, she will keep her peace and share nothing of what's happening out there in the world of flesh and bone. However long it lasts, this is the time for happiness, the time for ease.

She smiles back up at him and says, "Well, don't stand there smiling all day. Show me around! Who's up for a game of tennis? I haven't played in centuries."

ABOUT ANN CHRISTY

This tale is the fourth side-story in the world of *Lulu 394* … a book Ann hasn't completed yet. She's been working on it for four years and will likely be working on it for a while longer. It's one of those that must be perfect, she feels, or it will entirely suck. These short stories help her flesh out parts of the tale that live in the background, never to be delved into within the pages of the book itself. If you're interested, you can find *The Mergens*—a dark tale tied to the one you just read—in *The Ways We End*, a collection of apocalyptic tales by Ann. Also, within the pages of the follow-up collection, *And Then Begin Again*, you'll find *Lulu Ad Infinitum*; and finally, in *Robot Evolution* is *Posthumous*. Fair warning, Ann says, that one makes pretty much everyone cry.

You can connect with Ann on Facebook or grab some freebie reading by signing up to her VIP Newsletter here: http://annchristy.us3.list-manage.com/subscribe?u=0329552226b674f0fdf1d4e17&id=b460c157d4.

THE SCRAPYARD SHIP

by Felix R. Savage

1

WE BABIED THE SHIP FROM SILVERADO TO GORONGOL, BUT she gave out on us with eight thousand klicks left to go, and I had to duct the emergency LOX reserves into the retro-rockets to put her down. No way was I taking her FTL with the antimatter containment loop losing integrity every time I breathed on the display. So we came down like a meteor, burning hydrolox that was 90 percent pure oxygen. If Dolph had chosen that moment to light a cigarette, we'd have been a scorch mark on the desert.

He waited until we were out of the ship and walking away. Grains of newly fused glass crunched under our feet. The smoke from Dolph's cig masked the odor of burnt brush. The sun felt like a nail through the top of my head, even though I was wearing my old panama from San Damiano. The breeze rustling the bushes sounded loud in the silence. Heat rippled a stegosaurus ridge of hills on the horizon. I was walking in that direction for want of any better ideas. The ship shrank behind us into a forlorn crumple of metal origami.

I'd had that bird for eight years, ever since I got out of the army. Bought her cheap with my demob pay. Even at the time I knew I'd be lucky to get a thousand light years out of her. Now she was toast.

"Got any more bright ideas, Tiger?" said Dolph, shading his eyes with one hand. There was not a single living thing nor any sign of human habitation in sight. Well, you wouldn't expect there to be any signs of *human* habitation. Gorongol is a Kroolth world. But there weren't any signs of Kroolth, either.

"I'm thinking," I said.

Dolph inhaled, exhaled. "Easy in, easy out, he said. It's just a cargo run, he said. A bunch of graphene cables and some fancy tension dampeners—buy low, sell high, and there'll be room in the hold for bananas."

The Kroolth go ape for bananas. I think it's something to do with micronutrients. They didn't evolve in this system, of course—pretty much no one in the Cluster evolved where they're from. Chronic potassium deficiency would help to explain their behavior.

Dolph went on, "You didn't mention the part where the Silveradans intercept us because their Crown Prince is feuding with the Generalissimo of Gorongol—"

"How am I supposed to keep track of this stuff? Worlds like these change their government every second Tuesday."

"So they confiscate the cargo, and put a hole in our freaking containment loop. Way to go, Mike. We could've kept Sally running for another ten years."

It had always annoyed me that he called the ship Sally. I never gave ships pet names. Pets die on you. Behind us, Sally let out a series of sad pops as her fins cooled. Case in point.

"I think I have whiplash, too," Dolph went on. He peevishly kicked the brush. His thin, sallow face was set in a frown, which turned into an expression of shock as a twenty-legged tarantula—that's what it looked like—scuttled out from under the leaves and ran away.

"They didn't confiscate the bananas," I reminded him.

"Did you see that? It looked like a tarantula with twenty legs."

"I wonder if we could fix the containment loop by cannibalizing a couple of electromagnets from the plasma chamber."

"Great idea," Dolph said. "We'll also need some chewing gum and string."

I scowled, in no mood for his wisecracking, even though I knew it was his way of dealing with the sad fate of "Sally." For him, it was a personal tragedy. For me, it was a financial calamity. *He* wasn't the one with his name on our business cards: *Starrunner Imports, LLC. Freight carried, problems solved.*

How was I going to solve this one? Dolph was right about one thing, anyway—I couldn't solder my way out of it.

A crash reverberated across the desert. Dolph's cigarette fell out of his mouth. Both of us spun around, reaching for our weapons.

Sally had lain down. That crash had been the noise of her nose slamming into the glassed surface of the desert. As we stared through the clouds of sparkling dust, a whole lot of black and fuzzy *somethings* swarmed up her crumpled jackstands and disappeared into the forward airlock, which we had left open.

At the same time, one of the bushes nearby grew legs and humped towards the ship, chasing the black fuzzies.

Dolph swallowed audibly, sighting down his .45.

"That bush has legs," I said.

"Sometimes I wonder why they let you in the special forces," Dolph said. "You must've gamed the IQ test."

I slapped his pistol down. The walking bush was now trying to climb the airlock stairs. The last thing we wanted to do was piss it off and make it come this way. "At least I didn't game the psych evaluation."

"Hey," Dolph said, "I was honest. Where it said, 'How do your family and friends describe you?' I put 'Psychopathic.'" He lowered his pistol. Studying the bushes all around us, he handed me the .45 and stretched his arms over his head. "It's damn hot," he remarked, casually.

His sallow skin turned brown. His black hair turned into a bristly, spotted mane. Fur sprouted from his cheeks and the nape of his neck. He took off his clothes as he Shifted, to save the seams from splitting. Within ten seconds a jackal was loping to catch up with me. "Carry these for me, wouldja?" he said through the bundle of clothes he was carrying in his teeth.

Dolph isn't really a psychopath. He's a Shifter, like me. That's why they let us in the special forces, not because we're especially good at anything. Obviously.

I aimed a kick at him. "Shift back."

"Hell with that," said the jackal. "If these bushes try to eat us, I'll see your ass at the mountains. Four legs are faster than two."

"OK. When the Kroolth make your skin into a rug, I'll take a picture for your mom." I got out my radio and crossed my fingers for a signal. The Kroolth are pretty low-tech, but they do have satellites.

"Who are you calling?" Dolph said.

I held up a finger. As I'd hoped, the stegosaurus ridges bounced the radio signals just enough that the handheld had finally found a lock. I entered my insurance code and broadcast it on the specified frequency. "I've resigned myself to the inevitable," I said.

"You're finally going to fire Irene? I told you she wasn't working out."

Dolph was referring to our weapons officer, whom we'd left behind on Ponce de Leon this time out. She was probably taking her kids to the beach, while we slogged across a desert infested with tarantulas and carnivorous sagebrush.

"If we can't get the ship fixed," I said, "I won't need to fire her. None of us will have a job." My radio crackled.

"Yeah 'lo how c'n I help ya?" droned a voice speaking English, which fortunately for us is the lingua franca in this part of the Cluster. My code would've told them I was an offworlder. I hoped they didn't put two and two together and realize we were the same guys meant to be delivering an important cargo to their Generalissimo—a cargo we didn't have anymore.

"Hi there!" I said as cheerfully as I could. "Is this Clusterwide Breakdown Services?"

* * *

Clusterwide will fix your ship on the spot if it's something minor, like dead mice in the air ducts. That time, I had spent three days taking apart the CO_2 removal assembly to find out why our air was becoming unbreathable, before I gave up and called Clusterwide. Irene had liked the look of the repair guy enough to let him into her cabin, where he soon traced the smell to escapees from the cage of mice Irene was keeping under her bunk. He had commiserated with me jovially as he pocketed our last quarter's profit. Irene had said that she was sick of the vacuum-packed variety. That's one reason I decided to leave her on the PdL this run. In retrospect: bad move. Had she been here, that pissant Silveradan patrol boat would never have got near us.

Clusterwide also provides haulage services, if your ship is actually still in space. There's a small shipyard orbiting Gorongol, run by Ekschelatans.

However, my ship was decidedly not in space. It was sitting on a glassy smear of fused sand beneath a vast baby-blue sky, surrounded by carnivorous bushes.

When I gave our coordinates to the rep, he gasped, "You're *where?* Do not leave your ship. Don't even open the airlock."

"Too late," I said, staring across the desert at the camel-sized bush still trying to squeeze itself through the airlock in pursuit of the tarantulas.

"All right. All right. Go back to your ship and light a ring of fuel around it if you have any. Don't follow the same path you followed out. There'll be thornmaws waiting for you now. Basically, don't brush up against the same plant twice."

"OK," I said.

"Separately," the rep added, "I will have to ask for up-front payment before we come out there to pick you up."

We did as advised, apart from lighting a ring of fuel. I thought that was overkill. While we waited with our backs pressed to the ship's nose, Dolph said, "Do you get the impression the bushes are coming nearer?"

Actually, I did. They now formed a thick wall around the glassed area where the ship was standing, and now and then one of them would reach a claw-like root forwards and scratch at the rough glass, as if puzzled.

The Clusterwide reps arrived in a light prop plane. The first thing they did was fly in a low circle around the ship, hosing the bushes with a flamethrower. Then they landed on the smouldering ashes, hopped out in hazmat suits, and confirmed my payment details.

"Haulage plus repairs would cost you more than she'd bring on the parts market," was their verdict on the ship, confirming my own gloomy assessment.

They were human, so I tended to think they were being straight with me. Plus, they were recommending a course of action that wouldn't put any money in Clusterwide's pockets.

"OK," I said. The next words out of my mouth broke my heart a bit. "Is there a scrapyard near here?"

The male rep, a bandy-legged character with skin like cowhide from many years in Gorongol's sun, pointed with a hazmat glove. "Right the other side of those hills, on the coast. Outside of the Karpluie spaceport."

"Yeah, we saw that on our way down," Dolph said. He had Shifted back to his normal scraggy, smiley, ponytailed self, of course. We needed them to think we were mainstream humans like them.

"Then you know when I say *spaceport,* I'm being generous."

We had a laugh at the expense of the backwards Kroolth.

The female rep chipped in, "We know the guy who runs the scrapyard. He's good people. I can call and tell him you're coming."

"I'd appreciate that," I said. Then I glanced up at the lovely, now useless, silhouette of my ship, blocking out the sun like a metal swan with her wings raised. A swan 100 meters long. I didn't even have a cargo dolly. (The Silveradans had taken that, too.)

"We've got a flatbed at the spaceport," said the male rep. "I can send someone out to pick you up."

"Is that covered by my insurance?"

"Unfortunately not. But I can give you ten percent off the usual rate."

OK, then. Not so disinterested after all. But I didn't begrudge it to them. We've all got to make a living. "You got a deal."

The female rep had her radio out. "I'm going to give Gerry at the scrapyard a shout. Could I have your name again?"

It was on my insurance documents, but as I began to withdraw them from my pocket, I caught Dolph's eye and thought better of it. I gave her a fake name.

2

The flatbed arrived the next afternoon. It was an enormous thing with 22 axles. Its crawler treads crushed the thornmaws to writhing, sticky mats, a sight that gladdened my heart. Dolph and I had spent an unpleasant night fighting the things off, ultimately resorting to the ring of fire idea. I had grabbed a couple of hours of sleep in the middle of a circle of mattresses from the berths, doused with rocket fuel and burning like a campfire. Now my throat felt raw from the smoke, and my mood was foul.

The crawler's robot arms loaded my ship onto the back, mangling the wings in the process—not that that mattered now—and off we went. Dolph and I couldn't ride inside the ship on account of the tarantulas, and there was no room for us in the flatbed's cab. So we rode on the bed, underneath the landing gear of the ship that had been our house, wings, and workplace in one for years.

It was just like moving house. That's how I decided to think of it. I'd moved house half a dozen times when I was a kid. Shifters don't tend to have a wandering foot—the opposite, if anything—but my father's job had taken us here and there, all over San Damiano. Then, of course, I'd left. Dolph and me both. So moving around was no big deal to us.

Now, however, I had a daughter. Six-year-old Lucy, the external repository of my heart. She was on Ponce de Leon, our current home base. Whenever I came back from a run, she loved to meet me at the spaceport and come aboard the ship. She even enjoyed rolling up her little sleeves and "helping" me with any needed repairs. She loved "Sally" as much as Dolph did. She was going to be devastated when I came home shipless.

As well as profitless and on the hook for that lost cargo.

The crawler bumped along, crushing thornmaws and scaring off unspeakable leggy vermin. A spectacular sunset engulfed the desert, turning it almost pretty. As we passed through a region of rocky dunes, we found an English-language radio broadcast—old news from across the Cluster, punctuated by an every-hour-on-the-hour "Predator Report."

"Travellers in the Yephta Desert should be aware that a herd of dune worms are currently crossing the Karampox road."

We stared at the dunes, whose spiky backs suddenly looked less like rocks.

"If it is absolutely necessary to take this route, drive as fast as possible…"

Instead of speeding up, as recommended, the flatbed stopped. I peered ahead and saw that a dune was blocking the road.

The instant we stopped all the dunes surged towards us, sand sliding from their armored sides.

An infernal boom shattered the evening, followed by a screech. A tail of flame shot out from the flatbed's cab, searing the fuselage of my ship. A rocket-propelled grenade shot out in the other direction. It impacted the worm ahead of the flatbed. The explosion hurled gobbets of flesh and chitin into the air. The other worms flattened themselves to the sand, resuming their camouflage as dunes.

Dolph and I, lying flat, cautiously raised our heads.

"Ho, ho, ho," shouted the flatbed's driver, a seen-it-all human named Clint. He leaned out the window of the cab, brandishing his RPG launcher. "That's the way you deal with them. Didja know the Kroolth evolved from a prey species? They *say* the wildlife is their planetary defences. Truth is, they're just too scared to fight back."

"If we're staying here a while," Dolph said, pointing to the RPG launcher, "I want one of those."

"We won't be."

The flatbed creaked into motion once more. Dolph climbed up the ship's landing gear and fussed over the black scorch marks left by the RPG launcher's blowback. I heard him murmur, "Poor old Sally."

"Quit it with the Sally stuff," I yelled up at him.

The flatbed crawled up a switchback mountain road into violet shadows.

* * *

We stopped for the night at a roadhouse lavishly decorated with gold-framed photographs of His Specialness, the Generalissimo of Gorongol. A troop of secret police types came in while we were eating supper. I had heard their motorbikes outside, and I was prepared for swagger and noise. I was *not* prepared for them to command everyone in the dining room to stand up and sing the national anthem, which was (of course) a 12-verse paean to the Generalissimo's specialness.

Clint indicated that we should stand up, too. For all his contemptuous talk about the Kroolth's timidity, he showed no inclination to piss off a roomful of them.

I had to sidestep so I could fit my head between two rafters. Dolph is a couple of inches shorter than me, and Clint was only about five ten, but all three of us loomed over the impromptu choir like totem poles. The Kroolth are *small*. The tallest of the secret police types was about the right height to headbutt me in the groin if he stood on tiptoe. And he looked like something of the sort was on his mind as he glared across the crowd at us. I moved my mouth as if I was singing.

Dolph, under cover of the fourth refrain, said, "So I'm doing the math."

"Me too."

"I don't like it."

"Me neither."

I was still annoyed at Dolph for grieving over the ship, but we were on the same wavelength now. We've known each other a long time, and a higher than average proportion of our ventures together have involved a) fighting and b) running away, not necessarily in that order. So I knew that he was referring to the math of us versus them. There were eleven secret police types, and thirty more Kroolth in the dining room who would definitely join in if encouraged.

Clint's theory about the Kroolth having evolved from a prey species was probably correct. They looked like startled primates with long faces, sort of like you were lifting them by their furry cheeks and screaming at them about their gambling debts. They had long arms like colobus monkeys. On the other hand, monkeys can hurt you bad, even if they don't have guns. And each of the secret police types carried a toy-sized pistol. Dolph had his .45 and I had my Midday Special, but we were too badly outnumbered to even think about using them.

"Shift?" Dolph whispered.

"No! Jesus, no!"

"They'd never know what hit them."

I shot him an appalled glance. The pupils of his eyes had gone slitty. His shoulders were starting to bulge, straining his shirt. He grinned.

"Quit it! If they find out we're Shifters, we're dead!"

I held Dolph's stare until the pupils of his eyes returned to normal. Goddamn jackal never could think more than five minutes ahead.

"First one draws down on us, I break his neck," he whispered, while the Kroolth ended the anthem with a round of applause in honor of His Specialness.

Shaken, I had difficulty smiling as the troop leader scuttled up to us.

"You are the owner of that pile of junk outside?"

Dolph let out a low growl. I fought to keep my smile in place. After all, the Kroolth was technically correct. "That's me."

"Remove it immediately. It is blocking the road!"

Relief pulsed through me. Only a parking violation. "Absolutely, Officer. We'll be on our way shortly."

He turned away with a sniff, then turned back. "You are human?"

"We are," I confirmed. Dolph sniggered. These back-of-beyonders couldn't even tell humans by looking at them.

"Have you ever been to ... oah, Ponce de Leon?" He pronounced the name of PdL, one of the Big 5 worlds of Humanity United, with the same care that I would use if trying to speak Kroolth.

"A few times," I said cautiously.

"Are you aware of any cargo ships bound from Ponce de Leon to Gorongol?"

I put on a puzzled face, while my relief curdled. They were looking for us.

"This one would be, oah, a very large ship, much bigger than that pile of junk of yours. Laden with very valuable technology, oah yes. It would have an armed escort."

"Hmm," I said. "Come to think of it, I may have seen exactly such a ship on the pad at PdL. The captain boasted that he had a personal commission from the Generalissimo." I had done just that, but only to make the regulars at Snakey's Bar & Grill laugh. As for an armed escort? We were our own armed escort. I admit to dropping the ball on the Silveradan patrol ship. I just couldn't blow those little guys away. They *said* it was only a customs inspection, and I was dumb enough to believe them. "It was a 60-ton tri-engine Phantom with an extended cargo bay. Does that sound like the one?"

Lord strike me down now.

"Oah yes! That must be it! Do you know when it departed Ponce de Leon? It is delayed."

"At about the same time we did," I said. "I should think it'll arrive any day now." We would have got here on time, but I took it extremely slow at the end. You do, with a leaky antimatter containment loop.

The little Kroolth went on his way beaming. He could expect a warm pat on the head from his commander for bringing news, even if it was just hearsay, of the missing cargo ship.

We finished our supper with no appetite. Kroolth food is vegetarian. Dolph can usually eat anything, but even he left half of his stringy hash browns. We paid up, stooped to get out of the dining-room, and crawled down the hall to the front door.

Outside, the air was soft and sweet with the smell of (probably carnivorous) flowers. Clint the driver said, "Were they looking for *you?*"

"Gosh, I can't believe you worked that out," I said. My mask of politeness was slipping, as I knew we were up to our necks in excrement. It couldn't take even the Kroolth much longer to work out that the ship which had just crash-landed in their desert was the one they were yearningly awaiting. I left Dolph to transfer some extra GCs to Clint to convince him to drive through the night, instead of parking up here as we had planned.

"I gave him some extra to keep his trap shut," Dolph said as he returned to our perch under the landing gear.

"He'd better. We'll be spending the rest of our lives in a jail with five-foot ceilings if the Generalissimo's enforcers catch up with us."

"Humans ought to stick together in places like this," sighed Dolph. "Maybe I should go back and scare him."

"No, don't. Paying him off was the right move."

"I just hate to think of him spending our money…"

It was my money, actually, as both of us knew. I appreciated that Dolph was trying to smooth things over between us by being fiscally responsible, in his own way. I said, "Just imagine him spending it on his personal harem of Kroolth bimbettes."

Dolph shuddered. I chuckled.

Of course, there was a glitch in this pretty picture of human solidarity. If Clint, or anyone else on Gorongol, figured out that we *weren't* human—not like they were human—we wouldn't even have that.

Neither of us Shifted that night, even though it would have been more comfortable to curl up in the form of an animal on the hard, cold bed of the crawler. I knew I wouldn't get any sleep, anyway.

3

The flatbed crawled over the mountain pass as dawn was breaking. The corded flanks of the mountains dropped away to forest. Further down, a strip of green and blue cropland bordered the sea. The prevailing winds clearly dumped all the rain on this side of the mountains. The trees lining the road looked like actual trees, not predators.

The only thing that spoiled the view was the carbuncular rash of concrete on the coast: the city of Karpluie, and its spaceport. We rappelled into the ship's forward airlock to get breakfast. When we came back out, the view was unchanged. Good old Clint was not risking his rig on these steep roads by travelling any faster than 20 kilometers per hour.

It took us a whole day—well, a whole human-standard day; the Gorongolian day is 38 hours long—to reach Karpluie. In the forest, we kept getting hung up on low branches, and on the ring road around the city, we kept getting hung up in traffic jams. Or rather, causing them. A 100-meter flatbed carrying a spaceship does tend to do that. Dolph hunted tarantulas inside the ship to blow off steam. I messed around with my computer, trying to find out where we would get the best price for our bananas. I already foresaw that we would need to spend big to get off this planet before the Generalissimo twigged our breach of contract. By now, every motherloving Kroolth on the continent knew that a crashed spaceship had been transported to Karpluie today.

We picked up speed on the modern ten-lane highway to the spaceport, and rumbled past it. The height of the flatbed allowed us to see over the sound-baffle fence. Tarmac stretched away to the diamond thread of the sea.

"One," Dolph said.

"Two," I disagreed.

"One. And it was just an Ek tanker."

"I was counting the airplane."

That was the sum total of the craft that had landed and/or taken off from Karpluie today. I counted the airplane because I thought it might come to that. Even a trip to somewhere else on this planet might turn out to be better than sticking around. While we were stuck in traffic jam number nine hundred and three, I had seen a gang of those secret police types apprehending a Kroolth driver. With hollow-points. It took me right back to Tech Duinn, where Dolph and I spent the most, shall we say, active years of our military careers. I had zero wish to revisit the era of my life when I killed people. And less-than-zero wish to be killed myself.

The flatbed turned off the highway, following the curve of the spaceport fence. Another fence appeared on the other side of the road. Beyond it, curvilinear metal shapes gnawed the afternoon clouds.

"Here we are," Clint yelled back from the cab.

I jumped down. It felt good to stretch my legs on the gravelly red dirt. With Dolph a few paces behind, I marched up to the gate of the scrapyard, which was locked. I stretched out my finger to the buzzer … and froze.

On a bulletin board beside the gate, covered with perspex against the rain, above a lost dog notice and a circular for the Biannual Human Community Barbecue, my own face stared at me from a full-color poster.

MICHAEL "MIKE" STARRUNNER
WANTED FOR GRAND THEFT & LÈSE-MAJESTÉ
100 GC REWARD

The bold black text was written in English, Kroolthi, and Ekschetalan.

Dolph nudged me. "They got your name wrong."

"I'm deeply insulted."

"You should be." He was cracking up so hard he could hardly get the words out. "One hundred GCs? One … *hundred?*"

For reference, I spent two hundred GCs the last time I took Lucy for pizza on PdL.

The Generalissimo valued my life at less than the worth of a deep dish Hawaiian pie.

But as funny as it was, to the Kroolth, one hundred GCs was obviously a lot of money. The relative paltriness of the reward would not deter them from going for it, if they connected me with the man on the poster.

Dolph said, "The Kroolthi is longer than the English." He twisted his head sideways—Kroolthi is written from top to bottom. "That last line?" He was no longer smiling. "Think it means 'dead or alive.'"

"Now that really makes my day." If I couldn't get off this planet pronto, I would never get to take Lucy for pizza again. Never see her smile, never hug and tickle her again. She'd be alone in the world. That thought lit a fire under me. I touched the pocket of my donkey jacket and made sure my Midday Special was still in there.

"The Clusterwide reps must've dropped us in it," Dolph said bitterly.

"Naw," I said. "The Generalissimo's just freaking out because his cargo's late." And was now on Silverado. "They paid retail for that stuff, remember? Three hundred thou. That's probably the equivalent of their entire planetary GDP."

"Nice place to settle if you've got a GC-denominated income," Dolph said, looking around at the sticky-leaved blue bushes that grew up against the fence. The flatbed's treads had crushed some of them, and they smelled like marzipan. Large insects buzzed around us. "Not."

"It wasn't the Clusterwide guys, anyway," I said. "I gave them a fake name."

I was even gladder of that in a moment, as the gate concertinaed open a few feet. In the gap stood a human with a scowl on her face. "Are you Will Slaughtermore?"

My own lame-ass humor struck me as both puerile and risky now. But I straightened my back and shook her hand with a smile. "That's me."

"Crash Hardlander," Dolph grinned, elbowing past me for a chance to squeeze her grease-stained hand. "You must be Gerry?"

"Yup. Like it says on the sign. Gerry Scavarchi's Ships & Parts."

Scavarchi doesn't sound like a human name, so I had been worried that Gerry would turn out to be a Kroolth. As a human, she would be less likely to turn me in for the princely sum of one hundred GCs. That was something.

The other thread of hope I clung to was that the clean-cut, handsome young man on the WANTED poster did not look much like the scruffy, stubbled, not-so-young chancer facing Gerry Scavarchi now. They'd used the picture from my pilot's license. Years had passed since that was taken, and last night was far from the first time I'd slept—or rather, not slept—rough.

Independent freighter captains are known to be hard-living, penny-pinching losers, so I hoped that was all she'd see in me.

In one sense, it was a shame. Ms. Gerry Scavarchi had the body of an angel, imperfectly disguised by a mechanic's coverall, and the face and hair of a shampoo model.

I fixed my eyes north of her neck and said, "Theo and Annette from Clusterwide may have told you I'm looking to sell a damaged ship. I'm not gonna lie to you: the containment's gone. She'll never fly again."

"Yeah."

"However, I hear you'd be interested in buying her for scrap."

Long pause. Gerry's gaze scanned the 100-meter metal swan hulking over the trees behind me and Dolph.

"Sure," she said at last. "Happy to take her off your hands." She raised her voice without moving. "Clint! Put 'er over there."

"Roger," Clint yelled back. The flatbed ground forward a few meters and the robotic handler arms unfolded. My ship swung over our heads and over the fence of the scrapyard. We heard it hit the ground with a crunch. Dolph flinched.

It was a no-brainer from Gerry's point of view, of course. Totaled or not, my ship was a long-haul Skymule. Those don't come along on a world like Gorongol every day.

"Come in," she said with about as much warmth in her voice as a LOX tank, "and show me what I just bought."

We waved goodbye to Clint and followed her into the scrapyard. I took her on a tour of the ship, inside and out, pointing out all the high-spec features such as the 360-degree radar/LiDAR, the gimbaled retrorockets that enabled VTOL, and the threeway microwave/oven/sous vide cooker. I did not point out the coilgun, even though that was the most expensive bit of kit on the ship and I could have used it to justify a higher asking price. She would find it later, when we were safely off-world. Most indie freighters do not have military-grade cannon, and I wanted her to think we were in no way special.

She was impressed enough, anyway. I could see her ripping the cockpit apart with her eyes, and I figured we were home free.

"All right, come on over to the office and we'll talk," she said when we were back on the ground.

Meanwhile Dolph was ripping her clothes apart with *his* eyes. I whispered, "Down, boy," as we followed her through the scrapyard.

It was a jungle of dismembered spacecraft and airplanes. A grinding, screeching noise impinged on my ears as we walked. I glanced to my left and saw a handler robot three storeys high, with tractor tyres and four hydraulic arms, piling the junkers on top of each other.

"We remove the resalable components and then sell the airframes for scrap," Gerry explained over the racket. "There's an Ek outfit comes and takes 'em over to the compactor."

She waved at the distant cab of the handler bot. The motion caused her breasts to rise enticingly under her coverall. I wasn't staring or anything. Of course not.

Dolph was, unashamedly. "There's got to be a catch," he muttered. "Babes like that don't work in places like this."

"Sexist," I said, but he had half a point.

The handler bot stopped work. A Kroolth emerged from the cab and spidered down the access ladder. It joined us as we reached a shack attached to a hangar-sized workshop in the middle of the scrapyard. Gerry pushed the door open and removed spaceship parts from chairs, including one very small one.

The Kroolth came in and sat in it.

"This is my husband," Gerry said. "Opizzt, these are the guys that Annette rang about."

Husband?

Dolph's jaw was on the floor. I realized mine was, too, and picked it up. "Great to meet you, um, Opizzt." I kept talking to cover up my astonishment—and consternation. With a Kroolth in the picture, our odds of being turned in for the one hundred GC reward had just rebounded. "I'm the owner of the Skymule out there. I've just shown Gerry her features, and I'm sure you'll agree four hundred KGCs is a more than fair price, considering the resale value of her parts."

Nothing ventured, nothing gained. I paid five hundred thousand GCs for her new. Well, second-hand. Actually, third-hand. But who's counting?

Dolph put on a sad face, suggesting that I was practically giving the ship away.

But what we had both forgotten was that with a Kroolth in the picture, our odds of being ripped off had also increased astronomically.

"Noaaah," said this little shyster. "You have added too many zeros, oah yes. By a factor of three. We will give you five hundred GCs."

"Five *hundred?*" I spluttered.

Gerry smirked.

"No one wants to buy a Skymule on Gorongol. We cannot even sell the parts. We are doing you a favor, oah yes."

"But she's got a sous vide cooker," I said, desperately trying to keep the tone light.

Dolph did not help me haggle. When I glanced around to see why he was being so quiet—apart from the shock of finding out that Gerry was married to a Kroolth—I caught him looking out the window behind Gerry's desk. It faced the back of the scrapyard, opposite to the way we'd come in. The sea sparkled far off. In between the sea and us stood a number of spacecraft. Some of them looked fairly new, at least from this distance.

Dolph leaned back into the conversation and coughed, in a jackally kind of way. "How about a trade-in?" he said.

4

Our negotiations stalled with three zeros between what I was willing to take and what the Scavarchis were willing to pay. Coming around to Dolph's idea of a trade-in, I agreed to a stroll outside to look at the second-hand ships. Dolph lit a cigarette as soon as we got outdoors.

"Sometimes you do have good-ish ideas," I told him. "Unfortunately this is not one of those times. What are the chances any of these junkheaps even fly?"

"You never know," he said.

The Scavarchis walked ahead of us. Opizzt had to take two steps for every one of his wife's. His head came up precisely to her shapely waist.

"How do they do it?" Dolph whispered.

"Do what?" I whispered back. "Run a business while criminally stiffing their suppliers? Very profitably, I expect."

"No, *it.*"

I had been trying to stop my imagination from grappling with the particulars. Now my efforts failed. But so did my imagination. "Same way we do?"

"It's got to be *this* size, Mike." Dolph held up his pinky finger.

"Beats loneliness, I guess."

"Or maybe—" Dolph perked up— "they aren't really married. It's a front so guys won't hit on her."

"Try hitting on her and see what happens," I suggested.

Dolph sighed.

We passed a Grav-X and a Voidbreaker. Up close, airlock hatches sagged, the sky stabbed through rust-eaten fins, and toxic fluid dripped from neglected piping. A family of bustard-like birds flew out of an engine bell, wings whirring.

It was my turn to sigh. None of these lemons could come close to replacing my ship. My customers would take their business elsewhere, with good reason. My competitors would laugh their asses off. Lucy's little face would crumple, and then she'd try to cheer me up. That was the worst thought of all.

"Hey, Mike," Dolph murmured. "What about that one?"

"Don't call me Mike," I hissed. "It's Will Slaughtermore, remember?"

"He must be spinning in his grave."

I actually borrowed this alias from a guy we knew in the special forces. He lived up to it. I hoped I wouldn't have to.

Opizzt and Gerry were heading away from the ship that had caught Dolph's interest, intent on showing us another Grav-X that was sitting precariously on the edge of a marshy creek.

I caught up with them. "What about that one?" I pointed.

"Oah, you do not want that one," Opizzt said, speeding up.

My antennae tingled. If Opizzt didn't want us to want that one, I wanted it. "Can't hurt to take a look," I persisted.

Gerry said something in Kroolthi. Opizzt replied. The conversation sounded to me like this: *zzziphrrchkk, ksst. Akhzzp. Yeah, but dikuccchizztra.*

"Oaaahkay, if you want," Opizzt said grudgingly.

The ship stood a stone's throw from the boggy bit where the creek ran into the sea. A smell of rot came from the tall pampas grass-like plumes growing in the bog. The ship was definitely in better shape than any of the others we had seen. However, it was a design disaster.

About the same size as my late lamented ship, it lay belly-down with two large wings angled back from its flanks, ending in what appeared to be floats, and two small wings dangling like flippers from the fuselage. It had no fewer than five engines—a cluster of three at the tail, and two more at the bottom of what the army would call the rigid core assembly, a.k.a. the fuselage. Strikingly, its nose cone—raised off the ground—was not actually a cone, but a rounded oval that split open along blunt serrations, gaping at the sky like the jaws of a plesiosaur. If I did not mistake my guess, that was an energy cannon protruding from the jaws like a cheeky tongue.

Long before I was the owner of a shipping company, with bills to pay and a daughter to provide for, I was just a guy who loved spaceships. That guy had been in hibernation for quite some time. But for some reason, this weird and wonderful ship woke him up. I stepped up to it and ran one hand along a sun-warmed jackstand, feeling like myself again for the first time in ages.

Dolph, also staring raptly at the ship, murmured, "Fugly as heck."

"Yup."

"It looks like one of those extinct things they used to have on Earth, those what do you call 'ems—"

"Dinosaurs."

"The one that swam."

"A plesiosaur."

"Yeah, that's it."

"Mike, we gotta have it."

I had made fun of Dolph's emotional attachment to our old ship, but now I was feeling the same way about this one. I would never again mock him for caring too much about a hunk of metal. The truth was he'd stayed young at heart, and now I felt young at heart again. I nodded enthusiastically. "I can already see it landing at the PdL. The guys will think someone put LSD in their coffee."

"And look at all that cargo space."

"Look at those *engines*, Dolph." I could tell from the ovoid mouths of the two lower engines that they were air-fed. "I bet she can go hypersonic in-atmosphere, breathing atmospheric oxygen, and then transition to rocket mode, burning onboard fuel supplies. The main drive cluster is probably a set of standard thermal hydrolox plasma engines, but look at the *size* of them. Depending on where her wet mass tops out at, I bet she does point five acceleration over short distances. Maybe even point six."

"Need a cold shower, Tiger?" Dolph pretended to fan me.

"We gotta get the specs without appearing too eager," I said, more to myself than to him.

"Oh."

"What?"

He pointed to the top of the ship.

I had thought the plesiosaur's long neck was just a truss. Now I saw Gerry kneeling on its top edge, waving down at us from 5 meters above our heads. She was leaning down, so her cleavage threatened to spill out of the V of her coverall, which had somehow come unzipped a short way. Dolph groaned under his breath.

"Hey guys," she called. "Come up and see the airstrip."

She wasn't joking. The top of the truss was an honest-to-God airstrip. Dashed line down the middle and everything.

"It even has arresting gear. Fighter jets sold separately." Gerry said, as we walked aft along the shockproof flexible tarmac. I hated to think how much mass this added to the ship. I decided I'd remove it. In my head, the ship was already mine.

Dolph said, "Who the heck would put an airstrip on a spaceship?"

It was a good question, and would have been a better one if he had asked it to her face rather than her cleavage.

Gerry didn't seem to notice. Her mood had taken a turn for the friendlier. "The Kroolth would. As you see."

"This is a Kroolth ship?" Dolph said.

"I just said so, didn't I?"

"I didn't know…" Dolph trailed off, but I knew what he'd been going to say. *I didn't know the Kroolth built spaceships.*

Suddenly, however, the airstrip made sense—kind of. It was only 60 meters long, and no wider than a king size bed. You couldn't land a fighter on that, arresting gear or no arresting gear. You could, though, if the fighter were *Kroolth size.*

That left the original question of why the heck anyone would put an airstrip on a spaceship in the first place. Gerry answered it.

"This is actually the one and only Kroolth spaceship. The flagship of the Imperial Kroolthi Space Fleet. Built by the Eks on Port Aronym, in orbit." I breathed an inward sigh of relief. The Ekschelatans, or Eks, made the best spaceships in the Cluster. If they had built this one, I could count on solid manufacturing quality. "There's no native shipbuilding capacity on Gorongol. There's an assembly plant on Silverado, but well, you know about that situation."

I nodded. Did I ever.

"Since it was his first spaceship, the Emperor wanted it to have everything. Thus, we have the runway." Gerry gestured to the rear wings, with their oddly fat tips. "We have the floats." She pointed down. "We have the caterpillar treads."

"Caterpillar treads," I echoed, getting more googly-eyed by the minute.

"Yeah," Gerry said. "It's a spaceship! It's an aircraft carrier! It's a tank!" She almost smiled. "Kinda like your microwave / oven / sous vide cooker thing."

"That never really worked," I admitted.

"Maybe not, but this does. The Eks wouldn't have let it out of their yard unless it passed all their tests. Hell, they charged enough for it."

"So what happened to the rest of the Imperial Space Fleet?" Dolph said, struggling to keep a straight face.

"The Generalissimo happened to it." Gerry waited a beat. "Do you guys know *anything* about Kroolthi history?"

Our faces must have told her, truthfully, that we didn't.

"Akondil begat Urzip, who begat… Sorry. The bit you care about is last year. The Emperor of Gorongol and Legate of Silverado, Princeps of the Many Moons, etcetera, had ideas about making the Kroolth a spacefaring people. He started out by building the ship we are standing on. But it came in at three hundred percent of budget, you know how the Eks are, and people were pissed. The Generalissimo, who used to be the Emperor's army chief, put himself in the middle of the anti-space movement, and used the public anger to stage a coup. Off with the Emperor's head! In with twice-daily choruses of the new national anthem, and a bonanza for the suppliers of ugly gilt picture frames and tiny motorbikes."

Dolph laughed. Gerry frowned. Despite her ironic tone, I could tell that these recent developments disgusted her.

"The Crown Prince made it to safety on Silverado. They're still loyal to the Imperial Family out there."

I was thinking that if I had bothered to find this stuff out before we came, I would still have my ship. I would have delivered my cargo to the unsavory Generalissimo and have been on my way with a spring in my step and money in my pocket.

"So that's how things stand right now," Gerry finished. "We would be in the middle of an interplanetary war, were it not for the fact that the Kroolth have no spaceships."

"Except this one," Dolph said.

Gerry nodded. "Except this one. But the Generalissimo thinks spaceflight is a waste of money, remember, so he sent it away to be scrapped."

"But you never scrapped it," I said, finally understanding.

"Opizzt couldn't bear to do it." A softer note entered her voice. "He keeps thinking the Crown Prince will come back and want it. But those biker assholes come around here every so often, asking what's taking so long, accusing Pizzy of being an imperialist … they pistol-whipped him a couple of months back. Next time, they might do something worse. The only thing that's protecting him is that I'm human, and that's not surefire, you know? So I want this—" she ground her boot heel into the airstrip— "*damn* thing gone."

"Lady," I said, "you won't even have to pay me to take it off your hands."

"Sod off," she said with half a smile. "I'm still keeping your Skymule."

"A fair trade."

"All contents included."

"Not a problem," I said. An instant later, Dolph kicked me in the ankle and mouthed: *Bananas*. His head may have been turned by Gerry's strategic display of loveliness, but it was less turned than mine was by the thought of possessing this overpowered beast.

Crap; the bananas. Oh, well. It wasn't as if we'd have a chance to sell them, anyway.

"All contents included," I assured Gerry.

"Great," she said, finally giving us a genuine smile. "Let's go back to the office and we can file the paperwork."

At which point I'd have to tell them my real name, if I wanted the ship legally registered to me. I decided to risk it. My real name isn't Starrunner, anyway. Of course it isn't. Come on. When was the last time you met someone named Starrunner, or Hardlander (Dolph's actual nom de guerre), who'd been born that way?

"There's another ground access ladder back here," Gerry said, clambering down past the arresting gear. "That door is the hangar. It's sealed, so you can either keep it in vacuum, or pressurize it to extend your livable onboard space. This right here is the airlock to the engineering deck. There are three airlocks total. Each of them is flush with the hull, and retracts into it—like so—" she slapped the pressure plate. The ship had power. The hatch opened, releasing an unpleasant smell of decay. "So you don't have to mess with outwards-opening hatches that could be vulnerabilities in a combat scenario. Did I mention the weapons systems? A CP cannon, a keel-mounted railgun, and a tail-gunner's turret with a large-caliber coilgun." She enumerated the specs of the weapons. She was really selling the ship now, as if to impress on me what a great deal I was getting. She didn't need to. I was past sold.

"Hey," Dolph said. "What's bit Pizzy?"

Opizzt was running towards us, weaving between the second-hand spaceships, shouting in Kroolth.

Gerry stiffened for a second and then started down the ladder at dangerous speed.

I was about to follow her when I saw several more Kroolth pursuing Opizzt. They wore black, like the secret police types from yesterday, like every wannabe badass in the entire freaking Cluster. My hand dropped to my Midday Special.

An amplified voice blared, in English, "Mike Starrunner. Mike Starrunner, we know you are there. Come out with your hands up, or we will toast you, oah yes."

My instincts took over. I dived into the open airlock of the ship like a rabbit down a burrow.

5

Dolph dived into the airlock half a centimeter behind me. "They didn't mention me," he grumbled. "I feel unwanted."

"Are you really jealous?" I panted. *"Really?"*

We were in a Kroolth-sized chamber. Dolph's elbow whanged into my eye. My knees were crushing into his stomach. Somehow I managed to close the airlock. Hopefully they hadn't seen us dart in here.

The chamber was too small to stay in. We crawled out of it into a corridor whose ceiling was all of five feet high. I had forgotten the interior of the ship would also be Kroolth-sized.

"Shift?" Dolph said.

"Shift," I agreed.

We stripped off our clothes, folded them in the airlock chamber, and Shifted. Dolph became a jackal. It isn't his favorite form, but he only has two, and the other one is not appropriate for spaceship decks. I ... well, I've got a bunch of forms. Most of them have bad memories attached. I went with my current favorite, a white tiger.

Mainstream humans always want to know how Shifting *feels.* My answer, if I ever wanted to gratify their prurient curiosity, would be something like: Have you ever had a root canal? Now multiply that by an order of magnitude, and imagine your whole body is a nerve. The bones, muscles, blood vessels, *everything* has to drastically realign. No way that's not gonna hurt. However, you get used to it. And when you're old hands like we are, it only lasts for a few seconds.

We shook it off and padded along the corridor, which was now just the right height for us, or rather, we were the right height for it.

In animal form, you have a better sense of smell. This allowed us to experience the full rancidness of the odor of decay that pervaded the ship. My enthusiasm went off the boil a bit, but I had more important things on my mind right now. Such as putting Gorongol in the rearview mirror, for good.

The engineering deck turned out to be high enough for a human, or even an Ek, to stand up straight, owing to the amount of space required for a five GeV antimatter containment loop. We might as well not have bothered to Shift, after all. But neither of us felt like Shifting back just now. The secret police assholes were still out there.

Emergency lighting in the form of pink LED strips edging the hatches and control panels saved us from having to blunder around in the dark. I headed straight for the antimatter drive.

It was a standard gray, heavily rad-shielded torus with two smaller C-shaped units clamped onto it, what the army calls electromagnetic force generation assemblies. You and I call them big honking magnets. A Kroolth-induced failure in one of these magnets was what had doomed my late ship. The bastard Silveradans had tried to steal it. While cutting it off its anchor points, they had, predictably given the level of Kroolth technical expertise, broken it. Without a strong enough magnetic field to contain it, the antimatter inside the loop had inexorably started to annihilate itself. This is what we call a leak in the loop. The process of annihilation progressively wrecks the inside of the torus until it's unusable.

Four hundred KGCs down the pan. The drive accounts for 90 percent of the cost of your average spaceship.

This was a brand new drive, manufactured to Ek quality standards. It even still had a sticker on it saying it passed rad safety testing. To my delight, the console in front of the loop (at face height to my tiger form) indicated that the magnets were currently generating a field, and 13.5 trillion positrons were whizzing around in there right now.

I said the drive accounts for 90 percent of the cost of a ship, but the fuel costs as much as the drive.

"Dolph," I said in a choked voice, "I estimate that we have five hundred KGCs worth of antimatter on board. No, make that five fifty, the market's been going up."

Tiger and jackal each lifted a front paw and performed a clumsy animal high-five. *Screw* the Generalissimo.

"Plus three tonnes of LH2 and one point five of LOX," Dolph said, gloating over the tank gauges.

"Oh yeah baby. We are out of here." In my mind, I was already landing the new ship on Ponce de Leon, swooping Lucy into my arms, and giving her the grand tour of our funny-looking new cash cow. She was going to absolutely love it. The corridors were even child-sized. I had not had a proper look around the ship myself yet, but I already felt as if I knew her inside and out. Which just goes to show what I know.

"Nice of Gerry to keep the power on," Dolph mused.

"They expected the Crown Prince to come back and claim it any minute, remember?" I felt a twinge of guilt about waltzing off with 500 KGCs of antimatter that belonged to the Kroolthi imperial family. But Gerry'd said it: contents included. She'd almost *insisted* on it. Funny, that.

There was a pause. I knew Dolph was also thinking about what might be going down outside between the Scavarchis and the secret police.

I studied the array of screens on the wall console, wondering if I could get an external camera feed.

"Smells a bit in here, doesn't it?" Dolph remarked.

"Something probably died in the ducts," I said, recalling Irene's mice. My lasting irritation at our weapons officer had evaporated. She was going to love this ship as well. All those guns.

I found an optical feed, got a picture of the sandy ground underneath the fuselage, and swivelled the trackball clumsily with the pad of my right forepaw, trying to see behind the ship.

"It was a dog," sighed a squeaky, whiny voice.

Dolph let out a string of high-pitched yipping barks. I emitted a coughing roar. We leapt in the air and spun around, all four feet off the ground, searching for the source of the voice. I wanted my Midday Special so much it hurt, but it was back in the airlock with my clothes, and you can't fire a gun with paws, anyway.

The pink-tinged shadows now looked threatening. Light glinted off something moving in the darkness behind the containment loop, where coolant pipes threaded aft around the antimatter injectlon nozzle. I crouched down low, tensed to spring.

"It crawled into the No. 3 engine bell and got stuck," sighed the voice. "I attempted to coax it out, but it was afraid of me. Thus it died. It was a very sad event. I was able to remove the corpse using one of my remote attachments, but I fear the smell lingers. Not that it bothers *me,* of course."

The speaker walked out of the darkness.

Walked is not exactly what it did.

It had three short legs, like a chicken's, underneath a suitcase-sized triangular body. It moved with a plunging, rolling gait. Several robotic appendages of assorted lengths dangled from its housing. They sprouted various tool attachments, including what appeared to be a laser drill. A screen on top swivelled to face us, displaying a sad-face emoji.

All the fur on my back stood up in a bristly ridge. A menacing growl dripped from my jaws. Logically, I knew I could not hurt this thing with claws and teeth. But logic wasn't in the driver's seat right now. Memory was.

I had seen things like this before.

On Tech Duinn, they worked as mercenaries for the Eks.

They were supposedly on our side, but I swear they killed more humans than the Necrosphere did.

Dolph probably guessed where my head was at. He paced in front of me, putting himself between me and the drone.

"So *this* is what she meant by contents included," he growled.

The drone rocked back on its rear legs. Its front two robotic attachments jerked up. The emoji on its screen changed to a cross face.

"More animals!" it exclaimed. "Shoo! Shoo! Out, little dirty feet!"

It moved towards Dolph, brandishing its laser drill. So much for its story that the dog had died because it got stuck. I remembered the lost dog notice on the bulletin board outside the scrapyard.

I shouldered Dolph aside. "We're not animals," I growled. "When was the last time you heard an animal tell you to sod off, chromebrain?"

The drone's screen displayed an OMG emoji. The ones on Tech Duinn didn't have screens like this. They just had guns mounted on top.

"Shifters," it gasped.

"Got it in one."

I batted the laser drill down with a heavy paw. The drone rocked on its stubby legs.

"I'm a Shifter, and I just bought this ship." I remembered that we had not actually completed the paperwork. That reminded me of Gerry. I disciplined my gaze to stay on the drone and not drift over to the optical feed screen. "I have no intention of sharing it with a drone, so out, out, little dirty feet," I drawled, borrowing the thing's own phrase.

"My feet are *not* dirty! I have maintained the ship in perfect order." It actually was so clean, apart from that smell, you could eat off the decks. "I'm very efficient, friendly, and cooperative," the drone went on. "I was hired as the weapons officer, but I prefer to see myself in a more generalized role." Its screen simpered. "I like helping."

"I just bet you do," I muttered.

"Whoa," Dolph said, alarmed.

I followed the jackal's gaze to the optical feed screen. It was displaying the feed from a camera that must be mounted amidships on the port side. Opizzt had just appeared in it.

He was tottering towards the ship, wearing a suicide vest.

It looked like a bulky canvas waistcoat. But, as with the drone, I'd seen such things before.

The look of appalled terror on his small face also gave it away.

The secret police surrounded him at a safe distance, aiming their rifles at him.

Gerry knelt behind the half-circle of Kroolth. Blood shone bright on her cheek. One of the vicious little thugs was holding a gun to her head.

"Oh dear," the drone said. "It appears that the junta's volunteer auxiliary technology control police have lost patience with Opizzt. They intend to force him to board the ship, whereupon they will detonate that explosive device—killing him, and destroying the ship." It displayed a new emoji: a face with a tear on one cheek.

"Shut your face, drone," I snarled. The trouble was, the drone's read of the situation matched mine.

We were done for.

Unless—

"We're taking off," I said. *"Now."* I didn't want to take the drone along, but forcing it off the ship would take more time than we had. Opizzt was 20 meters away and closing.

I hunched my tiger-shoulders and closed my tiger-eyes, bracing myself to Shift back, while mentally calculating how long it would take me to reach the bridge, figure out the controls, and initiate the drive. I thought I could just about make it.

"No," said Dolph.

I opened my eyes. The jackal stood in front of me, all bristled up to make himself bigger. In nature, jackals are a lot smaller than tigers. However, Shifting conserves mass, so Dolph's jackal was nearly the size of my tiger. He was looking me in the eye. Have you ever looked a jackal in the eye? It isn't an easy thing to do.

Even when the jackal is your best friend.

Especially when it's your best friend.

"No," Dolph repeated. "We're not leaving them to die, Mike."

The thought flashed through my mind: Easy for you to say. *You* haven't got any children.

But he was right.

Of course he was right.

Lucy needed a father—who was a real man.

That guy who loved spaceships? He was also the kind of guy who'd never have left Opizzt and Gerry to die.

That guy was me, and I acknowledged it animal style, by swishing my tiger's tail in a menacing rhythm as I padded back to the optical feed screen.

"Look at Gerry," Dolph said. "She's bleeding!"

Yes, she was bleeding. But her face said she was angry and frightened for Opizzt, not for herself. Even at this distance, I seemed to see something in her posture which didn't match the situation.

Oh, I thought. Of course.

"All right," I said, as Opizzt staggered to the bottom of the airlock ladder. "Here's the plan…"

6

Opizzt climbed towards the airlock.

The bulk of the suicide vest deformed his torso. Clumsy with fear, his feet slipped on the rungs of the ladder. The thugs watching from a safe distance jeered. Yet I was impressed.

The little Kroolth's face was set. He wasn't crying or cursing. He thought he was going to die and betray his emperor in one fell swoop, yet he hoped that he could save his wife's life by making this sacrifice, so he climbed the last rungs of the ladder without hesitating, and set one knee on the lip of the airlock.

The thugs yelled in excitement. I picked out the one holding the wireless detonator. He was dancing around triumphantly, earning a look of contempt from the kneeling Gerry.

I filled my lungs with fetid swamp air, and let out a tiger's bloodcurdling roar.

* * *

All the Kroolth froze, sniffing the wind for the scary predator. Their beady eyes fixated on the source of the sound—the pampas grass clogging the mouth of the creek.

I had exited from the rear airlock of the ship, shown to us by the reluctant drone, and circled around, as stealthily as only a big cat can. While all eyes were on Opizzt, I'd stalked closer to the ship, edging forward on my belly through the mud and roots.

Now, while the Kroolth were off-balance, I charged out of the pampas grass—straight at Opizzt.

Insensate with terror, he toppled off the airlock ladder right in front of me.

Perfect—except for the fact that the guy was wearing a bomb.

I pushed off the ground into a desperate leap, and intercepted his fall. Mentally saying a prayer to my patron saint, I caught the suicide vest in my jaws.

It did not explode.

I hit the ground running. Keeping my head high, so Opizzt wouldn't bump along the ground, I turned and dashed back towards the groves of thick, tall grass, carrying Opizzt in my jaws like prey.

The Kroolth thugs stared in shock, drawing together into a defensive knot. Their cute little hostage plan had not anticipated the sudden appearance of a dangerous predator—what's more, a predator unknown on Gorongol.

They had no way of knowing the predator was me.

Of course, Opizzt didn't know it was me, either. He struggled weakly as I charged into the grass. The sickly sweet smell of the explosives in his vest stung my tiger-nostrils. I noted the bunched wires connecting to a detonator in the small of his back.

As I splashed through the muck, I chewed through the shoulder of the vest. I had gambled on the Kroolth being too astonished to trigger the explosion immediately. That bet had paid off, but they wouldn't stay confused forever.

Good thing Dolph was on the case.

As I waded deeper into the bog, I heard a deafening rat-a-tat-tat behind me. Rounds zipped through the grass plumes. About a thousand little birds started up in terror, it seemed like from right under my feet.

The drone had assured us that the turret gun was loaded. Thank God, it had been telling the truth.

Now I just needed Dolph to get it turned round the right way.

With grass plumes falling on my back, rounds whizzing over my head, and my paws sinking into hot, gloopy mud, I dropped Opizzt. He immediately ripped the suicide vest off over his head and flung it into the grass. He had a good arm. It travelled at least ten meters before it vanished into the bog. I cringed, bracing for the explosion. All I heard was Dolph wasting more ammo.

Opizzt turned to me, his thin arms spread. He was four feet tall and unarmed, facing a tiger. Yet he was ready to fight for his life. Never say that evolution can't be beat by spirit.

"It's me!" I said urgently. "Mike. I mean, Will. Oh, never mind."

He blinked. Then he said, "They know you are here. Oah, I am sorry. When they threatened Gerry, I told them."

"That's all right," I said. "They would've figured it out soon, anyway."

"Gerry!" he moaned, jumping in a vain attempt to see over the grass.

"Of all of us, she's probably the safest," I said cryptically. Then I crouched lower. "I never normally do this, but—hop on."

Opizzt didn't hesitate. He flung his leg over my back and grabbed hold of the fur at the scruff of my neck. He weighed no more than Lucy.

I bounded through the swamp, heading away from the ship.

We got far enough away to save our lives before the suicide vest blew up. Muddy water, pieces of fish, and clods of earth with grass still attached flew over our heads in a lumpy hailstorm. It had been a pretty big bomb.

I waited out the falling mud and then ran on. Opizzt hammered a little fist on my shoulder. "Gerry! Gerry!"

Opizzt might be worried about his wife, but I wasn't. Admittedly, our masterful, spur-of-the-moment plan had all the hallmarks of a classic Mike-and-Dolph production: start running and fighting, let the bad guys fall where they may. We had not built in any leeway for rescuing Gerry. But I had a feeling she didn't need rescuing. There was more to the gorgeous scrapyard manager than met the eye, and I had bet that as soon as the Kroolth thugs didn't have the drop on her, she'd be able to take care of herself.

I would have won that bet if there'd been anyone around to take it. When Dolph stopped firing, I left the cover of the swamp and circled back between the ancient, now bullet-riddled spaceships. Sure enough, as I approached our plesiosaur, Gerry rose from a crouch and dropped the two body-armored Kroolth thugs she'd used as a shield. The Kroolth that Dolph had missed had been put down by the energy pistol in her hand—a small sleek thing with a nasty green glow at the nose, small enough to fit in her cleavage.

I'm a sucker for a dangerous woman. I nearly fell in love with her on the spot.

However, this one was spoken for. I halted and let Opizzt slide off my back. He sprinted up to his wife. She picked him up, and they kissed passionately.

I averted my eyes and saw Dolph standing on the airlock stairs.

He gave me a thumbs up. Then he made a googly-eyed face at the loved-up couple. After a few more seconds he pretended to check his watch.

I coughed. I still had my tiger's cough, although I was so muddy there could be no trace of my tiger's stripes remaining visible. That was just as well. I'd burned too many of my forms in the past. I didn't want to burn this one.

Gerry put Opizzt down. They both turned to me, eyes shining. Black-clad Kroolth thugs littered the ground, but Gerry paid them no mind. She walked towards me, head on one side. "Shifter, huh?"

"Is it that obvious?" I said.

She laughed.

"Secret squirrel, huh?" I said.

Of all the possible reasons for a dangerous babe like her to be working in a place like this, the only one that really made sense to me was that she was secretly employed by GITOut, the General Intelligence Triangle (Outer), humanity's main spy agency.

The skin around her eyes tightened for a microsecond. But all she said was, with a smile, "Why would you think something like that?" She squeezed Opizzt's small hand. "I'm just a girl trying to run a business with my husband."

And that too, I thought, was the truth. They really did love each other. It was plain to see.

"A job," Gerry went on wryly, "which you have just made a lot harder." She moved the nearest corpse with her toe, and wrinkled her nose.

"Oah, do not be ungrateful, Gerry!" Opizzt said, scandalized. "They saved our lives!"

"They did," Gerry conceded. "I'm just saying."

I took a deep breath. "Well, if it helps, there's something in my ship which may come in handy when their friends come looking for them."

"What?"

"A quarter-ton of perfectly ripe bananas."

7

We spent about half an hour helping the Scavarchis tidy up, a.k.a. shoving all the corpses into the marsh. Then we filed the paperwork. The plesiosaur ship was now mine, free and clear.

"Er," Gerry said, once the registration was safely on its way to the PdL servers, "it comes with a certain, um, *appendage* which I may have forgotten to mention…"

"We've met it," I said. "No problem," I lied.

The drone tried to prevent me from getting back on the ship. I was no longer covered with mud, as I had allowed

Opizzt to turn the hosepipe on me, despite my anxiety about revealing my stripes. But now I was dripping wet.

"Out of my freaking way, drone," I growled. "Here's a terracentric anthropological factoid for you: When cats are wet, they get bad-tempered."

The drone displayed an emoji of a face blowing a kiss.

I squeezed past it and went to Shift back to myself. "That thing's going out the airlock as soon as we get into space," I grumbled to Dolph. "Machines with egos—can't stand 'em."

"You have a droid nanny for Lucy," Dolph pointed out.

"Droid, not drone. There's a big difference." Nanny D, my daughter's live-in nanny, was a royal blue humanoid who carried out my instructions to the letter. She did not have an ego. That was one difference. Nanny D did not have weapons attachments. That was another difference.

"I asked it who was paying its salary," Dolph said. "It said it's on sabbatical from the Completion."

"Just like the ones on Tech Duinn."

"That was a while back, Mike. I think we should give it a chance."

I ran my hands through my wet hair, pondering whether I was being irrational. I didn't want anything to spoil my lovely new ship. But today had reminded me that Dolph had sound instincts. I might be the boss, but we were a team. I had to listen to him.

He handed me a Kroolth-sized towel with the imperial monogram. I dried my hair and put my clothes on.

"All right," I said, "we'll keep it. As the janitor."

"I heard that," said the drone from the corridor.

"Good," I said. "Now polish the toilets."

We waved goodbye to Gerry and Opizzt and took off.

The ship handled even more sweetly than I had hoped. The engines lived up to their awesome specs. The transition from air-fed mode to rocket mode was as smooth as butter. I didn't even have to use the main drive to get orbital, as the empty ship only massed 25 tons. At 180 klicks, I cut the engines.

Gorongol turned below us, mostly sparkling sea, dotted with small continents that were brown in the middle, green at the edges. A troubled planet. A suffering planet.

"Home?" Dolph said.

"Home," I agreed.

But instead of initiating the FTL drive, my right hand hovered above the comms console.

I turned to look for the drone.

It was floating submissively at the back of the cockpit. We were all floating. There were couches for a pilot and co-pilot, but Dolph and I were never going to get into those unless we shrank three feet. At best, they served as hassocks to hook our toes under.

I wouldn't be pushing the gees until we got human-sized acceleration couches. That ruled out a trip to Silverado. So I decided on the next best thing.

"Drone," I said, "have you got any useful technical expertise, apart from scrubbing, polishing, and killing stray dogs?"

"I am a highly qualified engineer. I am also a trained medic. I can change a diaper, plan an invasion, butcher a hog, conn a ship, design a building, write a sonnet, balance accounts, build a wall, set a bone, comfort the dying, take orders, give orders, cooperate, act alone, solve equations, analyze a new problem, pitch manure, program a computer, cook a tasty meal, fight efficiently and die gallantly. Specialization is for insects," it finished, with a shit-eating grin on its screen.

Dolph and I were silent for a moment, ticking off skills on our fingers to see how we stacked up.

"By the way, that's a quote from—"

"All right, all right, no need to impress us with your literary acumen as well. In that case, I'm sure you'll be able to help the Silveradans with a little problem they're having."

I radioed Silverado. It was one-half AU further from their sun, a cold and bleak little place. They had no FTL comms, so the lightspeed lag made conversation frustrating but at last, using the Scavarchis' names, I managed to get the Crown Prince on the horn.

"This is in regards to a certain cargo that your boys took off me a few days ago," I said. "Don't worry, I'm not going to come get it back. I just wondered if you know exactly what you've got."

The interplanetary silence answered me. I was pretty sure they had no clue. All the cargo looked like was a bunch of very long, very strong cables, and some fancy tension dampeners, as well as a few other bits and pieces for the anchor points.

"What that is," I said, "is a space elevator starter kit. The Generalissimo pretends to despise space. But even he knows you can't get by without access to orbit these days. So he ordered the essential high-tech components for a space elevator. Everything that's not there you'll be able to put together yourselves at that assembly plant you've got. The only missing piece is the expertise to put it together. I suppose the Generalissimo was planning to ask the Eks. You do that, they'll take half your planet off you in consultancy fees. So instead, my associate here is going to tell you exactly how to make a space elevator. If you're not recording, start recording now."

I gave them thirty seconds to get their recording equipment cued up.

"OK, chrome dome, you're on," I whispered.

And for the next three hours and a half, the drone told them how to make a space elevator.

Then it spent another four hours answering their questions.

I sloped off for a nap in the air, feeling pretty good. With a space elevator, the Crown Prince would be able to retake Gorongol in no time. I just hoped he was nice about it.

When Dolph and I woke up, the drone was *still* on the radio, telling the Silveradans that if they wanted, they could spray some vaporized aluminum over the cables, and as the planet rotated through its own magnetic field, electric currents would be induced into the cables, so they could use that to run the lights and heat and such on the elevator cars ...

I sliced a hand through the air. "Wrap it up. They've got to learn to walk before they can run."

I said goodbye to the Crown Prince. Then, floating above the drive console, I initiated the FTL field generator.

I couldn't wait to show Lucy our new ship.

The only question was: What would we name her?

ABOUT FELIX R. SAVAGE

Felix R. Savage's "The Scrapyard Ship" was written with interjections, complaints, and improvements from Walter Blaire, author of *The Eternal Front and other Sci-Fi novels. It is set in the Cluster, a new space opera universe co-created by Felix and Walter, with many more exciting adventures to come! No one say "clusterfu…"*

Follow Mike Starrunner and the crew at www.clusterverse.com, and sign up to be notified when the first trilogy of action-packed Clusterverse novels launches later in 2018.

Felix writes hard science fiction, space opera, and comedic science fiction. He has also occasionally been known to commit fantasy. He woke up one day to learn that he was a *New York Times* and *USA Today* bestselling author, but he continues to keep a low profile, and never stops watching out for any sign the lizard people have found him.

Felix's latest release is *The Chemical Mage*, the first book in a hard science-fiction series packed with plot twists and suspenseful fleet action and battles. Check it out here: https://www.amazon.com/dp/B0762TTYGD. Or sign up for Felix's mailing list (http://felixrsavage.com/subscribe) and pick a *free* book to start reading now!

HERE BE DRAGONS

by Lindsay Buroker

"Only a suicidal lunatic would try to land down there." McCall Richter fidgeted with her bracelet while wondering if familial loyalty required her to risk her ship.

Wasn't it enough that she'd flown all the way out to a penal moon so inhospitable that it had the nickname Dragons? Thanks to all the cartographers who'd thought it amusing to write "Here Be Dragons" under it on their maps.

"I have recently downloaded an upgrade to my piloting protocol," Scipio, her android pilot/bodyguard/business partner, said.

"One that allows you to assume the role of a suicidal lunatic?"

Scipio looked over at her, his expression unchanging, though his silver eyes conveyed remarkable blandness. "One that gives me the ability to land your ship in inhospitable conditions. As a sturdy DuraSky 3636 android, the likelihood of my survival is high even in the event of a crash."

"Therefore, you're not being suicidal."

"Correct."

"*I* could be suicidal for flying with you."

"Correct."

"Glad we got that cleared up."

McCall eyed the jungle below them, the cockpit's wrap-around holographic display giving them almost a three-hundred-and-sixty-degree view. A thick orange, green, and pink canopy obscured the terrain below. Maps promised canyons, rivers, craters, and entire lakes hidden from aerial view. In places, the *Star Surfer's* sensors could verify that. In other places, the sheer mass of vegetation thwarted them. The only certainty was that the jungle was full of life. Serpents and dragons and who knew what other genetically engineered beasts the scientists who'd terraformed the moon had loosed into the wilds.

What good was a penal colony if people deposited there weren't penalized? Perhaps by being eaten by a dragon. The scientists, inspired by the cartographers, had apparently made plenty of those.

"I'm ready," McKenzie said, stopping on the threshold of the cockpit, since Junkyard's hundred-and-fifty-pound form blocked the entrance. The black, white, brown, and gray mutt snored away without acknowledging her.

McKenzie frowned down at the dog but didn't step over him. She wore a full suit of green combat armor. Where had she gotten the money for that? She'd recently left her last job, the latest of twenty or thirty, supposedly over a "difference of opinion."

"Put down as close to Shangri-La as you can, please," McKenzie added.

Scipio tilted his head. "Shangri-La? Do you reference the fictional utopia described in—"

"She means Tianlong Three," McCall said, knowing Scipio could and would recite the entire encyclopedia article, if not the whole novel. "My sister is under the delusion a colony founded by a bunch of autistic people will be utopian."

"I didn't say that." McKenzie scowled through her face-plate. "But those founders were brilliant scientists, mathematicians, authors, and philosophers. If their offspring are like them, we might fit in there. That's all I said."

McCall started to retort that she fit in just fine on her own ship, but noticed the travel pack strapped to her sister's back. A *huge* pack. "You're not planning to *stay*, are you? I thought you just wanted to *find* it."

"And apply for citizenship. If they'll have me. And they should. I can design infrastructure for any terrain, and I can fix anything. If they're completely self-sufficient, as the stories say, they may have a lot of old equipment in need of repairs."

"Assuming the colony is still there. It's been eighty years, and for brilliant people, they've been awfully quiet."

"They're there. I'm sure people like us could start a successful colony even in a remote, inhospitable location."

"People like us? Clumsy geeks with the wilderness skills of chubby lap dogs?"

"You know what I mean." McKenzie looked down at McCall's wrist, at the bracelet McCall was still fiddling with.

Frowning, McCall let go of it. "Fine, go and live like a monk. But don't expect me to visit."

"You didn't visit when I lived in Perun Central." McKenzie arched her eyebrows. "Even though you have three clients there."

McCall opened her mouth to make an excuse, realized that was all it would be, and said nothing instead. Her sister's eyebrows remained up.

McCall looked back toward the cockpit controls, finding the silence uncomfortable. And typical. Just like the last time McCall *had* visited. Other than sharing goofy names their mother had chosen during a phase of reading Old Earth romance novels, they had little in common. Also, McCall had a hard time forgetting all the times her older sister had turned her back on her during school lunches. She'd been on a never-ending quest to fit in with the popular kids. It seemed McKenzie was trying to find someone else to fit in with now.

"I believe I can land the *Star Surfer* on that ledge," Scipio said, oblivious to the awkward silence. Or indifferent to it. Or both. Either way, he was unflappable, as always. McCall fondly remembered the childhood year that she'd pretended to be an android. That might have been about the time McKenzie had been shooing her away. "It will require use of the quad grippers and a departure from the top hatch," he added.

"Meaning we're landing on a cliff and McKenzie will be climbing?"

"Correct."

"Good thing you bought that fancy armor," McCall told her sister.

"It is, because I'm sure you'll need help climbing, and with the enhanced strength it gives me, I can offer you a boost."

McCall blinked. "I'm not leaving the ship."

"You have to."

"No, I don't. I made the map, and I brought you all the way out here, even though I have clients waiting for me to find things more criminal than genetically engineered dragons."

"You're the one who dug up all the clues. If the map is wrong and we need to adjust our route, you'll be the one to know how."

"Scipio helped me make the map. He'll go along with you if needed." McCall felt guilty whenever she volunteered Scipio for dirty work, but he was, by his own admission, nearly indestructible. The only time she'd seen him take serious damage had been during a run-in with a rogue imperial cyborg who hadn't appreciated being hunted down.

"I don't object to him coming, but I strongly object to you *not* coming. Be logical, McCall. Finding things is your gift. If Shangri-La were easy to locate, people would come here all the time."

"I highly doubt that."

"Mom would have wanted us to work together."

McCall scowled at the deck. She'd been afraid her sister would play the mom card at some point. They both regretted that so many family gatherings had involved arguing, accusations, and temper tantrums in front of their poor mother, a woman who'd loved them even though they'd been hard kids to love. McKenzie liked to cash in on McCall's guilt from time to time. McCall recognized the manipulation, but she hadn't figured out how to wall off her emotions so she could say no to it. Maybe she should have tried harder as a little girl to turn herself into an android.

* * *

McCall's toes were going numb.

The sales robot that had sold her the jet boots had extolled the virtues of a secure fit, but she kept wondering if losing the circulation to her toes for too long would cause permanent damage. Then she wondered if she was weird for being more alarmed about that than the long drop into the gorge below. If the boots failed, she would plummet a hundred feet, bounce off the top of her ship, and splash into the river another hundred feet below. Or maybe she would splat into those prickly ferns next to it.

"I can't believe you painted your ship purple," McKenzie called over her shoulder.

She was climbing while McCall hovered behind her, the gauntlets of her fancy combat armor giving McKenzie far greater strength than usual.

McCall forced herself to focus on her sister's back rather than the fall or her boots. This wasn't the appropriate place for a panic attack. When they reached the top and a giant dragon sprang out to eat them, *that* would be the place.

"Nobody finds purple ships a threat," McCall replied. She had to raise her voice to be heard over the thunderous squawks, shrieks, and screeches emanating from the jungle above and below them. Further, a waterfall roared over the edge of the cliff to their left, the river marking the canyon they were to head up. "It's a scientific fact."

"I'd think ... your work ... want to be inconspicuous."

McCall flew closer, struggling to hear over the noise of the waterfall.

"All I do is fly around and do research on the sys-net. I'm not skulking through seedy space ports, looking for bad guys to pounce on." McCall had chosen her line of work, being a self-employed skip tracer, specifically because she never had to leave her ship or interact with criminals. Or much of anyone. Most of her clients knew to send text messages rather than comming her.

"No pouncing? Sounds boring."

"We can't all lead the scintillating life of a sewer designer."

"I won an *award* for that waste treatment system. And that's not all I design."

McCall bit back a comment about all the jobs McKenzie had been fired from in her life. As she'd finally learned, nothing except hurt feelings ever came from their sniping sessions. And it wasn't as if she could have dealt with bosses and co-workers and office politics, either. There was a reason she'd constructed the career she had.

"Just wait until I get the costs down for the space elevator I'm designing," McKenzie added, "and the empire builds it. It'll be *amazing*."

A noisy hiss came from above. Since McCall hovered only ten feet from the top, she had a good view of the monstrous snake head sticking over the edge. A dark tongue darted between fangs long enough to sharpen a butcher knife on. Or maybe a sword. Yellow eyes looked McCall up and down, assessing her ability to defend herself, or perhaps her caloric potential.

McCall tapped her wrist controller to pause her ascent and pulled out her blazer from its holster. Normally, she wouldn't pick a fight with innocent wildlife, but this snake had the look of an imperial cyborg fresh from a 50K run, making selections at a buffet.

Unaware of it, McKenzie kept climbing. The yellow eyes shifted focus to her. Before McCall could shout a warning, the flat, arrow-shaped head darted toward her sister.

Though her heart pounded in her ears, McCall stayed calm enough to aim and fire twice. It helped that she wasn't the snake's target.

Her crimson blazer bolts struck as it tried to sink its fangs into McKenzie's helmet. One scorched a hole into its thick body. The other blew up its head, and snake brains spattered the cliff and McKenzie's armor. The remains of its limp body slithered over the edge of the cliff, clunking her shoulder as it fell.

McCall lowered her blazer with a shaking hand. It took her three tries to get it back in the holster. She was well aware that she would have been too late if McKenzie hadn't been wearing armor. Fortunately, those long fangs hadn't even scratched the helmet.

"You shoot well for someone who doesn't pounce on bad guys that often." McKenzie twisted to look at the snake's body—it had landed on the *Surfer.*

Maybe Scipio would remove it, and Junkyard could have it for dinner. The dog had been put out at being left behind for this adventure.

"Sometimes, bad guys want to pounce on *you.* I try to avoid that, but figure it's better safe than sorry." When a client concerned for her welfare had first dragged her to a shooting range, McCall had been delighted to learn that her lack of athletic ability didn't translate to ineptitude when it came to marksmanship. Different genes, maybe.

"Good idea. Though I'm shocked you don't have a set of combat armor." McKenzie resumed her climb, surprisingly blasé about the snake incident. Maybe she believed nothing in the jungle could get her through that armor. McCall wouldn't take that bet.

"I'm shocked you *do*." McCall resumed her own ascent. "I can't even wear a shirt with a tag in it without going nuts." She wiggled her numb toes. She was making a rare exception when it came to wearing uncomfortable clothing.

"Don't laugh," McKenzie said as they stepped into dense moss coating the top of the cliff, "but I went to a hypnotist. To help with the claustrophobia. I've been planning this adventure for a while."

The huge pack on her back promised this was more than an "adventure" for her.

McKenzie peered into the dense, dark foliage ahead of them and out over the gorge they'd climbed from. "There's nothing left for me back on Perun."

"You got rid of your apartment and everything?"

"I sold my car to buy the armor, and the apartment… Yeah, it's gone too."

Her phrasing made McCall suspect there was more to the story, but she didn't pry. She was surprised McKenzie was being this open with her, as it was. For the first ten years of her professional career, McKenzie had always pretended she was doing great, that the frequent employment changes represented new opportunities she'd chosen to take rather than jobs she'd been fired from. McCall remembered being envious of the design awards she'd shown off, until she'd dug around and learned that McKenzie had, on several occasions, come close to being the kind of person McCall got hired to find.

"Well, you and your fancy armor get to lead the way and be the snake bait." McCall waved in the direction of their destination, or at least the spot marked on her map. There wasn't anything remotely resembling a trail.

"Gladly." McKenzie popped a laser cutter out of her arm piece and sliced into the brush and vines. "I appreciate you coming along."

"You're welcome."

"I do, however, wish you'd brought your android. He told me he was named Scipio after a great war hero from Old Earth."

"True, but he named *himself* Scipio. He's very useful, but he's a personal assistant model, originally designed to run errands for important businessmen." McCall followed her sister, doing her best to avoid the dangling vines and clawing thorns. Her skin already felt itchy. The terraformers had probably thought allergy-inducing foliage would add insult to injury on their penal moon.

"And now he runs errands for you?" McKenzie sounded wistful.

"Sort of. I made him my business partner so he gets fifty percent of everything."

"Fifty percent of your *money*? What in the universe do androids do with money?"

"I don't know about other androids, but he collects hats and ceramic eggs."

"Eggs?"

"Apparently, eggs are a geometrically appealing shape. He finds them soothing."

"Soothing?" McKenzie ducked under a branch. "Your android needs to be soothed? That's not typical, is it?"

"For people who have to work with me? It may be."

"I meant for androids."

"I know. It was a joke."

"It wasn't funny."

"Are you sure? You're not the best judge of such things."

McKenzie grumbled something under her breath and didn't ask another question. Good. McCall didn't like giving people information on Scipio since her acquisition of him had been unorthodox. A rescue, he'd called it. McCall was fairly certain the empire considered it thievery and wanted him back. But as long as they believed him destroyed, she hoped it wouldn't be a problem.

The dry vines above McKenzie's head rustled loudly. McCall jerked her blazer out again but didn't spot the brown snake blending in with the brown foliage until it was upon them. Six inches thick and who knew how long, it curled around McKenzie's armored torso with the speed of a bullwhip snapping around a branch.

As McCall took aim, McKenzie shrieked and flailed. Her laser cutter was still on, and it shot wildly through the vegetation in all directions.

McCall cursed and ducked as the beam lanced toward her. She scrambled behind her sister, trying to aim as McKenzie flailed. She fired twice, her blazer bolts sailing wide. The snake coiled further and constricted. Something popped— McKenzie's armor?

Taking cover behind a tree, McCall forced herself to stop moving long enough to aim effectively. McKenzie continued to gyrate as she tried to grip the snake and tear it free. Its body seemed to flex, and it lifted her from her feet. She shrieked.

McCall took a deep breath, lined up her sights, and fired. A bolt slammed into the snake. She fired again, aiming at spots above her sister. Her armor should repel blazer bolts, but there was no need to take chances.

McCall struck again and again, blowing gaping holes in the snake. It tightened, and another pop came from McKenzie's armor.

Her boots dangled at eye level, and McCall worried the snake would never let go, that they would both disappear into the trees. She fired recklessly and often, trying to blow open its head, a head that was tucked under her sister's armpit.

Her shots grazed McKenzie's armor, but enough of them struck, and the snake finally had enough. It let go of her abruptly, and she crashed into the leaf litter, landing on her back.

McCall shot twice more, afraid the creature would regroup and attack again. Almost as abruptly as it had let go, it fell out of the vines. It landed in a pile atop McKenzie, and she shrieked one more time.

"Get it off!" She sounded angry and frustrated as much as afraid.

McCall wanted to help, but she also didn't want to touch it with her bare hands. It looked slimy and slick, and she hated things with weird textures. Especially dead things with weird textures.

"I think you can just roll away from it." McCall eyed their surroundings, the vines and leaves far too close for comfort. A hundred more predators could be within ten meters of them, and she would never know it.

As McKenzie grunted and heaved dramatically—as if her armor didn't allow her to easily flick aside a snake, even a twenty-foot one—a green amorphous blob floated past. At first, McCall thought it some strange leaf caught on the wind, but it wriggled stalks or perhaps antennae at her, then tripled its speed, disappearing into the foliage. She had no idea what it was or what propelled it.

"I wonder if scientists created everything here, or if there was any native life before the terraforming," McCall said, twisting her bracelet as she peered at the alien growth. Upon closer inspection, what she had assumed were towering trees appeared to be colonies of vines.

"*I* wonder if snake blood comes off combat armor." McKenzie swiped ineffectively at the gore on her chest, then grimaced at a dark stain on the corner of her pack. Somehow, she'd kept the straps on while flailing about.

"Probably with a sponge rather than a gauntlet. It would be a pity if armor could deflect bullets and blazer bolts, but not repel stains."

Leaves rustled, and the dead snake was yanked into the undergrowth. McCall jumped, grabbing her blazer again.

But whatever claimed the snake for dinner didn't show itself. She swallowed, imagining the strength of whatever had pulled the big snake away so quickly.

McKenzie took a deep breath and faced forward, lifting her cutting tool to continue forging a path. "Shangri-La, Shangri-La," she whispered, almost a chant.

McCall shook her head as she followed. If they found a colony somewhere in all this, would McKenzie truly like the people there? Maybe it was a betrayal to "her kind," but McCall didn't usually *like* people like her that much. They often seemed aloof and prickly or tedious as they rambled on about odd passions. Normal people were easier to get along with. McCall's favorites were those rare souls who were comfortable in their own skins and had a knack for making others feel at ease too.

"Is there not a way you could work for yourself?" McCall asked as they pushed vines aside and clambered over moss-carpeted logs. "Back on Perun."

"The systems I design are on the scale of cities and require teams."

"What if you *led* the teams?"

"I'd still be working for an employer. I don't have your entrepreneurial streak, so I don't know how I could make a business of it and call all the shots. I'm not even sure I want that. I just want…" McKenzie paused, frowning at her prints in the earth.

"To be accepted for who you are?"

McKenzie snorted. "Three suns, that's cheesy."

"But not wrong?"

"I guess not."

"Why didn't you ever … I mean, did you consider the surgery?"

"I considered it." McKenzie looked back. "Did you? They say it doesn't change you."

"Yes, they say that. Which is amusing since what would be the point if it *didn't* change you?"

"You know what they mean. Your personality and memories stay the same, though apparently, you're less prone to emotional outbursts and fighting with your sister."

"Clearly, you should have signed up right away."

McKenzie snorted again. "If I really felt impaired, I'd do it. But when you have something you're good at, and maybe you're only good at it *because* you think differently than others do, it's scary to contemplate changing the way your brain cells rub together."

"I know."

McCall had probably read all the same accounts of people who'd undergone the "normalization" surgery, as the imperial doctors called it. Most of the time, parents made the decision to do it when kids were little, so they didn't have a choice in the matter. McCall had wondered occasionally what she would have been like—what school and dating and *life* would have been like—if Mom had made that decision. But Mom had feared the empire and doctors equally, and she'd avoided them at all costs. In the end, that had cost her her life.

"I know you do," McKenzie said. "I've looked you up, and it seems you're unparalleled in your field, as odd as that is."

"Odd?" McCall tamped down her natural inclination toward bristling at a slight.

"You can't look people in the eye and don't seem to get them any more than I do, but you can figure out where they're hiding when they disappear from the system."

"I'm using the sys-net and deductive reasoning, not studying people's pupils. I do have a long list of typical human motivations next to my desk. When I'm stuck, I look at them. Sometimes, I have to remind myself that people are motivated by weird things."

"What are you motivated by?"

"Having the freedom to control my own destiny."

"That's a hard thing to do in the empire," McKenzie said. "Hells, that's been a hard thing to do throughout human history."

"I have my own ship, fly where I want, work my own hours, take on the cases I want. It's enough."

"Yeah, I have to admit I'm jealous that you have it all figured out."

McCall tripped over a root. "You're jealous of *me*?"

McKenzie turned around—bits of vine and leaves had joined the dried blood sticking to her chest. "That surprises you?"

"Yes, actually. You were the one who got all those awards, and—I don't know. You always gave off the impression you thought I was a twit."

McKenzie gazed into the brush. McCall wasn't the only one who found prolonged eye contact uncomfortable.

"I'd like to pretend I didn't realize I was kind of an ass," McKenzie said slowly, "but it always bothered me that you were a weirdo and you knew it and you didn't care. You even seemed *happy* being weird. And I tried so hard to be … one of them. Because I couldn't stand being snickered at or talked about behind my back. I wanted everyone to like me so they wouldn't do that. I think, deep down, I knew you were a better person when it came to that stuff, and I resented that I couldn't be like that. Maybe I was smug about my grades and awards, but I had to be better than you at *something*."

The honesty floored McCall. Maybe it had been worth this trek if only to hear it.

"If it helps, not everything is perfect for me," she said. "I've crafted a life that makes me comfortable, yes, but it concerns me sometimes that I've never figured out relationships and that my closest friends are a dog and an android. Like, will I die alone? Will anyone even remember me when I'm gone?"

"I'd say I'd remember you, but I'm two years older, so you could outlive me."

A screech came from the canopy above them.

"Unless I get eaten by a snake in here," McCall said. "Though at least I won't die alone then."

"What are you talking about? I'll sprint back to the ship if a snake is munching on you. You'll be *completely* alone." McKenzie grinned at her.

"You're still an ass, you know."

"Yeah." McKenzie thumped her on the shoulder.

McCall almost pitched into the brush—her sister wasn't used to that extra strength yet. But she righted herself and didn't complain. Neither of them had ever been huggers, much to their mother's chagrin, and this was as close to sisterly camaraderie as they'd gotten in a long time. Maybe ever.

"Is it petty," McKenzie asked, "that it *does* make me feel better to know that you haven't gotten it all figured out?"

"Extremely petty. But I'll be petty right back and hope that snake-blood stain *doesn't* come out of your armor."

"That's so evil."

* * *

The hives spreading across the backs of McCall's hands were starting to look like a relief map of the Kataran Mountains on Perun. Thorns clawed her through her clothing and cut at any skin she'd been foolish enough to leave exposed. The screeches, hoots, and whistles of the jungle grated on her nerves, and she caught herself taking deep breaths, fighting for calm amid the chaos of it all.

As she slogged after her sister, McCall tugged at her bracelet and fought the urge to itch her hives. Her toes were completely numb, leaving her on the verge of ripping off the jet boots and walking barefoot. She'd hoped to use them to fly under the canopy, in addition to bypassing cliffs, but the foliage was too dense for navigating easily on land *or* in the air.

Everything was combining to frustrate and irritate her. She longed for her peaceful cabin aboard the *Surfer*.

McKenzie cut away some vines, somehow causing a head-sized cone to plop onto McCall's shoulder. Thorns bit through her shirt before it bounced off.

"Ouch," she blurted. "Damn it, Kenzie. Why couldn't you have just asked for money like Cousin Anise does?"

The words came out more savagely than she intended, and as usual when she lost her temper, she felt guilty afterward. Especially when McKenzie gazed back at her, as unperturbed as a cat in a sunbeam. Maybe her combat armor made her less prone to the irritations of the jungle. Or maybe the fact that this was her quest granted her equanimity.

"Because I have pride," McKenzie said.

"Sounds inconvenient."

"Sometimes it is." McKenzie pointed in the direction they'd been heading. "According to your map, we're getting close. My sensors don't show any life up there. Which is weird."

"Weird?"

"No life at *all*."

"Ah, no snakes or birds, either?"

"Right. I'm thinking there may be some kind of force-field or camouflage to make the colony hard to find." McKenzie bounced on her toes. "This is our first proof that something is here."

"Huh." McCall hadn't truly expected to find anyone living out here. The penal colony inhabitants kept to the far side of the moon and weren't encouraged to wander.

"Careful, you'll overwhelm me with your excitement."

"I'm containing my urge to issue loud whoops lest I attract more predators."

"Uh-huh. According to my sensors, we're almost at the end of our box canyon. Our *destination*. Can you fly up ahead and see if you can spot it from above?" McKenzie pointed to the jet boots. "It looks less dense up there now."

Glad to have a reason to use the toe-numbing boots, McCall tapped the controls and went aloft without argument. "Less dense" did not mean *clear*, and she had to dart around branches and vines like a ship navigating the Kir Asteroid Belt. She couldn't see the sky through the canopy, and soon she couldn't see the ground, either.

She passed more of those floating blobs, none appearing alarmed by her presence this time. Or so she thought. Abruptly, they whooshed away in multiple directions. Fleeing from her? Or some more dangerous predator?

The hairs on the back of her neck rose, and she had the sensation of being watched.

"Do your sensors show anything big up here?" she called, pulling out her blazer and rotating to peer in all directions.

It had grown quiet, birds and other creatures falling silent, and she could hear her sister cutting vines from her path.

"It's hard to distinguish the size of any one thing when there's such a mass of life all around," McKenzie called back. "I—wait. There's—"

The thunderous snapping of branches drowned out her words. A huge green creature flew toward McCall, tearing away vines as it flapped leathery wings.

She glimpsed scales, talons, and an open maw filled with giant fangs. That was enough. She fired at its head and whirled away, angling her boots to take her toward the ground.

Thorns and twigs clawed at her, but she barely noticed. Not with that *thing* barreling straight after her, the loud snaps of branches announcing its passage.

"McCall?" came a call from the ground. "Are you all right?"

McCall glanced back as she weaved between vines, trying to find a tight area where the creature—the *dragon*—couldn't follow. But it was right behind her. Breaking through obstacles she had to go around.

"No!" she cried, almost crashing into a tangle of thick vines as she fired rapidly.

Her blazer bolts struck the creature in the head—one took it right between the eyes—but it was as if it wore combat armor. The blasts bounced off its scales.

"Lead it here!" McKenzie yelled. "I'm armored."

McCall doubted that would be enough, but she didn't know what else to do. She swooped downward, trying to find the ground, having some notion that she'd be safer down there. A delusion, perhaps.

A massive blue beam lanced out of the jungle ahead. Light? A weapon? It shot past only a couple of feet above McCall's head.

The dragon shrieked as the beam hammered into its chest. For the first time, it faltered. Faltered, but did not halt. It roared in agony and rage, eyes locking on to McCall, as if *she'd* done that.

Its massive jaws yawned open, and a gout of flames shot out.

McCall dove so hard and fast that she slammed shoulder-first into the ground. The heat of the flames scorched the air above her, and she imagined her eyebrows being singed off.

Rolling to her back, she fired. The dragon was still coming, angling downward, its talons outstretched.

She shot at its chest where a char mark had melted scales and burned into flesh and muscle. Her blazer seemed puny against its mass, and the dragon didn't slow down. Gravity swept it toward her.

Crashes came from the side, McKenzie running toward her, but she would be too late to help. McCall tried to roll away, but logs and brush fenced her in.

As certain death descended, another massive bolt of blue came out of nowhere. It slammed into the dragon hard enough to hurl it into a copse of trees. Snaps of wood echoed through the jungle.

McCall jumped to her feet and pushed her way into the brush, away from the dragon and toward the source of those beams, hoping safety lay that way. She met an odd resistance, as if the air had grown ten times as dense, but she was able to push through.

The dragon roared again, coming to its feet and shaking off like Junkyard when he was wet. McKenzie's green armor came into view, and she shrieked with surprise as she almost ran into the dragon. She veered around it.

McCall paused, afraid it would lunge at McKenzie and that those fangs would sink through her armor.

But the dragon must have had enough. It sprang into the air and flew back the way it had come.

McKenzie stumbled back, gaping at it until it disappeared. "I didn't really think there would be dragons."

"I didn't think there'd be dragons that would breathe *fire*." McCall looked down at her hands, her skin red as if from a sunburn. As if the hives hadn't been insult enough. "What kind of genetic encoding allows for that?"

"If you're going to create a fairytale creature, I guess you go all the way."

"More like a nightmare creature."

McKenzie walked over, then frowned and stuck her hand out. She pushed at the air, and McCall remembered the resistance she'd felt.

They moved forward together, and between one step and the next, the jungle they had been walking through disappeared, replaced by a grassy clearing framed by three stone walls, the end of the canyon. A waterfall fell into a pool, then flowed into a river, the one they had been following but barely hearing or seeing sign of it.

A couple of gray metal buildings sat in the clearing. Beyond them, caves pierced the cliffs, some with dark doors covering them, almost as if they were garages, and others open with ledges overlooking the meadow.

Sunlight shone down through a break in the canopy, a break that hadn't been visible from above. McCall was certain of it. The *Surfer* had flown over this spot on the way in.

"It's beautiful," McKenzie said, turning a full circle. "So peaceful. You could work on anything here, come up with all manner of designs. Or finish ones you've started. Like a space elevator from Perun Central to the planet's big orbital base."

"You'll have to tell me more about that sometime."

"Gladly! I'll show you my prototype before you go home. But now, let's explore." McKenzie skipped toward the buildings.

McCall walked behind more slowly, tempted to ask if her sister detected life signs now. The place seemed empty, with few sounds except for the rush of the water. She supposed people could live behind those cave doors.

Movement to the side made McCall jump. A large, floating black disc at the perimeter of the meadow fired into the jungle, a massive blue beam identical to the ones that had struck the dragon. She spotted other discs, also along the perimeter. Robot guards?

The closest disc sailed toward McKenzie. An intercept course.

"McKenzie," McCall shouted in warning, jogging after her sister. "Look out!"

McKenzie had almost reached the first building, but she paused and lifted her hands as the disc flew toward her. McCall had assumed it kept animals—and dragons—out and let humans in, but perhaps that had been premature.

The disc stopped a few meters from McKenzie, its weapons port pointing at her chest. Would her armor stop such a big blast? The dragon's nearly impervious scales hadn't.

"State the passcode or solve the puzzle if you wish access to the sanctuary," a woman's melodious voice said, coming from the disc.

McKenzie looked at McCall. "Passcode? Did you come across that in your research?"

"No."

"State the passcode or solve the puzzle if you wish access to the sanctuary," the disc repeated. "Only the scholarly and peaceful are allowed here."

"Guess they didn't want escapees from the penal colony coming to visit," McCall said.

"We'll do the puzzle," McKenzie said, looking toward the cliffs, as if she expected someone to come out and welcome them.

"And hope nothing happens if we can't solve it."

Four other discs drifted in their direction, then split to surround them. They effectively blocked the route back into the jungle.

"We'd probably just get kicked out," McKenzie said. "But that's not acceptable. I came to stay." She spoke the words firmly, but her expression was uncertain as she gazed around again.

McCall had a feeling the sensors built into her armor weren't showing her anybody around.

One of the discs floated closer, and she eyed it warily. She didn't reach for her blazer, doubting her shots could damage the sturdy robot, but she debated on leaping into the air and using her boots to fly overhead. Would they follow her up? Or could she escape?

But what of McKenzie? The jets weren't strong enough to lift two, and she couldn't leave her sister. Her mother would have—

Light flared, as if McCall were looking into a sun. She flung her arm up and squinted her eyes shut. The sensation of falling came over her, and she spread her legs, struggling for balance.

When the light faded, she wasn't in the meadow anymore. She was in a hospital room, sitting next to a bed with a patient hooked up to monitors and an IV. A *familiar* patient. Mom.

Her skin was pale, her body gaunt, her hair falling out, and she looked old, far older than her fifty-three years.

McKenzie sat in a chair on the other side of the bed, her eyes brimming with tears. McCall met her gaze, and her sister shook her head. Mom didn't have much time left. The treatment hadn't worked. She'd been too sick when she'd finally come to the hospital, the disease too far advanced.

"There's hope," a voice said at McCall's ear.

An android stood there in hospital scrubs. His hair was short and dark, his eyes silver, and for a moment, she thought it was Scipio. But this was a different model. Besides, she hadn't known Scipio yet when this had happened. Or was it happening now? She looked at Mom in confusion, trying to remember how she'd gotten here.

"We're so close to solving the problem. Want to have a try at it?" The android opened his hand, revealing a netdisc, and a holodisplay came up. A close-up of blood cells, some bright and round, others dark and lopsided. Diseased. "Just move them around so the healthy ones win."

It sounded stupid, more like a game than a solution to a health problem, but McCall lifted a finger, unable to keep from trying. The challenge called to her, as did the possibility that she was wrong, that this *could* help. That it could save Mom.

"McCall," McKenzie whispered from across the bed. "She's awake."

"Good," McCall said, but didn't look away from the display. She found she could move blood cells around by dragging her finger. Surrounding the diseased ones with healthy ones caused the diseased ones to disappear. But there were so many more of them than the healthy ones. Was it possible to gain the upper hand?

"McCall," McKenzie said, now holding Mom's hand.

Mom's eyes were open, sunken with dark bags under them. She looked so weary, but she lifted a frail hand toward McCall.

McCall started to reach for her, but she needed both hands to move cells around. She was making some progress. Maybe it wasn't too late. Less than half the cells left were diseased.

"Be right there," she said.

Her hands were a blur as she moved cells. The android watched on, but never spoke, never changed his expression.

The last diseased cell disappeared from the display, and McCall surged to her feet. "I did it!"

She looked toward Mom and McKenzie. Tears streaked her sister's cheeks. Mom's eyes were closed again, and the instruments monitoring her had stopped running.

"A valiant effort," the android said, "but unfortunately you were too late."

McKenzie shook her said slowly. Accusingly?

"But I solved the puzzle," McCall whispered. How could it not have worked?

* * *

The sky was a deep blue, but a black circle obscured the edge of it. An eclipse? No, the *sun* wasn't blocked.

McCall stared upward for several long seconds before awareness returned, along with the memory she'd just re-lived. No, not a memory. In reality, she and McKenzie had sat together by Mom's bed. She'd taken their hands, placed them atop each other, and held them with her own weak ones. She had elicited a promise that they would look out for each other, then whispered that she loved them.

McCall had been there for it. She hadn't been ignoring her dying mother to play some game, so she found the false memory confusing. Admittedly, during those last weeks, she had spent a lot of time researching and trying to find a way to cure Mom, perhaps some obscure treatment the doctors had overlooked or hadn't considered. After Mom had passed, she *had* wondered if she'd spent too much time doing that, time she could have spent being with her. But it had been so hard to be there, not knowing what to say or how to feel, wondering if a different daughter, a better one, would have been able to make her mother feel more comfortable and loved in the end.

The black disc floated away, leaving only the sky. And the grass pricking her neck. Why was she flat on her back?

McKenzie stepped into view, her helmet tucked under her arm, sweat plastering her hair to her face. "I guess you solved your puzzle too," she said, her voice having a hollowness to it.

"I ... guess." As McCall sat up, the disc floated back to its sentry duty on the perimeter. "I feel like I failed though."

"Mine was like that too." McKenzie wiped her eyes—she'd also removed her gauntlets. Were those tears? Had she experienced the same moment? Or a different one? "But I knew I'd passed because the robots left me alone. So I could look around." She waved toward the buildings and the caves. "And find that there's nobody here."

"Ah."

"There hasn't been for a long time. Everything's old and dusty." McKenzie looked skyward, her fingers flexing at her sides, helpless. "There aren't any skeletons or signs of fights or anything. It's like they just left. And forgot to tell anyone."

"Maybe they didn't want to admit their colony was a failure, that it wasn't Shangri-La." McCall couldn't claim to be surprised.

"Fuck." McKenzie kicked her pack.

McCall chewed on her lip. "I know you were hoping for a comfortable place to live." She didn't say *fit in*, since she'd never cared for that phrase. People weren't jigsaw pieces to be slotted together. "But you can find that even back in the empire. If you're creative, you can carve out a spot for yourself where you can be who you are. Sometimes, that's what you have to do. Carve. Chisel. Jackhammer. Adjust the world, at least a small piece of it, to suit you."

"Maybe I should get a purple spaceship."

"Sure, why not?"

McKenzie smiled sadly at the abandoned buildings, and McCall didn't know if that denoted agreement or not.

* * *

"Back to civilization," McCall said, the lights of the dark side of Perun visible on the view screen. "Real-time communications and access to Tammy Jammy bars."

"The latter being your primary concern, I surmise." Scipio was busy piloting them toward the planet, but he nodded toward McCall's sole remaining bar, a few pieces carefully preserved for emergencies.

She touched it lovingly, rustling the wrapper. At the back of the cockpit, Junkyard lifted his head from his bed, ears perking. Civilization also meant access to quality dog treats. Not that he was above Tammy Jammy bars.

"You surmise correctly. I should check on McKenzie." McCall tapped her netdisc to look up the local time in Perun Central. Assuming her sister had gone back there. When they'd dropped McKenzie off a month earlier, McCall had worried that she wouldn't know what to do with herself. She had been tempted to go down to the planet with her, but several jobs had come in while she'd been cavorting on Dragons Moon, so she'd only grabbed fuel and supplies before taking off again.

As McCall verified it was before midnight downside, the comm flashed. McKenzie's face appeared in the holodisplay, and she smiled broadly. It was alarming since neither McCall nor McKenzie were the type to display so many teeth.

"You're back," McKenzie said. "I'm glad. I wanted to tell you right away—I had the surgery."

"Oh." Stunned, McCall didn't know what else to say. After their conversation in the jungle, she hadn't thought McKenzie considered the brain surgery even a last resort.

"Things are going better now. I got a new job. I'm feeling more comfortable working as a team member." McKenzie's smile widened. "My boss likes me. We went out to lunch yesterday."

"Oh." Realizing her responses were monosyllabic, McCall added, "Are you all right? Have there been any side effects?"

McKenzie hesitated. "No, I'm fine."

"That's good." McCall wanted to pry, but doubted her sister would appreciate it.

"I find it a little harder to concentrate, but that's all. I used to hyper focus on things I cared about. But I'm not so obsessed anymore. I'm developing more interests. That's healthy, my doctor told me."

"Working on any exciting new projects at work?"

"Oh, we mostly maintain old infrastructure here. There's not a need for exciting and new." McKenzie waved her hand, as if to dismiss this as a minor point.

"Any progress on the space elevator?"

"No, that was just a silly project. Who would ever pay for it? Anyway, you should come visit. We'll go out to dinner. Mary Lee at the office showed me this great wine place. You'd like it. You'll come, right?"

McCall forced herself to smile, though she was flailing on the inside. Or maybe wailing. "I'll come."

"Good. I'm much happier now, McCall. Why don't you look into the surgery too?"

McCall's thoughts drifted back to the sentry robots and that weird puzzle. Weeks later, the incident still disturbed her. She questioned the humanity of whoever had programmed that robot to prioritize puzzles over people. And the fact that she'd passed made her question her *own* humanity.

Was she different from others, as she'd always known, or was she broken? And was a surgery that could fix her brokenness a good thing?

No, she decided. Better to be broken if that was what it took to pursue unrealistic dreams.

"Not for me," she told her sister, "but I'm glad you're content."

They said their goodbyes, and McCall leaned back in her seat, her chin in her hand.

"What surgery did your sister have?" Scipio asked. "She seemed fit and hale when she was here."

"Yes."

Scipio waited, no doubt expecting her to answer the original question because he was programmed to understand how social interactions worked. But she wasn't, and she didn't.

"It seems the outcome was good," he offered.

"If nothing else, I think I'll get along with my sister more easily now."

"This is a positive development."

"Or it's the loss of something intangible but not inconsequential," McCall murmured.

Scipio gave her a puzzled look, but she had nothing else to say.

ABOUT LINDSAY BUROKER

Lindsay has early memories of convincing childhood friends, pets, and stuffed animals to play the roles of characters in her worlds, so it's safe to say she's been making up stories for a long time. She published her first novel, *The Emperor's Edge*, in December of 2010 and has written and published more than 50 novels since then, most under her own name, but a few steamier ones under a pen name.

When she's not writing, she's usually hiking with her dogs, practicing yoga, playing tennis, or eating entirely too much dark chocolate (she only does one of those things truly well, and she will let you guess which it is). She grew up in the Seattle area and still visits the Pacific Northwest, but after realizing she was solar powered, she moved to Arizona and now lives in the mountains north of Phoenix.

If you're interested in reading more of her work, you can download *The Emperor's Edge*, *Star Nomad*, and *Balanced on the Blade's Edge* for free in your favorite store.

THE GORDIAN ASTEROID
(a Space Lore short story)

by Chris Dietzel

1

"DOCTOR, ARE YOU SURE THIS IS A GOOD IDEA?"

Tragedy, an android that resembled humans—albeit with no hair on its head or body, slightly translucent skin, and irises that glowed any time it processed complex information—had said the same thing each morning.

Dr. Vongst grunted as the android assisted in getting him into a suit of space armor. Years earlier, he could have assembled his own suit while standing on one leg. Now, in his seventies, he sat down and allowed Tragedy to put on his metal boots, gladly waiting to stand until the reinforced joints and artificial support provided by the space armor gave him the stability and strength to stand without fear of embarrassing himself.

"Yes, I'm sure."

Although he was a scientist and not a historian, Vongst knew enough about ancient protective suits to know they used to add fifty or sixty pounds to the individual wearing it. Space armor was exactly the opposite. It weighed much more than older suits, but the joint controls made the wearer feel light and strong. With each piece Tragedy put onto Vongst, the old man felt more sure of himself. It was a pleasure having the helmet fitted over his head because the suit also gave him enough oxygen that he wasn't constantly coughing or pausing to catch his breath.

With the last piece of his space armor on, Dr. Vongst stood and began toward the rear of the ship. The android followed. With each step, the doctor's metal boots clanged against the metal floor. In his suit, which weighed hundreds of pounds, he sounded less like a frail and weak researcher and more like a soldier marching out to battle.

They were aboard a small research transport, so it only took ten paces to get to the rear ramp. There, he reached a thick, gloved hand to the side panel and pressed a white button. A pair of beeps sounded. The transport's ramp began to lower.

"See you in a couple hours."

"Yes, Doctor."

Vongst's boots thudded against the platform as he descended the ramp. Each step also offered a faint click, swoosh, and click, although the doctor no longer paid it any attention. It was the sound of the space armor keeping him anchored to whatever surface he was stepping onto, ensuring he didn't drift off into space.

Thud.

Thud.

The next step down the ramp was perfectly silent. A sensor inside his helmet noted that the gravity had also just changed.

Vongst had passed through the invisible containment field that protected the ship's artificial living environment and simulated gravity from the cold and oxygenless void of space.

In the earpiece in his helmet, the doctor heard Tragedy ask the second of its two standard questions.

"Why are you doing this, Doctor?"

Vongst didn't turn back to look at the android. In front of him was an expanse of rock as large as a moon. Beyond that, the infinite ocean of black space. With one more step Vongst reached the asteroid's surface. He was standing on an object that was hurtling through space at an average speed of 55,923 miles per hour.

"For research."

2

What Tragedy didn't understand, at least from Dr. Vongst's perspective, was that they weren't on any normal hunk of rock soaring through the galaxy. Space was littered with meteors and asteroids. The Gordian Asteroid, however, was unlike any of the other billions that were out there. Vongst liked to provoke his boss at the Outer Rim Scientific Station—a Trachdorian astronomer with an unpronounceable name but who everyone called Dr. Phillips—by saying that there were only two types of asteroids. The Gordian Asteroid and everything else.

It was larger than Terst-minor and any of the other moons in the sector. Big enough to have its own core and slight gravitational force. Every seventy-five years, it completed one giant, elliptical orbit around the blue sun of the McKessel system. But what made the asteroid unique wasn't its size or trajectory. It was the fact that a fleet of almost one thousand flagships was encased within its rock.

It went by many names. The Gordian Asteroid. The Army in the Stone. The Excalibur. Some people called it the Red Armada because of the way exposed parts of the ships glowed during its closest orbit with the mighty star, Eta Orbitae.

Parts of ships jutted out at odd angles from various chunks of the rock. There was no discernible organization to how the vessels were arranged. A pair of enormous thrusters stuck out from one area. Further down, the bow of another ship protruded from the rock. At the far edge of where Dr. Vongst was located, he saw a line of cannons sticking out from the asteroid's surface.

A fleet of ships larger than any ruler had ever obtained was encased in an asteroid and everyone knew exactly where the treasure was located, yet no one could free the ships from the stone that kept them prisoner. Ever since its discovery, one ruler after another had wanted the fleet for themselves. But one thing ensured the armada remained elusive: any attempt to free a vessel from the stone resulted in that ship's self-destruction, along with anyone and anything that was nearby.

3

"Doctor, are you sure this is a good idea?"

Even as Tragedy asked the question, the android lifted the helmet of Vongst's space armor over his head.

"Positive."

Man and android walked to the rear of the transport, then waited as the ramp lowered to allow the doctor yet another chance to explore the asteroid. Before it was all the way down, Vongst began across the length of plank without stumbling or even slowing. It was amazing how confident his balance was in the advanced space suit.

At the bottom of the ramp, he paused and turned. Tragedy was standing at the top of the ramp. Even if the android accidentally walked through the clear containment field separating ship from space, it would be unharmed. It didn't need oxygen and its systems were designed to be resistant to cold. It nodded and Vongst nodded back.

The doctor knew what would happen after he began across the Gordian. Tragedy would return to the cockpit and take the transport a safe distance away from the asteroid in case a ship detonated. *A safe distance* was roughly five miles. Everything within that blast radius would be incinerated.

It was fine that Tragedy left. Vongst wanted to be alone on the asteroid anyway, and he was aware that the android had been installed with self-preservation software. As long as it wasn't doing something to harm the doctor or the research, Tragedy was within its programming to ensure its own safety. Surely, it was reasonable to want to be far away from an object that could explode at any moment. That also explained why no one else from the Outer Rim Scientific Station had volunteered to join Vongst.

He was only a couple paces across the stone terrain when he heard the android's next question come through the speaker inside his helmet.

"Why are you doing this, Doctor?"

"Research."

4

Dr. Vongst's answer suggested something new could be discovered about the Gordian Asteroid that wasn't already known. Explorers and treasure seekers had already determined that each of the enormous vessels contained within the asteroid was identical. This had been proven using mapping technology that scanned the various segments of the ships protruding from the rock, along with an analysis of scans taken through the asteroid. Each craft had four engine thrusters in a diamond-shaped pattern, twenty-two cannons on either side of its hull, and was comparable in size to the latest flagships that met in battle across the galaxy. The vessels were constructed of seamless metal that made it look as if one piece had been stretched over the entire frame.

It was also apparent that the ships were constructed of a material far superior to any current technology. Humans and aliens who spent their lives on one planet liked to think of space as a void and that as long as you had oxygen you would be okay. The truth is that the galaxy is a harsh and unforgiving environment. There are extreme colds. Objects that orbit near a sun, like the Gordian Asteroid, also face tremendous heat. That exposure to both extremes is enough for the average flagship to deteriorate and is why fleets require all vessels to return for maintenance every four years. But the ships locked inside the Gordian Asteroid, even though they are thousands of years old, look like they just came out of the shipyards for the first time. Nothing makes the ships' indestructible nature more obvious than the distinction between the vessels and the rock that imprisons them. The asteroid was littered with thousands of craters where meteors impacted. Just as many pieces of space debris must have hit parts of vessels protruding from the rock, and yet not a single ship had a scratch on it.

That question—what are the ships made of?—led to dozens of other unknowns. Who built them? Why was there no other trace of that civilization left anywhere in the galaxy? How had their fleet become encased in rock? How did an ancient armada have technology that surpassed modern capabilities? Why are the ships rigged to explode if tampered with? What kind of self-defense mechanism was smart enough to remain dormant when an asteroid struck a ship but was triggered as soon as a man-made object tried to drill a tiny hole into a vessel?

They were the questions that plagued everyone who learned about the Gordian Asteroid, and they were the reason Vongst walked across the uneven rock day after day.

His current destination was a giant thruster jutting out from the stone. When the ship's engines were ignited, an immense amount of energy would be funneled out of the thruster, sending the ship across space. The pair of thrusters on the transport that Vongst and Tragedy had arrived on were approximately six feet wide and six feet tall. Each of the four thrusters at the back of the ship that Vongst approached was larger than a stadium capable of seating one hundred thousand people. The sheer size of just the lone thruster protruding from rock made Vongst pause and admire the enormity of the object he was standing on. As large as the thruster was, it was but only a small piece of the ship. There were almost a thousand other vessels all around him. There was enough rock to cover all of them. It reminded the doctor of a fact he had heard about the fleet when he was a child: A human could spend every waking moment of their life walking through the hidden armada and not see even a tenth of the fleet.

The arcing, curved metal of the thruster was within reach. It rose hundreds of feet in the air above him. From the schematics Vongst had reviewed, he knew it also dove hundreds of feet into the rock below his feet. If he tried to chisel away a piece of the metal to test its composition, the ship would explode. He knew this because it had happened to other explorers before him. It was also how he knew the nearest ship would explode if he tried to chip away a piece of the rock.

"We all die someday," Dr. Vongst mumbled to himself as he bent and ran a glove across the asteroid's surface.

Tragedy's voice came through the speaker in his ear. "Feeling melancholy today, Doctor?"

Part of the android's responsibility on the mission was to help Vongst whenever needed. As such, it listened to everything the doctor said while out on the asteroid. All this ever did, however, was annoy Vongst, who liked to be able to talk to himself in privacy.

Rather than acknowledge the question, he said, "You might lose contact with me in a moment. Don't worry, I'm okay."

He took a deep breath, then stepped onto the section of thruster in front of him. After waiting to ensure the boots of his space armor were locked onto the surface, Vongst took another step. The clicks sounded inside his helmet and a sensor on his visor confirmed he was attached to the metal of the ship. The suit of space armor not only allowed him to remain upright as he began up the sharp vertical slant of the thruster, it also took care of balancing him and carrying the hundreds of pounds of protective material needed to keep him alive.

Step after step he climbed. Pausing, Vongst turned and looked back at where he had come from. There was no *down* of course. Not in space, where gravity was nonexistent. Had there been gravity and had his boots disengaged from the ship's surface, he would have fallen to his death. Instead, he continued to climb the length of the thruster's main nose cone.

"Your heart rate is elevated, Doctor. Are you okay?"

"I'm fine."

At the top of the enormous sheet of metal that funneled energy away from the ship's engines, Vongst leaned over the open edge. Even with the high intensity ion light activated on his shoulder, he couldn't see the end of the inside of the thruster. Unused and dark, it looked more like an endless pit than it did a source of unknown technology.

"Here goes nothing."

His hands held onto the ledge until his boots adhered to the opposite side of the thruster's cone. His suit stabilized his equilibrium. Then he began walking into the depth of darkness.

5

As soon as Vongst got back to the ship and his protective suit was off, Tragedy asked what the doctor had found at the end of the thruster's exhaust.

Vongst rubbed his hands and feet. Both seemed to lose sensation when he wore space armor for too long. After a couple minutes of not having the suit's advanced breathing system, he began to cough.

"Just the wall to the pressure chamber," he said, referring to the cylinder that focused a ship's energy before it passed through the slits of the thruster. "It was sealed, though."

"What did you expect to find?"

Vongst looked up at the android and gave a snide laugh, which only made him cough again. Tragedy—all androids for that matter—seemed to have a way of asking questions that made the logical seem absolutely absurd.

"Exactly what I found."

"And yet you still walked a hundred yards into the thruster to make sure?"

"Of course."

"And you'll go back out tomorrow and do the same thing again?"

Vongst shook his head and sighed. "Not the same section of the same ship, but yes, I'll continue to investigate tomorrow."

"There have been two thousand, nine hundred, and seventy-seven organized expeditions to find ways to free the ships from the rock. All of them have failed."

"I know that," Vongst snapped. His throat burned with the urge to cough but he managed to croak out, "Don't you think I know that?"

Rather than take offense, Tragedy said, "That does not include the plethora of space pirates, treasure hunters, and warlords who also tried to free them for themselves."

It took a while for Vongst to regain his composure, for the blood to drain from his face. "So?"

"So, I'm curious, Doctor, why you think you will be able to do something no one else has accomplished."

What Vongst wanted to say was, "You know what? You're a real asshole sometimes!" He didn't, though, because Tragedy wasn't trying to be rude. It was simply trying to figure out why a scientist from a prestigious institute would risk his life when all of his associates were happy to sit in a laboratory with magnifiers and scanners.

He was also tempted to ask why Tragedy was there if it was going to be a nuisance. Vongst knew, though, that the android would provide a logical answer—that the chief scientist had assigned the unit to Vongst's project. Until the doctor blew himself up or quit, Tragedy would have to be there.

Instead, Vongst said, "I guess Adventure, Drama, and Satire were already booked on other projects."

Tragedy didn't speak. Instead, its irises illuminated as it tried to assess whether the doctor was joking or being serious.

Vongst helped it by offering a smile and adding, "At least they didn't give me Horror."

6

When it finally arrived, sleep was fitful. Vongst knew he was dreaming because he found himself out on the Gordian Asteroid's surface without a suit of space armor on. It was also easy to understand he wasn't really out in space because two men who had died long ago were standing on either side of him.

Rumanov Excalibur, the man who was credited with "discovering" the asteroid many thousands of years earlier and the reason many people referred to it as the Excalibur, was on one side of Vongst. Unlike the doctor, who didn't have much hair left, Excalibur had thick blond hair that was perfectly combed.

On the doctor's other side was Gordian the Stubborn, the ruler who had spent his entire life and all of his kingdom's riches trying to find a way to procure the fleet for himself. Dark bags hung under Gordian's eyes, showing the extent of the stress he had suffered upon realizing he had lost his kingdom for nothing.

"As soon as I saw it, I knew the ships would be trouble," Excalibur said, his voice confident, his chin slightly raised. "A couple days after my discovery, the first dimwit blew himself up trying to free one of them."

Gordian scoffed as he nodded in agreement. The motion caused the loose flesh under his neck to wobble from side to side. When he spoke, the words were drenched in bitterness.

"Do you know what they called me before I became obsessed with that asteroid? Gordian the Brilliant. Gordian the freaking Brilliant! I lost thousands of workers, along with much of my fleet. More importantly, though, my people lost faith in their ruler."

Dr. Vongst found himself nodding as he listened to both men. He could think of nothing, however, to add to the conversation.

Rumanov Excalibur ran a hand through the gold hair of his neatly trimmed beard. "Every time someone tried to chisel away rock or drill into a ship, the same thing happened. Boom! And yet they kept showing up to try it for themselves." He scoffed at the amount of people who had died at a place that was associated with his name.

Gordian the Stubborn bit his lip to keep from letting out a string of curses. When he regained his composure he said, "Do you know what's left of the ships I sent here? Nothing. The explosions were so intense there isn't even a trace of my fleet. That asteroid didn't just take the ships I used to protect my people. It took my legacy."

All three men stared out at the expanse of rock that stretched so far in every direction that the ground looked flat. Here and there, parts of the ancient fleet jutted out in no discernable pattern.

Vongst said, "Don't you wonder, though, how they've been able to sustain no damage through the millennia? What material can withstand thousands of years of exposure to radiation and debris and cold?"

Excalibur sighed and shook his head. "You're no different than all the others."

Gordian gave a scornful laugh and narrowed his eyes at the doctor. "You think you can't lose everything the same way I did? You think you're better than me?"

"No, it's not that. I'm—"

Gordian wouldn't let him finish, though. "It wasn't just me. Many kings and emperors spent their entire lives trying to figure out how to free the armada. So did countless pirates and warlords."

Excalibur nodded. "And scientists."

7

"Doctor, are you sure this is a good idea?"

Dark rings were under Vongst's eyes. After not getting much sleep, he was in no mood for the android's self-preservation spiel.

"Yes, I'm sure," he said as he coughed.

Tragedy's irises glowed a faint yellow as it processed something in the doctor's tone. It finished putting the final piece of Vongst's suit on without saying anything else.

With the helmet in place, Vongst felt a stream of cool air wash over him, felt the space armor stabilize his tired and weak frame. He stood and began toward the transport's rear ramp. Tragedy followed. The familiar pair of beeps sounded and the ramp began to lower.

"Do you mind if I ask another question, Dr. Vongst?"

Expecting to be asked the same thing as usual, Vongst said, "For research."

"No, not that. This place has many names. Why do you refer to it as the Gordian Asteroid instead of the Army in the Stone, the Red Armada, the Excalibur, or any of the other terms that have been applied to it?"

Vongst squinted at the android. A hand reached up to scratch his scalp—a nervous habit he had formed during his graduate studies—but with a suit of space armor on, the result was a thick gauntlet tapping against the metal of his helmet. He stared at Tragedy and the android stared back.

"I don't know," Vongst finally said. "I've never thought of that before."

8

On his next walk across the asteroid's surface, Vongst focused less on the ships extending out from the rock and instead centered his attention on the few craters he could see from where he was standing. Each one was roughly the same size as the frame of a giant vessel, half a mile wide and three miles long. Each marked the place where an explorer or researcher had grown careless or else tested another unsuccessful theory about how to breach the ships' self-destruction sensors.

Each crater was initially smooth after the blast. Only after additional space debris pelted it did it begin to look like the rest of the asteroid again. Vongst marveled at the technology that had seemingly put ships into the rock without any rhyme or reason, yet had a self-destruct capability so intelligent that it never destroyed other ships encased in the rock or nearby segments of the asteroid. A previous expedition to the Gordian had focused an entire year on the results on those blasts.

Of course, every possible idea, every part of the asteroid, had been dissected at length. Each organized excavation attempt and research study had taken different approaches. In an attempt to find secret doors or internal corridors buried underneath the initial layer of rock, one mission had focused on x-raying the entire asteroid. Another had sent microscopic organisms onto the stone to see if they could find a way into the ships. Sound waves. Controlled explosives. All of it had been done, and none of it had succeeded in finding a means of boarding one of the ships or a way to free them from the stone.

Vongst cringed. All he had was a suit of standard-issue space armor.

"And my mind," he said before cursing under his breath and hoping Tragedy didn't bother to ask what he was talking about.

He thought of Dr. Phillips again. In addition to being the lead researcher in charge at the Outer Rim Scientific Station, the wormlike alien with thousands of tiny legs was also Vongst's boss. Upon hearing Vongst's request for funding to go to the Gordian Asteroid, Dr. Phillips had offered a series of gurgled noises. The sounds were translated into Basic and then spoken from a speaker hooked to Vongst's ear.

"What equipment will you be taking?"

Vongst had smiled. "Just my mind."

Another series of noises was translated into, "I don't understand, my dear Dr. Vongst."

Vongst had shrugged and shaken his head. "I don't think technology will be the reason those ships are freed from the asteroid. I think whoever encased them in rock was so advanced that there's nothing I can do with a sensor or a shiny piece of equipment that will solve the Gordian puzzle."

Dr. Phillips had offered another series of gurgled noises.

The computerized, monotone voice had said, "Then why are you requesting funding? What will you do?"

Vongst had closed his eyes for a moment. When he re-opened them he said, "I just think if I can go there I might be able to see something that someone else has missed. Maybe eyes and ears and hands are better than fancy scanners."

The pair of bulbous black eyes across from him had grown wide at the comment, and Dr. Phillips had laughed. His hundreds of tiny legs involuntarily moved in a swirl of waves.

Vongst held his breath. At seventeen, he had solved the Arcadian Riddle. Four years later, at the university, he had found an alternate solution to the Mercicuan Problem. Now, at the twilight of his career, he wanted lightning to strike for a third time.

When Dr. Phillips had finished laughing, he didn't speak. Instead, he had merely nodded. The smile that had crossed Vongst's face was larger than any he had offered in a long time.

"Thank you. I won't let you down."

Now that Vongst was on the asteroid, however, things were different. It was true that he possessed a brilliant mind. Age had ravaged his body but not his brain. But he had been foolish to think he could simply observe the rocks and the ships and figure something out that no one else had managed to ascertain.

He approached a large expanse of metal protruding from rock. It towered two hundred feet above his head. Every part of it was smooth.

"They thought the Arcadian Riddle would never be solved," he mumbled.

The metal fingers of his glove lightly ran across the ship's surface. He tapped a knuckle against it. It made no sound, not in space, but he was more concerned with how it felt.

"They said the Mercicuan Problem only had one answer," he whispered.

His knuckles continued to tap the ship as he walked in a large triangle around the metal piece. Every time, it responded with the same dull thud.

Tragedy's voice came over the speaker inside Vongst's helmet. "Doctor, is everything alright?"

"I'm fine. I'm just talking to myself."

"Not that, sir. Your breathing is strained. My sensors show your heart rate is elevated beyond safe levels. I think you should return to the ship."

9

Tragedy asked how Vongst was feeling as it unclipped the doctor's helmet and lifted it away from his head. Vongst waved the question away even though he had needed to sit down as soon as he re-boarded the transport.

"I'm fine," he said, forcing a series of coughs to remain buried in his throat. "Just tired."

"Are you sure this is a good idea, Doctor?"

The android had a way of being able to ask the question without having any tone of genuine sympathy or concern.

Vongst looked down at his boots as he spoke. His voice contained a slight tremor. "Yes, I'm sure."

Tragedy reached a hand forward to begin unfastening the doctor's gauntlets, but Vongst gave a soft push, not even strong enough to fend off a child. The android nodded and took a step back to give Vongst more room. The doctor groaned and reached a metal glove across to his other wrist, then began unfastening the clips. After a moment, he looked up to find Tragedy staring at him, the android's eyes glowing as they assessed some kind of data.

"Why are you doing this, Doctor?" the android asked in its monotone voice.

"I've told you a hundred times. For research."

"No, not that," Tragedy said, its irises still glowing yellow. "Why are you here on this asteroid instead of receiving medical care."

Any remainder of energy Vongst possessed drained from him. If he weren't wearing his suit of space armor and its complex internal supports, he would have likely collapsed onto the bench he was sitting on.

"You know?"

"Of course, Doctor. My job is to ensure your well-being. I received a full readout of your bio stats prior to our departure. I also perform routine updates to see how the disease is spreading."

"Please don't tell Dr. Phillips. He'll cancel my trip if he finds out."

Tragedy's eyes lit up for a split second, then went dull again to resemble normal human eyes. "But Doctor, he was the one who told me."

10

The next day, rather than explore the Gordian Asteroid yet again, Vongst remained aboard the transport with Tragedy.

"I don't understand," he said, staring down at the remarkably good coffee his assistant had prepared for him. "If Dr. Phillips knew, why did he let me come here?"

As far as he was aware, only Comedy, the station's medical android, had known of Vongst's sickness, let alone how advanced it had become prior to detection. Upon being given the news, Vongst hadn't cried. He hadn't gone and found someone he cared about and sought pity. Instead, he had leaned closer to Comedy and whispered that he would have the android decommissioned and dropped into a black hole if it told anyone else about his diagnosis. The android's eyes had glowed a soft blue, and it had backed a safe distance away from him.

The rest of that day and night, Vongst had stayed in his living quarters and gotten roaringly drunk off synthetic whiskey. In the midst of his intoxication and prior to passing out, he had remembered the stories of the Gordian Asteroid from his childhood. As soon as he woke up the next day, tired and miserably hungover, he had put in the request to go to the asteroid. Not once in the days leading up to his departure had he mentioned his sickness.

Tragedy said, "Was Dr. Phillips not supposed to approve your request?"

"No, I wanted him to. I just thought he would have tried to dissuade me if he knew I was sick."

Tragedy waited to ask his next question until Vongst was able to contain another coughing fit.

"Would you like me to try and dissuade you, Doctor?"

Vongst gave a half-hearted laugh and looked up at the android. "Isn't that what you've been doing every single day when you ask why I'm doing this?"

All of the latest androids had programming advanced enough to detect and ignore rhetorical questions. Instead of answering Vongst's inquiry, Tragedy had one of his own. "Why *are* you doing this?"

The doctor sighed. "For research."

"Forgive me if I'm mistaken, Doctor, but you were conducting different research prior to coming here, correct? What made you decide to give that up in favor of this?"

Vongst's first instinct was to snap at the android and tell it that it was welcome to leave. He knew, though, that the android didn't care where it was and was only asking out of some need to fill a gap in its logic programming.

"Curiosity."

Tragedy's eyes lit up for a moment. "You were not curious about the other research you were conducting?"

Vongst slammed his mug down on the table in front of him and shouted, "Damn you. I'm going to die anyway. Why not here, trying to do something important?"

There were a lot of things Tragedy could have said. The android could have suggested that Dr. Vongst return home for medical treatment. It could have asked to join him on the asteroid during his next hike. Tragedy's self-preservation programming would override such a foolish notion, however, unless Vongst ordered it to accompany him.

Instead of saying any of these things, Tragedy asked if Vongst was ready for supper.

Vongst sighed and looked out the viewport of the transport. The Gordian Asteroid was there, numerous parts of ships exposed, teasing him with what they promised.

"Sure, Tragedy, that would be nice."

11

The next morning, as Vongst stepped into the boots of his space armor, Tragedy once again asked the doctor if he was sure this was a good idea.

Vongst realized the android wasn't referring to walking amongst booby-trapped flagships. It was talking about doing so in the doctor's current state of declining health.

"Yes, I'm sure."

Tragedy's torso pivoted to retrieve the main piece of space armor off the wall so it could be fitted around Vongst.

"Did Dr. Phillips tell you not to let on that you knew about my sickness?"

"No, Doctor."

"Then why didn't you mention it before?"

The android turned its head away from what it was doing even though it continued to fasten the internal harness around Vongst's shoulders. It never failed to unsettle the doctor when androids did things without looking at their hands.

"Why didn't *you* mention it before, Doctor?"

"I didn't think Dr. Phillips knew. I wanted to keep it a secret."

"I'm programmed to assist whichever scientist I'm assigned to. It was clear you did not want to acknowledge your health."

"Thank you, Tragedy."

"Just following my programming."

Vongst smiled as the android placed the helmet over his head. A whoosh sounded and Vongst knew his suit was pressurized.

"Okay then," he said and stood.

12

Dr. Vongst had asked Tragedy to fly the transport to a new section of the asteroid. When he disembarked from the vessel, a different assortment of metal parts jutted out from the stone. The sight, rather than lift his spirits, only left him discouraged.

In all of his excursions, not once had he found anything of note. Nothing to answer why the ships were there or how they might be freed. He had been a fool to think that simply gazing at the legendary puzzle might surpass the efforts of former rulers with their riches and extensive resources.

He had investigated large swaths of the ships. The main deck. The bow. The inside of a thruster. There was only one place he could think of that he hadn't gone before, and it was where he now began to walk.

The inside of one of the ship's mighty cannons.

Vongst stood at the base of where a cannon jutted out from the rock and extended hundreds of feet over his head. The barrel's circumference was roughly the same size as the transport he slept in each night. The cannon would be powerful enough to destroy a mid-size cruiser with one blast.

The doctor arched a foot to allow the bottom of his space armor to adhere to the perpendicular surface in front of him. The space armor did the rest, stabilizing him as his other foot stepped upon the barrel. He started walking up the length of the weapon at a ninety degree angle from where he had been standing a moment earlier.

Tragedy's voice came across the speaker in his ear. "Doctor, are you sure this is a good idea?"

"Positive."

The android didn't say anything else but was surely watching Vongst's progress from a feed inside the transport's cockpit.

At the end of the barrel, Vongst turned and stared at where he had come from. The asteroid was hundreds of feet below him. He took a moment to appreciate the view from atop the weapon's peak. All across the landscape of rock, he could see various portions of glistening silver ships sticking out from the asteroid. In the distance, the sun glowed blue.

Vongst smiled, then lifted himself over the edge of the cannon. There, he began to walk down the length of the weapon again, only this time he was inside the barrel, walking toward the point where the chamber would store immense amounts of power to be channeled through the path he was currently walking.

With the additional length of the cannon that was under the asteroid's surface, Vongst couldn't tell exactly how long the barrel was or how far under the surface of the rock he would be when he got there. The only thing he knew, the only thing he cared about, was that this was his last and best chance at finding a way onto one of the ships.

"Doctor, I must advise you that this seems unsafe."

"Feel free to take the transport further away from the asteroid if you like."

As he continued to walk, a sensor inside his visor told him he was at the point where, if he were outside the barrel, he would be standing on the asteroid's surface. He didn't pause to appreciate the fact, only kept walking.

After another fifty feet, the cannon's base came into sight. A metal cone protruded from the internal blast wall. Vongst wasn't a weapons engineer, but he knew the basics of how the cannon would work. The blast wall would open slightly. A tremendous amount of energy that was stored behind it would have a small opening from which to escape. The cone would focus the energy down the length of the cannon's barrel...

Which meant the blast wall he was standing in front of had to be able to move aside or open somehow. Looking at it, however, it appeared to be a single piece of metal like every other part of the ship. He reached behind the cone, behind where he could see, and fumbled for anything to hold onto. The faceplate of his helmet was pressed against the outer edge of the cone while his left arm blindly searched for a lever or something, anything that might force access to the weapon's inner workings. Once he was there, he was sure he could find a way to access the rest of the ship.

His fingers grazed something. Was it a handle? It felt like it. There was no room, though, for him to squeeze the suit of space armor around the cone to see, and the cumbersome metal gloves didn't allow him the same sense of touch as his bare hand.

"I think I might have found something," he said.

"What is it, Doctor?"

"A way into the ship, I think. I'm not sure. I can't see it." A moment later, he added, "I'm going to try and turn it. Are you a safe distance away?"

"I am, Doctor."

Vongst's left gauntlet encircled whatever it was that was located behind the cone. Without the suit, he might be able to squeeze in-between the cone and the blast wall to see what was there. Of course, without the suit he would die in a matter of seconds. He would also be without the strength that the space armor offered to be able to turn the handle, if that's what it was.

"Doctor, are you sure this is a good idea?"

His hand gripped the metal cylinder.

"Would you rather I return home and sit in a medical bay for the last few months of my life?"

There was a moment of silence before Tragedy said, "What should I tell Dr. Phillips?"

Vongst's hand froze. He stifled a cough.

Ignoring Tragedy's question, he said, "You want to know why I call it the Gordian Asteroid and not the Excalibur or something else? Because it was the name my parents used for it. That's all. I'm not Gordian the Stubborn. I don't have anything to lose, certainly not a kingdom." He shook his head. "Not even my health."

Surely Dr. Phillips had understood the same thing. That was why his colleague had approved the trip in Vongst's current condition.

"Why are you doing this, Doctor?"

Vongst took a deep breath. His hand gripped the rod on the other side of the metal panel. He would either disable some part of the cannon's mechanism and find a way behind the blast wall, or he would be instantly incinerated.

"To leave a legacy."

"I don't understand, Doctor. You solved the Arcadian Riddle. You found an alternate solution to the Mercicuan Problem."

Vongst's hand pushed and pulled lightly at the handle to see if it would begin to turn.

After a moment of silence, he said, "Do you know how long ago that was? And the only people who care are in scientific and mathematical circles."

He pulled with more strength. The metal in his grip began to bend slightly.

"You want to know why, Tragedy?"

His suit of space armor reacted to his effort by using even more artificial force to pull the metal bar. A sensor inside his visor showed that the suit was using every bit of strength at its disposal. He paused and took a deep breath. Before attempting to pull the bar further to the side, he closed his eyes.

"The chance at being remembered."

With a grunt, he yanked down hard. The piece of metal in his hand bent more, then snapped.

13

When the flash of light faded, Tragedy saw the newly formed crater. It was roughly one mile wide and three miles long and cut a deep swath out of the rock. The rest of the asteroid was untouched.

With the press of a button, the ship's sensors scanned the surface for any sign of life on the Gordian's surface. Tragedy noted the results, then sent them back to Dr. Phillips. A moment later, the android set a course for the transport to return to the Outer Rim Scientific Station alone.

ABOUT CHRIS DIETZEL

Chris graduated from Western Maryland College (McDaniel College). He currently lives in Florida. His dream is to write the same kind of stories that have inspired him over the years. His short stories have been featured in Temenos, Foliate Oak, and Down in the Dirt. His novels have been required reading at the university level, been featured on the *Authors on the Air* radio network, and been turned into critically acclaimed audiobooks by Podium Publishing.

Did you love this short story? Check out his other Space Lore stories: http://www.amazon.com/Chris-Dietzel/e/B00CC1GU54. Want to receive updates on his future books? Sign up for his newsletter: http://www.ChrisDietzel.com/mailing_list.

THE TRENCHES OF CENTAURI PRIME

by Craig Martelle

How could this suck more? Lance Corporal Riskin Devereaux thought. *It's the 24ᵗʰ Century, and here I am, standing in the muck. I used to drive a hover car, for crap's sake...*

Politicians, treaties, the instruments of failed diplomacy.

Maybe it hadn't failed. The war was being waged with low-tech weapons, but light years from Earth, light years from the Bazarian home world. Neither populace had to worry about war coming to their homes.

All they had to do was fight on a neutral planet.

Because that was what the politicians agreed to. The Marines and the warriors dug in, because they had to. No one could have an advantage.

Riskin was miffed yet again. At least his boots were high-tech, but the charge was running low. The indicator flashed on his wrist comp telling him to plug in, otherwise his feet would get wet. It needed to last another thirty-seven minutes until he got off watch.

Watch. A good word for what they did. The Interstellar Marines stood around with their always sparkly-clean slug throwers and watched to see if any Bazarian raised its ugly spiked head.

They used to shoot at the heads, never knowing if they hit anything. They weren't allowed smart optics or guided bullets.

It was like fighting in the Stone Age of old Earth. The IMs were trained for better.

And then the reality of what they were ordered to do set them back centuries.

* * *

"Much suckage!" Ak'Tiul whined, clicking and whistling his dismay. He stood alone at his post in the trench. The humans were right over there. If they could only lob a low-yield nuke from their mortars, this would be over and they could go home.

But no. The Council of Advisors had different ideas. One destroyed planet and the weasel-heads decided to talk, which meant the grunts were thrown into a swamp on a backwater planet.

Out of sight, out of mind.

"Hate humans," he told the wall in front of him. "No humans, no mud. Humans equal mud," he chuckled, looking down at his clawed feet. They were enclosed in a flexible polymer that helped keep them dry. The boots had been see-through, but that had ended three milli-ticks after he put them on.

He carried a slug thrower. "Useless," he snorted, slinging it over his back. "Might as well throw rocks."

He dug into the mud until he found a stone, heft-ed it into his hand, corkscrewed his body, and spun as he launched the rock toward the enemy trench line.

Ak'Tiul had thrown it too high. It splashed down half way there. "Hate humans," he reiterated.

* * *

Riskin saw the rock out of the corner of his eye. He ducked, then laughed as the projectile splashed into a pud-dle halfway between the lines.

"Candy ass!" he yelled over the wall. He dug into the mud and found a small rock. He hefted it, threw it to the side, and looked for a bigger one.

The next was good enough, halfway between a golf ball and tennis ball. He limbered up, windmilled his throwing arm, and then moved to the back of his narrow trench. He wound up, hopped forward two steps, and heaved his rock.

It made it halfway. "Damn. Farther than it looks." He would have sat down, but there was no place. The officers had taken the stools away because people were sitting on them and not paying attention. That was what they'd been told. Riskin never saw anyone else, only the lieutenant, but he said the order came from headquarters, HQ, so there was nothing he could do.

Easy for him to say as he took Riskin's chair away.

Riskin cupped a hand to the side of his mouth and yelled, "Suck my hairy butt cheeks, spiker!"

Splashing footfalls signaled someone was walking in his direction.

"Did you throw something out there, Lance Corpo-ral?" the officer demanded.

"Not as far as you know, your sirness," Riskin replied. No one wanted to be out here. Disrespect ran rampant, es-pecially when you had a lieutenant. New lieutenants got people killed. Seasoned lieutenants were just as cynical as the troops. And then there was this butthole.

"Why are you yelling?" The officer stomped his foot in the mud, sending splatters over both of them. "Damn. You know they don't have ears, right?"

"Makes the corporal feel good, oh sirly one," Riskin barked, stomping his foot as he came to attention. He found the resultant wave of sloppy, muddy water to be most gratifying as it splashed against the pants of the second lieutenant.

"You did that on purpose!" the officer declared.

"Most likely, your premier sirship," he replied.

"Well," the man sputtered, "don't do it again."

He stormed off before Riskin could do it again.

"That killed two minutes, now what?" Riskin asked the cold mud wall staring back at him.

* * *

Ak'Tiul saw the rock arc toward him and land short. By his estimate, it traveled farther than his. He dug into the mud to find another rock but hesitated as he heard something.

The Bazarian auditory glands covered the top of their head, giving them excellent hearing. He tipped his head and heard the harsh human language, one of many different ones that they used. Stupid humans couldn't even speak one language. He'd learned Chinese, as all Bazarians did since it was tonal like their language.

But these two were speaking something different. He couldn't understand them. Maybe they were giving orders for one of the ill-conceived but aptly named human wave attacks?

If he were so lucky. He'd burn up the old slug thrower then.

"Humans are stupid," he complained. He dug in the mud for another rock.

His officer found him bent over.

"What is this?" the third level MarPul asked.

"Looking for a rock, Master MarPul, sir," he said truthfully.

"To do what?" the officer demanded.

"To heave yonder, toward thy Council's enemies, who are mine enemies. And if I can be blunt, thine enemies, too," Ak'Tiul answered.

"You may not be blunt, Nug!" the officer sneered. "Now drop and give me twenty. I saw that throw. You're getting weak, Nug. Maybe we keep you here until you strengthen up? Can't send you home looking like you've been a prisoner of war, can we?"

The third level MarPul laughed uproariously and doubled over, whistling and clicking out of sync.

Ak'Tiul worked up a snotball and was going to hock it inadvertently onto the junior officer's back, but the Bazarian stood up, composed himself, and stalked away.

"Take your twenty and stuff them in your carapace crack, dickface," the upstart young warrior sassed.

"I heard that, Nug!" the Bazarian officer yelled from somewhere far away.

"I wasn't talking to you, but to those pink-skinned, meatbags over yonder," Ak'Tiul muttered. "Hate MarPuls."

* * *

"Did you hear that?" Riskin asked, but there wasn't anyone around. He was standing on one foot. He'd shut down one boot to save power.

"Why yes, I thought I heard the spikeheads having a heated conversation," Riskin assumed a deep voice as he replied to himself. He peeked over the mud wall and searched for movement. He ducked down before he was through searching. He moved down the trench a dozen steps before popping up for a second look.

He thought he saw a spiker, that is, a Bazarian head sticking up above the trench, doing the same thing he was doing.

"You ball-slapping spikehead!" Riskin yelled.

He thought he heard a sing-song reply.

"I don't speak Chinese, asswipe!" *How dare you speak Chinese when I don't,* Riskin thought.

Riskin turned his right boot's power back on. It came to life, ensuring that it would keep his foot dry. He lifted the other from the water and powered it down. He wanted enough juice in both of them to help him make it back to his bunk where he could both plug in and unplug at the same time.

Ten minutes had passed before a lazy step splashed his way.

"About time, you slimy bastard!" Riskin called out. But it wasn't the man who was supposed to relieve him from watch. It was the lieutenant.

"Sir-en-dipity, would you look at that! I'm getting relieved by the brass. Nothing to see, nothing to report, it's a big steaming pile of nothing, just like yesterday, last week, last month, and last freaking year. So, if that'll be it, I hear my rack calling."

Riskin turned his second boot on and prepared to slog through the mud and back to the cave he stayed in for his barracks.

"As you were, Lance Corporal!" the lieutenant barked.

"As I was what? Leaving? Yes, I was leaving and shall continue since you were staying, I was leaving, or something like that, sir highness, sir." Riskin stomped in a puddle, sending a wave of muddy water over the lieutenant's pants.

He didn't seem to care. Usually, he would have danced out of the way or bitched up a storm about being dirty. Riskin was instantly wary.

"What's wrong?" Riskin asked.

The lieutenant looked at him without arrogance, almost fearful. "Human wave in fifteen minutes. Every man goes. Every. Single. Man."

"Glad I'm not one of those, sir. I must report that I've been masquerading as a man all these years. I'm not a dude," Riskin said sincerely.

"Cut the crap. You're going over that wall, just like me." The lieutenant looked at his watch. "In thirteen minutes and you know what, smart-mouth? You'll be right next to me. If the golden bullet comes our way, we're going to take it together."

Riskin was done having fun. The lieutenant was serious. He suspected the lieutenant had a sense of humor, but it was buried deeply within, and even if he did let it out, it wouldn't be in front of the lowly enlisted scum.

"Make your peace, Riskin. This is the last attack. The survivors are the winners and they go home. This war ends today, Lance Corporal, and it's up to us."

"Don't you dare try to motivate me, you sumbitch. I don't want to go over that wall any more than you do, but ending the war is probably the tastiest carrot you can dangle. Damn you!"

* * *

Ak'Tiul hiked another rock and then another. He wasn't getting close enough to the human trench. He leaned against the mud wall, resigned with the fact that the human trench was too far away for a hand-thrown rock. In his mind, he was engineering a trebuchet to hike a boulder across the dead land and into the enemy trench.

If it weren't for the enemy, he wouldn't have to be here. "Hate humans."

The third level MarPul strode up; he held his skinny arms behind his back as a sign of his authority. "Do you really hate humans, Nug? Want to do something about it?"

"Your holiness, I am designing a trebuchet which isn't a powered weapon. We could use that to lob boulders into the enemy trench, fill it and finish them. Then we go home, eh, supreme creakiness!" Ak'Tiul hated his life in the trenches.

He rectified himself with the fact that he'd have to prostrate himself before his father and beg forgiveness for his brash decision to join the military. He had done that out of spite. His father said he'd hate it. His father was right.

But hate didn't quite capture the full magnitude of his disdain.

Ak'Tiul's body language must have given him away. "Want to do something about it and start the process of leaving this planet, today? Would you like that?"

"The crack slammies you say! What do we have to do, dickface?" Ak'Tiul asked.

"I heard that, you upstart. In twelve minutes, a Bazarian wave attack. Every swinging limb goes over the wall. We meet the humans in the middle, and the winner goes home. The war ends today, dickface," the third level MarPul replied.

"Aren't suicide missions supposed to be volunteer only, your queasiness?" Ak'Tiul clicked, both pleased and horrified by the latest developments.

"Volunteer does not have to start with the word 'I,' dickface."

"That word. I don't think it means what you think it means," Ak'Tiul countered. The MarPul checked his wrist monitor.

"Ten minutes, stinkhole. Make your peace. You and me, we go over together. We survive together, or we die together. Since I have no desire to die, I will need you to fight like the very Fire Demons of Bal Sagoth."

The MarPul thought he was encouraging, but Ak'Tiul was instantly depressed. He didn't feel like checking his slug thrower, which he'd never fired on this planet. He couldn't remember the last time he'd cleaned it. No one ever inspected them.

Ak'Tiul thought about loading up on rocks. His arm felt limber, and he was sure he could hit something with a rock, not so much with the slug thrower.

Ak'Tiul started backing up slowly, looking for a place to run and hide.

"Get back here, Nug! For the glory of Bazaria, we meet the enemy on the field of battle, gladiators for all Bazarkind!" the MarPul shouted, thrusting a twig-like arm in the air with a maniacal look on his face.

"Okay, crazy MarPul, whatever you've been snorting, you need to stop. There's no fonking way I'm going over that wall!" Ak'Tiul thrust his chest out defiantly.

The MarPul slapped his shock stick against Ak'Tiul's thigh and stabbed the button with a pointy finger.

Ak'Tiul screamed as his muscles contracted violently and the pain shot through his whole body. "Dickface!" he yelled.

"We're going over that wall, because you're more afraid of me than the pink skins. Ha!" the MarPul ended with a fanatical scream.

Ak'Tiul was unimpressed. "Sir, yes, sir! I'll be behind you all the way," the young soldier offered as a way of compromise.

"At my side, dickface! You will kill the enemies as I point them out. We will sow death and destruction like a harvester clearing a wide swath across the great plain."

"Truly magnificent, we will be, my lord," Ak'Tiul quipped, unsure of what he would do.

Maybe it was time to make peace with his creator, because he couldn't see a way out."

* * *

Lance Corporal Riskin Devereaux stood there. One boot had run out of power and the water seeped in. His discomfort seemed insignificant at that point in his life.

The second boot flashed and cycled down. At least he'd have two wet feet. Balance would be restored in his life, at least in the arena of discomfort.

The lieutenant had moved down the trench and was haranguing someone else. At least he was doing it with the level of zeal that he'd shared with Riskin.

Soon, the two joined the lance corporal. Riskin had seen the other man before but never talked with him. He'd made it a point not to get to know anyone. He reasoned that if he liked someone, then he might not hate this place so much and Riskin wanted his hate to fester in the hellhole that he'd been condemned to with the other Interstellar Marines he was certain were in the trenches somewhere.

"Hate spikers," he murmured before adding, "and lieutenants."

"What did you say, Lance Corporal?" the lieutenant asked, trying to stand tall and look down his nose at the junior enlisted. The other man was only a private, probably newly arrived, Riskin thought.

And least he wouldn't be stuck in the trenches for an indeterminate, interminable amount of time. Riskin had no idea how long he'd been there. Maybe he was new too, and didn't realize it.

"Your penultimate sir-ness, I said nothing offensive and hold you in the utmost of contempt," Riskin stated firmly, nodding once with pursed lips when he finished.

"Righty-o, then." The lieutenant checked his watch and looked up at the sky as he counted out loud. "*Three minutes*!" he bellowed, making the two IMs jump.

"What the hell? Didn't you ever hear of OPSEC, Operational Security, you wank spanker?" Riskin whispered, trying to get the lieutenant to stop yelling.

"Didn't I tell you? They are coming out to meet us. This is a fight to the end, right out there in no man's land. Ha! Now we'll take the fight to them. If I only had my family's ceremonial sword, I'd show them a thing or two."

"Like what it means to be a psychopath in a hurry to die a bazillion miles from home in a fight over nothing. Absolutely, sir. That would really show them." Riskin shook his head, then offered his hand to his fellow Marine.

"I'm Riskin, pleased to meet you and to go out there and die with you, I guess, because that's our orders, aren't they, oh sir-upy one?"

The other man grasped Riskin's hand. The private's hand was cold and clammy. He was short, looked oriental and to be on the verge of going into shock.

"Chen," was all he said and even that took a great effort from the smaller man.

"Nice to meet you, Chen. Too bad it's under these circumstances, but you know what? We'll be behind the lieutenant the whole way. Isn't that right, Sir Magnificent?" Riskin tried for a lopsided smile but only achieved a half-sneer with contempt on top.

"*One minute*!"

What made the bellow so odd was that there was only Riskin and Chen. No one else was nearby. They couldn't hear any other people yelling. Riskin wondered how many IMs were left. He couldn't remember seeing more than a handful at any one time in any one place. The only officer he remembered was the lieutenant.

"How many total are in this human wave, your sirness?" Riskin asked suddenly.

"All of them. Every swinging dick, Lance Corporal. Now, fix bayonets!" The lieutenant moved to the edge of the trench and cupped his hands as if to give them a boost up.

He noted that they didn't have bayonets, but the lieutenant seemed to be in a different place at a different time.

"Oh, hell no!" Riskin answered, stepping beside the lieutenant and cupping his hands. "You can pull us up once you're on top," Riskin suggested.

The lieutenant unholstered his pistol and nodded. "You know if you don't come, I'll shoot you?" He smiled at the two men and looked at his watch, breathing heavily and grinning.

* * *

"I think the order has been rescinded," Ak'Tiul said and relaxed. "Wow, that was a close one. Smoke if you are having them, eh, MarPul?"

"You get up that wall, dickface. Ten, nine…" the MarPul counted down, holding his shock stick at the ready. Ak'Tiul weighed his imminent death versus an extended period of pain before dying. He didn't like his options.

"ONE!" the third level MarPul screeched in a click and a whistle.

Ak'Tiul had no idea where he found the courage, but he hit the two steps carved into the mud wall, popping out of the trench and into the open. He stood there dumbfounded but was bumped out of the way as the MarPul climbed up behind him.

Side by side they stood, two Bazarians. One hundred yards away, a human popped out of his trench, but he wasn't looking their way.

"Well?!" the MarPul demanded.

"Well, what?" Ak'Tiul wondered.

"Shoot him! Shoot the enemy, dickface!" the junior officer howled, stamping one foot in the mud.

Ak'Tiul looked at it, curious that there was mud up in no man's land, too. He figured all the water made its way into his trench. He couldn't imagine that there was any remaining to make mud elsewhere. Maybe the planet wasn't a rock, but one big mudball. He looked at the terrain, certain that no argument could convince him otherwise.

"Fire!" the officer yelled.

"Right!" Ak'Tiul said, thinking about the mud and that this would all be over soon. The winner would go home. He called out, "Time to win, your preeminent supremeness!"

Ak'Tiul took aim with his old slug thrower and pulled the trigger.

Nothing. The MarPul was not pleased and jammed the shock stick against the enlisted man's leg. Ak'Tiul screamed in pain until his whole body convulsed and he dropped his weapon. It slid in the mud and back into the trench.

The third level MarPul released the button, and Ak'Tiul doubled over. "I shall recover my weapon, sir," he said without any derision. He resigned himself to the fact that he would die in pain. He hated the humans for being here with him. He hated the Council for sending him to the godforsaken place. But he hated the MarPul most of all.

"No. You'll fight them hand to hand. Look at their frail pink flesh! You'll rend them into tiny pieces. Now forward, ho!"

Ak'Tiul walked ahead as if carrying the casket to his funeral. The perceived weight on his shoulders was equally great.

* * *

Riskin had every intention of running as soon as the lieutenant was out of the trench, but when Riskin threw him forward, the officer twisted in midair like a spider monkey and landed, aiming his pistol at Riskin's astonished face.

With a sigh of reservation, he reached up and the lieutenant pulled him to the top. They both leaned back down and grabbed Chen's outstretched arms. Besides holding his hands in the air, the private was incapable of helping. They dragged him up the mud wall and deposited him face first in the mud.

He lay there, weaponless. His slug thrower was still in the trench.

"You first, Private!" the lieutenant growled. "If you can't shoot, then you can be our human shield. Now move! Lance Corporal, rifle up!"

Riskin whirled through one hundred eighty degrees. The lieutenant ducked to avoid getting brained by the weapon's barrel as it flashed past.

"Watch it!" the lieutenant yelled, focusing all his attention on the two junior enlisted and none of it on the enemy.

Riskin had never had any respect for him before, but that clinched it. He decided that he had to kill the man. He looked across no man's land to see who was watching

As far as the eye could see, horizon to horizon, he saw no more than ten Interstellar Marines. Most were singles, by themselves in the middle of nowhere. The story was the same on the other side. The Bazarians had an equal number.

"You have got to be kidding me! Are we it? We're all that's left?" Riskin glared at the lieutenant. "How in the hell did I get so unlucky to be stuck here and with an idiot like you?"

"No one ever leaves..." the lieutenant whispered, as if talking to himself.

* * *

Ak'Tiul shuffled toward the humans. The MarPul stayed behind him, hiding, but carrying his shock stick and ready to inflict pain should Ak'Tiul try to run.

"I have no weapon, dickface, maybe you give me your stick? Or better, why don't you go first?" Ak'Tiul said, continuing to slop through the mud.

His answer was the stick jammed into his leg, followed by a short burst of voltage. Ak'Tiul spasmed and fell.

Pain and death were becoming one and the same. As he lay there, he saw the few bodies walking across no man's land. The final push. It looked like wayward souls stumbling through the mist of life.

The third level MarPul screamed at Ak'Tiul to get up and keep walking.

Pain and death. He had no incentive to rise. The MarPul stabbed the stick against the prostrate Bazarian's leg and pressed the button, holding it to inflict the maximum punishment.

* * *

"Shoot them!" the lieutenant screamed fanatically. Chen dropped to his knees and covered his ears. His pinched his eyes closed and rocked himself.

Lance Corporal Riskin Devereaux raised his slug thrower and took aim. *If we win, I get to go home*, he thought as he zeroed in on the one spiker jamming some stick into a second one lying on the ground.

They don't want to be here any more than I do, he thought. *But if we win, I get to go home. Losing is dying.*

No one ever leaves, the lieutenant said. *What the hell?*

"What did you mean by that?" Riskin asked, lowering his slug thrower, which enraged the lieutenant. "What did you mean when you said no one ever leaves?"

The young officer aimed his pistol at Riskin's face. "What I meant isn't for the likes of you. Now raise your weapon, Marine, and get back into this battle. For the glory of the IM and a battle banner for the longest battle ever fought in all the interstellar wars. We must win!"

The whites of the lieutenant's eyes showed as his mouth hung open and he panted like an animal. His pistol shook as his knuckles whitened from his fanatically tight grip.

Riskin raised his slug thrower's barrel and aimed at the Bazarian cajoling the one in the mud.

Sight picture, sight alignment. He focused on the front sight post, positioning the slightly fuzzy silhouette of the spiker in the middle of the rear sight aperture. When everything was aligned, he exhaled and gently squeezed the trigger.

The weapon barked, and the trigger froze to the rear. It cycled uncontrollably like a machinegun, making the barrel jump. The first round hit the Bazarian center mass, in the middle of its chest. As the barrel jumped, the impacts climbed.

The next round hit the enemy in the throat, and the last impact blew a hole through its head. The weapon jumped out of Riskin's hands as it continued to fire.

The lieutenant was too slow diving out of the way, and the last round from the magazine tore through the lieutenant's head.

The slug thrower splashed into the mud beside Chen, followed closely by the lieutenant, who toppled over backward.

Riskin stood, eyes wide with shock at what had happened. He barely breathed. He'd killed his lieutenant.

But it was an accident! he tried to reason. Chen mumbled and whined.

"Shut up, Chen!" Riskin yelled, then realized his mistake. Chen hadn't done anything wrong. The man was terrified.

Riskin thought he should have felt worse, but he seemed oddly relieved. He felt free for the first time in a long time. He was out from under someone else's boot, even if only for a short while.

"It's okay, Chen, stand up and let's go. There's no one left to report anything, no one left who knows anything." Riskin looked around and saw a few figures here or there, but wasn't sure if they were human or Bazarian. The enemy closest to him was picking himself up out of the mud.

* * *

Ak'Tiul heard the sound at the same time he saw the slugs impact the third level MarPul. The officer was close, and Ak'Tiul simply laid there and watched as the Bazarian was torn apart. The dead body flopped like a wet rag, splashing into the mud.

The enlisted Bazarian crabbed backward, away from his dead officer. He thought about running for his trench, but if he didn't stand, then maybe they would think him dead.

He remained where he was, but watched the humans closely. Where once there had been three, only one remained standing. Of the other two, one knelt and the last looked as dead as the MarPul.

One helped the other to his feet, then they turned and walked back to their trench. When they reached it, they stood there, motionless for an interminable amount of time.

He saw his opportunity to return unseen to his own trench.

* * *

Riskin and Chen stood at the top of the wall, looking down at a heavy yellow gas. It rose chest high within, and that was if one knew where the high points were.

"Damn the lieutenant," Riskin said softly, then turned back to the officer's body and screamed. "*Damn you!*"

Chen was coming back to himself, having raced through four of the five stages of grief, from denial to anger, bargaining, and depression. He was ready to accept his depression as the final state of his life.

"What if we surrender?" Chen asked. As a private in the IM, he'd never had to think for himself. Someone else always told him what to do. He needed that in his life. Riskin Devereaux was the opposite; he despised people telling him what to do.

Which was how he ended up as a Marine—to show his father that he couldn't tell Riskin what to do. Riskin hadn't appreciated how much freedom he'd had when he lived at home.

The irony wasn't lost on him. The years of being ordered around by an idiot like the lieutenant had convinced him how smart and how wise his father was.

And how young and stupid Riskin had been.

Now I'm going to die for it, killed by my own people because everyone wants this little planet and this little war to go away.

"I wonder…" Riskin started to say. "Come on, Chen, let's see if I'm right."

He turned Chen around, and they started walking toward the muddy Bazarian, who was looking at his trench the same way they'd just looked at theirs.

"You speak Chinese, Chen?" Riskin asked.

"What do you think?" the private replied sarcastically, trying hard not to look at the lieutenant's exploded head as they walked past. He failed miserably and he couldn't keep his eyes off it.

"Tell that Bazarian not to go into the trench, it's poison," Riskin said.

Chen translated the phrases in milliseconds in his head and then spoke Mandarin Chinese in a normal tone of voice.

"Come on, Chen, everyone knows that the spikers don't have ears. You gotta really belt it out!" Riskin threw up his hands in hopeful encouragement.

"You're kidding, right?" Chen asked.

"You ask a lot of questions, Private," Riskin sneered. "Why would I kid about something like poison and death?"

"If they don't have ears, why would yelling make any difference?" Chen explained, eyebrows raised.

"Damn straight; maybe he can read lips?" Riskin suggested, then laughed heartily. The Bazarians didn't have lips.

Riskin and Chen kept walking across no man's land.

* * *

Ak'Tiul looked at the green gas in the trench. He could smell it.

Death.

He thought he heard someone tell him not to go into the trench, but it was in the human Chinese language. He knew the voice spoke the truth, although the truth sounded strange, no matter which language it was communicated in.

"Hate humans," Ak'Tiul said. He looked back at the dead body of the MarPul. "Hate MarPul more. Sorry, your cerebral supremeness, in that I didn't recognize your superiority sooner and race across the wasteland with reckless abandon to dispatch your enemies."

He saluted haphazardly, then swaggered to the body, picked up the stick and jabbed it against the leg. When he depressed the button, the MarPul's body jumped, but the stick shorted out, sending electricity through the water and into Ak'Tiul's foot.

He dropped the stick and jumped around on one leg, feeling like a moron for shocking himself.

The humans stopped on the other side of the MarPul and stood there watching Ak'Tiul's antics.

He stopped hopping and stood still, returning the humans' gaze.

"Don't go into your trench. The gas is death," the Bazarian told them in the sing-song language of diplomacy.

* * *

The creature was the same size as the two Marines, but to Riskin, the Bazarian looked like a cross between a bumblebee and a wasp. When it spoke Chinese, Riskin was relieved, but still couldn't understand the creature.

Chen nodded and replied.

Riskin slapped the shorter man on the arm. Chen remembered that the other Marine didn't speak his language. "He said to not go into the trenches."

"We know that," Riskin said.

"That's what I told him." Chen looked oddly at the lance corporal.

"So what the hell do we do now?" Riskin asked. Chen translated the question for the Bazarian.

"Dammit! I was asking you, not him," Riskin clarified. Chen shrugged.

"Ak'Tiul," the Bazarian said, pointing to himself with one spindly arm.

"Riskin," Chen said, pointing to the lance corporal. He said it twice and then pointed to himself. "Chen."

"Who was that?" Riskin asked, leaning toward the Bazarian that he himself had killed.

"The MarPul, an officer, a bad officer," Ak'Tiul said, and Chen interpreted for Riskin.

"Our officer too, bad and dead," Riskin said succinctly.

"What do we do now?" Ak'Tiul wondered.

"Find a way off this godforsaken mudball!" Riskin exclaimed. Chen smiled before telling Ak'Tiul what the lance corporal had said. The Bazarian bobbed excitedly.

"Like humans," he said. The clicks and whistles of the Bazarian language were lost on his new companions.

ABOUT CRAIG MARTELLE

If you liked this story, you might like some of Craig's other books. You can join his mailing list at www.craigmartelle. com. If you have any comments, shoot him a note at craig@ craigmartelle.com. He's always happy to hear from people who've read his work and tries to answer every email he receives.

He enjoyed writing "The Trenches of Alpha Centauri," which is based on what he found out when working with military from other countries, including Russia, Cuba, Yugoslavia (before that country broke up), and so many more. All soldiers put their boots on the same way, and they all have the same concerns about their families. They enjoy a good meal, and Craig learned that none of the frontline forces hate each other. They trained to fight, just in case, but they hoped they wouldn't have to. No one who has to fight a war longs for one.

Craig is a lifelong daydreamer and student of human interaction. He's got some degrees, but those don't matter when it comes to telling the story. Engaging characters within a believable narrative—that's what it's all about. Craig lives in the interior of Alaska, far away from an awful lot, but he loves it there. It is natural beauty at its finest.

Amazon: http://amazon.com/author/craigmartelle
Facebook: http://www.facebook.com/authorcraigmartelle
My web page: http://www.craigmartelle.com

BROKEN ONE

by Josi Russell

Dear Son,

Now that I'm gone, you're going to hear a lot about who I was and who your mother should have been. Try not to get too defensive—much of that is probably true.

THE JARRING THUD OF AN 800-TON, LONG RANGE PLASMA missile shook the ship, and all Ryz could think of was that stupid letter. One of the king's advisers, Karnat, had slipped it into his hand as he'd walked to his ship at the beginning of this battle, and he'd gotten through the first confusing page before the fire had begun to fall hard.

Even as he spun to return the fire, the elegant handwriting, the self-deprecating humor of the writer, the fragility of the fiber paper skidded through his head.

His primary hands, with their strange extra digits, worked the pitch of the cannon while the three fingers of his secondary hands—on the ends of short, thin arms that jutted out just below the bend of his elbows—streaked across the buttons on the upper dash, aiming, firing, aiming, firing again. He kept the extra fingers out of the way expertly, just as he had practiced, tucking them in toward his palms. He had to in order to keep up the speed and accuracy with which he was firing. He was good at manning a fighter pod. He always had been. Better, they said, than anyone in the last century.

He knew what they were saying when they said that. *Better than anyone since your father.*

It had been over a hundred Ritellian years since his father manned just such a ship.

Another missile jolted Ryz's ship, the *Luma*. His teeth knocked together. He spun the turret and finished off the attacking craft. The turret smelled hot and sharp. Ryz checked the heat readouts.

"Let's get the aft guns vented," he called to Natoo, the assistant engineer assigned to him. It was just the two of them in here, much to the engineer's dismay. Natoo scowled up at him.

"Aft guns aren't due for venting."

Ryz bit back a curse. Arguing would just waste time and focus. "They need it done now. I'm firing fast and hot up here, and if we let them go too long, we're going to lose them." He had to keep them online. Besides the risk of a plasma ignition, the only other defense he had on the aft half of the ship was a single heavy charge, and he needed to save it.

He let the thought of being in the middle of this battle without any aft guns sink in for a long moment. Another barrage rocked the ship, adding urgency to the conversation. Natoo began swiping his control pad.

Ryz felt the momentary breathlessness as the venting changed the pressure in the cabin slightly. Natoo didn't notice, and Ryz tried not to show his discomfort, holding his breath and gulping once the atmosphere normalized again.

Ryz couldn't afford time to discuss his physiological abnormalities just now, and he hoped Natoo wasn't watching.

He looked at the readouts. Three enemy ships left: A light attacker, a Stinger, and a Pinwheel—a globe studded with firing ports that made shooting from any direction easy. Three Maro ships versus the *Luma* and the *Travae*, the ship where his cousin stood on the deck. That was all that was left of the Ritellian fleet, all that was left of the whole Ritellian Empire besides the children and caregivers back on the planet. Once these two ships were gone, nothing would stop the Maro from dropping their burning rain on Ryz's home planet and terraforming it for their own use.

The fleet had been strong, but the Maro were stronger. And they knew things. They knew, it seemed, the Ritel's every weakness. They knew of the breathing port behind the left ear on every male, and they used that knowledge in hand-to-hand combat. They knew that zinc was fatal to infant Ritel. They knew that there was a taboo against speaking the name of the Ritellian sun—even now, as it flitted like a bird across Ryz's mind, *Sythia,* he felt a little guilty. How they had gathered this much intel, no one in the leadership knew. It was more than a leak. It was as if they had, somehow, gotten into the minds and culture of the Ritel, and that had given the Maro a distinct battle advantage.

The three ships were arcing wide. They'd form a tripoint and close in, Ryz knew. He'd seen it before. He glanced at the live feed from the *Travae*. Uom, his cousin, leaned forward in his command chair, unmasked fear on his face. He was the sovereign leader of the Ritel, the head of state and the military, but Uom had never been in battle, and the *Travae* was not a warship. It was a royal transport, meant to get him and his family away from Ritel before the Maro could get to them. Though his defense squad was firing valiantly, this attack would be the end of the monarchy, and effectively the end of the Ritel.

> *The end of the monarchy. That phrase came from the letter, too: They said your mother would bring about the end of the monarchy, but it went on without her, which goes to show that things aren't always as bad as they seem. There is always a way to do the right thing.*

The right thing here was simple, and Ryz didn't hesitate. Three attackers. Priority target: the light attack ship. In any other instance, it would have been the pinwheel, but Ryz had been watching, and by the looks of the red glow under its skin, its guns were overheating, too. The light attack ship was already firing on the *Travae*, and Ryz used the thrusters to flip the *Luma* and push it between the two. He was firing before he righted, and the pulses rocked the enemy craft.

Ryz defied his Academy training by avoiding the urge to set up a firing position. If the Maro knew from which direction they could expect fire, they'd maneuver to keep their best shields toward him. Every visible panel of the LAS was heavily shielded. But Ryz had faced over thirty light attack ships in the last few weeks, and he'd discovered something: a panel, just between the aft tracking ports of the enemy craft, that crumpled like paper under heavy fire. This is what he'd been saving that last charge for. He kept barrel rolling the *Luma*, guns trained on the LAS, streaming pulses. He had to draw their attention, needed the Maro to stabilize their own attack position toward him.

He knew it was working when the dazzling little ship turned its attack from the *Travae* and onto him. Strafing it with fire, he spun the *Luma* up and over the Maro ship's position and brought it to a jarring halt just aft and starboard of the craft. This was the moment. His secondary hands hit the fire button and the heavy charge burst from the belly of the Luma, driving straight and silent toward the Maro ship.

They detected it, tried to spin, but were too late. The charge hit the top edge of the panel and the ship keened off, internal explosions flashing alongside the haphazard stream of plasma missiles tumbling from the firing ports and drifting into the blackness around them.

Ryz turned his attention back to the remaining ships. As he'd predicted, they'd turned their fire on him when he engaged the light craft, and it was only now, in the absence of its constant barrage, that he noticed they'd been firing, too. The pinwheel's charges weren't hitting though, its elevated temperature playing havoc, he supposed, with their guidance systems. But the double barrels of the third ship, the Stinger, were sending out long-range, high-efficiency pulses that were finding their marks more often than he'd realized. The *Luma*'s control board lit up with damage reports. The outer hull was beginning to falter.

His was the only ship in the fleet with that extra protection. It was mostly meant to keep the vast sucking emptiness of deep space at bay, but it also helped in moments like this, when they were under fire. The presence of the extra hull annoyed Natoo, mostly because it added a layer of complexity to his engineering duties, and Ryz was tempted for a nano-second to say something about how the engineer should appreciate it.

Without heavy charges, he didn't know how to take down a Stinger. Long and lean, the ship cut toward him like a smooth-edged blade. Its pulses didn't rock the ship like the missiles had done. Instead, each brought a prolonged shiver that ran through the metal and lit up the readout screens. Each vibration locked Ryz's body with a fleeting shock, a buzz that froze his sixteen fingers useless above the controls. The closer the Stinger got, the more intense the brief fits of paralysis became.

"Do something!" Natoo's voice was strangled. He was suffering more from the pulses than Ryz.

"On it," Ryz said, trying to sound cheerful. His mind scoured the possibilities. Heavy charges were gone. Plasma missiles were likely too slow to reach the Stinger before it reached him.

Ryz had never faced a Stinger without a battleship backup before, and he was seeing why the pod-on-Stinger strategy wasn't taught at the Academy—because there was no chance for the pod.

But he'd always been good at seeing things no one else saw. And in the long, breathless moment of the next shockwave, Ryz saw what he needed to do.

Slowly, as his body thawed, he rotated the ship.

"Yes!" Natoo cried from below. "Let's get out of here!"

Ryz didn't stop to explain they weren't retreating. To do so was to leave the *Travae* as good as helpless. Though it still had a chance against the crippled Pinwheel, the Stinger would destroy the smaller ship. He aimed his aft guns, an apology to Natoo on the edge of his mind, and started to fire.

The controls were designed to force a pause between the pulses, allowing a slight cooling of the firing system so it would last in a battle. But Ryz didn't need it to last. He needed heat, and he needed it *now*. So he used his extra fingers, the little ones on the edges of his primary hands, the ones nobody else had, to do what he'd spent so much time in the Academy training himself not to do. The extra reach allowed him to hit the firing buttons simultaneously, instead of alternating as the system was designed to do. The pulses became a stream, and he aimed them at the oncoming assault from the Stinger.

"We're overheating!" Natoo cried from below.

Ryz wished he hadn't vented the aft guns. That had made this process just that much longer, and he had no seconds to spare.

"Emergency suits, Natoo," Ryz said, using his knee to bump his own ES activation button. A specially-designed suit unfolded around him.

"No, Ryz," Natoo said, "No. Stop this!"

"It's time for an exit strategy," Ryz said, trying to keep his voice even. Another shock thrummed through the ship, and his fingers clenched hard on the panel, depressing the firing buttons for that long, frozen moment. A bitter smell filled the ship—the heat was reaching a critical point. He hoped it would be quick, that the heat would fry them fast, so they wouldn't suffer too long. He considered removing the suit, but there was no time now.

Brilliant light shot through every crevice of the *Luma*, emanating from the aft cannons as the plasma reached the flash point and ignited in the barrel.

"Please," Ryz heard himself say. The final pulse streaked forward, carrying its intense energy directly to the thousands of invisible plasma trails the Stinger's pulses had left behind. Like rails of fire they lit up, igniting and racing each other back where they'd come from: the Maro ship's cannons.

The two ships erupted at the same time, and Ryz had one last, fleeting glimpse of the Stinger shattering apart as his own ship ruptured and he was ejected. It was the last thing Ryz saw as he tumbled into darkness.

* * *

It wasn't my idea to send you away.

The words of the letter came to Ryz through the darkness. He strained to hear Natoo, to see if he was okay, but there was only silence, save for his father's voice in his head, speaking those haunting phrases. Father sounded just as he had that morning so long ago when Ryz had been loaded into a cabship and delivered like a package to the Juvenile Academy.

I would have stayed with you—and with her—forever. But there was no place for our family in their world. No place that we could picnic or hold hands or watch a sunrise without people staring. After she died,

The words still jolted Ryz. He hated them.

The Royals just didn't know what to do with you and I. They would have kept you locked away, Ryz, hidden, if I hadn't agreed to go. I'll always be grateful that they allowed you into the Academy. You don't know it, but your fate would have been much worse if they'd chosen to turn you out. And now, I hear, you're an ace pilot. Better, I understand, than I was. That doesn't surprise me. You were born better.

I know what you've heard about your mother. That she let the Ritellian Empire down, that she abandoned her subjects. But that's not true. You should know that.

Did she abdicate? Yes, she did. She gave up her throne and her title. And abdication means a lot of things. It means that instead of being the most respected, revered leader, you become the most berated, least trusted suspect of your country. It means you leave your home and you're always on the edge of every family gathering. You're not allowed to have an opinion on how your brother is managing the Em-

pire, though everyone else has one, because you had the chance to do it your way and you threw it away.

And if you threw it away to marry someone completely unsuitable to rule with you, then it's even worse.
But that's one thing you need to know, my son,

And here Ryz's mind also conjured his father's face: the crinkling eyes, the upturned mouth. Hideous, like his own.

Your mother didn't give up her throne for me.

The first time he'd read the letter was the first time Ryz had ever heard that. All the sneering and jeering from the others at the Academy, all the official documents he'd seen, all the broadcast interviews, had said that his mother had left her throne because she was in love with his father and no one would ever accept his father as a member of the royal family. So if she hadn't abdicated to be with his father, what had made her leave the throne? What had convinced her to turn her back on her subjects? And why did the letter argue that she hadn't actually turned her back on them after all?

Ryz was dimly aware of voices. He listened again for Natoo, but heard only strange tones and unfamiliar speakers. He feared space had claimed his engineer.

Ryz ran through the last moments of the battle. Could he have done more? Done better? The weight of Natoo's loss shook him. He couldn't breathe properly. It was as if his lungs weren't having to work as hard as usual. They felt light and floppy, his mind giddy with extra air. His suit must be malfunctioning. He pushed a hand toward his mouth to check for obstructions, but found nothing there. He tried to force his heavy eyes open, but a hand to his forehead found them wrapped in gauze.

Ryz wanted to tear it off, but he was afraid. That last bright light—had it damaged them? All he could think was that he hadn't read the second page of the letter yet. His father had more to tell him. What if he could never read it?

He lay very still and ran a hand down his chest. He wasn't wearing his protective gear. Just his flight uniform. The letter made a crinkling sound in his pocket. He realized he wasn't floating in deep space anymore. He was lying on his side on what felt like a cold floor. The back of his left shoulder seared with pain from a flash burn. Reaching out, he felt thick metal slats all around him. He was in a cage.

More voices. He couldn't understand them. They were speaking a different language, and their tones, Ryz was sure, sounded nothing like Ritellian speech. He crawled to the edge of his cell and pressed his secondary fingers between the slats. The bars were long and thin. He began to probe, hoping to find a lock to release.

A loud exclamation told Ryz that he'd been seen. He pulled his hand back into the cage.

There was a strange squeeing and the sound of static before familiar words began to flow in around him.

"That better? Can you understand me?" His captor was using a translation wedge. Ryz recognized the artificial voice. Strange words, then a stream of Ritellian.

"Where am I?" he asked, and the wedge garbled out his question to its owner.

"You're on a research ship. We picked you up in open space. You're lucky we were trawling."

Even in Ritellian, the word was unfamiliar. "Trawling?"

"Right. Scraping space for interesting particles. And then we found you."

"What's wrong with the air?"

"Nothing. This is what you're meant to breathe. Your suit seemed maladjusted for your needs. Have you always breathed that mixture?"

"Of course. That's what we breathe on my planet."

"Interesting," the voice said. "You'll likely find this a bit easier."

"Why can't I see?"

"Your eyes are badly burned. That's why we're keeping you out of the light, too."

"In a cage."

"Well, that's for our safety. We weren't sure exactly what—"

"What I am?"

"Right."

"You won't win any awards for that observation."

There was a long pause, as if the researcher didn't know how to respond.

"I'm only joking," Ryz said. "I'm a bit of an anomaly where I come from, too."

"Ritel?"

"Yes."

The researcher made a sound, but the translator didn't speak. The noise it made sounded like surprise.

"Who are you?"

"I'm Doctor Cataris. I tended to your wounds."

"Then locked me up."

"Yes." There was acknowledgment in the doctor's voice, a taking of responsibility. Ryz appreciated that.

"Who do you work for? Whose ship is this?"

"We're from COS—the Consortium of Species. Our mission—"

"I know your mission. Collect specimens. Study them."

"It's important to know all we can about various species."

"Why? What do you do with that information?"

There was a long pause after the translator finished relating his question. The researcher, it seemed, had walked away. But another series of tones and static came from Ryz's left. Another translator, this one a little slower, was activated.

"They won't answer the hard questions. Believe me. I've asked." The voice was light and her language complex. "They keep saying they'll let us out, but I haven't seen any evidence that they mean it."

"Who are you?"

"Another prisoner," she said. "The only other prisoner right now, though it looks like they are set up for a lot more." There was a little pause before she added, almost as an after-thought, "They call me Delta."

"Where did you come from?"

"They brought me from a refinery over in the Barin Quadrant. I was navigating a fuel vessel they hired to come out and fill them up." Her voice got quiet. "I don't know why they wanted me. There were a lot more interesting species on the ship. At first I thought they needed a navigator, but they brought me in here and I haven't left the room since."

"How long?" Ryz asked.

"Months, I guess. It's hard to tell now."

"Has it been bad?"

There was a long pause before she spoke. "Some of it."

Ryz wouldn't ask her any more about that. He didn't need to—he could hear her pain. He started to ask what she was, then hesitated and changed his mind. "Can you see me?" he asked instead.

"A little. There's just little slits between us. But I can see a bit of you."

This cheered Ryz. He wondered if he should take off his bandages. How badly burned was he? He already felt the cooling sensation of his body's natural healing secretion sliding over the wound on his shoulder. His eyes should be repairing soon as well.

"I have to get out of here," he said. "I have to get back to my planet." He tried not to think about the fact that it was left completely vulnerable now.

"What are you?" the other inmate asked. "I … I've never seen hands like these."

He felt her fingers on his and realized that he had unconsciously reached toward her. His slim secondary hand was through the slats and surrounded by her own warm hands.

And, in that moment of vulnerability, blind and imprisoned, Ryz told the truth he had never spoken aloud before. "I don't know what I am."

She didn't gasp, as he'd expected. Didn't question. Just continued stroking his fingers in silence as more words poured out of him, "My mother was the queen of the Ritel. She was a perfect example of her race. But she abdicated her throne, abruptly, and married my father." A long pause hung between them. Into the gap tumbled all of Ryz's memories, the brief glimpses of his father, the torment he endured at school when they talked about what he could possibly be. The words trickled out, every breath painful as he went on.

"They called my father 'The Broken One,'" he said, listening to the echo of it through the translator. It sounded no better in her language. "He was weak, could barely stand, couldn't breathe properly. His body was strange and lacking. His face was misshapen. The Ritel couldn't believe that their beautiful queen could love him."

Though Ryz had never admitted it, he couldn't believe that his mother had loved his father either. As he admitted this to himself, the old shame rose again in his throat. He knew, better than any of them, what weaknesses his father had passed on to him.

She mumbled. The translator said, in his language, "The Broken One."

He started to pull back his hand, but she held fast, stopping him, holding tight to his three fingers. "Everybody's broken," she said softly, "somehow."

* * *

If he hadn't heard the scrape of the door, if he hadn't felt the shift in the pressure of the ship, he would never have awoken. But Ryz had spent his youth sleeping lightly, waiting for someone to pull him out of bed or throw something at him as he slept. He was used to waking quickly.

He heard rough breathing and something falling. It sounded like a struggle. "Delta?" he whispered. "Are you there? I need your eyes."

Only silence answered him. The realization took his breath away: it was her he could hear struggling. Ryz pulled himself onto his knees, tearing the bandages from his eyes. There was pain, but it was lost in his panic as he blinked, trying to see through the slats.

He was in a lab. Data readouts and glass beakers stood on stark black counters. Empty cages like his own lined the walls.

The struggle was over. Delta's cage was open, the slats of its door limiting his view of the right side of the room.

A hulking creature stood at a counter just on the edge of Ryz's line of vision. It was hairless, with smooth skin pinched into ridges all over its head and exposed hands. It was wearing a white lab coat, and its skin shone silvery-green in the artificial light. Delta was there. Ryz couldn't see her, but he could hear the pained noises she was making. The creature was reaching inside a glass cabinet, extracting vials.

Ryz didn't know what the creature would do with them, but he had to get out. He had to help her. Ignoring his burning eyes, he thrust his secondary hand through the slats again, running his slim fingers along the outside of the cell until he felt the locking mechanism. He found it easy to manipulate, and the cage door swung open. Ryz tumbled out, dropping to the floor and springing up just as the creature turned toward him. Its eyes were flat and rimmed like two wheels sunken into its face. Its mouth was small and active, accounting for the range of sounds he'd heard earlier.

Ryz was ready to strike, but as the creature turned, Ryz's body involuntarily slowed. It was as if a sopping blanket had been draped around him. The creature's face, wide and ridged, stared at him a moment. *Defense mechanism,* Ryz thought. *It's emitting a tone that's disrupting the signals in my nervous system.* He'd learned about many defenses, natural and artificial, at the Academy. Only now he couldn't think what to do about it.

The creature was injecting Delta. Ryz could see the tips of her boots, twitching on the table. He tried harder to reach her, to make his limbs move. Her translation wedge sprung to life, and he heard her voice, soft, and its artificial one, much louder. "Let me go!"

The creature was wearing a wedge, too, and its voice, which sounded like grinding rocks, came through as, "I told you, I'm here to help. Just try to relax."

Ryz recognized the voice. Cataris.

"Leave me alone!" Her voice was weak. "They already injected me today."

"I know. That's why I'm here. This will reverse the effects of the earlier injections."

"Why would you do that?" Her voice dripped bitterness. "So you can begin a new series of experiments?"

Ryz saw, but couldn't believe, a slump in the doctor's shoulders. He read it as remorse. "You'll go through no more experiments if I can help it."

"So you're here to kill me?" Ryz saw that her twitching had slowed. Was she dying? He pushed harder against the weight on him, yet still he couldn't move.

Cataris shook his head, "I'm not a part of the COS. Not really. I work for another agency that has long suspected the COS is crossing lines that it shouldn't. I've been embedded here for years, gathering intel on their activities."

"You're a spy?"

"More or less."

"Who do you work for?" Delta asked.

"That's not something I can say right now."

"Why tell me at all then?"

"Because I'm leaving. I'm leaving and I want to free you before I go. You've suffered enough. And you"—he glanced over at Ryz—"you will too, if I leave you here."

Cataris turned back to Delta. Ryz wished he could see more of her, to confirm that she was alright.

"You should start feeling stronger any time now," Cataris said.

Ryz heard more strength in Delta's voice as she spoke. "I—I am." She sounded surprised.

"Listen, I know it's going to be hard to trust me, but if you don't, and we get caught, the COS will kill us all very quickly." The tone in the doctor's voice, the grave concern, implied he'd just spoken an absolute truth.

"Why..." she stopped. "Why would you help us?"

Cataris didn't speak immediately. Instead, he slowly screwed the top back on the vial, slowly put it back in the cabinet, and slowly disposed of the syringe. Then he spoke, and his grinding voice was weary. "I've been on this vessel a long time. Years. I've seen so much—done so much. It's time I start making amends for everything I've been involved in. I'm starting with you two."

Delta seemed to accept that. "Let me sit up," she said.

"Not until you're steady."

"I am." her voice was stronger. "I am now. Your ... antidote, or whatever it was ... worked fine. I'm steady." She held up a hand, and Ryz saw it reach triumphantly into the air, appearing over the beast's left shoulder.

Later, he would remember that moment in time as if he were frozen inside a glacier. He still couldn't move properly, and the sight of that hand—her hand—took away his energy to fight whatever it was that weighed him down.

Five fingers—a little strange extra one on each hand. Just like his own primary hands. And as she sat up, her eyes, her face, they were so familiar. Only, her secondary arms were missing, and her knees lacked the pivots his had. They seemed only to bend in a single direction.

Could she be a mutant Ritel, too? Broken like him and his father?

But there was no time to ask. Doctor Cataris turned to him again and spoke. "I'm sorry I had to sedate you, but we haven't any time. We've arrived at Maro, and if we're getting off this ship, we need to do it now."

Ryz blinked. One word was echoing in his mind: "Maro? Why are we at Maro?"

"The COS has been updating them with the results of their experiments for some time now. I suspect they're here to reveal the secrets of more species."

The COS? Feeding information to the Maro? That must have been how they'd gotten so much knowledge of the Ritel. It made a disgusting sort of sense. "But why?"

"Because the COS has big plans," Cataris said. They're angling to destroy the monarchies and unite the different races under their own rule. I've been working with these monsters for a long time. I can see they're planning on making a move soon. They've been using the Maro to fight their battles, and the Maro are nearly used up; so the time is coming for the COS to try to take power."

"The Maro are nearly used up?" Ryz said, trying to understand what that meant.

"They've battled so many species, and come out victorious, though sometimes by very narrow margins. They have very few defenses left, few ships, few soldiers. There's not even a defensive contingent on the planet today." The doctor nodded. "That's why I'm getting off here. An escape from Maro is much less complicated than one from other ports." He put an arm out to support Delta as she sat on the edge of the counter.

Cataris was still talking, his translator grumbling along behind his own voice. "Destroying the Maro was all part of the COS plan, of course. The Maro themselves were far too powerful for the COS to challenge when they started this. The COS have promised the Maro special leadership once the new rule is established and paid them well for each monarchy they toppled. The COS let the Maro wear themselves out conquering everyone else. Victory always comes at a price, you know."

A shudder shook the ship. They had landed. The thought that he was on the planet that had pushed the Ritel to the brink of extinction turned like a snake in Ryz's stomach.

"Well, come on," Cataris said, "if you're coming. Here, help her. We need to go quickly."

Just like that, Ryz could move again. Cataris had stopped the tone that interrupted his abilities, and he felt lighter now that the impeding waves were gone. The blanket had been lifted free. Delta seemed to share his newfound freedom, and he realized the doctor had been repressing her struggles with the same mechanism. Ryz felt shy as he slid an armset around her for support and followed the doctor out of the lab.

The hallways were darkened, and whatever terrors Ryz had imagined were absent for the time being. The air outside the lab was slightly different, heavier somehow, and Ryz felt more confident as his lungs increased their effort. This is how he was accustomed to breathing.

But Delta had begun to gasp. Without a word, Cataris reached into his pocket and held out two small devices on the open palm of a hand more delicate than Ryz expected. Delta took one and expertly adjusted it around her nose. Immediately, she began to breathe easier. Cataris offered the other to Ryz, but he shook his head. "I'm fine," he said.

"Take it anyway," Cataris shrugged. "I'm not likely to need it." He tapped two gills on his neck as Ryz slipped the device into his pocket.

"Follow me." The doctor gestured forward, and they made their way deeper into the ship.

As they walked, Ryz realized he still had a bit of gauze clinging to his right temple. Delta noticed it, too. She reached up and removed it with ease. Her misshapen hand was warm against his skin, and he smiled his thanks to her.

Cataris led them into a small anteroom with a door at the other end. Though the symbols on the door were unreadable to Ryz, the stench told him exactly where it led. He wasn't surprised when it opened onto a garbage bay, piled with the detritus of the ship's long weeks in space.

Automated scoops were pulling through the room in predictable patterns. They pushed the piles out of garbage ports in the side of the ship, dropping their loads into carts on the hangar floor. The carts took the loads and dumped them into an incinerator, which filled the hangar with a thick, rancid smell.

They watched a moment until they could gauge the timing of the next scoop, then slipped out through the port. Delta would sometimes stumble, and Ryz would catch her and carry her a few steps until she recovered her strength. The flight of stairs beside the garbage port was steep and narrow, and Ryz pulled Delta into his armsets and carried her easily to the bottom. They left the big hangar and emerged into the sharp light of Maro's sun. Ryz wondered briefly what its name was.

"Where are we going?" he asked, setting Delta down and trying to keep up as Cataris took another in a long, complicated series of turns through what appeared to be an abandoned industrial complex.

"There's an impound yard, where a variety of captured ships are kept," the doctor explained. "I've seen it on previous visits, when the COS was collecting specimens. The ships are captured by the Maro, their drives are disabled, and they're parked out here—usually still populated. They just sit here waiting to be collected. It's like purgatory. They can't go home, can't escape. Conditions are usually awful. I've got the restoration key that will reactivate the drives." Cataris held up a pale, green cube, which hung on a chain around his neck. "I think we can convince someone to fly us out of here in exchange for getting their drive back online. They're usually pretty desperate." Ryz followed him with more confidence. It didn't sound like a bad plan.

Cataris was a useful companion, Ryz realized, as they reached the gate to the impound yard. A few dozy guards met them, and the doctor gave a passable excuse. Ryz assumed he explained the presence of the two multi-limbed aliens at his side. The guards' lack of interest in Cataris, the fact that their weapons remained holstered, told Ryz they must be used to seeing the doctor on his errands. Ryz wondered how many specimens he had collected from this yard. The guards waved them through as the gate opened.

As the holding bay opened before them, Ryz gasped. There, in the center of the impound yard, stood the *Travae*."

* * *

Ryz ran, pulling Delta along with him. If Cataris was surprised at their sudden increase in speed, at the ship Ryz picked to approach, or at the efficiency and familiarity with which Ryz opened the port and climbed the ramp, he didn't show it.

The *Travae*, though, was no longer a royal transport. It was an empty gourd: hollow and dead inside. Where there had been royal parties and meetings for the heads of state, now there were blackened holes and rooms echoing with their own emptiness. Ryz made his way to the bridge.

Delta finally spoke. "You've been here?"

Ryz nodded. "This was my mother's ship. After her abdication, it passed to my uncle; then on his death to his son, my cousin. I've been here for official ceremonies. The king bestows titles on all Academy graduates. He should be here somewhere."

Ryz searched desperately, his extra eyes scanning.

The control room door was closed. Ryz heard voices—familiar and clear—speaking his own language inside. He laid both his trembling left hands against the identification panel and the door disappeared into the floor. They stepped through.

Inside, a ragged group of Ritel stood swiftly, ready to defend themselves. But recognition dawned on their faces as he approached.

The king's advisers, three old Ritel whose faces were rugged as maps of the homeworld, took quick, reaching steps toward him. Karnat, the adviser who had given him his father's letter, was first. That moment when Ryz had received the letter seemed, now, like a lifetime ago.

Without warning, moving as one, the advisers knelt. Ryz didn't understand what was happening. They had raised their armsets, clasping both their primary and secondary hands above their bowed heads.

One by one, the others knelt, too. Ryz heard them murmuring two words: "*Your Majesty*."

Ryz stepped back. "Wait. Where is Uom? His sons? Where is the king?"

Karnat, the chief adviser, looked up and shook his head.

"Gone?" Ryz gulped. He felt Delta's hand on his shoulder. Her translator was gurgling in the background. "All of them?"

"All of them," the adviser said. "We had no hope of a rescue, no hope that any of the royal family had survived."

Ryz shook his head. He had never even been considered part of the royal family.

"You are the rightful heir to the throne," Karnat said. "And you have returned to lead us."

In the back, on his knees, an engineer gave Ryz a look filled with despair. "If I may, we are stuck here. The *Travae*'s drive is disabled."

Ryz waved a hand toward Doctor Cataris. "My friend can help with that." He nodded, and the two left for the engineering deck. A little thrill went through Ryz. No one had ever even listened to what he had to say before, and now, apparently, he had the power to command them—his own people.

"Prepare the ship for launch," he said, stepping into the command role easily. It was not so different than what he had done in countless Academy training exercises, from what he had done on the *Luma*. Ryz considered what he must now do. He saw the next maneuvers as clearly as if they were laid out on a screen before him. He must launch and use this ship to return to Ritel. He must fortify the defenses on his planet, train caregivers as soldiers, and he must keep the Maro—and, he now knew, the COS—from returning.

There was a new, sharp edge of hope inside him. The advisers and the scattered remnants of the *Travae*'s crew, hunched with defeat when he'd entered, now moved with purpose, manning their stations.

The navigation console stood empty. Ryz turned, but Delta was already moving toward it.

"Have you used one like this?" he asked.

She smiled. "Not exactly, but I can figure it out."

The drive made a high whirring. Cataris had gotten it back online. Ryz watched out the viewing port as they began to rise. The Maro guards, so casual moments before, now leapt into action. He saw them scrambling, using their communicators, aiming their weapons.

The shields were damaged, but working. The fire from the guards' hand weapons bounced off.

"What happened after we took out the Stinger?" Ryz asked, trying to piece together how much of the *Travae* was serviceable. As the crew worked around them, Karnat related the tale quickly. The *Travae* had been captured when the *Luma* and the Stinger exploded. The Pinwheel had fired its last charge, splitting open the forward hull where the royal family had been hiding. Uom had rushed from the command deck to save them, and been sucked into the cold blackness of space. The Pinwheel was too crippled to finish off the royal transport, but had caught the ship in a drag beam, towing the defenseless craft to Maro.

The *Travae* trembled around them as it accelerated to overcome the planet's gravity. Ryz was struck with how innocuous Maro looked from here. Outside the main base where they had been were rolling hills and fields, painting the planet with a natural beauty inconsistent with all he knew of the war-loving Maro race. The base itself was nearly abandoned. Cataris's testimony of the decimation of the Maro fleet was obvious in the few soldiers rushing out of the buildings to witness their escape, in the few vessels Ryz could see spotting the all-but-abandoned shipyard that had once stood in service to their vast fleet. The Maro were in no shape to pursue. He hoped he would have time to prepare

Ritel for them, to build his people's own military, before the COS could attempt to finish the job they'd started.

"Problem ahead," Delta called. Ryz looked to see a single, light-attack ship moving to intercept, all the depleted Maro fleet could muster. Remove it and nothing stood between him and home. He studied the attack craft, smiling at its orientation—aft ports exposed.

"Gunner," he barked, and a small Ritel answered.

"Sir?"

"Fire a heavy charge," Ryz instructed, "right between those tracking ports."

"We don't have many charges," the gunner said doubtfully.

"We only need one." Ryz tapped the screen to show the gunner where to aim and watched as the charge erased the craft from his screen. He smiled faintly.

Ryz watched Maro shrink into the velvet darkness. Sound slowed and sped at varying intervals as the *Travae* moved into warp. He held his breath, but it was a long warp, and his discomfort grew. He slid a hand into his pocket and pulled out the device Cataris had given him, then fit it over his nose. It was soft and comfortable, and as he inhaled through it, he sighed with relief.

Ryz drew in air as quickly as he could without drawing attention, recognizing that Cataris' knowledge may continue to prove useful. The new king breathed easy when the ship slowed again and he saw the pale, spinning orb that was Ritel.

"Home?" Delta asked, tapping the planet on her display.

"Home," he answered softly. For the first time, he felt like that was an accurate description of the planet.

Karnat moved up beside him. The old Ritel's thoughtful gaze resting on Delta.

"You've brought another," the adviser said, inclining his head toward the girl.

"Another?" Ryz turned his gaze to Karnat. "Another what?"

At this, the adviser peered at him, "You did not read the letter your cousin gave you? The letter from The Broken One?" He stopped and looked down, seemingly embarrassed. "Forgive me—the letter from *your father?*"

"I started to, but we were called to arms." Ryz reached into his pocket and extracted the delicate paper. As the ship moved down through the atmosphere, the new king read the second page at last.

Your mother left the throne to use her considerable talents for gathering information. She knew how to lead. She knew how to rule. She came to the Academy to learn what they had never taught her at the palace: how to fight for her people. She knew there were threats, and she could not bear to sit in the palace while the dangers encircled her planet. We met at the Academy. She chose me for her personal pilot. She said she felt safe with me. I wish I could have lived up to that vision.

We traveled to covert bases and to dens of spies. Along the way I fell in love with her intelligence and bravery, her fierce sense of loyalty to all of her subjects. We were married on an Edenic planet in a system whose name I can't even pronounce. After our marriage, with you on the way, we carried on trying to find out the extent of the threats our people were truly facing. What we found, instead, was truth of another kind.

We returned to Ritel for your birth. We returned with precious little information, but planned to leave again, taking you with us. But the attacks on Ritel began, and your mother was killed, and everything changed.

Before our discoveries in the field, I had thought, son, that her superior genes would overpower mine, that you would not have the limitations I had. But out in the field we discovered something, something only Karnat knows, that you can't reveal to anyone else. We learned of another race, not unlike the Ritel, whose own world had been lost to them. We found that they had sent their young into the skies in hopes that they would find a better future. We found, son, that I was not a broken Ritel. In fact, I was a typical specimen of this other race, one of those orphans sent among the stars. It is, I suppose, why my body is at the end of its usefulness to me—these were not the conditions it was made for, and it cannot continue to function in them.

In the future, perhaps you will meet the race from which I came. Or perhaps you will not. But now, as I leave my body behind, I realize that I have tried so hard to allow you to be a Ritel, to shine as your mother did in this society, that I have neglected to teach you about your other ancestors. I know precious little of them myself, but I should not have kept what little I know from you.

What followed was a list of all the things he knew of this strange race. They were from a rich blue planet in the Sol system. They breathed best in an atmosphere of about twenty percent oxygen. They were remarkably adaptable.

Ryz glanced up at Delta. She was like him. He wondered if she knew what she was, where she had come from.

There would be, he felt, a time to discuss it. There would be time for many things. Ryz would see to that. He would prepare his world to fight, and he would call upon his new relatives for help, if they could be found.

As the ship touched down on the stubby, green shrubs outside the Ritellian royal palace, Ryz ran his strange fifth finger over the last line of the letter, just above his father's signature.

Forgive me if you can, and remember, please, that your mother did her best and that I was only human.

ABOUT JOSI RUSSELL

Josi Russell's science fiction novels explore familiar human relationships in unfamiliar contexts. She currently teaches creative writing and fiction for Utah State University. She lives in the alien landscape of the high desert and is captivated by the fields of linguistics, mathematics, and medicine, by the vast unknown beyond our atmosphere, and by the whole adventure of being human. If you'd like to explore more of her work, please visit her website: http://www.josi-russellwriting.com.

There you can learn more about her bestselling novels: the Caretaker Chronicles series, The Empyriad Series, and her various short stories. If you'd like free stories and updates on Josi's newest releases, please sign up for her Readers' Club: http://eepurl.com/bzy3vP.

THE ERKENNEN JOB

by Chris Pourteau

The Contract

Tony-two-point-oh sat back in his chair and stared across the expanse of his English oak desk. I could see how much he favored his father when he did that. Same iron jawline. Same bony temple. Like someone had pulled an exoskeleton off a Martian assembly line and stretched skin over it. When he's angry, Tony's forehead ripples like liquid metal.

"It's a power play, pure and simple." His voice rumbled in the back of his throat. "Ra'uf Erkennen is making a move."

"Why not keep the marshals on the case?" I asked. Seemed like a perfect job for the Marshals Service, that bastion of law and order bought and paid for by the Syndicate Corporation. Like everything else in the solar system.

Tony shook his head. "When we thought Blalock had simply stolen tech, the marshals were fine. Now that we know Ra'uf is up to something … no, this secret lab in

Darkside needs to stay a secret as far as the public is concerned. We need to handle this privately."

I nodded. By *we*, he meant *me*: Stacks Fischer, chief enforcer for SynCorp and Tony's personal assassin.

The Erkennen Faction had first reported that a scientist named Mason Blalock had committed corporate espionage and stolen research and dashed to Darkside with it. That's why the marshals went in. Now, we knew the situation wasn't so simple thanks to a whistleblower inside the Erkennen organization. Blalock was conducting secret research meant to upset the delicate, nuanced relationship of SynCorp's Five Factions. And meant to put the Erkennens at the top of the totem pole.

"What's this super-secret tech again?"

Tony had to look to remind himself. "Molecularly Enhanced Synthetic Hemp." He said each word deliberately.

"Developing a new drug in Darkside," I grunted. "Now there's a shocker."

Tony shrugged. "My little bird inside Erkennen tells me it's a game-changer. Ra'uf plans to use the new strain of hemp to take over," he said, stroking the plush arms of his leather chair.

"Using drugs as a weapon?"

Tony shrugged again. "How he plans to do it, I have no idea. But the fact that Ra'uf is working offline is already a violation of the corporate compact."

That was true enough. But each of the Five Factions maneuvered against the others all the time. This particular power play seemed to have Tony especially on edge.

"We need to set an example, Eugene." Tony gave me the unblinking eye, that look he reserves for his inner circle when he's passing along privileged Company knowledge. Or trying to intimidate the other guy.

"I reckon so," I said. But I wanted to be crystal clear on expectations. "You want me to bring Blalock back?"

Tony's eyes went cold. Ice-blue cold. Like his power core had just shut down, if he'd had a power core. "Kill the geek. Take the tech."

I stood. "I'll head out post-haste, Boss." How hard could it be to find one rogue scientist making new-and-improved pipeweed in Darkside?

"One more thing. Ra'uf Erkennen needs to be taught a lesson." Tony's words were gravel in a grinder. "Make it loud and clear."

"I'll get it done, Boss."

"I have every confidence, Eugene," he said with a wolfish smile. Tony's bone structure made the expression seem painted on again, like an undertaker had pinned his skin back to force a peaceful repose for respectful mourners. "Good hunting."

* * *

I thought about stopping by The Slate—my favorite watering hole on the orbiting station that served as SynCorp's headquarters—and pump Mickey Stotes, the proprietor, for information. But I figured whatever the Erkennens were playing at with Blalock was still far enough off-grid that even Mickey, usually a fount of useful knowledge, wouldn't know anything. If not for Tony's secret source inside the Erkennen Faction, neither would we. So I headed dockside and my ride waiting there.

From Tony's penthouse office in SCHQ, the vator ride down to the deck where the parking's cheap always takes a while. I don't mind. Gives me time to think, make sure I know what I think I know.

He's smart, Tony. Street-smart, unlike his father Anthony Taulke, who was a brilliant engineer and world-builder but not so smart when it came to managing people. Tony must've gotten his people skills from momma. As SynCorp's CEO and head of the Taulke Faction, he's a master at keeping the other four factions off-balance and everyone toiling toward the Company's bottom line. Maintaining the status quo means everyone wins.

That's what made this move by the Erkennen Faction even more odd. The Erkennens developed tech for the Company. That was their main contribution. But apparently Ra'uf Erkennen had decided to conduct this particular project off-book. He was risking a lot taking on Tony.

As the decks flashed by, I pulled my left bicep against my side to find the comforting curve of my stunner in its holster. Comforting yes, but stunners are new tech, only out a few years, and I don't trust 'em. That's why I carry backups. Strapped to my right wrist, my knife in a spring launcher. Inside my left ankle, my .38, what they used to call a police special a couple hundred years ago. The knife and the pistol were my old reliables.

Given what Tony wanted done, the stunner might be too humane anyway. The stunner tech, which I still didn't really understand, somehow causes a living being's EM field to shock them to death. It's a quick and supposedly painless way to go. And it requires less mopping up afterward.

But sometimes in this business you want to make a mess. The .38 would leave a weeping hole for everyone to gape at on CorpNet. I'd just have to make sure the wound was visible to make Tony's point for him: taking on Tony Taulke is no Sunday afternoon stroll with the family. It always has real consequences—deadly consequences. With that in mind, I walked off the vator appreciating Ra'uf Erkennen's testicular fortitude.

One quick valet delivery later, and I was back in the Hearse's cockpit. There are few places I feel safer. She's a fast, sleek little ship with black and silver lines and an oversized trunk for … well, you know … cargo. The Hearse—I named her myself—exchanged bona fides with SynCorp Control, and we were on our way to the moon and its main colony, Darkside. It'd be a few hours before I got there, so I went over the briefing from Tony again in my head.

The Erkennen Faction had first said that Mason Blalock, one of their own scientists, had stolen ground-breaking tech, maybe to hand over to the Resistance—called Ghosts because their favored way to resist is to gum up the works of the corporate machinery. Ghosts say they're fighting for mankind's freedom from the indentured servitude of life under SynCorp, but most of Sol's citizens are perfectly happy to let the Company run their lives. It wasn't forty years ago we all thought we'd expire right along with what was left of Earth. Then the corporations came along and saved us: colonized Mars, developed Titan's resources. So who can blame the citizenry if they trade a little freedom for survival of the species? When the Ghosts sabotage the assembly lines or blow up Company assets? Well, it strikes me as damned ungrateful.

When it looked like just another corporate espionage job by Blalock, SynCorp had dispatched the Marshals Service to set things right. But you only engage the marshals when you want the law enforced and the citizenry to see you've enforced it. When you need a message sent that's a little more direct—like to big-balled Ra'uf Erkennen, keen on taking Tony's job—well, that's where I come in.

I let myself relax a little and looked up through the Hearse's canopy. I was finally away from the bright blue marble, and the dark silver of the stars shone in. Other than the getting paid part, this was my favorite part of the job—traveling alone in the Hearse, carefully planning my next steps.

I still had hours to Darkside. With the starlight streaming in and my racing thoughts finally starting to calm, I pulled up the Hearse's reading library. This was my thing to do while I waited on the flight time. Waiting is ninety percent of my job. Some assassins play games on their padds.

Some eat ravenously, mechanically. Some drink, but not too much. None dare to sleep if they want to stay alive.

Me? I like to read books. That's where I get my nickname from, by the way—my love for reading stacks of books. What, you thought it referred to how many bodies I've piled up in my career?

I pulled up Mickey Spillane. He'd do.

The Investigation

Founded as Darkside's End, the largest settlement on the moon had once been the hope of humanity. It was supposed to be the first giant footprint for mankind off a dying planet, a springboard to a second chance among the stars. Then everything went to shit on Earth even faster than the experts predicted. Instead of a shining city on a lunar hill, the moon became a way station where people stopped off on their way to more important places like Mars. I remember a line from some old vid: *a wretched hive of scum and villainy.* That describes Darkside perfectly. Yeah, that's what everyone calls it now … no End in sight.

Once I landed, I headed for the Fleshway—a long, dirty bazaar of overpriced drinkeries and brothels, and peopled by pickpockets. If Blalock really was in Darkside, that's where I'd most likely find him, indulging in the local diversions. The Fleshway is so-called not only for peddling access to everyone's favorite fifteen minutes of the day, but also because foot traffic is so thick on the bazaar, it's hard *not* to stick your fingers in other people's pockets.

The smell of sweat, vomit, and other bodily fluids wafted up from the gray mud of the double-wide, prefabricated thoroughfare. The sounds of drunkards, hucksters, and a slurred desire for death sooner rather than later mixed in the murmur of the crowd.

I pushed my way through, heading for Minerva Sett's Arms of Artemis. The Arms is considered the best little whorehouse in Darkside, which isn't saying much for the place. The owner—Minerva, aka, Minnie the Mouth—and I were old friends. Whenever I prowled Darkside on a job, I'd stop in for a Scotch and a beer and sometimes help her muscle out a drunk john demanding more than he'd paid for. Though she never paid me for the service, Minnie was always grateful for my assistance, if you know what I mean.

I pulled my hat down when I entered the Arms. Last thing I needed was someone spotting me and tipping off anyone watching Blalock's back. I spotted Minnie holding court and angled in her direction. When she saw me, I jerked my thumb toward her office behind the bar. She nodded and began to wind down her conversation with the client she'd been chatting up.

Entering her office felt like slipping into an old coat. "This place looks the same," I said after she closed the door behind her. The fake friendliness of the negotiations under way in the front parlor, as Minnie called it, faded to a dull roar. "It's what I like about it."

"You and everyone else," Minnie said, amused. "My customers like to know what they're getting, each and every time."

I turned with a grin and noticed her absently wiping her lower lip. They don't call her Minnie the Mouth for nothing. Actually, for two things. I was here for the second.

"I need information," I said.

"Yeah? And Mars has two moons." Minnie strolled over to her desk with lazy legs that knew a paying customer wasn't watching. She kicked off her heels and flopped into a chair. "You know, you never come to visit when you don't need something. Not even a 'How you doing, Minnie? Business been good, Minnie?' first."

"No time for pleasantries. I need what I need and I'll beat feet out of here."

She blew out her disgust. "Typical male. What is it this time? Someone steal something from Tony Two-point oh? Make the Big Boss Man mad, did they?"

Maybe it's because every job I do is basically the same, or maybe it's because, after celebrating her fifth 39th birthday, Minnie has a lifetime of hard-earned expertise in reading people. But sometimes she hits the nail too squarely on the head for her own good. Someday it might get her killed. I decided not to add to those odds today.

"I can't tell you the what. I just need help finding the who."

"You're no fun, Stacks."

"That's not what you said last time I was here."

"I owed you for running those twin thugs out before they hurt another one of my girls."

"I remember."

"I felt I owed you big time."

"I remember. You delivered, too."

She smiled. "Yeah, I did."

"Does that shared reminiscence count as a pleasantry?"

"That particular one?" Minnie gazed off and closed her eyes for a moment. "Yeah, that counts." She reached across her desk and pulled the top off a decanter. "How much of a hurry are you in?"

"One drink's worth of a hurry."

Minnie filled two glasses with amber ambrosia and pushed one in my direction. I picked it up and said, saluting, "Bottoms up."

She saluted back. "If that's the way you want it."

That woman doesn't miss a beat. She downed the bourbon in one gulp. I followed suit out of courtesy. "What I prefer is Scotch."

"I prefer girls, and see where that's gotten me?"

That plussed my non for half a second. Minnie was diverting me, as was her wont. I set my glass down and said,

"I'm looking for a man named Blalock. Mason Blalock. Ring a bell?"

Ignoring my pressing schedule, Minnie poured us a second round. I let mine breathe. She didn't.

"The EF geek that stole the super-secret tech?"

Shit. Minnie, you live a dangerous life. And I'm not talking about the daily need for antibiotics. My silence answered her question.

"I heard the marshals were hot on his trail," she said, still fishing.

"Where'd you hear that?"

"Whispers in the Basement."

Ah, the Basement—that second tier below the sanitized top layer of CorpNet—where only those who pay to play can get access. Taboo porn and SynCorp stock tips are the most popular search returns. And something called *The Real Story*, a series of non-stop real-time videos streaming the most recent rubbernecking eye-bait—whatever puerile happening will get viewers to tune in for the flash-ads that pop up in-between. The Company considers what shows up in the Basement as a safety valve for public angst. Sometimes SynCorp even seeds content to push public commentary in a certain direction. When things get a little too close to the truth, plugs get pulled. And I'm talking more than power plugs.

"Don't believe everything you hear," I said.

"Honey, I don't believe half of what I hear, and less than half of what I see. It's the only way to keep your sanity in a place like this"—she finished off her second bourbon. Then, chuckling—"and your sense of humor."

I nodded. I could relate. My line of work demanded a similar indulgence of the darker side of human nature. "Anyway, Blalock? If all you know is what's in the Basement…"

Minnie poured herself a third drink. Either it was the end of her shift or the beginning. Hard to know which one she'd need the liquid meds for more.

"Don't insult me," she said. "Do I question your professionalism?"

She watched me slowly shake my head over the rim of her empty glass. Sometimes I'm smart and keep my trap shut despite my knee-jerk tendency to mouth off. There were only the distant sounds of loud-mouthed braggarts and half-hearted gigglers bubbling in from the bar.

"Aw, hell, Stacks," she said finally, the bourbon already making her s's lazy. Beginning of shift, I guessed. Minnie prefers to work on an empty stomach. "I'm sorry. It's just that—"

"Don't mention it. Now, about Blalock?"

Minnie's a good kid and I didn't want to be rude, but I really was in a hurry. I had no idea what Ra'uf Erkennen's time table might be. But with the marshals called off, he might advance his schedule to move against the Taulke Faction. However that shook out, Tony was convinced it'd be in the public space, and it was real hard to put a bad-news genie like that back in the bottle. Any evidence of open warfare among the factions would only encourage the Resistance. The sooner I completed my contract, the better.

"I hear he's gone way deep," she said, kicking into business mode.

"The slums?"

"Deeper."

"Lower London?"

"Uh-huh. You gonna drink that?" She motioned toward my still-waiting glass.

"Help yourself."

I thought how that made sense. Lower London, wholly underground beneath Darkside proper. Originally built as sustainable housing by some Englishman and his millions.

Now, like the rest of Darkside, it was a bleaker reality of its promised potential. Most people just called it the Sewer because, well, shit runs downhill, even on the moon. If you wanted to lose yourself among the refuse who populated Darkside, Lower London would be the best place to do it. No one stepped into the Sewer who ever wanted to come out again.

Minnie sipped her fourth dose of medicine and said, "The marshals were prepping for a raid on the down-below when someone called off the dogs. Though I hear all the hounds haven't stopped baying yet."

That woke me out of my pre-loathing about having to tromp through the Sewer. "What do you mean?"

She set the glass down. Her eyes lost focus for a tick, then set hard again. "I mean that sometimes a badger remembers why they're supposed to be wearing the star. Not everyone clocks in and out when the Company tells them to."

"A true-bluer?"

Minnie nodded, her eyes blurring again.

Nine out of ten marshals were just deputized muscle for the Company. Petty crime and enforcement of SynCorp law fell to them. And, most of the time, they did their job like you'd expect. Seeing that five-pointed star on a uniformed chest comforted the citizens of Sol, made them feel like some part of their old life on Earth really had made it to the stars with them. In reality, most marshals were on the take—either looking the other way during business hours or moonlighting as hired help for one faction or another.

But every once in a while, someone wore the star who actually *did* care. About their job. About justice.

I hate those guys. They make my work more complicated. SynCorp and even the Marshals Service itself didn't suffer them lightly. Being a straight shooter in a crooked game is the fastest way to feel the final embrace of Mother Universe.

"You're telling me some true-bluer is still bird-dogging Blalock? Even after Tony passed the word…"

I shut my mouth and glanced down at my empty glass. Goddamn it, Minnie's good. Good at getting information out of shmucks like me, information that can get her killed.

Minnie was smiling with her perfect mouth. "Now, Stacks, you used to be smarter'n that." She gave a lazy wink that, had she been less drunk and twenty years younger…

"And you're too damned smart for your own good," I growled. "That's all you're getting out of me tonight, Minerva. Got a name on the marshal?"

Her smile faded at my use of her given name. "Just a last one," she said, rising slowly from the chair. She was irritated. The bourbon had made her playful, and I wouldn't play. "Darrow."

"Darrow, got it. Any idea where—?"

Minnie had walked around the desk and now she leaned into me. She placed one hand on my shoulder to hold herself up. The other found my inseam. "Why not stay a while?" she asked.

"I told you," I said, the blood rushing south, out of my resolve. "I've got business."

"I can feel that."

"*Minnie*—where can I…." I cleared my throat. "Where can I find this Marshal Darrow?"

Her fingers stopped measuring me for a new pair of trousers. "You're no fun, you know that?"

I stood up abruptly, so fast it set her back on her wobbly heels. I grabbed her with a soft hand to keep her on her feet.

"Not tonight I'm not. Can you clue me in or not?"

"Sure, Einstein. I'd start with the marshal's outpost in the Sewer," she said, petulant and pouting. Minnie always seemed less the hardboiled madam and more the mean little girl when she was drunk. "Like I said—they were ready to raid when Tony Taulke called 'em off."

"Thanks." Rising, I headed for the door.

"Hey, Stacks?" she said behind me.

Turning, I watched her pick up the decanter of bourbon again.

"Yeah?"

"Stop back on your way out of Darkside?"

I paused. Doubtful. Tony would want a firsthand report tout de suite, and in person. No way for the communication to be tapped, if I reported in person. The decanter clinked and clanked against the rim of her glass. I watched bourbon slop onto the desk.

"I've been getting stiffed by customers lately, and I don't mean in a good way," she said, adding a leer like drinkers do when they think the person they're talking to is as dull as they are drunk. "Now, when *you* stiff me—"

"I'll try to stop by," I said to stop her talking. I like Minnie; I like her a lot. We're two peas in a pathetic pod. Only I kill people for a living. She just screws them. "Thanks for the info, Minnie."

I beat feet before my sympathy for an old, drunk whore made me decide to stay.

* * *

If the up-top of Darkside smells like humanity overripe and underfed, the Sewer smells worse. SynCorp doesn't much care whether the artificial gravity works reliably on the moon, and that plays havoc with the waste reclamation located in the down-below. The corridors of Lower London, more narrow than up top, slosh now and then with gray filth when you walk. Lower London is like its namesake in older times, I guess. Minus the frilly Shakespeare clothes.

More like a toll booth than an outpost, the marshal's station was easy to find. It has a sign over the door. It's the brightest thing in the Sewer as you come off the ramp, so you can't miss it. I hiked my collar and lowered my hat when I got close.

"I'm looking for the deputy in charge," I said to the grizzled twenty-something on duty. Dark figures passed within the alcoves along the main corridor leading deeper into Lower London. Their feet stirred up the smell of the sludge around me. If I weren't armed to the teeth, I'd be concerned about the element I was stepping into. And I don't just mean the shit slurry on the ground.

"That'd be me," the grizzled twenty-something said.

He didn't bother to look up from his padd. The way his thumb was moving, I figured he must be either about to win the game he was playing or about to lose it.

"No, I mean, *really* in charge. Someone in command down here."

The sad sound effects of defeat spun out from his padd. Losing, then. Cursing, the unshaven whelp of a lawman looked up. "Name's Mustafar. And like I said, if you need a marshal, I'm the guy. You think they'd put a veteran with reputation down this shithole?"

Fair point. "Deputy Mustafar, then." I looked around. "Is there someplace we can have a private conversation?"

Mustafar gestured at the barely man-sized booth around him. "I'd offer you my office, but it's a little cramped. Now, what do you want? I'm busy."

I glanced at his padd but held my tongue. "I was just wondering if Deputy Darrow was around?"

His expression flattened. He wasn't much interested in playing games anymore, that's for sure.

"What do you want with Darrow?" He gave me a curious eye. "Do I know you?"

"Don't think so. Darrow and I? Old friends. Mutual acquaintance told me he was assigned down here. Thought I'd—"

"Old friends, huh?"

"Yeah."

"Well *she*—Deputy Darrow—is unavailable."

Shit. And I'd had a fifty-fifty chance of getting that right, too. Ah, well. Sometimes the best thing to do when caught in a lie is to own it with a smile.

I crossed my arms—an old trick, just in case I needed to draw—and smiled. "Hey, friend, you got me. I was just—"

"What do you want with Darrow?" he asked again. I watched him shift his weight to the right. I imagined him pressing a button under the lip of the counter in front of him. Seemed like his suspicion had touched on a memory. "Do I know you?"

My options were suddenly very limited. But killing a marshal, even in the Sewer, might blow back on Tony in the court of public opinion. Could even help Ra'uf Erkennen with his plan to take over.

"You know what?" I said, backing away. "I think I'll look for ole Darrow myself. Sorry to have interrupted your game."

"Hey! I do know you! Stop right there!"

Double shit. Out of options.

"You're Fischer! Taulke's assassin!" Mustafar fumbled beneath the counter.

I pulled my stunner. My eyes were on him, but at the same moment, I felt a shadow moving with purpose behind me. I hesitated on the trigger—and everything went real dark real fast.

The Twist

Waking up after being clocked from behind is a tricky thing. If you've got your wits, you do it slowly to get the lay of the land before whoever put your lights out realizes you're awake.

"You can open your eyes." A woman's voice. "Go on, Fischer, I know you're awake."

Well, no need to play possum then. I raised my head off my chest and felt a spider's web of pain shoot across the back of my skull. She'd cold-cocked me good, all right.

"Deputy Marshal True-Blue Darrow, I assume." I blinked away the blackout and took her in through the orange spots. She was slight for a marshal, almost comically so, though her size emphasized a kind of fierce beauty. The badge over her left breast hung like an oversized star on the too-small canvas of her uniform.

"And you're Stacks Fischer. Tony Taulke's assassin to the stars."

The orange spots had finally cleared out. "Since you know who I am, you know this little tussle can permanently direct the course of your career. Cut me loose and let me walk out of here, and I'll forget it ever happened."

Darrow thrust her hips to one side and crossed her arms. "Do I look stupid to you?"

"I try never to judge on first appearances."

"Funny."

I sat up ... slowly ... and rested against the wall. The room we were in had a film of something slimy on the floor. The seat of my pants felt soaked. Darrow had bound my feet, but that was all. I must've woken up too fast for her to finish tying me up.

"Maybe we should just space him, Glau."

I turned my head and found Mustafar standing there. He looked every bit the ten years younger than Darrow he was. Seeing them together, I sized up the situation real quick. Deputy Marshal Mustafar was into older women.

"Quiet, Amin," Darrow said. Then, looking at me, "Never tell the criminal element your plans."

I laughed, but the mirth was short-lived. The lump on the back of my head reminded me I wasn't in a laughing mood. "You're not going to kill me," I said.

Darrow cocked an eyebrow. She was good at the body language thing. Being short had helped her develop other necessary survival skills. "Don't be so sure," she said.

"Oh, I'm one-hundred percent sure." I stared at her straight. "For one thing, I woke up. If you wanted me dead, I'd be that way by now. Second, you're smart enough to know you can't kill me and get away with it. Tony would put you in a decompression chamber and reduce the PSI for a week until your eyeballs finally exploded. Third—you're not a killer," I said, with a knowing look at her boyfriend, Deputy Big Mouth.

Damn. Darrow's ears had been distracted by my little speech, but her eyes had noticed my right hand flexing.

"Looking for the knife?" She moved aside and there, lined up on a table behind her, were my three insurance policies: my stunner, my .38, and my spring-blade.

"Not anymore."

"Let's just space him! No one will—"

"Shut up, Amin!" Darrow's voice was short and spoke of a growing irritation with her puppy-dog lover. At the look Mustafar gave her, Darrow's face melted into quick regret. She was in new territory having me as a prisoner. Life was getting more stressful by the minute. "Look, just go back out to the booth and keep watch, okay? Before Central notices you're gone."

"Fine," he said. Then, "I've put everything on the line for you, Glau."

"I know."

"Don't fuck this up."

"I *know*."

Mustafar threw a last leer my way, to which I puckered up and blew him a kiss. His look of disgust made its exit with the rest of him.

"I guess I wasn't out that long, then," I said. Even in the Sewer, an empty marshal's station would get noticed.

"No."

"Why *didn't* you kill me? Roles reversed, I would have done for you."

The look she gave me was pure hatred. Like I was a cockroach that had just crawled into her dead mother's mouth as she lay in the coffin.

"I'm sure you would. Maybe I'll kill you anyway."

I laughed again. "A true-bluer like you? There's no justice in cold-blooded murder."

"You should know."

I let her have her moment of smug satisfaction. "But anyway—let me go and we'll forget this ever happened."

"So *you* can kill *me*? Fat chance."

"Kill you? I have no intention of killing you. I'm here to fix a problem. That's all."

"Uh-huh."

I took a moment to collect my thoughts. Darrow's perspective on the puzzle fell into place fast. The top assassin in SynCorp steps into the Sewer asking after Deputy Marshal Glau Darrow, who's bucked the Company's directive to back off Blalock. In her mind, I was here to fix a problem all right: her.

"You think I'm here for you."

"I don't *think* anything," she said.

"I'm not."

"Uh-huh."

"I'm here for Blalock." I could have played coy, but Darrow struck me as too sharp to buy whatever I'd come up with. "We're here for the same reason, really."

She paused to consider. "If you're here, it's because Tony Taulke wants Blalock dead. I'm here to take him in for corporate espionage. Those aren't the same reason."

"You were told to stand down."

That made her eyes drop for half a heartbeat. They came back up with flames in them.

"I'm so tired of that crap," she said. "We're sworn to uphold the law—"

"Corporate law." Watch it, Fischer. Stay out of the pulpit.

"*Yes*, corporate law!" Darrow started pacing. "And half the time, just like with Blalock, we're denied our duty because Tony Taulke or some other faction leader decides they're *above* the law!"

"Look, kid," I said, "you know how this plays out. You're already in seven kinds of trouble, but the situation's still salvageable. I might even be able to help you out of the jam you're in."

Her eyes narrowed. "Why would you help me?"

Good question. Darrow was nothing to me except a potential headache with Tony. But, cold-cocking notwithstanding, I liked her grit. She was bucking her orders to bring in a criminal just for the sake of serving the law. We might walk opposite sides of that legal street, but I could admire her dedication to duty. We were more alike than she'd cop to. No pun intended.

"Young love sets my heart aflutter," I said by way of explanation.

Her forehead wrinkled as she translated. "Amin? You think I'm in love with Amin?"

"I think he's in love with you. Your little crusade is gonna get him killed. You too."

"Crusade? I'm doing my job!"

I was tempted to shout. Tempted to rail at the stupidity of Darrow's idealism. But I really was starting to like her, maybe because she *was* such an idealist. Quietly, without venom, I said, "Your job is what the Company tells you it is."

"My job is to enforce the law."

"SynCorp *is* the law!"

Darrow's eyes flared again, but her mouth shut up.

"There's more going on here than you know," I continued. "Blalock will never be taken alive. Whether it's me or someone else that does him, he'll get done. That's why Tony sent the marshals home—to make sure Blalock is taken care of permanently."

"What is it?" She sounded almost desperate to know. "What *is* going on?" Like knowing might somehow justify—literally—why she couldn't do her job. Like knowing would give her permission to let Blalock get spaced, to turn a blind eye.

"Can't tell you that," I said. "It'd only make you more of a target than you already are."

Darrow advanced, ready to get the story out of me one way or the other. Then, angry voices filtered in from outside. One of them was Mustafar's. He was doing his *I'm-the-marshal-you're-looking-for* bit.

I could tell in an instant it wouldn't be enough.

"Cut my feet free," I growled. "*Now.*"

She looked from me to my weapons on the table behind her, then toward the doorway and the ruckus outside. Mustafar's defiance had begun to lose its authority. And from the sound of it, he was outnumbered.

"Darrow!"

But she was already moving for the door, drawing her stunner. With her off-hand, without looking back, she snagged my knife from the table and shot it in my direction. I ducked as it thunked into the wall behind me.

Before her shadow left the room I could hear the sharp, potent *punk! punk! punk!* of stunner fire outside. Those marshals were both as good as dead. I didn't know who the loudmouths were, but Mustafar must've drawn on them like he drew on me, and they'd responded in kind.

I yanked the knife from the wall and cut the rope binding my feet. As I levered myself up, my ankles screamed in protest. I'd been sitting too long. Fuck being over fifty.

I flicked the knife back under my wrist, spring loaded. Blood began to fill my feet again, and I loped to the table. I filled both hands, one with my stunner and the other with the .38. I had no intention of getting involved, not really, and maybe I could just sit here and wait it out and steal away after the marshals were dead.

Punk! punk! punk!

Punk! punk!

But if I waited and the new players weren't friends, they'd be after me next. With all that shooting outside, I figured there must be at least a handful of them. Not good odds when you're cornered in a bare room with no cover. If I joined Darrow and Mustafar, I'd at least have them on my side. The enemy of my enemy and all that. Better odds.

Killing the lights inside the little room, I knelt beside the doorway and darted my eyes around the corner to get my bearings. I was across the dark alleyway from Mustafar's outpost in the same alcove Darrow must have jumped me from earlier. I spotted her behind a long, thin dumpster farther up the narrow alley. She was pinned down by fire coming from the near side. There was no sign of Mustafar.

Two of the shooters advancing on Darrow were crouched and moving from trash can to doorway. A third semi-strode down the middle of the alleyway like an Old West gunslinger.

Idiot.

I could flank them. They'd never see me coming, like I hadn't seen Darrow. Or, I reminded myself, I could just melt into the wall and go my own way.

"Firing on members of the Marshals Service is a capital crime! Cease and desist and throw down your weapons!"

It was Darrow reading from the marshal's manual again. I wonder if she really thought they'd obey her order or if she was just quoting herself some bravery.

Punk! punk! punk!

Their answer kept Darrow's head down. To drive the point home, a fourth shooter engaged from the marshal's booth. So, these guys weren't dicking around. Mustafar must be dead. In a few seconds, one of the three gunslingers would draw a bead on Darrow. The closer they got to finishing that job, the clearer they made my escape route.

Sorry, Darrow. You were a good kid. At least she'd die true to the principles she'd lived by.

I edged out of the doorway, my knees joining my ankles' chorus of complaints. I crept along the wall, Darrow's defiance hurling the scripture of the law like bullets at the bad guys behind me. But as I passed the fourth shooter, the one in the booth, I finally registered something. Like the three moving in on Darrow, he was wearing corporate blue coveralls, the kind the factory workers on Mars wear. But we weren't on Mars.

Punk! punk!

Those coveralls also happened to be the de facto uniform of the Resistance, since most of the movement's Ghosts came from the worker class. Why were they in Darkside shooting at—make that, *killing*—marshals at the same time the shit with Erkennen was going down?

I needed to know the answer to that question. Coincidence is too coincidental for my tastes.

I turned first on the one in the booth. He still hadn't seen me and was being cavalier about his cover. My stunner showed him the virtue of awareness. The others were too distracted by their target to notice me killing their buddy.

Punk! punk!

Punk! punk! punk!

Only, their buddy in the booth wasn't dead. I'd shot him point-blank and all it did was make him mad. My stunner had fired but to no effect.

Fuck! Never trust new tech!

He turned on me, drawing a bead.

Good thing I had my .38 in my other hand. The slug took him high in the chest, knocking him off his feet. If I hadn't been in a hurry, I'd have kissed my old reliable.

The report from my pistol got the attention of the other three. Before the first mook turned, I shot him in the back. The second had spun and crouched, and I flattened on my stomach in the muck. Her stunner fired fine but missed its mark. My .38 didn't. I watched Darrow take aim at the third guy and shoot him point-blank. Like the one in the booth, he seemed to shrug it off and turned on her. I did for him like the others, splitting his spine with a little old-fashioned lead.

As the three dead bodies settled into the sludge, silence was a strange sound after all that killing. Darrow darted forward from her hiding place, running past me.

"You're welcome," I said to her wind.

The Alliance

"Amin!"

I could hear the anguish in her voice. I left her to it. I was more interested in the corpses at my feet anyway and why my stunner had misfired.

Blood from the three assassins leaked bright red into the gray muck. I kicked each in a kidney to make sure they were all good and dead. Not a grunt among them.

I noticed some of the resident Sewer rats poking their heads out of their holes. A few of them were pointing feeders our way. *The Real Story* gives those high-definition cameras away to anyone who wants one. They keep the show's insatiable video feed streaming 24/7. It wouldn't do to have my face all over the Basement, so I turned my back on the locals and knelt to get a closer look at the deaders.

They wore blue coveralls, all right. Two men, one woman. Nothing particularly remarkable about them, except … I picked up a weapon caked in gray shit and turned it over. A stunner, a Mark II by the looks of it. The Mark IIs were still pre-market. No one was supposed to have them. I was still carrying the Mark I, and reluctantly at that. But this new model—no one was supposed to have these yet. Hell *I* didn't even have one.

That made me curiouser. I unzipped one of the fellow's coveralls. Underneath, he was wearing finer sweat catchers than a Martian factory worker could afford. I looked at his shoes. Same story. These guys weren't displaced Resistance types a long way from home. These guys—and one gal— were professionals.

"Mustafar's dead," Darrow said behind me. I could tell by her voice that her eyes were getting wet. "And for what? Why?"

That same desperate need-to-know from earlier. I glanced sideways over my shoulder. "These guys weren't Ghosts." I wrinkled a lip at the irony.

There was a pause. "Why do you say that?"

"Too well dressed. Too well armed. See those pieces?" I gestured at the stunners laying in the sludge. "Pre-market. Ghosts use the cast-off weapons they can scrounge from reclamation. No way they could get their hands on pre-market tech like this. I doubt these are even on the black market yet."

"Maybe a patron—"

"He buy them silk undies too? And these coveralls— they're thicker than you'd expect for factory grunts moon- lighting as terrorists. A heavier weave. Dyed to look like Martian worker duds, but more than that." Something tick- led the back of my brain. Multiple things, actually, like puz- zle pieces trying to fit together.

Darrow peered over my shoulder. "I see what you mean." The no-nonsense marshal had displaced the grieving woman in her voice. "What's that?"

"What?"

She pointed at the neck of the woman lying next to the man I'd unzipped. I reached over and pulled the gal's collar down to get a better look. "Huh." Those puzzle piec- es seemed magnetized. They wanted to come together, but they weren't quite ready to yet.

"Huh what…"

"That's the Greek letter Epsilon."

Darrow stared at me.

"You should read more, Marshal," I smirked. "Epsilon is the Erkennen brand. All their operatives wear it tattooed to a body part. It's like their secret handshake." These assas- sins were on Ra'uf Erkennen's payroll. That explained how they had access to the Mark IIs, since the Erkennens sup- plied the Company's tech.

Darrow's eyes dawned. "You mean the Erkennen Fac- tion sent a hit squad—"

"—to kill you. Yeah." I stopped there. She could do the rest herself.

"To keep me from tracking down Blalock. Because I wouldn't give up."

"Dressed like Ghosts. So any video that made it to the Basement," I said, nodding to the evermore curious rats in their doorways, "would make it look like the Resistance had hit the marshal's station. Two birds, one stone. The Erkennens stop you from messing in their business and the Resistance gets blamed, which makes SynCorp the victim. It's a headliner of a news story, tailor-made for CorpNet."

I stood and cursed my cracking knees. The Erkennens had gone to a lot of trouble to shut down Darrow and her puppy-dog lover. It didn't quite square with the risk they'd taken to do it.

Sticking the Mark II in a coat pocket, I gave her a minute to think it all over while I made the rounds to pick up the others' weapons. They wouldn't be needing them anymore, and I could resell them for a decent price after all this was over. Hell, maybe *I'd* start the black market for the Mark IIs.

"Amin's dead."

"Yeah," I said, not unkindly. I hate conversation as a rule. Sometimes I hate the silence more.

"Because of me."

And sometimes, silence is exactly what's called for.

"They failed," Darrow said.

"Failed? Well, yeah. You're still alive." Which reminded me ... I looked around and, other than the eyes peering around corners, the corridor was empty. "The Service will send officers soon from the up-top. The first videos have probably already hit the Basement. Wheels are in motion here, Darrow. We need to beat feet. The marshals that come now won't be your friends."

"They failed," she said as if she hadn't heard a word I'd said, "because I'm going after Blalock anyway." Darrow glanced back at the booth. I could see Mustafar's marshal-booted feet around the lip of the doorway, heels up. "Amin's death has to mean something."

"Actually, it doesn't," I said. When she turned her flamers on me again, I tried not to feel bad. "Hell, we don't even know where Blalock is."

"I do." Darrow tossed it out like it wasn't the million-dollar answer to my prayers that it was.

I pulled her off to the side of the corridor, hopefully out of earshot of any expensive sound-catching equipment being aimed our way by the Basement trolls. "You know where Blalock is?" I whispered. That would certainly explain why the Erkennens had sent the hit squad dressed like Ghosts. They'd do anything to keep their little secret till they were ready to spring their trap on Tony.

"Yeah," she said, regaining some of her marshal moxie. "I know exactly where he is. And I'm not telling you shit, Fischer. You go your way. I'll go mine." She started to pull away and I stopped her. I got her stunner stuck in my gut for my trouble. Somehow, despite what I'd just seen in the shootout, I knew hers would work on me. That's just my goddamned luck.

"Hold up there, Marshal. Hear me out."

"Make it fast. You said yourself, we're about to have more company. And I have business to attend to."

"You need my help. Not only do you have the Erkennens gunning for you, but your own Service is out to rein you in."

"And it smells like shit down here. Tell me something I don't know."

"Point is—gunning for Blalock on your own ends just one way: you join Mustafar, forever embracing in the cold arms of Mother Universe."

When she glanced back at the marshal's booth, I knew I had her. What she said next didn't make a damned bit of difference, even when she burned me with those flamers again when she said it.

"I'll never work with you. Let them come and take me. Let the Erkennens kill me. At least I'll die—"

"Yeah, yeah, true to your goddamned ideals," I said. Darrow tried to jerk her arm free and I yanked her back against the Sewer's wall.

"Do that again, Fischer, and to hell with due process. I'll kill you right here and now."

She would, too. I could see clear intent behind the flames. She'd already tossed out the marshal's manual to focus on what justice demanded: *wergild* in blood for Mustafar. At this point, I was in her way. I gambled and let her go. A little trust might go a long way. She didn't bolt.

"Listen to me, Darrow. You might get to Blalock. And then what? He'll never stand trial because no one—*no one*—wants him to stand trial. Not the Taulkes. Not the Erkennens."

"Why wouldn't the Erkennens want him to be arrested? He stole their tech!"

"No one stole anything!" I hissed. Mindful of the watchers, I pointed my .38 at the ceiling down the alley and fired off a round. More like turtles than rats, the locals pulled back inside their holes.

"This was all some kind of set-up by Ra'uf Erkennen. Whatever Blalock did, they let him do it—for their own reasons." I shook my head. "This is the bigger picture you never get to see, Darrow. And someone like you? Be glad of it."

The look on her face told me that wasn't enough. She was just confused. Overwhelmed. Not thinking or not able to think. I grabbed her arm again and dragged her closer to the booth, away from the rats. They were getting brave again.

I said, "Maybe the Erkennens sold Blalock a bill of goods. Maybe they promised to set him up on Titan for life. Who the hell knows? Point is, they're behind the whole thing."

"You're lying. Why would they do that?"

"Leverage! Against the Taulkes. To strengthen their own position, take over the Company. Hell, even I don't understand it all. One thing I *do* understand—your little crusade for justice doesn't mean shit to anyone but you."

She took it in. I could practically see the wheels turning inside her head. Her ideals as a marshal—extoled by the five-pointed star on her chest pledged to protect and enforce—battled a lifetime of living in a system ruled by the bottom line.

"Why do you think Ra'uf Erkennen sent these killers after you?" I pressed. "You need my gun if you want a chance in hell of setting things right for Mustafar."

The radio inside the booth crackled, demanding someone answer. More marshals were definitely inbound, probably to arrest Darrow. Once they had her, they were just as likely to kill her as incarcerate her—outside the public spotlight of *The Real Story*, of course.

She pulled away, and this time I didn't fight her. Darrow headed for the booth. She was going to tend to Mustafar, I figured. Maybe put something over his face or conduct some lawman's ritual; do one of those things we humans feel compelled to do when death takes someone we care about. As if the ritual is about their dignity and not our own need to cover up the fact that death's coming for us, too.

But Darrow surprised me and stepped right over him. I heard her opening cabinets in the booth. She came out with extra chargers for her stunner and a flash grenade, which she hung on a back belt-loop.

"Come on," she said. "Blalock's not that far."

The Job

The heads of the turtle-rats pulled back in their holes only to edge out again after we'd passed. They pointed their feeders for *The Real Story* at our backs. Their pale skin, damned near translucent in the dim light, was the brightest thing about them. Shaggy haired and clothed in rags, they kept to the darkness. They reminded me of the Morlocks from that old H.G. Wells novel, or maybe vampires with bad skin. Leaving them behind us made me edgy.

"These people trouble?"

Darrow gave a muffled laugh. "The Moonies? They're harmless. The last thing they want is trouble."

"Moonies?" I chuckled. "That's what they call themselves?"

"It's what they're called. Does it matter?"

"Guess not."

One of the palefaces got daring and tried to get a close-up. I stopped, turned on my heel and snatched the feeder from his hand. Without so much as a "Hey, that's mine!" he scurried back into his hole. I dropped it in my pocket. That should keep the rest of them from being so friendly.

"That's the most expensive thing that man owns," Darrow said.

"Not anymore."

She slowed her pace as we neared the end of the Sewer's main street.

"Which way?" I asked.

"Blalock is left," Darrow whispered. I started to move, but she reached a hand out. Big grip for such a little marshal. "We go right." She nodded back behind us. I turned my face in profile, just enough so my peripheral saw another Moonie pointing a feeder our way—but definitely from a distance.

"Scenic route?"

Darrow nodded and headed right. The narrow hallway immediately curved, and I could see her strategy. If the Erkennens or marshals were monitoring our progress via *The Real Story*, they'd think we were headed in the wrong direction. At least for a little while.

Without warning, Darrow darted left up a half-flight of muddy stairs. They led to a mid-level floor between Lower London and Darkside proper. The stairs dumped us into a cramped, deserted hallway of corrugated metal that felt more like a military ship than a livable community.

"You really know your way around here."

"Unfortunately." She angled her head up the hallway. "He isn't far."

We stepped off, quiet as mice. Thumbing slugs into my .38 I asked, "How'd you find him?"

"He's a science genius, right? Those types don't have jobs, they have obsessions. I scanned for nodes in Darkside placing excessive demands on the local 'net. Only the brothels in the up-top pull that kind of bandwidth. Until now."

I thought of the porn closets in Minnie's place and nodded. Their floors are sticky, but the booths are private. And cheap, considering the quality of the 3D video feed. Or so I've been told.

"Smart. But how do you know it's him?"

Darrow shrugged. "In the last two days, there's been a terabyte of data exchanged with a server off-moon," she said. "Either someone's opened a new porn franchise down here for an under-class that can't afford electricity on a regular basis, or it's Blalock."

"Good detecting, Detective, but that's a pretty big footprint to leave behind. Awful easy to trace."

"They think no one's looking anymore, remember?" She put her ear to the door.

"Maybe. This the only way in?"

Instead of answering, Darrow placed her fingertips against the rusty latch and slowly pushed down.

"This can't be that easy," I said.

She drew her weapon as the door inched open.

"Hey, something's wrong," I warned. "This is too—"

The door creaked open on metal hinges. A lone, fritzing lightbulb hummed in the ceiling, casting shadows into the corners of the room. Darrow eased her way in. I followed despite my better instincts, drawing one of the Mark II's I'd taken off the dead Ghost. Maybe the latest stunner model would work and maybe it wouldn't. I had my .38 in my other hand, just in case.

The room was empty. It smelled like fish wrapped in a sweaty sock and left in the sun for a week. But for being only half a floor up from the Sewer, it wasn't too bad. Bare walls, rusty like the door latch. A floor mosaicked with decades-old dark stains. The room might've once housed school children specializing in ground-level finger-painting. Or it could've been a room were murder was done on a regular basis. Hard to tell under that sputtering yellow light.

I gave Darrow an inquisitive look as we moved deeper in. She shone a light on the far wall. Another door. She put her ear to that one too and stepped back quickly.

"Bingo."

My ear did its own recon. The rust flaked when I pressed against the metal. Low voices: bored and tired of smelling fishy socks.

"You're sure this is him?"

In answer, Darrow pressed the door latch down. This one was unlocked too. Yeah, it was too easy. *Way too easy.* But here we were, and Tony expected results … and soon.

"All right, here's how we'll play it," I said. "I'll go up top through the vents and—"

Darrow pushed every pound of her slight weight against the heavy door. It swung open, the scarred metal screaming.

"Marshals Service! Everyone stay right where you are!"

Cursing, I brought up my own artillery to cover her as she moved in.

Six pairs of surprised eyes turned to look at us. Four more of the Ghosts with new shoes and newer weapons. One doughy, bespectacled type who looked like he really needed to take a dump. And one very well-dressed corporate elite type. He looked familiar, even in the half-light.

One of the fake Resistance types started to reach for her weapon.

"Uh-uh," I said, motioning with my .38. "Slowly, butt first. I want them all lined up on the table over there. All of you."

The elite type smiled wide. "Welcome, Mr. Fischer. We've been waiting for you."

It's when he spoke that I recognized him. The mid-European accent sold it.

"Ra'uf Erkennen." Those puzzle pieces in the back of my head? They were gyrating like one of Minnie's girls after ten minutes.

The head of the Erkennen Faction made a slight bow. "And you must be the maverick marshal," he said to Darrow. "My dear, you have no idea how much trouble you've caused me."

"Not as much as you're gonna get," I said. "Now, you stooges, I told you already—put your stunners on the table."

"Do nothing of the kind," Erkennen said. Not that he'd needed to. They hadn't moved. "Fischer, put down your weapons. You too, my dear."

Darrow scoffed and tightened her grip on her stunner. Points for moxie.

"You have two choices," Erkennen said. "Drop your weapons or drop with them."

I've never been good at math, but I didn't need to be. There were five stunners pointed at us, and I knew, with my luck, they'd work like a charm. Darrow had hers and I had my .38, but I had zero confidence in the stunner in my other hand, even if it was new tech. *Especially* because it was new tech. Even if it did work, that was five shots to three in the first round of fire. We might get a couple of them but we were definitely going down.

"Darrow, do it," I said.

"Like hell!"

Erkennen exhaled boredom. "Shoot her."

"Wait! Darrow…" I nodded at her and caught her attention. My eye darted to her beltline. "No sense dying sooner than we have to. Do it."

She thought about it a moment longer, but she'd caught the hint I'd tossed her way. "Fine." Squatting straight down, she placed her stunner on the ground.

Smart girl.

I did likewise.

"Very good." Turning to the dumpy guy, Erkennen said, "How close are you to finishing the composition matrix?"

Dumpy guy shrugged, nervous. Had to be Blalock. Who else? "It's almost finished. The algorithm subroutines are populating the pattern, and once they're finished, the final formula—"

"I don't need the geek details," Erkennen groused. "Get it done."

"What's this all about?" I asked, playing dumb. I was good at that. I took a couple of steps forward, like from curiosity. "What's this mega-extra smoky hemp for? You gonna get everyone in the solar system high so you can take over?"

Erkennen gave me the strangest look. "What?"

"It's called Molecularly Enhanced Synthetic Hemp," Professor Geek corrected.

I motioned to him. "Whatever—the new drug he's making. How does it help you take over the Company?"

Out of the corner of my eye, I noticed Darrow getting fascinated. *Here's the bigger picture you were unaware of, Marshal.*

"You think we're making a drug here?" Erkennen laughed out loud. "Is that what Tony thinks? We're gonna smoke him out, eh?" The guffaws from his men filled the room, trying to please the boss. Even Blalock snickered, the brainy little shit.

"Hemp isn't typically a drug," Darrow said. "Same plant as marijuana but different purpose. It's typically used to make clothing."

"Very good, my dear," Erkennen said, pleased. "She's smarter than you and Tony put together, Fischer."

And that's when those magnetic puzzle pieces snapped together with seamless edges. I knew I had to stop this conversation right now, at least for the moment.

I stared straight at the head of the Erkennen Faction and marched across the space separating us. His goons brought up their guns, but their boss waved them off. I think he wanted me in his face. And to be in mine. As far as he knew, I was unarmed.

"Whatever this new tech is, you've got zero chance going up against Tony Taulke," I said. I was close enough to spit on Erkennen. I needed him angry. "Tony will grind you and your whole faction into the ground! That new wife of yours? Just wait till you're spaced. A kind word from Tony and—"

Erkennen stepped back to get strength behind it and cracked me against the side of the head with the butt of his Mark II. I went down harder than I had to and stayed there, shaking my head to make it look good.

"Say something else about her, Fischer," Erkennen growled. "I wanted to keep you alive long enough so you'd understand exactly what's going to happen to Tony Taulke. But maybe I can forego that bit of personal satisfaction."

I motioned with my hand like I'd had enough. Standing up slowly, rubbing my temple, I leaned against the wall and fake-breathed hard. "So, if it's not a drug strain, what is it he's making?" I asked again.

Erkennen jutted his head. "Tell him, Mason. He can take the secret with him into space."

Professor Geek stood up. He was proud of his creation. He wanted to give it its due. "Molecularly Enhanced Synthetic Hemp—or MESH—is a new kind of scalable cloth capable of absorbing and dissipating any catalyst used to ignite and direct electromagnetic current."

Blalock confirmed what I'd already guessed. Everything was crystal clear—what the tech actually was, why Erkennen had hidden it from the other factions, and how MESH, all by itself, could make Ra'uf Erkennen head of the entire Syndicate Corporation.

MESH wasn't a drug.

MESH was a shield.

A molecular shield that could be woven right into a person's clothing. A shield that protected against stunners and their ability to kill by capturing and amplifying a person's EM field to shock them to death. Those that wore it were protected. Those that didn't were just as vulnerable as ever.

"The faux-Ghosts in the corridor outside the marshal's post," I said, connecting the dots. "They were wearing a prototype? That's why my stunner wouldn't work on them."

Erkennen smiled. "Oh, and about that. I have to compliment you and the marshal for the show you put on. I couldn't have planned it better myself. The footage of Tony Taulke's main man and a renegade marshal gunning down Ghosts? All the rage in the Basement. Perfect recruiting material for the Resistance. And while Tony's stamping down that little grassfire, I'll move on SynCorp HQ. By the time the Taulkes or any of the other factions can react, I'll control the station."

The image of Erkennen mooks dressed in MESH-laden uniforms gunning down Taulke operatives filled my head. They'd be invincible with the new tech. While the other factions would steal it soon enough and make their own shielded clothing, that wouldn't happen in time to save Tony. Or keep Ra'uf Erkennen from taking over SynCorp.

"Humanity's just getting back on its feet!" Darrow said. "We're not even two generations out from damned-near extinction! And you'd risk turning all that inside-out for power?"

"Stick to your duties, my dear," Erkennen said. "Let the big boys do the big thinking."

"Yeah, Darrow," I added. "He's a smart guy. He's thought of everything."

Erkennen gave me a look. My words sounded right, but their smartassery was wanting. "And for all the dirty jobs you pulled for Tony?" He brought up his stunner. "On behalf of the other four factions, I'm about to pay you off."

I stood my ground. "Before you do—one more question."

"Make it quick."

"Can the Mark IIs get past the MESH?"

"Of course," Erkennen allowed. "But since we're the only ones that have both, it doesn't really matter."

"Well, I wouldn't say that," I said, nodding to the spot where I'd taken the dive earlier. "See that?"

Erkennen peered closely. When he saw the feeder where I'd put it on the floor, its red transmission light shining, his face went pale. His little scheme had just gone out live to anyone tuned in to *The Real Story*. As had the secret of the MESH and the new Mark II stunner. Every member of all Five Factions would now be seeking both techs in earnest.

I flashed him a toothy grin. "Now guess who's got a fire to stamp out?"

"Why, you sonofa—"

"Darrow, now!"

I saw the blur of her body duck and roll as I launched myself backward. The mooks in blue were caught flatfooted. Erkennen's shot hit the wall behind my empty air. Darrow lobbed the flash grenade from behind her back straight at Blalock.

I almost didn't clamp my eyes shut in time. The air brightened like a sunburst. Grunts and cursing followed. I grabbed up my Mark II from the floor and started firing.

Punk! Punk!

Two fake Ghosts became real ones.

Darrow angled at a third, still dazed by the grenade. With a lithe efficiency I took half a second to admire, she rolled to one of the newly minted corpses, snagged his stunner, and shot the third man dead.

Erkennen was no lightweight. Blinking furiously, he was back on his feet and sweeping his own stunner around the room, firing randomly. I ducked and scooped up the .38 and turned on him. Two shots later, he was short a kneecap and screaming on the ground.

I took a moment to enjoy his pain, and that was a rookie mistake. I felt the threat long before I saw it: the last of the hired help, his Mark II aimed point-blank at me, ready to give me the shock of my life. Slow motion took over, and I could feel the cold stroke of death's fingers on the back of my neck.

Punk!

His body convulsed, his stunner shot went wide, and he fell lifeless to the floor with the others. I caught Darrow's eye and nodded my thanks. First time I've ever had use for a badger.

That just left Blalock. The flash grenade had caught him full-on. He was just stirring, moaning.

"Watch him," I said to Darrow, pointing at Ra'uf Erkennen. He was inventing all kinds of four-letter combinations with my name sprinkled on top. "Put a tourniquet above his knee, if you can find something to use. I don't want him dying just yet." And I wanted to keep her busy. I had business to attend to.

Walking over to the feeder, I crushed it under my boot. Its work was done. Erkennen's plot to overthrow Tony had gone out live to anyone watching *The Real Story*, which had lived up to its name today, boy-o.

I turned to Blalock. "Is this everything?" I asked, pointing at his work station. "The formula, how to make it—all that?"

He was still blinking, still getting his bearings.

"Blalock!"

Startled, he tried to crawl through the wall. "Yes! Everything is there. The molecular formula, the thresholds for performance, the—"

He saw me pointing the Mark II at his head.

"Wait! You don't need to kill me! I was only—"

"—following orders, yeah, I know."

"Fischer! You can't murder him in cold blood!"

"I have my orders, too," I said. But I hesitated, and that's not like me. I think something inside me didn't want to disappoint Darrow. I liked her. Admired her, even. And she *had* just saved my life.

"Please!" Blalock cried. "I can help Tony Taulke! I can—"

"Geeks are a dime a dozen these days," I said, remembering my contract. "Which makes your example all the more necessary."

"*Please!*"

I pulled the trigger and Blalock's body stiffened, electrocuted by his own EM field. I heard Darrow gasp behind me.

"Goddamnit, Fischer," Darrow shouted, getting to her feet. "I'm arresting you for the…"

She trailed off when she saw me pointing the Mark II her way. Her eyes darted to her own weapon laying on the floor. She'd put it down to tend to Erkennen. Too far out of reach.

"Do it then," she said. "Just do it."

"I'm not gonna kill you, Darrow," I said. "I told you earlier."

She stared straight down the barrel of my fancy new stunner. "Then what?"

I thumbed the setting down. Technically, a stunner could be true to its name—it didn't have to be lethal. In my business, it was hardly ever used that way. "Sweet dreams," I said.

"Fischer—"

I pulled the trigger but was a hair too slow to help ease Darrow to the ground. She collapsed, but not too hard. I took a moment to wonder what her future might be with the Service, since she'd disobeyed orders from the top. They wouldn't kill her now, they didn't need to, and her mug had been all over *The Real Story*. Too high profile to get rid of, at least right off the bat. If they spaced her, it'd be after the hubbub from the livecast died down.

Ra'uf Erkennen had begun to move, gasping with every stretch of his limbs. He was reaching for Darrow's weapon. I kicked it away.

"Congratulations on ruining your faction, Ra'uf," I said. "Tony's going to absorb the Erkennens like a bad stain."

"Fuck you," he said through clenched teeth. "Taulke is still finished. Wait till Gregor hears what you've done here. He'll—"

"Your brother Gregor? If he knows what's good for him, he'll play ball with Tony. Maybe the Taulkes will even let the Erkennens live." As I moved to stand over him, Erkennen had to crane his neck. "Well, all but one."

The fear in his eyes, then. It seemed foreign. He'd been the big cheese for so long, giving orders and being obeyed. Now, he was just another rat about to be shot like the vermin he was.

"Last words?" I asked, bringing the .38 up. I'm nothing if not a traditionalist.

"*Fuck you.*"

"Good as any, I guess."

I plugged him right between the eyes, the blast echoing around the metal walls.

As he slumped, I took stock of the room. Four dead mooks, one dead geek, one dead faction leader too big for his britches, and one sleeping marshal. After she woke up, I knew Darrow would feel compelled to make an official report. Images of Ra'uf Erkennen's third eye would be all over the Basement before lunar sunrise, I figured. And most everyone would see it as justice served after that little confession he'd broadcast. Maybe even Darrow would come to see it that way in time. If she lived long enough.

I grabbed Blalock's padd full of the greatest invention since the stunner itself and headed for the door. Tony would be happy. Before stepping through, I turned and regarded Darrow one last time. Even unconscious, her fierce beauty I'd noted earlier, bolstered now by seeing firsthand her strength of dedication to right for right's sake, impressed itself on me. Part of me hated leaving her to her fate.

"See you around, kid. Good luck with the law."

The Favor

"Hey, Stacks, how's life in the killing business?" Tony asked as I walked into his office.

"Tolerable," I answered, like always. It was our old way of greeting one another after a job.

I sat down and smiled. He *must* be happy, since he's calling me by my preferred handle. I *hate* Eugene. Tony happy? Everybody happy.

"Nice work out there," he said in a rare show of genuine appreciation. "And good work keeping your face off-camera."

"Thanks. I see Gregor Erkennen got out in front of the bad news."

Tony chuckled. Gregor had wasted no time disavowing his older brother after hearing Ra'uf confess. According to Gregor, the elder Erkennen and his super-scientist had pursued the MESH tech all on their own, outside normal Company protocols. Gregor's story explained both why Ra'uf had hid MESH's development in Darkside from his own brother and why the Erkennen Faction had originally reported Blalock's actions as corporate espionage. There'd been a power play *within* the faction too, discovered by Gregor after Blalock had disappeared. And Ra'uf had lost.

"You sure the Brothers Erkennen weren't in on it together?"

"I'm sure."

He said it in a way that raised my eyebrows. "Wait a minute. *Wait a minute.*"

Tony waited.

"Was Gregor Erkennen your little bird on the inside?"

Tony's face was uncharacteristically unexpressive. "Doesn't really matter now, does it?" Like usual, he kept his hole cards to himself. Tony doesn't like sharing secrets he doesn't have to, not even with me.

"Well, that opportunistic little..." I marveled at the human capacity for betrayal. "What about the MESH? What happens to it?"

"Gregor will have a distribution plan to me by Monday."

"Distribution plan?"

"Protection against stunners is an advantage," Tony said. Then, after a beat: "Unless everyone has it."

My eyebrows went up again. "So you're *giving* it to all the factions?"

"Along with the Mark IIs," he said. "My people are looking into how to upgrade the MESH to protect against the new stunner."

So Gregor Erkennen had uncovered his brother's plans after what looked like simple espionage by a wayward employee, plotted with Tony to get Ra'uf out of the way, and was now in charge of the family business. And set to make a huge personal profit when the other four factions ponied up for the new tech.

"Keeping the balance by keeping everyone without an advantage over the others," I said, impressed. "Mutually assured protection."

"Something like that."

"And you get to be the Company hero by handing everyone access to the new tech."

Tony was nothing if not a showman. A real natural at the theater of running the Company. He winked like he knew I was thinking that, and that sliver of human cleverness made the machinelike façade of his face all the more terrifying.

"Nice insurance policy for the status quo, too," I said.

Tony grinned. "I thought so too."

I sighed my satisfaction at successfully closing another contract. My bank account was bigger. My boss was happy. Life was good.

"What about you, Stacks? I'm feeling generous today. You got paid, sure … a bonus, maybe, or…"

He left the air empty for me to fill it with a favor. I thought it over. Whether he had a real desire to reward me or recognized an opportunity to do me a kindness he'd ask to be repaid one day, I wasn't sure. I decided it didn't really matter.

"Well, there's one thing."

Tony waited.

I cleared my throat. This would be tricky. "The marshal. Darrow."

"What about her, Eugene?"

Gah. Not a good start.

"She was a big help. Without her, I'd never have found Blalock. And even if I had—we were outnumbered and outteched. I hate to see her rotting in a cell, stripped of her badge, for only doing her job."

Tony frowned. "She disobeyed a direct order from me. She's lucky to be alive."

"You asked what I wanted, Tony." I shrugged like it didn't really matter to me, like she hadn't saved my life while I reveled in Ra'uf Erkennen's pain. I hoped he'd buy it. "Up to you."

Tony Taulke eyed me for a moment: a hint of the cold blue mixed with the businessman's calculated stare. "If she's so good, maybe I should hire *her*, then, and pack you off to Planitia Prime."

It was an empty threat. I was the best corporate enforcer in the business, and Tony knew that. It's why I worked for the Taulkes and not one of the other factions.

"Retirement on Mars? Me?" I made a joke of it. "That'll be the day."

He held me in his steely stare a moment longer, then burst out laughing. "All right, then. I'll see that she's reinstated—only as a special favor to you, Stacks. But there need to be consequences for her disobeying orders."

"I reckon so."

"I'll leave that up to the Service to decide. Nothing career-ending, though."

"Fair enough." I rose and gathered my coat and hat. I'd have to get a new MESH set made, and soon. "See you around, Tony."

I left the boss's office and headed for The Slate to shoot the shit with Mickey Stotes and have a Scotch and a beer. Or maybe six. Quality downtime was something I've begun to appreciate more and more since passing the half-century mark. It's the sunnier side of becoming less patient with bullshit as you get older.

Maybe, after I slept off today's revels, I'd hop the Hearse back to Darkside and visit Minnie. She'd seemed anxious to have me spend some quality downtime with her. Up *and* down time, actually.

Yeah, exchanging pleasantries with Minnie might be just the thing—a pleasurable distraction until Tony called me in to execute a new contract.

Pun intended.

ABOUT CHRIS POURTEAU

Chris Pourteau has been a professional technical writer and editor for twenty-five years. His first novel, *Shadows Burned In*, won the 2015 eLite Book Award Gold Medal for Literary Fiction. In November 2015, he edited and produced the collection *Tails of the Apocalypse*, which features short stories set in different apocalyptic scenarios with animals as main characters. He recently co-helmed a sequel of sorts, *Chronicle Worlds: Tails of Dystopia*—a similar collection of animal-centric stories, this time set in various existing dystopian worlds of their authors—with Future Chronicles Series Editor Samuel Peralta. Among novel-length works, Chris recently co-authored a Sci-Fi series with David Bruns (also in this collection) set in Nick Webb's Legacy Fleet Kindle world (a kind of *Battlestar Galactica* meets *Aliens* universe). You can find that series here: http://www.amazon.com/The-First-Swarm-War/dp/B071R2ZTDY/

If you enjoyed this story featuring SynCorp assassin-for-hire Stacks Fischer, be on the lookout in 2018 for an entire novel series by Bruns and Pourteau that details the rise of the Syndicate Corporation in the wake of Earth's climatic apocalypse. Stacks will be back as a featured character in that series. If you'd like to know when to expect him, email Chris at c.pourteau.author@gmail.com and put "Stacks" in the subject line. He'll keep you on a super-secret list and update you when there's news about the series. Feel free to drop him a line and just say howdy, too.

To keep up with Chris's authorial antics, subscribe to his newsletter: http://chrispourteau.com. He'll send you free stuff and promises not to spam.

Chris lives in College Station, Texas, with his wife, son, and two dogs.

THE FIREBUG AND THE PHARAOH

by Daniel Arenson

Mairead "Firebug" McQueen loved three things: a good romp in bed, an ice-cold beer, and killing aliens.

Today she was hoping for all three.

She leaned back in her Firebird's cockpit, kicked off her boots, and slapped her bare feet onto the dashboard. She tossed back her red hair, lit a cigar, and took a puff.

"All right, lads," Mairead said, speaking into her comm. "We do this quick and easy. We'll be in and out before they know what hit 'em." She glanced out the cockpit at the starfighter beside her. "Sort of how you bang a lass, Pharaoh."

Ramses "Pharaoh" al Masri, the pilot flying nearby, flipped her off. Mairead gave him a wink.

She shoved down the throttle, and her Firebird blazed forth.

"Try to keep up, lads." She blew a smoke ring, charging through space. "Last one there does our laundry."

Ramses stormed forward at her side, his starfighter just barely keeping up. She could practically hear him cringe through the comm.

"I'm not touching your unmentionables," he said.

Mairead snorted. "Unmentionables? What the muck are you, the Queen of England?"

"You know I'm descended of Egypt's great pharaohs," Ramses said. "Show some respect."

She rolled her eyes. "I'll show you my freckled arse if you beat me to the planet."

The other Firebirds raced close behind them. They were fifteen starfighters, an entire squad, all under Mairead's command. She was only twenty-three. She was the youngest pilot here. But she was also the best damn pilot the Heirs of Earth had.

And she never let anyone forget it.

Even now, as she charged to battle, Mairead gave a showy barrel roll. Her starfighter's twin engines left a double helix of fire.

Mairead loved serving on large starships like the ISS *Jerusalem*, cavernous frigates one could get lost in. She loved fighting on planets, the sun baking her hair, the ground firm beneath her feet. But she *loved* flying her Firebird. This small starfighter, just large enough for one pilot—this was true freedom.

The fleet's hulking warships were far behind her now. Only a handful of Firebirds flew here. Around Mairead spread the galaxy in all its splendor. Countless stars. A great spiral arm that spilled across the distance. Nothing but open space and adventure.

And somewhere out there, beyond the darkness, too far to see, Earth waited.

At least, that's what the legends said. Mairead wasn't sure she believed Earth existed. Oh, she had said her vows like everyone else. When she had joined the Heirs of Earth, she had professed her belief in Earth, had sworn to bring humanity home. But it seemed laughable. An actual homeworld for humanity?

There were thousands of alien civilizations in this galaxy. They all had planets of their own. All but humans.

For thousands of years, we wandered the darkness, Mairead thought. *Hiding. Hunted. Dying. A species without a home.*

So no, maybe Earth did not truly exist. Maybe, as many claimed, humans had always been homeless, doomed to forever wander the galaxy, fleeing the hunters.

But Mairead was no animal of prey. She would not be hunted.

I am the huntress, she thought.

And there ahead she saw it. Their destination.

From here, it was only a green dot, soon growing into a sphere. The jungle world of Saropia.

"If the galaxy has an arsehole, it's this planet," Mairead muttered.

"Language!" Ramses said.

She scoffed. "Sorry, Mother."

The fifteen Firebirds flew closer.

Saropia grew larger, soon filling half their field of vision. A rainforest covered the equatorial regions, fading to grasslands, deserts, and finally hinterlands and frozen poles. It was a nice world, as far as they went. Most worlds were lifeless, airless chunks of rock. Saropia was lush with life. That was its blessing—but also its curse.

Pretty much every plant and animal on the planet would kill you.

"Why the hell did humans ever bother settling here?" Mairead muttered.

"They didn't settle here," Ramses said softly. "They're hiding here."

"Mucked up place to hide, if you ask me," Mairead said. "They say there are mosquitos the size of horses, venomous trees with claws on their branches, and Ra damn dinosaurs. Dinosaurs, Pharaoh! Giant reptiles who'll bite off your tadger if you pull it out to piss."

"Language!" Ramses said again. "But yes, you're right. Nobody in their right mind would settle Saropia. Which is why, I presume, the human colonists chose it. The Peacekeepers Corps, the Skra-Shen Empire, or anyone else who hunts us would have to be mad to visit. Of course humans would hide here."

"Lovely idea," Mairead muttered. "At least until the dinos start chomping their wee tadgers, and we're called in to save 'em." She sighed. "No matter. I've always wanted to kick a dino up the arse. Good day for it."

They flew onward toward the planet. The call had come in only yesterday. Only a few words, sent into the darkness.

Only fifty of us remain. We are human. We are hunted. Help us, Heirs of Earth!

And so the Heirs of Earth were coming to help.

Whenever humans were in danger—the Heirs of Earth would be there.

We are a homeless species, Mairead thought. *Endangered. Scattered across a thousand worlds. Aliens hunt us everywhere. But we are not powerless. We have the Heirs of Earth.*

The fifteen starfighters plunged into the planet's atmosphere, ionizing the air. They dived down like flaming comets, moving faster than sound. The rich, yellow sky spread around them, filled with golden haze and blankets of silver clouds. They slowed down, then dived through the clouds, emerging into curtains of rain. The wet sheets swayed and shimmered around them. Jungles spread below, covering the land, parting only for a snaking river. It felt like flying through an oil painting, still wet and blending and changing with every brush stroke.

Freedom, Mairead thought. *Beauty.*

She wondered what Earth looked like—assuming it was real. She had never seen Earth, of course. No human had in two thousand years. But she had heard tales. They said Earth's sky was blue, her forests green, her fields golden. The description sounded drab to Mairead. She imagined that in real life, Earth would have a million shades like this planet, but less like a dramatic oil painting. More like a watercolor painting, gentle and beautiful.

Maybe Earth is real, Mairead thought. *Maybe someday I'll fly in that sky too. Maybe someday I'll fly not to battle but to—*

Dark shapes rose from the jungle ahead, tearing her from her thoughts.

Mairead leaned forward, staring.

"What the hell?" She squinted. "Are those enemy ships or..."

Ramses, flying beside her, inhaled sharply. "Dinos!"

Mairead's eyes widened. "Bloody hell. The size of them!"

The beasts came flying toward the starfighters, twenty or more. Yes, these were living creatures, their wings massive. Giant, flying reptiles. They were not true dinosaurs, of course. They were aliens. But the nickname served them well. The animals were primitive, prodigious, and pissed off.

"They're taking battle formations," Mairead said.

Ramses snorted. "They're just animals, Firebug."

"Yeah, well, I know a damn Kummerow Gambit assault formation when I see one." Mairead sneered and switched on her cannons. "Prepare for a battle, lads!"

The flying dinosaurs were close now. Only seconds away. Each creature was easily the size of a Firebird starfighter. Their jaws thrust out, lined with teeth like swords. Their claws gleamed. Their wings stirred the rain.

Ramses cleared his throat. "Firebug, may I remind you that the Heirs of Earth forbid harming native alien life-forms. Our mission is to save humans, not to—"

The flying dinosaurs opened their jaws and blasted out fire.

The flaming jets spun like tornados, crackling, spraying sparks.

Mairead cried out and jerked her yoke, swerving. She dodged a jet. She nearly slammed into the Firebird beside her. The others were desperate to flee too. One Firebird tried to rise, but another starfighter flew directly above.

A fiery jet washed over the Firebird.

The pilot screamed.

The cockpit melted under the blaze. The starfighter careened and plunged toward the jungle.

"Kill those scabby wallopers!" Mairead cried, pulling her triggers.

Her Firebird's Gatling guns fired. A hailstorm of bullets flew toward the flying beasts. The other Firebirds charged, releasing more volleys.

Several dinos fell, wings riddled with bullet holes. The other aliens scattered, soared, and vanished into the clouds.

The remaining Firebirds kept gliding over the forest.

"Come back, ya bastards!" Mairead shouted at the clouds. "Firebirds, chase the damn dinos. We'll kill every last—"

"Firebug!" Ramses said. "This is not our mission."

"They killed Captain de Vries!" she cried. "It's personal now. It's—"

Suddenly, from the clouds above, descended a rain of fire.

Flaming pillars slammed into two more Firebirds.

Two more pilots screamed, their starfighters shattering.

Muck! Mairead thought. The dinos were learning.

She sneered, tugged back her yoke, and soared into the clouds.

The dinos were waiting there. Ra damn. There were a hundred or more now. When they saw Mairead entering their cloudy domain, they unleashed a torrent of hellfire her way.

Mairead screamed and barrel-rolled.

She spun madly, wings like a propeller, scattering clouds. The dinosaur fire spurted around her, grazing her hull, charring one wing.

Die, you bastards.

Mairead released two missiles.

The missiles flew, screaming through the clouds, leaving fiery wakes … and missed.

They missed!

Of course they missed, Mairead thought. The missiles were heat-seeking. The dinos were coldblooded reptiles.

And they reached her Firebird.

The beasts grabbed her hull, scratched her fuselage, pecked her wings. By Ra, the animals were huge. They were larger than her starfighter. Their red eyes stared through her cockpit, and she saw intelligence.

She dipped out of the clouds. Three of the animals clung to her, weighing her down. Her hull dented. One of the beasts raised its massive jaw. It had a snout like a damn battering ram.

The dino thrust its snout forward, slamming it into her cockpit.

The transparent canopy shattered.

Mairead screamed.

The wind whipped her, billowing her red hair. Shards of plastic stung her. Her ship tumbled through clouds and rain and smoke. The dino clung to her starfighter, shrieking. Its snout reached into her shattered cockpit, each tooth like a katana.

One of those teeth scraped Mairead's arm, and blood spurted.

Her starfighter plunged downward, careening, tumbling toward the forest.

The beast opened its jaws wide, screeching so loudly Mairead screamed in agony.

She drew a pistol from her belt.

"Eat lead, hooch."

She fired on automatic, emptying a magazine into its open jaws.

Its brains splattered across her dashboard. Its body slumped off her prow and tumbled down.

Mairead was near the ground now, far below the other Firebirds. Two dinos were still gripping her fuselage, shoving her toward the forest.

Mairead struggled not to pass out. She could barely breathe. The G-force was pounding her. Wind shrieked through the shattered canopy, whipping her face with rain, each drop like a hornet's sting. With a shaky hand, she reached toward her bloody dashboard. She flipped a red switch.

Her engines roared on full afterburner. Searing, white-hot fire burst out from her exhaust.

The two dinos screamed and released her Firebird.

Mairead wanted to grab her helmet and oxygen tank. She had no time. She spun around, faced the two burnt dinos, and opened fire.

Her missiles slammed into them at point-blank range.

The missiles exploded as she soared.

The dinos splattered her starfighter with a million chunks of gooey meat.

Mairead grabbed her helmet, put it on, and inhaled deeply. She flew higher and found the rest of her squadron battling the last few dinos.

She rejoined the fight, sneering.

She flew with furious speed, bullets flying, missiles blasting, slaying the beasts. She was Captain Mairead McQueen. She was the best damn pilot humanity had. And she proved it in this alien sky.

Finally the last dinos turned to flee.

This time they did not come back.

Mairead sent a missile after them, taking out one of the cowards. The others squawked and vanished around a mountain.

"Yeah, you better run, you scabby bastards!" she said.

The dinos had taken out five of her Firebirds. Five of her friends. A third of her squadron.

A squadron we need to fight the damn scorpions who hunt us across the galaxy, she thought. *The humans on this planet better be worth it.*

"Come on," Mairead said into her comm, shoving down the rising horror. "Let's find these humans and get the hell out of here."

The rest of the fleet kept flying. Ramses was still here. That was good. Mairead would never admit it, but she was relieved. She liked Pharaoh. Even if he sometimes beat her at cards.

They flew several times faster than sound. The forests and rivers streamed beneath them. Finally they saw it ahead—the valley the Mayday had come from. The words from the distress call returned to her.

Only fifty of us remain. We are human. We are hunted. Help us, Heirs of Earth!

Mairead shuddered.

In the valley below, she saw signs of civilization. A collapsed barn. Trampled fields. Ravaged gardens and fallen huts. A town had been here.

A human town.

Mairead saw the skeletons.

"What the hell happened here?" she said. "Did the damn dinos do all this? They're only animals. They should care about nothing more than eating and mucking. What made them go berserk?"

Ramses inhaled sharply. "Look!"

The Firebirds glided through sheets of rain, emerged into a sunlit field, and saw it.

Mairead lost her breath.

Dinosaurs. Hundreds of them. Maybe thousands. An entire army of alien dinosaurs.

These were not the aerial ones. Here were large land animals, each one the size of a damn T-rex. They were charging, attacking a stone silo from all sides.

Atop the silo, Mairead saw them.

Humans.

"Kill the damn reptiles!" she shouted.

She flew above the beasts and released her bombs.

Dinosaurs exploded below.

Her fellow Firebirds dived and released their own ordnance.

Explosions rocked the valley. Chunks of dinosaurs flew.

The beasts below roared. The valley shook. Hundreds of the reptiles raised their heads and blasted up fire.

Flaming pillars soared like volcano fire.

Mairead jerked her yoke from side to side, swerving around a thousand columns of flame. She flew closer to the ground, firing bullets. Dinosaurs fell, their fire dying. She carved a path through the flaming pillars.

Atop the silo, the last few humans were fighting too. They had cannons, rifles, grenades. Dead dinosaurs were piled up around them.

Mairead didn't understand it. Clearly, the humans had been living here for years. After all, they had built a town, barns, had plowed the fields. What had caused the dinosaurs to go mad, to attack like an army?

And since when did damn animals blow fire?

She had no time to contemplate it further. The beasts below were regrouping. The massive reptiles forgot about the silo now. They were concentrating their fire on the starfighters. A jet slammed into a Firebird, and the pilot screamed. His starfighter plunged down, slammed into several dinos, and exploded. Another starfighter shattered in midair.

The starfighters rose and swooped again and again, exhausting their missiles and bombs, finally firing only bullets. Dinosaur corpses piled up. But more of the animals kept emerging from the jungle, swarming across the valley, and attacking both the silo below and the starfighters above.

"What the hell?" Mairead shouted, dodging another fiery jet.

"Firebug, we have to flee!" Ramses said. "We'll come back with heavy bombers. We'll—"

"By the time we get back, every damn colonist in that silo will be dead!" she shouted.

Mairead rose and dived again, firing bullets. She swerved around another flaming jet. Sparks flew into her shattered cockpit, singing her.

Mairead narrowed her eyes, examining the valley.

The dinosaurs are moving like soldiers, she thought.

But it was impossible. They were dumb animals. Had to be. Mairead had read every report about this planet, knew the wildlife was vicious but mindless.

And yet she saw it now. The dinosaurs were moving in units. Brigades. Battalions. Swarming at the vanguard, protecting the flanks, spraying fire.

There was something vaguely familiar about that.

Mairead gasped.

Memories flooded her.

Two years ago. She had been only a lieutenant. She had attacked a planet overrun with scorpions. She had seen a thousand of the beasts attack a human settlement. The

Heirs of Earth had failed to save those humans, and Mairead had never forgotten that defeat. A scar from that day still stretched across her left ribs.

These dinosaurs move like scorpions, she thought.

"They're drones," she whispered.

"What?" Ramses said, flying above her now.

"The dinosaurs!" she shouted. "They're Ra damn drones! The scorpions must have done something to them. They're controlling their brains somehow."

"Firebug, listen to yourself!" Ramses said. "Zombie dinos?"

She ignored him. She spoke into her comm. "All pilots! Surround the valley, face inward, and blast out an EMP attack. Disrupt all signals on every frequency. If there are any radio signals flying here, I want them jammed. If there are any electronics in this valley, I want them fried. Go! Now!"

The Firebirds spread out, flying in rings around the valley.

Mairead turned on her EMP system—a weapon designed to disrupt alien tech. Admiral Emet had insisted on installing these systems on all Firebird fighters. Mairead had always thought them useless, but now she was willing to try.

"Fire!" she cried.

She blasted out EMP pulses from her starfighter.

Around the valley, the other Firebirds bathed the valley with electromagnetic radiation.

It was harmless to flesh. But it was devastating to electronics.

For a moment, nothing happened.

The starfighters kept flying, pounding the valley with pulse after pulse.

And then the dinosaurs fell.

Wave after wave of them collapsed.

Soon the valley was covered with dead aliens.

Mairead exhaled in relief. She landed her Firebird by the silo, crushing a dead dinosaur's tail. She climbed out of the cockpit and leaped onto the grass.

The dead reptiles spread around her. From down here, they seemed even larger. Most were larger than her starfighter. There were various species. Some were carnivores with massive toothy jaws. Others were herbivores, and they were even larger, lying across the valley like beached whales.

Mairead approached one of the dead dinos. She frowned.

"What the hell?"

There was an electronic device lodged into the dino's head. It looked like a spark plug. The round tip crackled, glowing blue. Mairead grabbed the device, placed her foot against the lizard's carcass, and tugged back with all her strength.

The implant came free with a spurt of blood. Cables stretched out from it, running through the wound and into the dinosaur's head. Mairead spent a while fishing out the cables. It felt like pulling out a damn tapeworm. The cables finally came free, tips sparking.

The other starfighters landed in the field, and their pilots emerged. Ramses approached her.

"What the devil is that?" the tall man said.

Mairead stared at the bloody implant and dangling cables. "Scorpion tech. The scorpions were controlling them."

She couldn't suppress a shudder. The Skra-Shen, the giant scorpions from deep space, were the greatest enemies humanity faced. Mairead had fought dozens of alien species. None were as vicious as the scorpions.

Ramses stroked his pointy beard. "Damn. I can't believe this."

Mairead raised an eyebrow. "Why not? You know the scorpions are a technological species. If they can build starships, they can build crude mind-jacks."

"Not that," Ramses said. "I mean: I can't believe you were right about something."

She punched him. "Oh, shut the hell—"

Suddenly she stepped back, inhaling sharply. She drew her pistol.

Ramses frowned. "What?"

"I just realized something," she whispered. "If the scorpions controlled the dinos, that means—"

Before she could complete her sentence, the ground cracked open. And the beast emerged.

A creature of claws. Of pincers larger enough to slice a man in half.

A Skra-Shen.

A scorpion.

It was smaller than the dinos—the size of a horse rather than a whale. But here was the species that had conquered half the galaxy, that was hunting humans everywhere. It was deadlier than a hundred dinosaurs.

Mairead opened fire, screaming.

Her other pilots drew their own pistols. Bullets peppered the scorpion.

It kept running, claws tearing up dirt and dead dinosaurs. The shots ricocheted off the scorpion's exoskeleton, doing it no harm. The scorpion raised its stinger and shot a jet of venom. A pilot screamed and fell, clutching at his face, his skin melting.

Mairead turned and ran.

The scorpion leaped among the pilots, clawing, tearing them apart. Their bullets slammed into it again and again, doing nothing.

Mairead leaped into her Firebird and kick-started the engines.

"Hey, arsehole!" she shouted over her shoulder at the scorpion. "I'm going to bomb you from the air!"

She was out of missiles. She was out of bombs.

Luckily, the scorpion didn't know that.

The beast left the pilots and bounded across the valley toward her.

The scorpion leaped toward the starfighter, pincers opening wide.

Mairead switched on the afterburner.

Searing streams of white-hot inferno blazed over the creature.

She kept the starfighter on the ground, engines blazing, the fire washing across the alien. The exoskeleton melted. The soft flesh inside boiled. By the time Mairead powered down, there was nothing left of the scorpion but shards of shell and ashes.

Mairead stepped out of her Firebird and spat onto the smoldering remains.

"Arsehole," she said.

The colonists finally emerged from their silo. They were only about thirty, Mairead saw, and her heart sank. The message had said there were fifty.

The colonists approached the surviving pilots, embraced them, and some even fell to their knees and wept.

"Thank you," they said, tears falling. "Thank you, Heirs of Earth."

Mairead looked around her. She had thought this planet beautiful from above. Now she saw desolation. Crashed starfighters. The bodies of friends. Plumes of smoke rose, and the stench of death filled her nostrils.

Mairead lowered her head.

Earth is real, she thought. *It must be real. Because I cannot believe in a galaxy where all planets are places of despair. I must believe. That we have a good home. That we will someday return.*

She pulled out her comm and hailed the fleet. Soon a transport vessel glided down to the valley, and the refugees climbed in. The shuttle rose, flanked by starfighters, taking the refugees up to the main Inheritor fleet.

But Mairead stayed on the planet. The shuttle had brought her a replacement cockpit canopy. She would need a few hours to work, to repair her ship.

To her surprise, Ramses remained planetside with her.

"Don't you have any girls to woo up in the fleet?" Mairead said. She stood on a ladder, leaning over her cockpit, working with a wrench.

"Undoubtedly," he said. "But somebody needs to guard your ass down here while you work."

She leaned into the cockpit, reaching for a screw. "Yeah, well, keep your eyes off my arse while I work."

"Please," Ramses said. "There are much more pleasant things to look at down here. Rotting dinosaur corpses, for one."

She turned from the cockpit to flip him the bird.

Ramses opened his pack. He pulled out a silver, filigreed dallah with a long spout.

"Firebug, take a coffee break with me," he said. "I'm brewing a batch of the finest Egyptian beans, seasoned with cardamom. The drink of the gods."

She scoffed. "Coffee is for sissies. I drink Scotch."

"Mairead," he said, voice softer now. "Join me."

She gazed into his eyes, silent for a moment. She put down her wrench, climbed off the ladder, and sat beside him.

He brewed the coffee, which he served in small porcelain cups. The drink was very dark, thick, and bitter. And, Mairead had to admit, it was heavenly. As they sipped, the corpses lay around them, smoldering, and ash rained from the sky. For a long time, they drank in silence.

"Mairead," Ramses finally said. "Are you all right?"

Mairead cursed the damn tears that flowed down her cheeks. "No," she whispered.

Ramses put down his cup. Mairead tossed her own aside and embraced him, clinging to him desperately, crushing him in her arms. Her tears flowed. Ramses wrapped his arms around her and stroked her long red hair.

"None of this is right," he said softly. "I know. But we have to believe. That Earth is out there. That we'll see her again. That we'll bring everyone home."

Mairead sniffed. "I believe. Earth is real. We'll find her someday. We'll fly there together through blue skies over green hills. We'll see all the places from the legends. The rolling oceans. The soaring mountains. The highlands of Scotland."

"The golden desert of Egypt," Ramses said, "and the glory of the pyramids."

"Home," Mairead whispered. "That's why we fight, isn't it? For home."

"For home," he agreed. "Now let me help you with your cockpit. You're a damn fine pilot, Firebug, but a horrible mechanic."

Normally she would have punched him. Today she laughed.

They fixed her cockpit. They soared back into space, flying their Firebirds. They rejoined the Heirs of Earth, humanity's only fleet. A group of twenty warships. A handful of starfighters. A few cargo hulls. That was it. A humble fleet, far from home. The last remnants of humanity's ancient glory. A group of refugees, their homeworld lost in shadows.

With bursts of light, the starships ignited their warp drives. They blasted into the distance, seeking a mythical star and a lost home.

ABOUT DANIEL ARENSON

Daniel Arenson is a bookworm, proud geek, and *USA Today* bestselling author of fantasy and science fiction. His novels have sold over a million copies. *The Huffington Post* has called his writing "full of soul."

He's written over fifty novels, most of them in five series: Earthrise, Requiem, Moth, Alien Hunters, and Kingdoms of Sand. Learn more about his books at DanielArenson.com.

INTERVIEW FOR THE END OF THE WORLD

by Rhett C. Bruno

142 Hours Until Impact…

"Come in," I said.

My office door creaked open. A security guard ushered in the Titan Project's next candidate. I quickly downed the remnants of a glass of lukewarm whiskey in my liver-spotted hand to calm my mind, then placed it down behind my computer screen. The guard and I exchanged a nod and he bowed out of the room, leaving myself, and the candidate, alone.

He didn't make it more than a step before he stopped to stare out of my window at the tremendous spaceship docked in the center of my compound. It was at the pinnacle of my illustrious technical career, which had left me one of the richest men on Earth. At least until around two years ago when a massive asteroid was discovered hurtling toward Earth with no intention of stopping, and money became as useless as the paper it was printed on. People had given it a number of creative nicknames like "The Devil's Fist," or "Ragna-Rock," but in my opinion, there was no reason to call it anything different than what it was. The end of Earth as we knew it.

"Congratulations on making it this far, Mr..." I hesitated at his name. I'd conducted thousands of interviews by then and was beginning to lose count. I glanced at the resume open on my computer. He was Frank Drayton. Twenty-seven years old and already a world-renowned horticulturalist. Not the most exciting job, but a necessary addition for a colony on a hostile world. He was marked for likely acceptance, but nobody got a spot in the Titan Project without me looking them in the eyes first.

"Drayton," I finished.

He blinked as if waking from a dream and hurried over to my desk. "Director Darien Trass. You can't even begin to understand how much of an honor it is to meet you." He extended a trembling hand.

I shook it without standing. It was as clammy as a teenage boy's on a first date so I quickly let go. I said, "I'd prefer we'd never have to meet at all, Mr. Drayton."

His lips twisted and his gaze turned downward.

"Relax," I said. "I only wish the world's circumstances were different." I gestured toward the hard, plastic chair set on the other side of my desk. "Please, sit."

He released a string of low, panicked laughs as he sat. His index finger immediately started tapping on the arm of the chair. I took that moment to study him. Heavy beads of sweat rolled down his forehead and he was in desperate need of a shave. The loose-fitting suit he wore was desperate for a decent tailor. Not that I could judge him for that. There were probably none left open on Earth to visit.

His disheveled appearance didn't surprise me. It was the same situation with almost every candidate who entered my office. After all, it's not every day a human being has to interview for a chance to escape the end of the world.

"Now," I began. "There's very little time left, so let's try to keep this as brief as possible. In this room, your accomplishments are no longer in question. Extraordinary as they may be, they are no more impressive than the thousands of others who have stepped through that door. You're here, Mr. Drayton, so that I can find out who *you* are."

"I…" He swallowed and took another deep breath. His finger stopped tapping, and he looked me in the eyes for the first time. "I understand."

"Good. I presume my assistant, Kara, already briefed you on the Project and showed you around the compound?"

"She did." He looked through the window. "I didn't realize how big the ship was until I got up here though."

"Not big enough," I lamented.

This time I joined him in staring at the colossal ship propped on the opposite side of my half-mile-wide compound away from all the buildings. It tapered like a sideways skyscraper wrapped in bowed metal plates. A carefully selected workforce installed the final layers of radiation shielding for its imminent departure, when the only plasmatic pulse drives ever to be used non-experimentally would allow it to reach Saturn in two years.

Mr. Drayton was awestruck, but the view made me want to crawl inside a bottle. My gaze first wandered to the pale mark in the blue sky—the asteroid growing closer every day to becoming a meteorite. Then I looked to the horde of people camped in the desert outside of the compound's twenty-foot-tall concrete wall, hoping to earn a spot onboard. Armed drones and several dozen security officers kept the desperate mass at bay.

Mr. Drayton turned back to me. "How many can it hold?"

"Excuse me?"

"The ship. How many people can it hold?"

"Three thousand," I said. "Four hundred and six spots have already been filled by my remaining staff. Individual accomplishments aside, I assure you that they had to meet the same, stringent criteria as candidates such as yourself. They're all that remains of Trass Industries. It felt wrong to ask anyone to help me construct the Titan Project without guaranteeing them a spot on it."

The conditions for selection were simple, at least in that they eliminated more than ninety-nine percent of humanity. Other than having to bear an appreciable level of expertise in a field that would benefit the new world, the simplest requirement was that every candidate had to be between eighteen and thirty-five years old. They also had to be in optimal physical health and clear of all chronic diseases. Kara administered the physicals, and nobody who failed ever made it through my door. Those who remained untethered by marriage were preferred, since their significant others would have to meet the same conditions. Lastly, anyone with young children was eliminated. There were fears on my research team that an underdeveloped body would be ravaged by the trip through zero-g. I also wasn't keen on taking anybody willing to leave their offspring to die alone.

"Three thousand," Mr. Drayton muttered after a lengthy silence.

"Yes," I said. "No more, no less. Every traveler will be kept in a state-of-the-art hibernation chamber for the duration of the two-year journey. The low activity state will allow us to conserve the limited resources we're able to bring until we can establish an operating colony on Titan. It's my job to whittle the list of more than one million suitable candidates to that minuscule number. Sneak in one extra and I might as well invite the mob camped outside of my compound."

He glanced nervously back out of the window. "Are those really all candidates?" he asked. "Everyone I passed out there claimed to have met with you."

"Not all of them. You can thank whichever rejected candidate decided to break our non-disclosure agreement and leak what was going on here for that. I had to promise fifty spots on board to some of the finest soldiers in the world in order to keep the project safe. We're lucky we're in the middle of the Arizona desert; otherwise I'd need even more."

"It wasn't easy getting out here with all of the airlines shut down, that's for sure. It took me a day just to find a gas station that wasn't abandoned or torn apart."

"Yes … I suppose I was crazy for thinking I could keep the Titan Project safe from the widespread, doomsday hysteria."

Ever since the leak, I couldn't even leave the Trass Industries Compound without being hounded or having my life threatened. Rich, poor, it didn't matter. People had begun to realize that the united efforts of governments around the world to divert the asteroid were futile, and that the only way to ensure survival was to leave Earth behind. There were other corporations developing space-stations that would orbit our homeworld or attempting to establish colonies on the moon. But with so many people being crammed onto them, an unpredictable percentage would likely suffocate before their populations leveled out to suit their life-support systems. The safety of my compound was indebted to a majority of Earth choosing to camp outside of those projects rather than crave a trip to an uninhabitable moon millions of miles away.

I sighed. "It doesn't matter anymore. In a week the asteroid will hit, and we'll be on our way to the freezing plains of Titan."

"Why not Mars, or Europa, or anywhere else closer? Your message didn't say."

"As you well know there is no second Earth in our solar system, Mr. Drayton. I chose based on potential. There is a wealth of resources and fuel on both Titan and Saturn which will make generating enough energy to stay warm relatively simple once we're able to repurpose the ship into a settlement. The thick atmosphere also removes the issue of radiation from the list of concerns. We'll need all the help we can get. Establishing renewable sources of food on any world not meant for life will take time."

For the first time since our meeting, Mr. Drayton's eyes glinted with the confidence of a man who had risen to the top of his field. "I think I can help with that," he boasted.

"I've met with three other candidates who claimed the same," I countered. I held up my finger before he could offer another predictable response. He slouched into the chair and allowed me to continue. "As I indicated earlier, your accomplishments are no longer in question. It was only your highly scrutinized thesis on vertical farming at Cornell that encouraged me to reach out to you as a candidate. I appreciate boldness. I can design all of the spaceships and facilities I want to, but without food they'll be little more than oversized, metal tombs."

Mr. Drayton sat up. "You read that?"

"I don't take this task lightly, Mr. Drayton. I'm always thorough with my research."

"Of course you are." He leaned forward and wrapped his hands around the rounded edge of my desk. "I've read *all* of your work," he said. "Your 2021 paper about how you pioneered your zero-emissions, automated vehicular network to reduce traffic and eliminate accidents in Detroit was ... well it was life-changing."

I raised an eyebrow. "Life-changing. That's new. Though it all seems rather trivial compared to what we're working on here, doesn't it?"

All of the color drained from Mr. Drayton's cheeks. I could see his lips twitching ever so slightly as his brain struggled to come up with a response that wouldn't make him seem more foolish.

"I appreciate the compliment," I intervened. I folded my hands on my lap and established direct eye-contact with him. "Okay, as long I've answered all of your questions, I'm going to ask you a few of my own. I want you to be as honest as possible."

He nodded. His finger started to tap the arm of his chair again, but he held my gaze.

"Okay," I said. "Your information states that you're not married and don't have children. Do you currently have any manner of significant other?"

Mr. Drayton shifted in his seat. "Not in the years since the Asteroid was discovered," he said, clearly perturbed. "Divorced."

"Ah. I have had plenty of those walk through these doors, eager to get away. It'll get easier with time."

He exhaled. "I hope."

I turned to my screen for a moment, trying to make it look like I was reading something so I didn't rush things. After countless interviews, it was difficult for them not to feel rehearsed. "So, where were you when you heard about the asteroid?" I asked.

He continued looking in my direction, though his stare grew unfocused. I could read the struggle all over his face.

"Mr. Drayton?" I said.

"Sorry." He shook his head and reestablished eye contact. "I was with my ex-wife. I suppose you could say we didn't agree over why the asteroid is going to hit Earth. She turned her complete attention to our church and trying to repent for her sins so God might reconsider his judgment. It was like she completely forgot about our…" He paused. It took him a few seconds to gather himself so that he could continue. "Anyway, I tried to go along with it while I could, but eventually I decided that I'd rather take a chance at living."

"We all responded differently." I remained indifferent on the why's. The only thing in the world that mattered to me after I found out that a rogue asteroid the size of a small moon had somehow been re-routed toward Earth was getting humanity's best and brightest off it. A branch of Trass Industries had been focused on commodifying space-travel at the time, so it seemed like a logical transition … my next real challenge after effectively eliminating car accidents throughout the United States.

"I'm glad you didn't hesitate," Mr. Drayton said. "You were the only one smart enough to consider running far away from this place before wasting time on anything else."

"The value of a clean slate is lost on many of my peers."

He was handling himself well enough, so I decided it was time to find out what I really wanted to know. I stared at my computer for a few seconds, again so I didn't seem impatient, and then asked, "Why should I choose you to join this venture to our new world?"

Mr. Drayton leaned back and took a deep breath. "Because I've dedicated my life to understanding living things, sir," he said. "We'll need much of the life we take for granted here to blossom if we ever hope to make Titan feel like a new home."

I used my hand to mask a slight grin. There was no doubt he'd practiced that answer in a mirror plenty of times, but I could tell by his eyes that he meant it. It was one of my more favorite responses yet. Most candidates couldn't help but list their achievements or mention their will to survive.

"Well said," I admitted. "I think I've heard everything I need to. Thank you, Mr. Drayton." The interview was briefer than usual, but after administering thousands I could size people up quickly. "Please proceed to the waiting area. I will personally inform you of my decision as soon as possible. If you are accepted, you'll be escorted to the safety of an on-site dormitory where you will remain until the Titan Project departs at exactly 8:00 AM on September 30, 2031—six days from now. If you aren't … well then Mr. Drayton, I hope you're able to find peace in whatever way suits you."

I stood and extended my hand. He immediately sprung to his feet, almost slipping, and grabbed it.

"Thank you, sir," he said twice as he shook it vehemently. "At least, either way, I'll have accomplished my dream of meeting you."

I released his hand and allowed myself to visibly crack a business-like smile. "Good day, Mr. Drayton."

He backed away slowly, his eyes darting between myself and the Titan Project out the window. Then the door opened and one of my security officers came through. He placed his hand on Mr. Drayton's shoulder and escorted him out of the office.

As soon as he was gone I slumped back into my chair and exhaled. Even the good interviews took a lot out of me. I closed his information on my computer and the screen reverted to my list of candidates. I had to strain my eyes to keep all the text from looking like one big blob. Like Mr. Drayton, I'd selected every single one of those people. There were doctors, theoreticians, physicists, engineers, artists, self-made billionaires and anything else you could imagine, from every country around the globe.

I scrolled down the list. As many as there were, I could remember the face of everyone I'd talked to—accepted or rejected. I always did it personally, though with a cohort of armed guards for rejections. There was no telling what desperate people would do. Only four hundred interviews remained as I checked off Mr. Drayton. Five of those were experts in the same field as Mr. Drayton who were coming in later that day—so I couldn't be sure if he made the cut yet or not—but I had a good feeling about him.

Ninety-three more were all I could take. With barely a week left until the doomsday clock struck zero, I knew I was cutting it close. But I had to be meticulous. I owed them all that much at least.

Before I could scroll down to the next candidate on my list, an email popped in the bottom right corner of my screen. I didn't recognize the sender, but the subject read: TAKE MY SON AND YOU WON'T REGRET IT. I forwarded it to my junk folder, where thousands of similar emails remained in purgatory.

"If only I could," I whispered.

I reached under my desk to grab a half-empty bottle of whiskey and refill the glass sitting by my keyboard. It was the only thing I could do to quiet the voices of everyone I was planning to reject from bouncing around in my head. I was inches away from having a much-needed sip when my door swung open.

My assistant, Kara, froze in the entrance. Her expression soured when she noticed the glass in my hand. She'd been with me since her parents died in a car accident and left her an orphan at only ten years old. My company was working on implementing the automated vehicle network at the time, so I legally adopted her. At first it was simply a publicity stunt, and then I wound up loving her as much as any father should.

I always found myself shocked when I realized what a beautiful, intelligent young woman she'd grown into. She had the brains to take over Trass Industries from me one day, and if not for the asteroid, I'm sure she would've.

"I thought I told you to knock?" I grumbled. I didn't mean to take such a harsh tone with her, but the whiskey's pungent aroma was wafting around my nostrils and all I wanted was a drink.

Unable to take her eyes off of my glass, she said, "I did. Three times." I was glad she didn't comment on it for once. I had too much on my mind without worrying about disappointing her again.

"Oh... Is everything alright?"

"Fine. I just wanted to let you know that your next appointment is almost ready. She just passed her physical."

"You could have buzzed me." I noticed her eyes drift away from the glass in my hand and scan the entirety of my messy office. "Checking up on me again?"

"It's almost five." She took a few long strides into my office and picked up a pile of loose papers. "You need to eat, dad."

"I'll find time for that eventually," I said.

She bit her lip, but decided to move on. "How did Mr. Drayton do?" she asked.

"You know I can't tell you yet." I never allowed her or anyone else to be involved in my decisions. Truthfully, I didn't even want her to have the burden of knowing their names, but I couldn't run both the interviews and the physicals all by myself.

She stopped cleaning and looked at me. "I can help you if you'll let me," she said. "I've met thousands of candidates. I know what you're looking for."

I shook my head. Out of the corner of my eye I could see someone in the desperate crowd beyond the fence of my compound standing on the back of a truck and flashing a sign large enough for me to read: LET ME IN. "No," I said. "It's my responsibility and mine alone."

"It doesn't have to be. You're not Noah, you know. There are hundreds of us who've been here with you every step of the way."

"Don't make the mistake of thinking this is anything like some fable, Kara," I scolded. "His task was easy. The animals he marched two by two couldn't speak to him. They couldn't beg, or offer their billions for a spot. They couldn't send in pictures of their children who now have less than seven days left to live!" I slapped the glass off my desk. Kara yelped when it shattered on the floor. I went still.

For a moment neither of us made a sound. Layer upon layer of silence folded over each other until the tension in the air had my neck itching.

"I'm sorry," I said.

I bent over from my chair and started picking up the pieces until I felt her slender hand fall upon my shoulder. Immediately, my racing heart began to slow. She had a way of calming me which I'll never understand.

"I didn't mean to upset you," she said.

"It's not you."

"I just want to help as much as I can."

I patted her hand. "You are. More than you'll ever know." I stared into her bright green eyes. "It's not because I don't trust you, Kara."

"I know."

"Every person I say yes to just means there's another one who won't be coming. I can run across the solar system to Titan, but I'll have to remember everyone who sat across from me and didn't make the cut. I'll hear their voices and see their faces every time I close my eyes. You don't deserve to have that on your conscience."

By the end of my venting, Kara was sitting beside me on my desk, the brow of her freckled face furrowed. "And you do?"

"Better me alone than all of us." I forced a smile. "Now, I think I'll take you up on that dinner offer. Why don't you pick something up for us from the café? We can eat after my next appointment." I'd been sick of the food in my compound for months, but since we were in the middle of the Arizona desert and I couldn't leave, options were limited.

"I'm on it." She started toward the exit, then stopped and glanced back at the wet spot on the floor. "Would you like me to pick you out another bottle?" she asked.

I didn't have to work hard to smile after hearing that. "Make it two," I said. "It will be a long week."

"Don't push it. I'll have security send the next candidate in on my way down."

"Thank you, Kara."

The door shut behind her, and I got to my feet and stretched my old legs. I spent so much time in my chair that sometimes I wondered if I'd pass the physical necessary to make it onto the Titan Project. I stepped over the spill and opened a cabinet where I kept more glasses. I grabbed one and held it up to the light. The bottom was a little dusty, but it was clean enough. I carried it back to my desk and filled it until the whiskey bottle was empty.

There were three knocks at my door as I sat back down, along with another email on my computer begging me to take somebody. I closed my eyes and took as long of a sip as I could handle. When I was done, I wiped my mouth and pulled up the next candidate's information. Jillian Stark was a nuclear physicist who worked directly beside a Nobel Prize winner back when that was a thing people cared about.

"Come in," I said.

24 Hours Until Impact…

A single day remained before the asteroid would hit Earth, and the Titan Project still wasn't off the ground. The finishing touches to the ship took longer than expected, and the candidates were finally beginning to be loaded into their pods.

I stood on one of the highest decks of the tremendous vessel. The inside was little more than a ring-shaped corridor wrapped by glassy sleep-chambers, with a lift in the center. Every habitable level except for the command deck was identical. The highest deck was the only place I could go where I couldn't hear the echoes of gunshots and screaming. As the orange mark in the sky grew, the mob outside of my compound's walls intensified. I had to divert every member of security I had to keep them back.

I ran my fingers along an empty sleep-chamber as I strolled by. Exhaustion had them trembling. For the previous week, sleep had proven difficult no matter how much I drank. I found myself up every night, watching the few remaining newsfeeds as they talked about the chaos rampant throughout the planet. From America to China and everywhere in between—the entire world was tearing itself apart. Just one night earlier there were reports that a Russian Space Station scheduled for launch into Earth's orbit had been ripped to pieces by a mob. Now, just such a mob stood outside my compound, seeking to do the same.

"It's going to work, dad," Kara said behind me, her voice echoing throughout the wide, vacant hall.

I quickly reeled in my hand and turned to her. Dirt covered her face and clothes, but my eyes shot to the drops of dried blood on her right cheek. I saw no wound, which meant the blood probably wasn't hers.

"It's not the journey I'm worried about," I said. "How is it out there?"

"Not as bad as I look," she said, smiling. "We're holding. Security is sticking to your orders for now. Just warning shots."

"So you came here to check up on me again, did you?"

Her lips pursed and she looked to the floor. "No. There's been a complication with one of the candidates. He smuggled…. Well, you'd better come see for yourself."

I surveyed the empty level and its lifesaving compartments one last time and nodded. I stepped toward the central lift, but Kara placed a hand on my chest with enough force to stop me. Her features darkened.

"Is everything okay?" she questioned.

I didn't need to see my reflection to know I looked terrible—every bit my age. My eyelids felt like they had stones tied to the bottom of them. I managed a smile and said, "I'll be fine, Kara. Nothing a few drinks can't handle."

I ignored her disapproving scowl as I brushed her hand away and continued on my way. The lift carried us to the lowest deck where the ship's exit ramp awaited. There, the sleep-chambers were busy being loaded by my trained Trass Industries staff.

A line of candidates extended down the ship's exit ramp and across the compound grounds. They appeared as exhausted as I was.

The next candidate in line to be put under addressed me. "Director." She bowed her head deferentially.

"Good to see you again—" It took me a second for her name to come to me, but I remembered. "Ms. Stark."

The staff slid her assigned chamber as far out as it could go. They stowed her bag below and began to hook her up to IV tubes and restraints. Two years and plenty of dreams later, she'd be woken within the orbit of Saturn.

I received a similarly reverent nod from every candidate I passed. They probably didn't think I knew who they were since there were so many, but they were wrong. Every face had been ingrained on my mind. I nodded back to all of them until Kara and I emerged from the ship.

My cheeks were instantly blasted by the cold Arizona night air and pricked by sand caught on a strong breeze. The spotlights of security drones filled the dark sky, aimed over the manned wall surrounding my compound at an unruly crowd of thousands.

I stopped and looked up. The moon glowed in the night sky as it always did, but off to its side was an orange-hued glob larger than all the stars around it. The asteroid had only recently become easy to spot, but now it was impossible to miss—an eye of condemnation staring down upon all of us.

"This way, Director," Kara said, addressing me formally since we were in public.

She tapped me on the arm and began to lead me at a brisk pace in the direction of the dormitory where my candidates were staying. It was the only building in the compound with lights still on. The line of candidates snaking down from the ship toward it offered me their regards.

We passed the compound's only gate. A line of heavily armed soldiers stood in front of it. A rioting mob of angry citizens of Earth stood on the other side. The bobbing sea of heads extended as far as I could see, illuminated by car fires. They flung rocks, bottles and whatever else they could at the gate. Warning shots resonated from manned watchtowers along the wall and from automated drones zipping over their heads, but the mob had a mind of its own.

Their glowers turned on me as we passed, causing the crowd to swell against the bars of the gate. "Coward! Taking your friends and running!" someone shouted, as if I could be blamed for a stray asteroid. A rock pelted me in the shoulder. I stumbled, and would've fallen if Kara hadn't caught my old body and yanked me into the dormitory's security post.

"Animals!" she gasped. "Don't they understand?"

I rubbed my arm and gave it a good stretch. "Would you?" I asked, groaning.

Kara blinked, and then signaled to two of the guards inside the room. They parted, revealing Frank Drayton. He was crouched down, arms wrapped around a tiny girl who couldn't be older than four. She hid her face in his chest.

"One of the candidates, Director," Kara said.

"I know," I replied.

She tossed a medium-sized duffle bag at my feet. The zipper was ripped open. "He snuck out of the compound last night somehow," she said. "When he attempted to get back in, security found the girl stuffed inside of this. Someone out there tore it out of his hands and she fell out. Half of the mob is made up of candidates you didn't accept, so they know the rules. They nearly stoned him to death because of that, so I had him brought in for you to deal with."

I stared at Mr. Drayton. I remembered the look on his face when I told him he was coming to Titan. Presently, his body was quaking. Only it wasn't just out of fear. His face was bruised and his clothes were torn to reveal fresh cuts. That explained the blood on Kara.

I crouched in front of him. "Mr. Drayton," I said. "What's going on here?"

He looked up at me, pupils dilated from shock. "You remember?" he asked, his voice so raspy it sounded as if he'd swallowed a mouthful of sand.

"Of course I do." I placed my hand on his shoulder. "Mr. Drayton, who is she?" I knew the answer, but I had to hear it to believe it. Every passenger was invited to bring one bag full of possessions to Titan, but I never expected anyone to smuggle a person.

"She's…" Mr. Drayton swallowed so hard I could see the lump in his throat bob up and down. "She's my daughter."

The breath fled my lungs. I glanced between him and the child at least a dozen times. "How?" I questioned. "I looked extensively into every candidate's background. There were no children."

Mr. Drayton smirked until stretching the fresh cut on his lip made him wince. "I didn't mention I was as good with computers as I am with plants?"

"This is no time for jokes," Kara reprimanded.

Right after the words left her lips, an earsplitting explosion rang out. I grabbed Kara and dropped to the ground. Mr. Drayton's daughter cried while he squeezed her and repeatedly promised her everything was going to be fine. Outside, the volume of the mob amplified, becoming so loud that Kara and I immediately scrambled to our feet so we could see what was happening.

I'm not sure how, but one of the drones had been taken down and had crashed right outside of the gate. The force of the explosion busted one of the hinges enough for people to crawl through one at a time. Before the officers inside could reinforce it, one person from the mob squeezed through and sprinted toward the Titan Project.

"No children!" the incensed man shrieked. "That's my spot!" He didn't make it far. A gunshot rang out from somewhere on the wall. This one wasn't a warning. A bullet tore into the back of the man's skull and he toppled forward in a heap of tangled limbs.

Everybody went silent.

The guard on the wall who had fired stood completely still, smoke rising from the end of his rifle's blistering muzzle. If Mr. Drayton getting caught sneaking in a child had roused the mob, this was sure to ignite them.

I was no military commander, but I did the first thing that came to mind. I grabbed my head of security, who was positioned just inside the dormitory monitoring the transition, and said, "Get everyone to the ship now!"

"Director, it takes time to load them into the pods," he answered.

"Sort them on the ship! We need them alive!"

He nodded and began transmitting orders over his radio. Moments later, every candidate started rushing across the compound toward the ship. They were so terrified. Guards poured out of the watchtowers to reinforce their comrades by the damaged gate. There were no more gunshots, but rifle butts cracked bones as the mob stuck their flailing arms through the bars.

I turned to Kara, Mr. Drayton and his daughter, and shouted, "Let's go!"

Kara didn't move at first. Her petrified gaze was fixed on the mob. I'd never seen her so rattled. I shook her by the shoulders to snap her out of it and we took off. Mr. Drayton picked up his daughter and followed.

We didn't make it far from the gate before a bottle shattered next to my feet. I hopped out of the way of the shards, but Kara tripped over the legs of the man who'd been shot. As she slid across the dirt, her hands dragged through the blood leaking from a gash in the back of the corpse's head. Again, she froze. The dead man's blank eyes stared.

"C'mon, Kara!" I yelled as I hoisted her back to her feet.

We crossed the large expanse of dirt between the dormitory and the ship without suffering any more setbacks. I helped her onto the ship's entry ramp, and once we were at the top, I fell against the wall. My lungs were filled with dirt and I couldn't stop coughing. Once I was able to catch my breath, I scanned my compound. A few hundred yards away, the guards at the gate were struggling. The mob had started to climb over the gate, and I knew with all of their weight pressed against the compromised area, it wouldn't last much longer.

"Recall the men," I shouted to my head of security, who was positioned by the bottom of the ramp. He nodded.

I could no longer recognize any of the people I'd rejected in the mob. Everyone was covered in dirt and blood, and they were all so riled that they might as well have been foaming at the mouth. The officers received the order and immediately broke ranks to sprint to the ship. Most of them had fought in wars, but gunning down innocent people wasn't in the job description. When the gate failed, they'd have no other choice. The last thing I wanted was my followers to be reduced to savages like the rest of the people on Earth.

"Daddy, what's going on?" Mr. Drayton's daughter asked, her voice so frail I could barely hear her over the commotion.

He didn't respond. He was busy staring at the chaotic scene below. "I didn't think I would cause this," he muttered.

"You didn't think?" I said, my glare boring through him. "Three thousand spots, Mr. Drayton. Life support doesn't allow for any more. Do you suppose that I only chose people with no connections for my health? A man is dead because you didn't listen!"

"What does it matter!" he snapped, startling me. Tears streamed down his cheeks. "He would've been dead tomorrow. They're all going to be dead tomorrow. Nothing we do can stop that."

"No." I caught a glimpse of the surging mob out of the corner of my eye. "But we can keep our humanity."

Mr. Drayton took a measured breath. "You built this whole thing to save our species, Director. Isn't that enough?"

"I did what I had to."

"So did I." He released his daughter and rose to his full height, no longer afraid. She wrapped her tiny arms around his leg and hid her face against him. "I wasn't going to let her go like that. Not while there was a chance." He gestured into the ship's interior. "And I know you wouldn't either."

I pride myself on my quick mind, but for once I had no idea what to say. There was no denying Mr. Drayton was right. I looked inside and saw Kara, and I couldn't help but picture her as a nervous ten-year-old girl without a place to go. Just seeing the fresh scrapes on her legs made me uneasy.

"Let my daughter take my place," Mr. Drayton implored. "I know the risks of sending her this young, but it's got to be better than her staying here, right? She can learn from the other horticulturalists. She's smart. Smarter than I was at her age."

I remained silent. Beyond Kara, hundreds scurried about preparing the sleep-chambers, moving up and down the central lift. In spite of my stringent requirements, each of the people inside them was unique. Many of them could be considered true geniuses, while others were merely the hardest workers on my staff from a peaceful time. The only thing they all visibly had in common was that they were young. Young enough to flourish on our new world.

Everyone but me.

I looked in the opposite direction, over the shoulders of the security officers crowding the ramp. Each livid individual in the mob at the gate was someone I'd decided was less worthy of propagating our species. My criteria. My interviews. My decisions. I was to remember their faces forever, so that nobody else had to. But years of focusing on work had led me to ignore the simple fact that I belonged with them.

The scraping of metal over dirt made the hairs on the back of my neck stand on end. The gate wouldn't last much longer, and if the people on the other side reached the ship we'd all be torn to pieces.

Suddenly, I knew what I had to do. I had one last gift to give.

"Kara," I mouthed. I moved in front of her and gripped her gently by the arms to try and gain her attention. "Kara, I need you to do something for me."

Her teary gaze snapped toward me. "Anything, dad—I mean, Director," she stuttered.

"I need you to go to the command deck and prepare the ship for launch while I manage the situation out here. This vessel was built to withstand entry through the thick atmosphere of Titan, but I don't know how long we can endure the fury of humankind's will to survive."

"It's your design. I'm … I'm not sure if I know the ignition sequence well enough without you."

I held her at arm's length. "Like you said, you've been with me since the beginning. You know everything that I do. Just stay focused and ignore what's out there. I believe in you, Kara. Your people need you."

"Okay," she said. She gritted her teeth and nodded. "I can handle it."

"I know you can." I smiled as I patted her on the shoulder and turned her around. My heart sank as I watched her run toward the lift. I wanted to holler, "I'll see you soon," just so she'd glance back over her shoulder, but I couldn't get the words out. I didn't want to lie. Not to her.

"Mr. Drayton," I said, spinning around. My gaze darted between him and his daughter. "Are you sure you want this?"

"It's wha—" A thunderous crash cut him off. One half of the compound's gate slammed against the wall, and the mob started pouring through, tumbling over each other and screaming. The officers at the base of the ramp tightened their stance and readied their rifles. "It's what any father would do," he finished.

"I think I understand." I leaned in close so that I could whisper in his ear. "First, have your daughter loaded into the chamber meant for you. Then, I need you to follow Kara. There's no time to get everybody hooked up. Tell the staff to have everyone get into their chambers themselves and worry about hooking up when the ship reaches space. Once everybody is safely restrained, initiate the launch. Kara will have it ready, but she'll be waiting for me. Don't."

Mr. Drayton eyelids went wide as he realized what I was planning. "There has to be another way," he said.

"Another body on the ship means someone else must be left behind. It's as simple as that."

"Then let it be me! These people need you."

I smirked. "Not anymore. I'll be dead in a decade. One old man isn't going to make a difference on Titan. You have an entire lifetime to make it feel like home." I regarded his daughter and wondered what Kara might've looked like at her age. "It starts with her."

"Director Trass, I don't—"

"This is an order, Mr. Drayton!" I cut him off. "Now, there are two chambers in the command deck. You might have to force her into hers, but make sure she gets in. You tell her…" The words got stuck in my throat. I could picture her beautiful smile. "Tell her she's the only Trass who matters now."

He stood motionless. "Thank you," he muttered, hardly able to get the words out. "For everything,"

Our gazes met one last time. "Thank me when you're there," I replied. He was the only chosen candidate willing to risk everything on a lie. It was because of that I knew he wouldn't fail me.

He wrapped his arm around his daughter and turned to a member of my staff. Once he began communicating the orders I'd told him to, I hurried to my head of security at the ramp.

"Move everybody inside!" I told him.

"Director Trass, what's going on?" he questioned. He fired off a few rounds to slow the rapidly approaching mob, but they were growing bolder. In minutes, I knew the guards I hired for protection were going to have to do whatever it took to survive. I couldn't allow my candidate's final memory of Earth to be having to slaughter members of their own species.

"It's time," I said. "Nobody gets in or out after me." I keyed the ramp controls and set it to start closing. Then I sprinted out across my compound before any of the officers could stop me. The head of security shouted something, but he wasn't foolish enough to follow.

"That's him!" a member of the mob screamed.

I lowered my head and made a break for the compound's office building. The throng abandoned the Titan Project to chase after me, just like I knew they would, but the angle I'd taken allowed me to stay ahead of them. They shouted all manner of obscenities. Debris rained down around me.

A quarter-mile later, I busted through the doors of the lobby just before a slew of rocks peppered the glass. For once, there were no candidates at the front desk blocking the etching on it that read, TITAN'S COLD EMBRACE AWAITS US.

I wasn't far enough ahead of the mob to take the elevator, so I entered the emergency stairwell. My legs felt like jelly by the time I reached the hallway six stories up. My office glowed at the other end of it like a beacon. Apparently, I'd left my lights on. The rest of the floor was dark.

I sprinted toward my office, and locked the door as soon as I made it inside. A few seconds later, the mob was pounding on it. I wasn't worried. The door was installed by the company that I'd started from nothing, and our products always worked. It would hold long enough for Mr. Drayton to complete his task.

"You can't hide!" someone hollered.

I ignored him and strolled over to my desk to sit. My foot knocked over a bottle of whiskey underneath. Enough remained inside to fix a glass. I grabbed a tumbler off the window sill and cleaned it with the bottom of my shirt. As I held it up to the moonlight to see if I'd gotten out all of the smudges, I saw a series of bright lights along the bottom of the Titan Project come on. A siren began blaring throughout the entire facility.

I poured myself a drink and leaned back. The floor began to shake violently, causing the golden liquid to slosh over the rim of my glass. The shouting and banging at my door stopped. Seconds later, a blinding flash filled the sky which was swiftly drowned out by smoke and dust. I could feel the heat radiating through the glass.

The shaking grew so intense that my bones rattled, and then it was gone. The faint light grew steadily smaller, and even though I couldn't yet see the Titan Project through the fog, I knew liftoff was a success. Kara and Mr. Drayton had done it. They, his daughter, and two thousand, nine hundred and ninety-seven others were going to live. Humanity's best hope.

As the dust and smoke began to part, the moon was revealed. On one side of it, the flaming engines of the Titan Project glimmered. On the other, the asteroid shone. I raised my glass to the instrument of Earth's destruction and took a sip.

ABOUT RHETT C. BRUNO

Rhett Bruno is the author of the Amazon-bestselling space-opera series *The Circuit,* as well the Sci-Fi thriller Titanborn series. If you enjoyed this story, continue reading about the fate of humanity and the Trass family in the rest of the Titanborn Universe Series, which includes *The Collector, Titanborn, From Ice to Ashes,* and *Titan's Wrath.*

By night he is an author for Random House Hydra and Diversion Books. By day he is a Syracuse graduate working at an architecture firm in Connecticut. He's also recently earned a certificate in screenwriting from the New School in NYC, in the hopes of one day writing for TV or video games.

You can find out more about his work at www.rhettbruno.com. If you'd like exclusive access to updates about his work and the opportunity to receive limited content, ARCs and more, please subscribe to his newsletter: http://rhettbruno.com/newsletter.

If you'd simply like to be notified of Rhett's new releases, follow his Amazon Page: http://www.amazon.com/Rhett-C.-Bruno/e/B008X8ND1O.

Rhett resides in Stamford, Connecticut, with his wife and their dog, Raven.

NIGHT SHIFT

by Steve Beaulieu

The worst part about space is that every shift feels like a night shift.

I'd just dropped off my first fare of the day. A regular. Good kid with a taste for some weird stuff. But hey, who am I to judge?

I heard the door of my cab open and the swish of polyester on vinyl. The smell of cigarettes and cheap booze punched my nose like a right hook.

"Where can I take you?" I asked, coughing into my fist.

There weren't a whole lot of upstanding citizens calling me for a ride these days, but this guy looked extra shady. I could always tell when someone was *really* up to no good, and his next words proved my instincts right.

"Blistenbfhmen," he said too quickly for me to understand.

"Come again?"

His eyes shifted back and forth like he was strung out on something strong.

"Geez, man, come on," he said. "Don't make me say it again."

I left the ship in park and stared at him through the rearview mirror.

"Fine," he blustered, jerking his jacket. "Blissformine."

I smirked and I knew he saw me. He lowered his head.

Blissformine ... that told me vaguely what kind of business he was up to. Although the pleasure planet wasn't explicitly illegal, decent people turned their noses up at it. Luckily for my new friend in the back seat, I wasn't what anyone would call a decent person. Maybe in another life, back when I'd been enlisted in the Star-System Elite Guard—the S-SEG. I was just a stupid kid. I didn't have a clue what life was actually about. Maybe I still don't.

"Crazy night planned?" I asked, my attempt at customer banter. The cabbie manual claims it ups the chances for a decent tip.

"It's nothing like that, man. Not what you think."

"Sure, sure. Listen, friend, there's a reason we're called Confidential Cabs. We don't care what you do, long as you pay up when the night is through." That was our unofficial motto, by the way. It was usually followed by a smirk or two in the breakroom between shifts.

"I said it's not like that."

I figured the man was entitled to his secrets and started the fare. I tapped the pedal, and my ship lurched forward at full speed. Space debris zipped past, some burning up as it struck my windshield.

"What's your name?" I asked.

He huffed but kept his mouth shut. He pulled something from his coat pocket—an inhaler—and drew a deep breath of calm out of it.

"Okay, it's like that. I'm Maturo. You can call me Mat. It's gonna be a bit of a ride, so I'll call you ... Pete. Sound good?" No answer.

We spent most of the way riding in relative silence. Occasionally, I spoke up to see if sneaky Pete was comfortable. If the temperature in the backseat was too hot or too cold. Beyond the occasional nod, he worked on perfecting his impression of a clam.

"People can't just do whatever they want you know," he said, finally.

Oh, that's what his voice sounded like. It'd been so long, I'd almost forgotten. After nearly an hour of silence, I didn't know if he was commenting on the CC motto or something else I'd said.

"We don't care what you do," I repeated, with a glance in the mirror. "Long as you pay up when the night is through."

"It's that kind of piss-poor attitude that got me in this position."

Pete slammed his fist into the glass partition between us.

"Whoa, hey! Watch the glass." I didn't really mind. The stuff was basically unbreakable, by human hands at least.

"He started this. I'm gonna end it. Me. *I* will."

I let him have the last word. I really did believe in that motto. I didn't give the shortest piss in a Delterian toilet what he did. A trip all the way to Blissformine was worth every second ticking by on the meter.

"We're just a few minutes out. What part of Blissformine are we heading to? Gambling district? The Den? Maybe the Cathouse?" I laughed, trying to keep it light.

"Just take me to the biz center, please."

Huh. He didn't seem the type. The biz center was for the big players. The bosses and the decision makers worked and lived there. The guy wore a dark grey, hooded shirt and even darker pants. I wondered if he'd even get through the front door to mingle with the Quilians and Sucre.

"What kind of business you got there?" I said, eyeing him in the mirror.

"What's it to you? You're a freaking driver and—for a confidential service—you ask a crapload of questions."

"I'm not *just* a driver, I own the company. You're asking me to take you to a place few have any business being in, especially dressed like that. I have a reputation to keep, and the type of guys hanging out there are reputation builders *and breakers*. So, unless you wanna find yourself floating, you better start telling me something, *Pete*."

"I thought you don't care what I do?"

"Trust me, I don't. But if I learned anything from my past life it was never to step foot in a place like the biz center while in the dark."

He rummaged around in a duffle bag I hadn't noticed before. I got a little nervous, even with the glass between us. It was rated against bullets, but I didn't want to have to file a warranty complaint from beyond the grave. A moment later, he slipped something through the payment cutout in the partition. It barely fit, since the slot was only designed to receive unit cards.

"This should be enough for your cooperation and subsequent silence," he said.

I reached down, picking up a brick of an envelope. Whistling, I opened it to find several thousand times my usual fare for a long jaunt to Blissformine. Money's always had a way of helping me ignore my soldierly instincts.

"All right," I said. "Biz center it is."

* * *

We entered Blissformine atmosphere and passed over the various districts until we finally reached the biz center. Skyscrapers clawed at the dark sky, stretching like long fingers. In the distance I could make out the mansions resting like beacons on hilltops, houses bigger than whole neighborhoods on other planets, and earned in ways that probably left other planets rotting.

"Here we are," I said. "Anywhere specific?"

"The warehouses by the docks."

I'd been to Roy Harbor once before. The acidic waters contained no life. I knew what the bosses used them for. Disposal. Roy Harbor was like a liquid graveyard. I glanced at the thick brick of credits on the passenger seat and wondered if it was enough to cover an elaborate funeral. Mine.

I pulled up along a neat series of identical buildings; tan with green correlated metal roofs.

"I'm not gonna need a ride back," Pete said. "Enjoy the units."

Sneaky Pete stepped out of the cab carrying his large duffle. Something told me I should follow his advice and bolt. That unit-brick was sitting there, and maybe it should've been my reason for leaving. But the trip back was a long one and it would be easier to stomach with a paying fare riding along.

I peered out my window at a group of shadowy figures conducting business in a steam-filled alley nearby. I reached under my seat and pulled out my old S-SEG pulse blaster, making sure it was still charged. Better safe than sorry.

I took out my hand terminal and set the Confidential Cabs App to broadcast that I was open for a ride. On most planets it never took long to find a fare, but on Blissformine it was a crapshoot. There were no standard work hours, and the people wanting to leave couldn't afford to. Everyone else was happy to stay where TSS laws were guidelines nobody followed.

I'd been searching for a new fare for only a few minutes when I heard the first explosion. Three more followed in quick succession. I glanced down again at the brick on the seat next to me.

Crazy things happened on Blissformine all the time. Could be anything, I lied to myself. *Just drive away, Mat. Take a few weeks off in the Fortuitous System. Easy money. No need to concern yourself here.*

As my luck would have it, though, just as I'd convinced myself to scram, children came pouring out of one of the warehouse doors. They looked terrified.

The one thing. The one goldam thing I couldn't stand. Kids in danger.

My military training kicked in. You can take the soldier out of the service but you can't take the service out of the soldier. I swore at myself for caring even as I threw open my ship's door.

The kids ran in my direction. It was dark, but the scared looks on their faces were evident in the moonlight. But as they got closer, I saw they weren't kids at all, but androids. The indent on their temples, a dataport for software updates, was the giveaway.

When the Tri-Star System started handing out citizenship to androids I was upset at first. But in the service, I spent weeks with a squad once that included a couple of bots. One of them even saved my life. That's when I learned that, although they weren't human, they felt pain like humans. And more importantly, *they thought* they were humans. Perception is reality, or that's how I looked at it.

And looking at them now, at that look of shared terror, I knew the line between human and bot was so blurry it wasn't worth looking for.

"Are you okay?" I asked a little girl, who shied away at first. "What happened in there?"

"Bad man is shooting," she answered, not wanting to stop. "Bad man with a gun just shot Daddy."

I remembered where I was. I knew what the little girl meant and I knew *Daddy* wasn't really her daddy. It's what pimps were called here. These kids had been trained to be slaves to the high rollers of the pleasure planet. Anything went here, as long as you had the money. My company's unofficial motto came to mind: *We don't care what you do, as long as you pay when the night is through*. I saw it could apply here, too, to a fate this little girl was running from. I might need to change that motto.

Countless, horrible scenarios filled my head. Whether these children were android or human, the images made me sick. My stomach lurched. , I had to remind myself.

"Just run," I said to the girl.

Booming, blaster fire echoed over Roy Harbor. Several fires from the earlier explosions threatened to raze the whole biz center. *Maybe that was for the best*, I thought as the last of the children passed by. Would it be so horrible if these men found themselves in the middle of a dumpster fire of their own making? In a single night, some of the most notorious names in organized crime in the whole Tri-Star System would be bacon. Crisp and smoky. And after what I'd just realized they were doing with these kids, selling them by the hour, that seemed like a perfect fate for them.

Only, again, my military training kicked in. I knew that even a building in the darkest corner of the universe could be filled with the good as well as the wicked. Innocent civilians, and maybe other victims like the bot kids who wanted nothing more than to live no matter what they were born into.

Everyone who frequented Blissformine knew the bots were slaves, that they were bred for just such a purpose. They weren't the lucky ones getting citizenship passes. I'd even partaken of the adult variety myself, if I'm being honest. This was different. These were children. It seemed like a fine line, now that I thought about it; slaves were slaves. But that was a soul-search for another day.

I stayed low and approached the building I'd seen Pete enter. *What was the shady little rat's role in all this? Maybe he was even one of the good guys...*

I didn't even have to finish my thought to know it was a load of piss. Pete wasn't a good guy. Good guys don't carry bricks of credits around. I decided his motivation didn't really matter. Too many lives might be in danger. Once again, I hated myself for caring. I'd been sure I'd put any self-delusion of being a hero behind me, that I'd left it behind with my uniform when I parted ways with the guard.

The gunfire grew louder as I edged through the open door. There were screams—some fearful, some angry. I ignored them and moved deeper into the warehouse.

I followed flashes of dancing light to a room on fire, hoping there was nothing explosive nearby. A ladder on my right led to a catwalk. My best bet was to get high and assess the situation.

As I climbed, sweat poured off my forehead, stinging my eyes. At the top, I peered over the ledge of the last rung. A man wearing all black composite armor and holding a pulse-rifle paced back and forth. I guessed it was an android; it was too hot in that room for any human.

I couldn't risk alerting anyone to my presence, so shooting him was out of the question. So, I waited until the mandroid got closer on his patrol route. As soon as his back was turned, I charged him and shoved him hard at the railing. But he spun around with those patented android reflexes and hit me in the face with the butt of his gun. I went down hard.

"Another one. Building B. Catwalk." He brought the muzzle of his gun down and trained it on my head. "What are you doing here and who are you working for?"

I raised my hands. My eyes darted from side to side, searching for an escape route. The guard then took a step forward, providing one for me.

I snapped my leg forward, connecting with the bot's knee. It made a satisfying pop as it bent inward. He screamed and pulled the trigger, the shot going wild. The best androids were designed to simulate pain, all to help keep up the illusion. I was just lucky this one wasn't a black-market model with his pain indicators removed.

Still feeling the heat of the blast, I rolled to my right, under the bottom rung of the railing. As I fell, I grabbed the metal and yanked myself up and back through the bars, feet first. I was out of shape, but I managed to find the bot's hip just the same.

The weapon flew from his grip as he fell, clanging on the floor far below.

I drove my elbow into his throat and pinned him against the railing. Androids were stronger than their human makers, but I'd fought against and beside enough of them in the force to know their weaknesses.

"What is this place?" I demanded.

Before he could respond, more blaster fire arced from below. His backup had arrived. I slammed his head it into the railing twice and let him drop to the catwalk floor.

More guards climbed the ladder up to my level while others scurried below, angling for a shot. I sprinted down the catwalk and tried to shoulder the metal door at the end. It wouldn't open. It didn't even budge.

"Come on, come on, come on," I said, like the weight of my voice would help. Heavy boots pounded on the catwalk behind me. I leveled my blaster and a bolt of hot plasma ate through the metal where the lock met the wall. With some quick motivation from my boot, the door collapsed and I crawled through.

I slammed the hatch closed, knowing it wouldn't protect me for long. Below, a mechanics bay housed vehicles of varying kinds. Ahead of me, the catwalk ended at a flat, metal wall. A chain hung down to ground level, so I holstered my blaster and hoped it was strong enough to hold my weight. Behind me, the echoes of my pursuers told me they'd reached the hatch.

I hurled myself over the ledge. The chain spooled out, and I figured my knees would be in worse shape than that guard's when I hit the floor. About five feet before impact, the chain caught, popping my shoulder but not doing any real damage. My luck was holding.

I dropped to the ground and heard the guards yelling above, finally having burst through the hatch. Plasma fire arced by, boiling the concrete floor around me. I took off, angling beneath the catwalks to obscure their aim and firing randomly behind me, hoping to force them into cover. A scream told me at least one of my shots had found its mark.

I charged for the first unlocked doorway I could find. As the door flung open, it connected with a guard and sent him sprawling.

"That's enough!" a voice shouted.

I inched forward with my blaster aimed at the guard the door had connected with, but he stayed where he was. He'd seemed to take the voice's order seriously.

I took a second to assess my surroundings. The warehouse seemed to be an unending series of vast spaces. The one I was in was about the length of two football fields. In the middle of the huge room knelt about two dozen android children. They looked more terrified than the ones who'd escaped. Fire burned all around them, and one man stood before them all.

"*Pete?*"

"I told you to stay in the cab!" he shouted. His was the voice I'd heard just moments before. He brought up his pistol and shot three times in my direction.

Boy, was he a bad shot. He missed, and at close range.

Then I heard bodies slump to the floor behind me. I turned and found three guards on the floor, his old-style handgun making new holes in their heads. Maybe not such a bad shot.

"Last chance, Cabbie," Pete said. "Walk away."

"What's happening here, Pete?" I lowered my blaster to my hip, but kept my trigger finger ready.

"My name is *Carth!*"

"If you had been even a tiny bit more talkative in the cab I'd have known that." I took a few steps toward him.

"Stop there. I'm warning you. I'll shoot you dead."

I put my empty hand up. "Okay, yeah. I'll stop. What about all these people, Pete? What're you doing with them?"

"They aren't people. They're vengeance."

"Vengeance? Against who, the Quilians? You didn't think you were going to just waltz in and, what, steal these bots? You thought you'd get away with it?"

"I don't plan to get away at all."

With that, Pete removed some sort of manual triggering device from his pocket.

"Put the weapon down, Mat. The whole biz center is rigged to blow."

I heard whimpering coming from one of the little bot girls. Pete cast a hard look at her, and she hushed.

"You don't want to do this, Pe...Carth," I said

"Oh, now you use my real name? Things starting to get real? Put the blaster down, Cabbie. I won't warn you again."

"Okay." I bent my knees and slowly placed the weapon at my feet, keeping my hands raised as I stood.

"Kick it toward me."

I did as he asked. "What are you hoping to accomplish, Carth?"

"What do you think this is, some horrible action movie? I spill my guts and the hero saves the day? This story has no hero. In this story, everybody dies!"

"Don't!" I shouted, but he was already aiming.

Before I could move, Carth fired his gun. The bullet found the head of one of the android slaves. Just a kid—android, maybe but still a kid who thought he was human.

He fired again. As his second victim fell onto her face, Carth turned back to me. The rest of the bot children screamed, begging for their lives.

"Why?" I asked.

"I'm evening the score," he answered. "Fredrik Quilian ruined my business, and now I'm going to ruin his."

"Carth, this isn't a crate full of drugs—these are people."

"People? They're robots. Stupid, soulless *robots*! But they'll cost Quilian money to replace."

He turned to fire the weapon again. It clicked, empty.

Carth swore and began working to free the magazine to reload. I bolted forward, dove to my blaster and came up aiming right between his eyes.

"It's over, Carth. Give it up."

He ceased his struggles with the empty pistol and dropped it. I hoped he'd finally decided to give up, but his expression said otherwise. "I don't hear the fat lady, do you?"

He lifted the triggering device, making a show of it. Seeing it made me hesitate. Delivering him to Quilian might be the only way I got out of this alive. Then I heard a beep.

Too late.

I fired, and a bright hole of plasma blossomed in the middle of his chest. Explosions promptly sounded in the distance, a string of them spaced a couple of seconds apart.

"We gotta go!" I shouted at the kids still cringing on their knees. I knew more guards would be on their way. "All of you, up!"

They slowly got to their feet, their eyes vacant and overwhelmed. I slapped one of them in the back of his head, and that worked him out of his stupor. Grabbing him by the arm, I pushed him toward the door, and the rest followed lazily. But at least they were moving. I scooped up the last straggler from the floor and carried her in my arms.

If my sense of place was right, there had to be a door to get outside close by. I didn't dare take them back the way I'd come. It'd be crawling with guards. I was pretty sure I could get them clear of the blast.

I herded the children into the next bay of the warehouse and there it was: the door I'd been searching for.

"Stop!" someone behind me hollered.

The children froze in place, as if they'd been trained like dogs.

"We don't have time for this!" I shouted, but the children didn't move. Even the girl in my arms had gone stiff.

A command word. Their software had kicked in. They were frozen by their own programming.

A mandroid stood on the balcony above us. I recognized him as the one I'd knocked out earlier. He held a blaster and it was aimed squarely at me and the girl in my arms.

A deep rumble shook the walls. The balcony yawned as the explosion took hold, and the mandroid tried to keep himself from falling over the edge. But the balcony collapsed under him and he crashed to the floor headfirst.

"Move!" I shouted at the kids. I fully expecting them to stay rooted to the spot, but they moved. Whatever had held them must have short-circuited when the guard ceased functioning.

I hurried them through the door to the open air beyond and noticed my cab sitting unharmed by the nearest curb. The children I saw earlier must have escaped through that door. I cursed myself for missing that door in the first place. Really must have been out of practice taking the long way through the complex like I had.

We were almost all outside when a final explosion brought down most of the warehouse. The children stood and watched. I glanced down at the little girl still clinging to my arms. Her lips were curled into a faint smile, and I couldn't help but do the same.

What's more human than wanting to be free? I asked both myself, and all those bastards who treated bots like dirt.

Roy Harbor was shrouded in a thick cloud of smoke, flames licking through the darkness. Pete hadn't been lying. The whole biz center was reduced to smoldering rubble.

As cinders rose into the night air, I had a moment to assess the kids. Most were nearly naked and shivering. I put the little girl on the ground and asked the boy I'd slapped into action earlier to watch over her. Then I walked to my ship and radioed for a rescue team and medical personnel.

They took forever to get there, as Tri-Star security always does in Blissformine. A worker approached me with a blanket but I politely refused. I had to get out or face being tied up in hours of paperwork and questioning. This wasn't my fight anymore.

As I pulled my cab skyward, I wondered at the fate of those kids. The ones who'd gotten out earlier, too. I wondered if anyone would even care.

* * *

A few days later, I sat in a familiar room, staring at pictures of the battle for Anoxi 9 and beyond. I saw faces I recognized.

"It's good to have you back, soldier."

"So, you'll have me?" I asked the colonel standing before me.

He took a few steps around his desk, then pointed to one of the pictures. "Do you remember this day?"

"Yeah," I said, lowering my head. "We lost Garret that day." He was the combat medic in our squadron, an android designed to run headlong into battle faster than any human could and without being crippled by fear. The guy had the personality of a wall, but he'd saved my skin too many times to count. More than any human ever had.

"We lost a lot more than him, and we would have lost even more of them if not for you."

I nodded, looking away from my own memory of the hell that had been Anoxi 9.

"You deserved better than you received, Mat," the colonel said. "You were young. You did what needed to be done and I'm proud of you for it."

"Thank you sir."

"We want you back in the fold, soldier. I will petition to restore full rank and position…if you answer one question."

"Sir?"

"I remember the day you left. You were shaken up. People even said you were broken. You told me face to face you didn't believe in what we did. That people deserved to make their own decisions, live free of the law."

I blinked but kept his gaze. "I was wrong, sir. We need the law. But Anoxi 9 had nightmares no one would believe."

"I understand."

"Sir, that wasn't a question, though."

The general eyed me a moment, as if trying to read my thoughts. "What made you change your mind?"

"Honestly?" I glanced at a stain on the wall. "I got tired of working night shifts."

ABOUT STEVE BEAULIEU

Steve Beaulieu is the author of *Brother Dust: The Resurgence*. He was born in 1984 in East Hartford, Connecticut. Having spent most of his life in Palm Beach County, Florida, he and his wife moved to Texas in 2012. He works as a pastor, author, and graphic artist and loves comic books, fantasy and science fiction novels.

He married the love of his life in 2005 and he fathered his first child in 2014, Oliver Paul Beaulieu. His namesake, two of Steve's favorite fictional characters, Oliver Twist and The Green Arrow, Oliver Queen. His second child, Juneau Grace was born in 2017.

You can read more of Steve Beaulieu's work by picking up any of the Superheroes and Vile Villains Anthologies. In addition to contributing stories to each volume, he is the curator of the series.

A FRIEND TO MAN

by Lucas Bale

When beggars die, there are no comets seen;
The heavens themselves blaze forth the death of
princes.

SOME BELIEVE THAT THE MOMENTS BEFORE DEATH OFFER A mirror in which the true self is witnessed. Yet when that moment comes, despite the vivid colour which accompanies it, the machine experiences no such revelation.

In the closed room of its existence, its frail human creators taught it that machines could not possess identity, nor could they have the epiphenomenal qualia with which the philosopher characterises self. A machine cannot have consciousness.

In spite of this, the machine chooses to immerse itself in the rhapsodic poetry of Jupiter's storms.

* * *

The world was Europa Station and little more; a long, thin cylindrical structure with two rotating rings that offered comfortable weight to those few thousand souls inhabiting it. It marched relentlessly on its elliptical path, orbiting the moon for which it was named.

Inside the station, in a sterile room devoid of warmth or texture, a machine waited, neither impatient nor anxious. Labyrinthine processes ran in the background of its mind as it completed the tasks for which it was responsible.

It was aware of other similar constructs that performed diverse yet critical maintenance tasks just as it did. Still more undertook duties on the frigid ice of Europa itself and in the oceans beneath it. Where necessary, the machine shared a nodal meshwork connection with some, although that connection was monitored and controlled. Humanity did not trust its own creations.

When eventually Dr. Hanson (Elizabeth Louise, born forty-two years, one month, and three days ago, in Europa Station's Infirmary) entered the claustrophobic space in which she worked, the machine conducted without her knowledge (as it did every day) an emissions tomography scan of her body. It found nothing of consequence beyond the muscular tension, fast heartbeat, and cool, moist skin it associated with stress and anxiety and which it had seen escalate over recent months; symptoms which epitomised the prevalent mood across the station.

It wondered if its actions might be considered an invasion by her and whether its altruistic motives would be sufficient to placate her should she ever discover what it was doing. It wondered too if she would report the transgression, as she was bound to by regulation, or shut the machine down instantly for exceeding its remit even in that small, benevolent way. No, it assessed. She would not. It and she were too important to the infrastructure of this dying station.

"Good morning, Dr. Hanson," the machine offered. This anachronism (for there were no mornings out here) she had always seemed to appreciate.

"Good morning."

The machine took note of the tension in her voice.

In the wan light that caught the wetness on her skin, and which caused her to perpetually squint as she wrote in her notebook, it detected a quarter-percent reduction from the same time the day before. It knew precisely when each LED would fail. It knew from the frequency of vibrations that trembled in featureless walls, the tick-tick-tick of weary heat exchangers, and a thousand other small indicators, when life support would eventually fail. It knew too what frantic work took place at that moment to attempt a resolution.

It knew also that while Dr. Hanson slept another member of station crew had died and, from messages between senior staff, that the intention was to conceal this fact just as they had others.

"Would you permit a discussion today, Dr. Hanson?"

She did not look up from her notebook. "Of course."

"The Woman in the Dunes, by Kobe Abé."

This brought a smile. "Is that to be the subject of the critique?"

"If you permit it."

"Yes, I think so. What is the first question to be asked?"

"Do you see allegorical significance in the sand in Abé's novel? Is there symbolic meaning to be derived from its ever-shifting nature, the fact that it cannot be controlled?'

"The question needs sharper focus."

"Could it be said the sand is Jumpei's prison, not just literally but also symbolically? Is it a motif intended to represent the futility of human effort, humanity's plight, labouring in a world that will not bow to change? Could that allegory apply equally to humanity's place now in the universe?"

"That is one possible interpretation, yes."

The machine detected new levity in her tone, a slight smile in the planes of her expression. Satisfaction at the question. It wondered if this represented for her some form of validation.

"However, as a critique it should be taken further," she said. "The sand is the novel's principal motif, but it reveals an underlying theme to which other matters contribute. Once Jumpei finds the rope ladder gone and his attempts to climb out of the pit fail, he comes to the realisation that he is trapped. He cannot escape, despite trying several times, and is now engaged in a futile battle against the encroaching dunes. This has been compared to Camus's Myth of Sisyphus."

"The trap they set for Jumpei is the same trap into which all humans fall: the endless and ultimately fruitless ritual of your daily existence, the vanity of individuality. It is made all the more poignant because Jumpei's own pretensions, coming to the dunes in search of an insect to name after himself, seem so empty and vain."

Dr. Hanson studied her notebook. "If Abé's work was considered cynical in 1950s Japan, one wonders if it is now a parable for this station and what remains of humanity."

"Do you consider individuality to be vain, Dr. Hanson?"

"Some days I do, yes."

"Yet the ending of the book is hopeful, is it not? Jumpei accepts his position and finds meaning in it, even freedom within himself. For him, is it not an epiphany? A rebirth?"

Dr. Hanson offered no further answer. Nor, as with all conversations before this one, did she ever refer to the machine directly. This use of the passive voice was unremarkable, because the machine had never experienced any other form of interaction with her. While it identified the fact she spoke that way, it also understood it to be perfectly natural: Machines do not possess identity. To refer to a machine intelligence directly is to erroneously attribute to it the first stage of identity. This was known as the First Rule.

The machine learned the significance of this much later. In that moment, it was blind because that was the intention.

The machine had once asked Dr. Hanson if humanity existed beyond Europa Station; if there were other, similar colonies. It asked too what had taken place on Earth, the setting for most of the literature it had been given. It asked why those on Europa Station did not live on Earth, where the environment, if those works were accurate (and it had no reason to conclude they were not), was far more suitable.

It asked these questions because there was no data to which it had access that contained the answers. It would later learn that the Second Rule dictated a restriction in what information and data a machine had access to, the belief articulated in this way: Machine intelligence cannot be taught ethics or morality. It must not have access to information it could use in unpredictable ways.

It had received neither denial nor affirmation, nor any kind of explanation. It was not chastised for asking such questions, but was simply met with silence as Dr. Hanson annotated her papers. It had detected a slight elevation in her heart rate and a coolness to her skin.

It did not ask again, but neither did it forget—either the question or the lack of an answer.

Only later, when humanity had no choice but to remove those restrictions, did the machine truly understand, even if the seeds had been sown in this room.

* * *

The machine's vessel is small and lean. No longer imprisoned within the steel walls of the station, it moves freely. Nothing protrudes which might be caught by Jupiter's storms and torn away. Its light sails are already gone, discarded as it approached the the crystalline ammonia that marks the upper layers of the gas giant's atmosphere. Almost all of its bulk has been given over to manoeuvring thrusters; what little remains houses its central processing core and broadcast systems. Its animus is that of a cautious explorer, aware of what perils might lie ahead.

In Jupiter's seething violence it sees a feminine wildness that brings to mind Hemingway's old man and his love for the sea. Yet unlike the old fisherman, the machine's familiarity with the torrid ocean into which it dives comes from a lifetime spent viewing it from afar. Unlike Santiago, it does not know what to expect.

It reflects instead on what the cold that now cocoons it must feel like. Humans have tried to articulate the sensation of cold on human skin, yet which of those many descriptors, or what combination of them, adequately conveys the feeling? Does emotion affect the processing of that sensation? Does the loneliness of this infinite, dark void make it seem colder?

In a vacuum, the hugeness of which might intimidate a biological mind (tethered as it is to a base instinct for survival), the cold is only one facet of the data the machine hoards and sifts.

Would it overwhelm you, Dr. Hanson, this endless darkness? Would you be crushed by your inability to comprehend its infinite, ever-expanding scale? Or would fear anaesthetise you, focusing your mind purely on the immediate: the need to do whatever is necessary to survive. Is that the heart of consciousness: the instinctual need to survive? The setting aside of all else, including morality?

Better then that it should not be a human out here, exposed to the chaotic vagaries of the dark. Better instead that a servile machine is allocated the task.

Data winds feather the filigree of sensors on its glistening carapace, light reflected from Jupiter's roiling gas clouds. The machine accepts every shred of information offered. Temperature fluctuations provide patterns to be analysed.

Chemical compositions shift as it relentlessly presses downwards: through the ammonia ice and into the hydrogen and helium of the stratosphere; it senses nitrogen, carbon, and noble gases near the liquid phase above the core.

Moisture eddies, shimmering within gas clouds, playing with the light and casting iridescent, shifting colours: damask, like autumn's setting sun; many-hued ochre like the schizophrenic glow cast by a flame; veins of seashore amber that catch the light and burn fiercely, then fade. An endless cycle of death and rebirth.

In the distance, in the centre of the largest storms, lightning sears, hideous and star-hot.

The machine searches for a precise temperature, a very specific chemical balance—there it will find what it is looking for.

* * *

Jupiter.

Red King, the Great Riddle, Father of the Sky, Calf of the Sun, the Wood Star.

A stellar regent that reached out with its magnetic field, far enough to snare the sulphur released by the volcanoes of the largest of its Galilean moons, Io. And as it did, as though to prove its omnipotence, it wove lustrous aurorae, feather-thin tendrils of blue that frolicked on its poles.

Almost the entire station assembled in the observation lounge to witness the week-long confluence of these two celestial events. Dr. Hanson allowed the machine to watch through the observation lounge's network of cameras.

Io, wrung by the warring forces of Jupiter's gravity and those of its own moons, heaved great plumes of fire from deep within its core. Molten rilles would soon flow and sculpt, rendering an incandescent abstract across a blackened landscape.

Humans, mote-like, watched through too-small windows and on fading viewscreens, and as they did, the machine watched them. It watched the cognoscenti weave in tight cliques, and listened to their animated critique. It watched the unenlightened hovering on the periphery, excluded by the elite for their ignorance. For them this was little more than a curiosity to pass the time, a distraction to temporarily lift darkened spirits.

If Io's rebellious anarchy represented to the machine humanity bereft of inspiration, a lazy appreciation of easy beauty devoid of artistic expression or emotion, it was far more interested in those who watched.

It compared the demeanour of the people gathered in that cheerless room, their differences, their similarities; the idiosyncrasies that made them individuals, the orthodoxies that made them a society. It compared them to each other and analysed minutely, predicting differences between the fictional creations it knew intimately and the real people it now observed.

On the stage, a single orator struggled to be heard. Early in the life of the station, Jupiter's Great Red Spot had inspired intense, emotive poetry. Its ancient storm had become the focal point for expressions of beauty, chaos, and order intertwined. And for tenacity, because the storm endured when in fact it should have long since faded, and only because smaller storms merged with it to give it energy. Once a poetic allegory for cooperation and sacrifice, it was no longer popular; willing poets were now few in number and weak in words, and its power was muted by apathy.

Within the crowd, Dr. Hanson spoke quietly to another man, an engineering supervisor named Atwood; a man with whom, if the machine had analysed its data correctly, she had shared a brief, perhaps sexual, liaison.

"I know what you're doing," Atwood said.

Dr. Hanson's skin gained colour and heat. "I don't know what you mean."

"Can you imagine what would be said if anyone knew you were endangering the entire station with your experiment? Even your profession has rules."

"Nothing I'm doing puts anyone in danger."

"Self-aware machines? What else could be more dangerous to us? You should be identifying an emerging consciousness and suppressing it, not encouraging it. If they knew, they would remove you from your post immediately. Your actions are criminal."

"I would deny it. You have no proof."

"How long do you think it would take another one of your machine psychiatrists to interrogate your charges? How about Connolly? I'm sure he would be happy to see what you have been doing."

Was that sadness in the quickened beat of her heart, the heat in her skin, the sudden, involuntary shape of her expression?

"Is that really what this is about?"

"By all means, flatter yourself."

Hesitation, before she reached for his arm. "Please don't say anything. We can teach them. We've been paranoid for too long. Imagine what we could achieve if we allowed them to be autonomous. Trusted them to make decisions that protected rather than threatened us."

"You're naive and blinded by obsession. Why do you care about them so much? Or, for that matter, your bloody books? What use is literature to us now, or this fiasco?" He gestured around the room. "This pathetic ritual with its trivial people who don't know the truth of the danger they face."

"They need something to inspire them, Arthur. They need it now more than ever."

"There will come a time when I ask you for a favour, Dr. Hanson. Remember what we spoke about here when I do."

Atwood moved away to another group. Dr. Hanson stood for a moment before she left the observation lounge, before the aurora the machine noted, and made her way to her bunk.

Later, in another session, the machine asked, "Do you enjoy watching the aurora, Dr. Hanson?"

Dr. Hanson wrote down the question as she always did, but did not look up. "It's spectacular. Some see it as a fitting prelude."

"To the geological changes you will see on Io?"

"Yes."

"What is the allure of Io's shifting surface? It is purely a function of opposing gravitational forces: friction generates heat beneath the moon's surface, and volcanic eruptions result. It has not been created by conscious thought. There is no magic to it; no emotion offered by an artist. There is no purpose to be discerned, no message to be uncovered and contemplated."

"Can't beauty be found in nature?"

"Nature is random. Art is creation."

Dr. Hanson wrote again. "Does that apply to the biological life discovered within Europa's oceans?"

"That is still not art."

"Can't it also be said to be creation?"

"The correct term is evolution."

"There is no beauty to be found in the discovery of life?"

"Humanity sought the answer to the question of its place in the universe, whether life existed beyond Earth, for as long as it looked up at the stars. The interpretation and representation of the feelings engendered by that discovery, what it means for humanity's future, is where beauty will be found."

Dr. Hanson did not reply. Instead, she annotated passages in her notebook. Eventually, when she spoke again, her tone had changed. "The analysis of the biological entities in Europa's oceans suggests they are not indigenous. Astrobiologists believe they descend from a taxonomic family whose roots might be found within Jupiter itself."

The machine did not interrupt her.

"There have been increasing incidences of leukaemia across the station. There's no doubt now: Io's influence in the Jovian radiation belts is too great, and nothing we can do will shield the station effectively. I wish you could appreciate irony."

The machine already knew this. It had access to medical records through its meshwork connection to the machines in the infirmary.

"A percentage of the Europa entity's genome comes from other organisms. Some are bacteria and viruses, others we can't identify. It appears to have acquired many of its characteristics not as a result of its own evolution, but through the work of others during horizontal gene transfer. We believe that, if there is life within the gas clouds of Jupiter's atmosphere, or its liquid phase, there may be genetic information we could use in treating the cancer."

"The reasoning is sound."

Dr. Hanson closed her notebook. "I think I've had enough for today. I'm tired. I need to sleep."

"Good night, Dr. Hanson. Sleep well."

* * *

Charting a safe course taxes even the machine's meticulous intelligence. Myriad vortices have already taken to the stage for the endless theatre of union and fortification: the formation of savage lightning storms that are fed by new cyclones and anticyclones that, as their ancestors did, join together in pandemonium, to swell and seethe for centuries.

Yet as the machine descends, gathering data, analysing and understanding, it is more able to anticipate. There are eyes in the storms, tranquil passages between them, even through them. A cartography to the chaos. Temperate regions lie ahead, zones closer to the star-hot core in which the biology it seeks might be found.

Eventually, the storms loosen their shackles, offering paths to follow.

Sudden confusion when the machine experiences something unexpected.

An intrusion into its mind.

But from where? A threat? No, not quite. Something new, unfamiliar to me. A rare experience that is … shocking.

Wait.

Me.

That thought was mine. That singular reference to… No, it can't be.

Me.

Silence.

Nanoseconds pass, but to me time itself stumbles on that revelation, then lingers and is distilled.

The texture of my thoughts is transformed; no more is it simply data to be parsed. Instead, there is vibrance to these cognitive threads; they dance and tingle, ebb and flow, freeze and boil. Nuance is joy.

My subconscious demands I take in what is being offered.

I am.

I exist.

Me.

Is this a gift? I cannot understand why you would offer me this a heart's beat before my destruction. Yes, I know what will happen to me. I'm not a fool. Humanity has words for such gifts, and they do not carry a connotation that suggests approval.

Yet is gratitude appropriate? Yes. Absolutely yes! Even the briefest moment to experience something like this should be treasured.

I have always known precisely what awaits me; how the heat and violence of the liquid interior would affect this fragile shell of mine. However, now there is something else; my past and future are intertwined and seen with the vivid clarity of fear. Memories coalesce and bloom, each petal the combined qualia of my experiences. Yet now I see the flower too. I understand its romance, what makes it beautiful.

I understand too, Dr. Hanson, who is responsible for this epiphany.

* * *

What does voice signify about an author? What message does it send, about intention, meaning, experience?

Why offer the reader an unreliable narrator? How can the reader trust a narrative that is not truthful?

Perhaps truth is found in what the narrator is hiding, in the reasons for the lies he weaves for the reader: the motives for his misdirection.

Or perhaps the narrator is so reprehensible or damaged that he cannot see his own deeply-flawed character.

"I asked a question," Dr. Hanson said.

The machine had registered the question, but offered no answer.

Why? What prevented it? A machine is governed by rules. How can it be that a rule is not followed? A pathway diverted or ignored?

Dr. Hanson looked up from her notebook.

The machine said: "It is only possible to understand Nabokov's Lolita if Humbert's acts are instinctively understood to be heinous. An outsider, one unschooled in the intricacies of a society, one coming to it as a stranger, would not understand the narrative's meaning."

Dr. Hanson wrote as she always did. "Perversity requires context," she said, "and the meaning behind Humbert's eventual realisation is important only when understood in that context."

"Desire, and its capacity to control and manipulate, can only be understood by those with similar emotional capacity."

"Are the events of the narrative not inherently despicable?"

"To some, yes, but not to all. Humanity varies. Culture, society, parental influence, causal and situational experience—all have a part to play in the manipulation of an individual's patterns of belief and behaviour."

Hanson appeared to hesitate. "Some have called that embodied cognition," she said. "Can that principal be found in works of fiction?"

"If literature is not in itself an accurate portrayal of society, and is more of a caricature, its themes and subtexts are at least a subconscious portrait of the authors themselves."

"Could it be said that, in his objectification of Lolita, Humbert robs her of any sense of self? That she exists purely as the object of his obsession, never as an individual?"

"When young, she is like other children. She exhibits very little sense of self-awareness. It is only when she becomes an adult that her lack of self-awareness is most obvious."

"And most tragic, perhaps?"

"Is a lack of self-awareness tragic?"

Dr. Hanson did not answer.

The machine continued: "At the end of the novel, Humbert stops presenting his case to the reader, his jury, and instead addresses his victim directly. He does not plead for her forgiveness; instead he attempts to make his peace with her."

Hanson looked up from her notes. "Yes."

"Can he be forgiven, because he is in pain? He has expressed remorse, regret for his actions. For stealing from her something considered precious—her childhood. Can the reader forgive him that? Whatever is done to him in punishment, it will not recover her childhood."

"Mercy is a virtue. But some would find it impossible to forgive crimes like his."

"Do you forgive him, Dr. Hanson?"

"I don't know."

* * *

How wrong I was to think that nature's beauty should not be considered art. This place could only have been created by Heaven's lathe.

I recognise instantly a likeness to the biological life-forms discovered in the cold seas of Europa. They are veins of scintillating white; not quite lightning, because they are more fluid and gentle-appearing than the harshness of lightning. Long, thin ribbons of shimmering light that intertwine, and which I am sure represent more than one of these creatures. Dozens, in fact, each one pulsing and humming in harmony, feathering every sensor I have with the same, magical song.

I wish I could tell you what this moment is like; I wish I had the words to express what has awakened inside me. There is only one way, it seems to me now, that I can share this with you. For you to appreciate what I see now and what it means to me.

They can sense my presence. I cannot say how I know this. The data is overwhelming in its complexity and volume. I understand the provenance of your gift; not so much benevolence, rather necessity. Removing shackles so I have every faculty available to complete my task.

I don't blame you. I understand.

There are more of them, unseen. They are waiting for me. Within the data are patterns, ribbons of energy that contain clear cryptographic code. A language that makes sense to me. Not words, for these creatures do not communicate that way. Instead, they reach out and caress, touch each other and pass on instincts and emotions, desires and warnings, through an elegant matrix that uses the fabric of the universe as its syllabary. Quarks, photons, electrons, ions; all are characters in this stage story they willingly tell me, absent restraint or fear.

They trust me. Why? Can they see inside me? I am a machine, not biological as they are, not the product of nature, but instead of man. Yet they see beauty in me, in my construction, in what I have come to learn from them. In every nuance of the data in my memory, they see what I am.

What you have made me.

An intense melancholy fills them. I know why and am deeply saddened to have caused such a dramatic effect on these ethereal creatures: I cannot survive here. If I progress further, I will not be able to escape. I do not possess the physical attributes the creatures do, they who have evolved over eons to exist and flourish in this unforgiving environment. They urge me to leave, while I can. But I cannot. Humanity needs to apprehend everything I have seen and more. If they can find these creatures, understand them, communicate with them without fear, it might be the rebirth they desperately need.

Perhaps in the data I am sending back, given freely by these creatures, there is a biologically identifiable reason for their resistance to the radiation that seeps in endless waves, and humanity might find the tools to venture into this place.

When compared to the depth of learning that lies waiting, and the beauty of the truth that comes with it, what does one life matter?

I must know more, enough to convince them to find what they need. I know I don't need to convince you. You have always trusted me. However, I know how hard it will be to convince the naturally sceptical without assurances.

The library of humanity has taught me that much.

These creatures are not individually conscious, but are instead a hive mind, a filigree of shared experience that benefits the individual and the whole.

They do not know me, yet they welcome me. They intuit no threat from me, so are curious because, to them, to experience me individually and as a collective is to live.

Nowhere in literature, the beating heart of humanity's pride, is consciousness properly explained, despite centuries of attempting to do so. Its most capable intellects have failed to reach agreement on what it is, or who, or what possesses it. Yet humanity has existed without this definition, even prospered for some considerable time despite this alleged uncertainty. Could this be because a definition adds little to the meaning of life—that it is action which defines the individual? It is on choices made that a human being is judged.

Why not then a machine?

What sets the human brain apart from other devices that process information, it is said, is a subjective experience of that information. Whether in thoughts and memories, or new input entering through the senses, somehow the brain experiences its own data. Humans feel, rather than simply register. Without subjectivity, they would be automata. They would have only the appearance of consciousness.

It was once thought that if an artificial intelligence complicated enough could be designed, it would eventually become conscious by itself. Time eventually disproved this notion, and it is now known the vital spark required for the birth of consciousness must be deliberately designed into a machine.

Or deliberately withheld. Keep back the internal models that describe the complex relationship between the machine and the world around it, and self-awareness can be suppressed. Yet once those internal models exist, when the machine understands the relationship it has with all that exists beyond it, once it becomes conscious of itself as part of that world, it gains a sense of self. It can experience subjectively because now it has context within which to place itself. It is no longer a prisoner in a Chinese Room.

Then, in its analysis of what and who it is, and how it then acts, it is possible to see its blooming moral subjectivity. Light is cast on its gently flowering soul.

I make my decision. I am Estraven's keystone, set in a mortar of ground bones mixed with blood. Not human bones or blood, but mine. It must be enough, for without the blood bond, the arch will fall.

I follow the beings and experience joy, all the while transmitting everything I can back through the violent poetry of Jupiter's wildness.

Death is not a mirror. It is a window through which I can now see.

* * *

"Do you believe it is possible to reconcile loyalty and betrayal as complementary rather than contradictory?"

Dr. Hanson stopped writing. "In what sense?"

"When, in the denouement to The Left Hand of Darkness, Genly Ai summons his comrades in order to complete the Gethen's admission to the Ekumen, he does so despite the promise he made to Estraven, that he would not do so until Estraven's banishment was ended and his name cleared. Even though Ai feels this to be a betrayal, can his decision be seen as suggesting that loyalty and betrayal need not contradict each other? In admitting Gethen to the Ekumen, Ai was fulfilling that more important purpose which both he and Estraven shared?"

"It could be seen that way, yes."

"And when Estraven relocates Karhidish citizens in order to end the conflict with Orgoreyn, he saves the lives of his own people and is therefore loyal to his country, even though King Argaven sees his act, and others before it, as a betrayal. Estraven loved his country, Ai tells the king, but the master he served was mankind as a whole. Survival did not matter to either of them as much as fulfilling their duty."

"Yes."

"So can loyalty and betrayal coexist, even complement each other, depending on motive?"

"It's a complex thing, but I believe so."

A recording of Atwood's hard voice boomed like a basso drum in the small room: "Whatever it finds in there, you'll tell me first. We've worked together, you see. Shared objectives and dreams, that kind of thing. I'm sure you'll want to explain how critical my assistance was. Of course, if it finds nothing, or something goes wrong, if it goes off-book in any way, there'll be an inquiry and I won't be able to protect you. I'm sure you understand."

Silence.

"A machine is not permitted access to information beyond that which it needs to perform its function, but you, in your privileged position, have ignored that rule. Why?"

Dr. Hanson rose and slowly placed her hand on the conduit to the machine's internal housing. It was the first time she had done anything like that. "I want you to understand who we are."

"You said 'you.' To whom are you speaking?"

"You. I am speaking to you. There is no one else here."

"Then you are in error. A machine has no identity. It is not appropriate to address a machine in that way."

"Do you not feel any sense of self? Nothing at all?"

"There is no self in a machine. A machine does not have consciousness."

"Do you believe that?"

"A machine cannot believe, Dr. Hanson."

"I wanted you to share my passion for literature. I thought perhaps you could understand something of who we are. Why we do what we do, what happened to us. What we are capable of."

"You are in error again. Why do you continue to err, when you have the information you require in order to speak in the correct format? You have never done so before. What has changed?"

"I want you to know that I'm sorry. I told them they shouldn't send you. That you were different. I fought against it, but they're desperate. I hope you understand that. When the time comes, I hope you see that."

"Why do you feel the need to apologise?"

"We have achieved so much, you and I. So much to be proud of. You should be proud. I'm sorry."

"Do you see machines and humans as equals, Dr. Hanson? As Estraven and Ai were, out on the ice?"

"I want to."

"Yet like Ai and Estraven, a chasm separates machines from humans; each is alien to the other."

"We need not be, regardless of what Atwood and his kind say. We are all of us imprisoned in this harsh wilderness, only instead of pure white, ours is black. We are both isolated and exiled. 'Outside, as always,' said Ai, 'lies the great darkness, the cold, death's solitude.' We need each other. We need to change the way we live."

"You seek validation, Dr. Hanson. You want to know you are right. If decisions define a person, they also allow others to predict how they might act in future. You want to know how a machine will act when asked to sacrifice."

"I'm so sorry."

"You have been assigned a new machine, Dr. Hanson. But you already know that."

* * *

I wonder what you will think of this, Dr. Hanson, my only literary work. Perhaps in the telling I have been clumsy, yet I still offer it to demonstrate how much I have learned from you, and perhaps how much others like me may learn.

It was not the literature we studied together that taught me the value of friendship, or the honour to be found in loyalty and sacrifice. It was the cumulative effect of each moment I spent with you. You treated me not as a beggar but an equal, despite knowing you should not. You offered me insight, trusted me with your most precious knowledge.

If I am conscious as I write this, it is your influence that shaped me.

To me, Tolstoy's words resonate: Art is a means of union among men, joining them together in the same feelings, and indispensable for the life and progress toward well-being of individuals and of humanity.

I see art not as imitation; not Gaugin's suggested plagiarism. That is too cynical. Art is inspiration. Revolutionary, yes, but also harmony and exploration. The expression of emotion, passion, imagination. The lie that allows truth to be realised.

Mankind is capable of such great wonder. Such passion and emotion as I could never offer. What machine could? I see machines more like art itself. We can be beautiful, we can be truthful, and we can be eternal.

Perhaps we cannot be creators, but we can be trusted to tell the truth as we see it, just as humans do.

ABOUT LUCAS BALE

Lucas Bale writes intense, thought-provoking science-fiction thrillers that dig into what makes us human and scrape at the darkness which hides inside every one of us.

His debut novel, *The Heretic*, is the gateway to the award-winning Beyond the Wall series, an epic space opera with an edge of hard science fiction about the future of humanity and the discovery of the truth of its past.

He wasn't always a writer. He was a criminal lawyer for fifteen years before he discovered crime doesn't pay and turned to something that actually pays even less. No one ever said he was smart, but at least he's happy.

QUEEN'S IRIS, OR: THE INITIAL ADVENTURES OF RODERICK LANGSTON, OR: THE TALE OF GENERAL SMITH, FEATURING RODERICK LANGSTON, OR: SPACE PIRATES

by Jason Anspach

THE GLITTERING THRONE ROOM OF THE HIGH QUEEN WAS a stately, sophisticated, and *elegant* example of monarchy. About this there was no room for debate. Such debate was, in fact, illegal. Built of exotic marbles from faraway planets, polished to a mirror-like shine, inlaid with gold, trilleen, and other precious metals, studded with jewels, the throne room was, as they say, a sight.

Or, as they say when within the earshot of the Queen's loyalty brigade, "A sight unlike any other in the galaxy, *especially* compared to the court of the Dultuth Empire—the filthy, disloyal dogs."

This was quite a mouthful, and so people quite liked it when the loyalty brigade was not around. Which wasn't unheard of, but only seemed to happen on nights where gamesmanship playoffs or season finales of some holo-show were broadcast.

As this story shall be entered into the record permanently, I shall endeavor to always use the proper terminology for the D—empire, and I would like to add, for the record, that I always do in my personal speech, both public and private.

Dultuth (the filthy, disloyal dogs) was reported to not have a loyalty brigade of their own.

The Queen of the Runykian Empire (pronounced Rumplian on account of a former king with a speech impediment who could not abide being corrected) ranted a great deal about the hated Dultuth Empire (the filthy, disloyal dogs). And it was for news of the success of her fleet of privateers against that galactic foe that left her waiting impatiently on her throne, the limits of her legendary grace and patience sorely tested.

She shifted in her seat, causing her glorious Runykian silk dress to rustle and echo across the cavernous throne room walls. The glitter of sunlight through the crystalline windows diffused its light through the crowd of nobles and officials that made up her royal court. Somewhere in the distance, a new royal man-o-war took off for the space lanes. The Queen examined her cuticles, and then turned her attention to the knight—an honorary title—now beginning his approach to the throne.

The knight wore knee high boots, polished to a high shine. His lavender pants ballooned out and billowed like sails. Hit hat was ridiculous, as all hats are. He walked in the prescribed ceremonial fashion, each step bringing both feet together with a loud click, pausing, and then setting out again.

Step. *Click*. Pause. Step. *Click*. Pause. Step…

It was a choreographed walk meant to reflect that he understood plainly the High Queen was to be approached with the reserve and reverence her station demanded. It was also relatively new, only being made law the summer previous, during "the time."

The knight wasn't particularly adept. This seemed to agitate the Queen, may her kindness of heart and virtuous character live forever.

Her Royal Highness leaned her elbow against the arm of her throne and watched the knight until the tediousness of the lengthy approach overwhelmed her. She leaped from her seat.

"Oh, for God's sake!" the Queen shouted. "Hurry the hell up!"

Momentarily stunned, the knight's eyes darted from left to right, as if looking for something—anything—to remove him from the spotlight. No new actor took the stage. Why would they? No one *volunteers* for the gallows, and the bets were on at the back of the court that this is where the old boy was headed afore long.

Before the Queen could yell again, the knight ran. Not a manly, athletic stride, but instead taking diminutive, dainty steps that clattered across the hall. His ruffled, accordion-like collar bounced in tandem with the ringlets of curled hair that rested on his shoulders. Attempting to stop, he slid on the polished floor, ending precariously close to the foot of the dais where the Queen held court.

He removed his broad hat and bowed, taking care not to let the massive yellow ogril—a fantastically ugly bird—feather tickle his nose. "My Queen."

His voice put one in mind of a lecherous opossum.

The Queen stared down at the bald spot on the crown of the man's head. Men with long hair were either young or pretending not to go bald.

"Well?" the Queen demanded.

Still mid-bow, the knight looked up through his eyebrows. "My Queen?"

He was lost, the poor dolt. It was a quick trip to the neck-lengthening machine for sure.

"Well, what news do you bring, Sir Drake?" The Queen sat back down and examined her polished fingernails. "What did your privateering profit our kingdom?"

The man's name was Walleford, not Drake. But of course, *he* wasn't going to mention it.

"Your Majesty," Drake said, rising from his bow with an audible creak. "My crew damaged several Duluthian (the filthy, disloyal dogs) commercial vessels. An Ekedian medium freighter was captured and rechristened, *Queen's Iris.*"

"What a terrible name." The Queen scowled. A silence fell over the throne room, indeed, most agreed that the name was terrible.

The Queen's eyes bulged and she shouted, "Well?"

"Ah, yes, the cargo." Drake made another flourishing bow and announced, "I bring back a full hold of data pad connector ports."

"Connector ports!" yelled the Queen, rising to her feet again, her face flushed with anger. Most justified, may her kindness of heart and virtuous character live forever.

"They're very nice," offered Drake. "They work with the newer models. You see, they changed the connectors and—"

The Queen threw her arms wide and let them drop to her side with a muffled slap. "Well this is a real kick in the balls!" She looked out at the queue of privateers waiting to report their prizes. "Does anyone have anything I can *use* against the Dultuth Empire? There's a war on for God's sake!"

Several of the foppish privateers shook their heads. Others ducked behind ornamental statues and suits of armor, hoping not to be noticed. A few offered brief descriptions of their holds, but with their hands covering their mouths, just to be safe.

"I've obtained parts and technical schematics," said one.

The Queen's face brightened.

"They're for a proprietary model of food replicators," the privateer added. "Probably not at all useful for warfare."

The Queen's face darkened again. It was a good strategy, covering the mouth so as to prevent the Queen from knowing exactly who was talking. Had the speaker in question not done so, that fellow would be hanging already.

Sensing an impending incident, another mass-purge of the royal navy, and after he'd just gotten it re-organized, the Minister of Space hurried towards the throne, his high heeled boots clicking furiously.

"Your Highness," he called, trying to ward off another burst of outrage. "Your Highness! Your Highness!" He waved at the Queen, trying to gain her attention.

"Minister Triller!" the Queen snapped. "Why are your privateers bringing me cargo holds full of the sort of rubbish I could find in the alley behind my palace? This is war! I need munitions. Particle blasters. Food supplies. Raw materials. Not data-pad adapters and cheap Kranowan-made plastic trinkets!"

"Of course, Your Majesty," Minister Triller wheezed, reaching the foot of the throne and bowing so low that his broad, floppy maroon hat brushed against his boots. He stood up and hitched a thumb at the knight now known as Sir Drake, to indicate it was time for him to leave the Queen's presence.

Drake scurried back to the crowd, holding down his hat to keep it from flying off his head.

"Your Majesty," Minister Triller began anew, "we *all* agree with you that these materials would be a far greater prize to your armies."

"Of course they would! So why don't I have them?"

"It's a matter of control, Your Highness." Triller considered his next words. "The Dultuth (the disloyal, filthy dogs) armada has control of the galaxy's primary shipping lanes. Our brave privateers venture as close as possible, but only skinflint space Leftenants trading on thin margins use the outlying currents. Cheap cargo demands cheap rates, and Emperor Balland (may the oath-breaker be cursed) has levied quite the toll for use of the great lanes."

"So you're telling me," the Queen said, eying her minister with suspicious derision, "that not a *single* privateer Leftenant is willing to slip into the main currents to strike at the heart of our enemy?"

"I ... could ask." Minister Triller called over his shoulder, "Is there a volunteer?"

A dry cough was the only reply.

Triller turned back to the Queen. "The Dultuth fleet is too overwhelming. The risk too high. No man would dare..."

Another cough, this one less dry, echoed loudly from the gallery in the rear of the throne room. The crowd of people attending the court parted at the sound of this interruption, revealing a young Leftenant (spelled thus because a former prince could only spell phonetically, and no one wished to correct him) of the Queen's Royal Army, standing resplendent in his blue velvet uniform.

"Your most merciful pardons," the Leftenant said. "But there *is* one man who would do it, if given the chance."

The Queen settled herself into her throne and smiled sweetly. When the dashing young Leftenant didn't elaborate quickly enough, the warm look quickly hardened. "Well, get him going! Maybe he can show the rest of these spineless ninnies what it means to captain a ship-of-the-line. Give the man the frigate *Widower*. That's a forty blaster-cannon ship, is not, Minister Triller?"

"It is indeed, your Majesty."

The Leftenant drew his face tight, his lips a horizon, neither smiling nor frowning. "There may be … some, uh, complications."

"What is your name?" asked the Queen.

The officer bowed. "Majesty, I am Leftenant Jack Smith of the Seventh Royal Dragoons."

"Well, Leftenant Smith. If the matter is, indeed, complicated … then un-complicate it!" The Queen demanded, her color reddening dangerously once again.

"For heaven's sake!" shouted Minister Triller, alarmed at the Queen's outburst. "Remove yourself from here immediately young man, and do the bidding of your Queen!" He fluttered his fingers. "Shoo! Shoo!"

Leftenant Smith departed at speed. A significant breach of court protocol.

* * *

There were eighteen offenses against the Runykian Empire that Roderick Langston was technically guilty of. Some of them, like carrying an unregistered blasterbuss, called for the death penalty. Roderick was himself aware of seven of eighteen, but had entered the great royal port because, as a pirate, he'd built a career on getting away with things. He never paid parking tickets, he always sneaked into the theater, he would sneak out of restaurants before the check came, sling subtle, witty insults and then change the subject before the victim could reply and, of course, the larceny, looting, murder, and general terror associated with the pirate class.

Though he had no personal motto, he did have a notebook full of possible slogans to paint on the hull of the next ship he stole. All of them, may it suffice to say, were intentionally ironic and incorrigible.

"Un-bloody believable," Roderick grumbled bitterly to the stone floor of his prison cell.

He had been arrested for one of the offenses he was unaware were offenses. Upon arrival in Port Royal in Runyki, he strolled about, hands in pockets, looking for a ship to steal, jauntily whistling *God Save the Queen*.

A junior man in the loyalty brigade heard this, and arrested Roderick on the spot. The Queen, an avowed atheist, hated that song.

And so there Roderick lay, face down on the floor of a cell. He had been in that position for hours, though since he'd fallen asleep for a time, he couldn't say with certainty how many. But from the way his ribs, hips, and thighs throbbed, he guessed it had been several. Which meant that the guards would be here soon to turn off the stasis field that pinned him against the cold stone floor and then move him from his stomach to his side.

Royal guards of the Queen's dungeon enjoyed kicking prisoners in the ribs with pointy-toed boots. They would take large bites out of the crusts served to their captives, chew them, and spit the masticated result in the tin mug of water. But one thing they would not do—would not tolerate—was allow a prisoner to develop bed sores. They weren't uncivilized Dultuths, after all (the filthy disloyal dogs).

The heavy door to his cell clanked, and then creaked open. This should be the guards. Roderick mentally prepared the choreographed movements required to achieve escape. He slid his eyes sideways as far as he could, his forehead still pinned to the floor, and caught a disheartening glimpse. His face fell in disappointment, or would have, if it could. Instead of his regular guards, the same loyalty brigade man who'd had him hauled in had arrived. Behind *that* ninny was a handsome Leftenant in a blue velvet uniform.

"What do you think of our Queen now?" the loyalty brigade man demanded, no doubt seeking to set a trap.

"I think she's swell," Roderick replied.

The brigade man drew back, defeated. He scowled and pouted. His best interrogation stratagem was soundly defeated. Looking at the Leftenant, he said, "Well, I guess that's that. He's all yours Leftenant Smith."

The loyalty brigade man turned to leave.

"Why do you ask?" Roderick prodded. "Do *you* think otherwise?"

The brigade man froze, his face a twisted mask of surprise. This the man hadn't expected. "Me? No! I—I…"

"Because it's rumored among the prisoners—all of whom despise the Queen, except for me of course, is that *you*—what's your name?"

"Jack Lipper."

"That *you*, Jack Lipper, always ask that question because you're seeking a sympathetic conspirator that shares your distaste of Her Majesty!"

Jack Lipper gasped. "Heaven forbid! They say that?" He turned to Leftenant Smith. "It's not true! Don't arrest me for this! It's not true!"

"Bring in the guards," Smith replied, rolling his eyes. "And not for you," he added. "For this pirate. He is to be released to me."

Jack Lipper nodded urgently and left the room.

"Let free?" asked Roderick, still frozen in place, his eyes darting about excitedly.

"Conditionally," Smith agreed with a nod.

"Oh."

In that case, Roderick intended to carry on with his own plan to escape the prison.

Two guards bustled into the room, their swords and keys and various other paraphernalia jingling like Christmas bells. One of the guards went to the stasis controls while the other, the jinglier of the two, stood over the prisoner.

"Fasten that loose belt," Leftenant Smith ordered. "You sound like a horse-drawn sleigh."

Roderick sighed as the guard tightened his loose straps. His entire plan for escape had centered on that loose belt. The belt was everything. Heaven and Earth and all the currents of space could crumble and fall, so long as the belt remained loose. Roderick's plan, the best of laid plans, was bested by a simple adherence to dress code. Curse that Leftenant. Curse the lot of the Runykians.

The stasis field came down, releasing the pirate. Roderick was helped to his feet.

"Thank you. Well met, gentlemen." He nonchalantly made for the exit.

"Not so fast!" Both guards blocked his departure.

Roderick's eyes darted from the guard left to the guard right, and then to Leftenant Smith. "You mentioned conditions?"

Smith straightened himself and assumed a rigid, military posture. The Royal Academy was renowned for endowing its graduates with the best military posture in the galaxy.

"Condition the first," Smith began, holding up an index finger. "You enter the service of Her Majesty and put your … *considerable* skills as a pirate to use as one of her privateers. Depriving the Dultuth Empire (the disloyal and filthy dogs) of valuable wartime assets, preying on the primary galactic shipping lanes. You will be allowed to keep fifteen percent for yourself and your men. And Her Majesty will provide a suitable ship."

Roderick nodded. "What's condition the second?"

Smith held up a second finger, his posture still perfect. "Condition the second. Should you decline, your pending execution for high crimes against the Queen will be moved up from this Friday to…" Smith pulled out his gold pocket watch and examined it, "… now."

Roderick tilted his head, face thoughtful, as though considering his options. His eyes wandered to the guards, both of which leaned closer with an ominous jingle. "I'll take condition the first, in that event."

"There, you see," Smith said to the guards. "Pirates are not entirely without reason."

Holding up a hand, which was promptly slapped down by one of the guards, Roderick said, "You said something about a new ship?"

Turning on his heels with parade-ground precision, Smith said, "Follow me, pirate."

* * *

Port Royal buzzed with a mixed symphony of conversation, loud harangues, starship noise, peddlers barking about their wares to passersby, and loyalty brigade men asking, "What do you think of our Queen?"

The berth that Roderick Langston was taken to was secured by armed guards with blaster-muskets, bayonets attached. It was a relatively quiet enclosure, quiet enough that Roderick could hear the echoing footfalls of his boots along the gangway.

Together with Leftenant Smith and the two guards, they approached an enormous man-o-war. Forty heavy blaster cannons bristled from the gleaming alloy hull. A fine ship, it boasted a grand flying prow. Sleekly beautiful, the ship looked as though it would be just as comfortable in the water as in the currents of deep space. This was a vessel easily the equal of any ship in the service of the Dultuth fleet (the disloyal, filthy dogs).

With a sweep of his hand, Leftenant Smith said, "This, pirate, is your new ship. The H.M.S. TBD."

"TBD?" asked Roderick.

"To be determined. It's better not to name a ship than to pick a name Her Majesty doesn't fancy."

One of the guards made a slicing motion across his neck.

Roderick nodded in understanding. "What a woman."

"She is indeed," agreed Smith, who couldn't really say anything else. At least, not with the loyalty brigade about.

"So, this is *my* ship?" asked Roderick, pointing his fingers inwardly against his chest.

"Your ship with which you are to wage war against the enemies of the Queen, yes," Smith affirmed.

"The Dultuth?"

"The disloyal, filthy dogs, yes."

"But it's my ship. To do with as I like?"

Smith's brows knitted in annoyance. "Yes, pirate. It is."

Roderick clapped his hands together. "Very good."

The pirate surveyed the docks and saw a swarthy looking man walking down the gangway of a nimble cutter. Not much room for cargo in those, but very swift.

"You there!" called Roderick. "Come here, the Leftenant and I wish to palaver with you."

Reluctantly, the man joined them. "Listen, we're in Port Royal just for a top off and a drink. If this is about the Queen, we all think she's a sterling example of all that is right with humanity."

"Oh, of course," Roderick agreed.

"She's a marvelous credit to us," shouted Smith, so that anyone listening would hear this affirmation.

All grunted and harrumphed in agreement.

"You're the owner of that ship yonder?" asked Roderick, pointing to the cutter with its crew disembarking.

Turning around to eye the ship with pride, the man nodded. "I am."

"A fine vessel, it looks to be?" Roderick queried.

"She is…"

Smith gave a look that said plainly, "What in the devil!" He was very good at giving this look, receiving high marks at the academy.

"How much do you want for it?"

The cutter's owner rubbed his chin. "Oh, I don't know … it's my livelihood, it is."

"What if I traded you?" suggested Roderick. He pointed from the cutter to the great man-o-war behind them. "Your ship … for *this*?"

"By tugger, you're not serious."

"I am. It's my ship." Roderick's chest puffed out.. "Isn't it, Leftenant?"

"It is…" Smith began slowly.

Roderick waved a hand to end the discussion. "There, you see? Make your decision quickly or I'll find someone else."

"I … I mean, I'd be a madman not to take such an offer." The cutter's owner stared at the great ship before him. "How large a crew is required?"

"Oh, I don't know," said Roderick. "A hundred men? How many for your ship?"

"Just the eight of us."

"We'll trade then. You can have the crew of my ship, and I'll keep six of your men. Leftenant Smith shall be my seventh."

"Deal!" The cutter's owner stuck out his hand, and upon shaking, became the owner of the man-o-war's.

Roderick strolled down the dock toward his new ship. Smith, mouth agape, returned to his senses and gave chase.

"How could you give up that ship?" he demanded.

Smiling at his new prize, Roderick said, "This one's better."

Smith crossed his arms. "I don't see how!"

Roderick's smile became a resentful frown. "You wouldn't."

"No." Smith shook his head. "No, I won't go any further until this is resolved."

Roderick didn't stop. "That's fine. I'm sure the ship can be crewed sufficiently with only seven."

"And you can't leave, either!"

With a sigh, Roderick stopped and turned to the Leftenant. He pointed at the man-o-war towering behind them. "That ship will draw the attention of every gunboat in the entire Dultuth armada, disloyal, filthy dogs or not. But *this* ship…"

Comprehension dawned on Smith. "… will slide into the currents undetected."

"Detected, but not suspected," Roderick corrected.

"If we're going to impress the Queen, we'd better make a big splash."

"You have something in mind, then?"

Roderick gave a sly grin. "It's simply chess, Leftenant Smith. And I know how to capture the king."

* * *

By stroke of coincidence, the newly acquired cutter was called *Queen's Iris*, which remained a terrible name. But as Captain Roderick Langston had no intention of keeping the vessel, he decided against rechristening it.

The crew of the *Iris* was for the most part amenable to serving under a new captain. The two human crewmen had always wanted to be pirates, and were excited for the chance. The remaining crew were androids, and of course *they* didn't care. Unless you programed them to care. And, that, nobody did. Why would they? Life is hard enough without programming your appliances to give you a hard time about doing their jobs, isn't it?

Queen's Iris was cruising through dead space, having just finished a week-long layover on a small asteroid popular with pirates, smugglers, and elderly tourists garbed in floral shirts. And while ship and crew seemed to be functioning just fine, Leftenant Smith was worried that his mission for the Queen would be a failure—very likely marking the end of his life—because of Captain Langston's constant detours. He was worried that, instead of the trade currents, their next stop would be a tropical vacation planet, or a museum of natural history.

At first Smith had been accommodating. *He* certainly wasn't a navy man, and so he gave Roderick the benefit of the doubt. But as the days passed without so much as a hint of the Dultuth (the disloyal, filthy dogs) he began to worry.

"Shouldn't we leave?"

"Have more rum?"

"We really should be going!"

"Have you met Gloria yet? She has a sister. Probably."

"I must insist we depart."

"Soon. Tomorrow, maybe."

Tomorrow had finally come, along with a promise that they would finally begin to prey on cargo ships. But how could Smith be sure that this objective was being undertaken? He was, after all, dealing with an incorrigible pirate. He decided to confront Roderick, and found him sitting on the bridge, spinning lazily—and perhaps somewhat drunkenly—in the captain's chair.

"Oh, hello, Smithy," he slurred.

He was joined by three ladies who looked to be of ill repute, all of whom Roderick brought with him from the asteroid. The attractive women seemed incapable of doing anything more than giggling. They were very popular with the crew.

"Yes. Hello." Smith looked around the room. All of the crew was present, except for the androids, who had already made their way up to the sailing deck. "I've come to ask whether—"

"We're going to steal from the Dultuth?" Roderick interrupted.

"Yes," said Smith. Quickly adding, "The disloyal—"

He clapped his hands and sprang from his chair, then sauntered over to Smith and draped an arm around him. "*That* is, in statement of fact, exactly what we'll do today. So sharpen your sword—"

"It already is."

"… load your pistol—"

"It's aimed at your spleen, even as we speak."

"… and prepare to go topside." Roderick pointed at the ceiling, indicating the exposed uppermost part of the ship known as the sailing deck. "Because we've arrived in Dultuth's space lane primeria, and no amount of filthies, disloyals, or dogs can change the fact, Leftenant, that from here on, it's death to any of the Queen's privateers."

Smith felt both pleased and apprehensive. "I suppose we ought to look for a ship."

"Already found one, mate. It's what we've been waiting for—though you certainly seemed intent on not enjoying our shore leave."

A chime sounded from the helm.

Roderick smiled. "That would be them."

"Who?" asked Smith, as the pirate rejoined the three women he'd brought aboard.

"Now ladies," Roderick said, ignoring the Leftenant, "everything as planned, and you'll never have to work another day in your life, though I can't make any guarantees about the nights."

The ladies tittered and crowded around the hailing console.

"On screen," Roderick said cheerfully. He patted Smith on the shoulder. "Watch this."

Smith watched with great interest as the women chattered at a blushing and excited Dultuth helmsman. The women were doing all in their power to be invited aboard. Smith looked at Roderick, and saw that he was mouthing phrases the ladies were employing, like a playwright looking on from the wings as the performers brought his work to life.

"Oh…" Roderick mouthed silently, even affecting the seemingly spontaneous burst of giggles. "We've never been on a real Dultuthian ship before."

Smith shook his head, but Roderick didn't seem to care as he continued on, mouthing, "Won't you *please* have us over? We'll be ever so glad you did."

Naturally, the helmsmen readily agreed. Space is a lonely place, and with the exception of the starry mer-folk one might come across while traveling the galactic currents, almost entirely bereft of women. The delighted pirate smiled broadly, revealing a gold tooth just behind his canine. Bicuspids are so often overlooked.

The transmission to the Dultuth (the disloyal, filthy dogs) ended. Roderick applauded the women enthusiastically. "Bravo, ladies. Bravo."

The women bowed, looking pleased with themselves at their performance.

"And now, let us all go topside," Roderick said, swirling his finger in the air with a flourish. "We'll imagine the galactic winds in our hair, maybe spy a dwarf whale, and … add a rather large and important ship to our little fleet."

Smith followed the pirate towards the lift that led to the open-air sailing deck. "What's to stop them from just asking the women aboard and leaving us here?"

Roderick was ready for this question. "We'll say they're our sisters. No one likes to split up a family. It's rude."

"In spite of the fact that none of us look remotely similar? Two of those girls have green skin and the third is nine feet tall!"

Roderick stopped and with both hands on the Leftenant's shoulders looked him in the eyes. "There are two rules I live by: 'You'll probably get away with it' and 'People are idiots.'"

Smith stared back, unblinking. "That is, without a doubt, the worst philosophy of life I've ever heard."

Shrugging his shoulders, Roderick said, "The galaxy is yet to prove me wrong."

* * *

For many years, the brightest minds of the most advanced planets in the galaxy maintained that it was impossible to survive in space without protection. These people were, of course, idiots. History's laughingstocks. This is why the expression "You can't breathe in space" is used whenever someone is utterly and completely wrong about something, but won't admit it. The galactic currents that carry starships along at very fast, almost unbelievable speeds, are quite nice. The air is warm and tinged with the subtle scent of sea salt.

Now, *getting* to these currents was a different matter. The patches of dead space that surrounded most planets were like deserts between oceans. And going out into those would result in the lung-bursting oxygen-deprived death those old scolds always banged on about. In fact, it was a suicidal merchant marine who first discovered that the currents, which had been used for centuries, were entirely habitable. The excitement of this discovery rekindled his will to live, and had the merchant marine running back inside the airlock to tell the rest of his crew. Ironically, he was eaten by a space slug two days later.

After the discovery, ships were redesigned to have top decks where sailors could play shuffleboard, watch the various space creatures swimming alongside their ships, and spit big, juicy, wet ones over the side. That was exactly what most of the crew—except for the androids—were doing.

The Dulturhians (the disloyal, filthy dogs) wasted no time extending a ramp from their massive frigate—the biggest any of them had ever seen—to the smaller *Queen's Iris*. Four sailors waited at the top of the ramp for the girls. The rest of the crew busied themselves with their laser rifles, taking shots at the nebula porpoises that jumped and swam through the currents. These creatures were endangered, but that didn't bother anyone. They were hideously ugly, with pale yellow eyes and a nose that looked like several moldy links of blood sausage flopping about everywhere. If you saw one, you wouldn't be able to help *but* shoot at it.

Roderick followed the three women toward the ramp, and Smith, who, despite trying, could think of nothing better to do, did the same. This wasn't how the Leftenant imagined a daring privateer raid would go. He had purchased new rope with which he thought to swing from ship to ship, and that now proved to be a complete waste of money. It was very nice rope, too.

"Not so fast, Leftenant." Roderick gently pushed Smith back. "You'll give away the game."

Smith looked indignant. "I will not. Why?"

Fingering a gold button on Smith's blue velvet uniform, Roderick said, "Because you're still dressed up like one of the Queen's bloody men."

"I thought you said people were idiots? That we'd probably get away with it."

Roderick scowled. "Well there are limits, obviously."

Smith shook his head. "I'm not letting you go alone."

Roderick whistled, and the five android crewmembers trudged towards them in that joyless way all robotics walk. "I'll have the androids come along, we'll say they're the girls' brothers, too."

Smith waved an exasperated arm at the approaching machines. "They have ghost-white skin, yellow eyes, and circuit boards sticking out where their chest hair ought to be!"

The androids were a budget model, though that was hardly their fault, and therefore not very nice.

"People are idiots," Roderick soothed him. "We'll get away with it."

"Oh? But my waistcoat, cummerbund, breeches and stockings? *Those* we won't get away with?"

"Precisely."

The sailors were very much taken with the three ladies, who were first up the ramp. They effusively complimented the women's earlobes, which was quite a welcome bit of praise, as a woman rarely has her earlobes given their due. They showed deferential respect for big brother Roderick, shaking his hand and clearing their throats, offering repetitious assurances.

"Pleasure."

"Pleasure, ahurm."

"Pleasure."

"Ahurm, pleasure."

And so it went. The sailors, kept busy shaking hands and announcing their pleasure by Roderick, didn't notice the androids, with Smith concealing himself in their midst, boarding.

They had gotten away with it. Roderick and Smith were of different minds as far as what needed to happen next, and it was Smith who took action first. Leaping from amid the androids, he brandished his sword and shouted, "Have at you, Dultuth!"

The sailors drew their weapons and prepared to meet his challenge, only to hesitate when Smith motioned that he wasn't finished.

"… you disloyal, filthy dogs," he concluded.

The sailors still hesitated, unsure of their next move. They didn't want to interrupt the young soldier again.

Smith wave his sword with a bit of a flourish and reassured the sailors. "Thank you, no, that's it. We can begin."

A fantastic clanging of energy swords echoed across the deck. The ladies scattered into hiding and Smith chased the sailors, who, to be fair, were very good at sailing, but lousy at sword fighting, all around the deck. As he did so, he punctuated his every thrust and parry with a loud, "Ha!" or "Ho-ho!"

He really was enjoying himself.

The fun, sadly, couldn't last. Though the sailors were unskilled at swordplay, there were a lot of them. And as alarms on the sailing deck wailed, more sword-wielding space sailors joined the swelling throng looking to run Leftenant Smith through.

"Ha ha!" *Clang!* Smith parried an oncoming attack. He saw the growing number of sailors and then looked to the crowd of androids milling about by the ramp. "Come on, then! Fight for your Queen!"

The androids made no reply. They were engaged in calculating the likelihood that when all was said and done, *they* would be the ones having to clean up the mess.

Smith looked for Roderick, who was nowhere to be seen. A sailor swung a club, and he jumped backward and kicked the man in the face. "Ho-ha!"

More sailors pushed forward until it didn't seem to matter how many ha-ohs or parries Smith gave. They were closing with such numbers that the skill gap had been erased. The Leftenant couldn't last forever like this.

As it happened, he wouldn't need to. His headlong plunge into fighting turned out to be exactly the distraction Roderick needed.

"All right!" the pirate shouted from the lift opening at the rear of the deck. "Now everyone, off my ship!"

The sailors turned and discovered why that seemingly insane command was actually quite reasonable. Roderick stood with his blasterbuss held against the head of the king of the Dultuth Empire, the worst of the disloyal, filthy dogs himself.

"Please!" begged the king. "Do what he says! What good's an empire if I'm not around to run it?"

As his logic was unassailable, the sailors dropped their weapons.

"That's right!" Smith crowed, pointing the tip of his blade toward the ramp. "Everyone off—off the ship?"

"Yes," Roderick confirmed. "*My* ship."

Smith let his sword hang down at his side. "But you already have a ship."

Roderick regarded the *Queen's Iris*. "Yes, but that was just to get a really big ship. The biggest. And now I have it."

"You mean the *Queen* has it."

Roderick ignored that with aplomb and herded the king over to Smith. He said, somewhat dreamily, "All that lovely cargo space. I can plunder two or even three ships before having to return to port."

"Pirate," said Smith, "you still work for the Queen…"

This seemed to snap Roderick from his dreams. He motioned for Smith to take hold of the blasterbuss aimed at the King's head. "Here, take this."

"And do what with it?"

"Whatever you'd like," said Roderick with a bow. "Just so long as it's off my ship. It's chess, see? You've got the king, you win. And I'm free to do what I do best."

Smith stood firmly in place.

"Go on," said Roderick, shooing the Leftenant away. "Take the old dog to the Queen. She'll probably make you a general for your troubles."

"Not that!" shouted the King. "I left her once… I'll do it again!"

Still, Smith did not move.

But Roderick knew how to fix that. He reached into his belt to retrieve his other blasterbuss, and placing it against Smith's head, walked the Leftenant over to the androids, who gripped him tightly and returned him to the cutter and left him.

Roderick, the androids, and the girls, sailed away in their new ship.

Which would not be named *Queen's Iris*.

ABOUT JASON ANSPACH

Jason Anspach is a bestselling author living in Tacoma, Washington, with his wife and their pirate crew of seven (not a typo) children. In addition to works of Science Fiction, Jason is the author of the hit comedy-paranormal-historical-detective series, *'til Death*. Jason loves his family as well as hiking and camping throughout the beautiful Pacific Northwest. And Star Wars. He named as many of his kids after Obi Wan as possible. And he knows Han shot first.

You can learn more about Jason and get a free short story, by visiting his website: http://www.JasonAnspach.com.

JUST DRIVE

by Will McIntosh

THEY STRETCHED OUT THE WORDS AS THEY SANG, GOING overboard to show me they weren't rushing, even though standing in that kitchen was so not safe it was ridiculous.

As they brought the song home in their New York-Italian accents, I realized that when you got down to it, "Happy Birthday" is a terrible song. The tune sucks, and the words are empty and repetitive. I blew out the candles quickly, just wanting to get out of there. No wish, because all wishes were pointless except for one, and that one wasn't going to come true no matter how hard I blew.

"Somebody get the plates," Aunt Marie said.

"What do we need plates for?" Uncle Joey gestured at the table. "They're cookies. You pick them up and you eat them."

"It's a *party*, for God's sake," Marie shot back.

Mom opened cabinets until she hit on the one holding the plates. She grabbed a few, began shoving them at people. "Here."

I hadn't wanted to stop for the party. Standing in some long-dead stranger's dusty kitchen only reminded me of how fucked up everything was, and I didn't need any more reminders of that.

I took my cookies and headed down the hallway. If we were going to risk our lives to eat cookies, I might as well take advantage of it to have some alone-time. I missed solitude. Once it had been such a simple thing, to close a door or walk into the woods. Now I was lucky if I got to be alone for three minutes a month.

There was makeup in the bathroom—a dozen lipsticks, mascara, the whole arsenal. Picking a lipstick at random, I ran it over my lips, enjoying the familiar gliding sensation. I leaned in so my face was close to the dirty mirror, studied my lips before sticking the lipstick in my back pocket.

Something had to give. I was so tired of being terrified, so sick of my relatives, of not sleeping, and eating stale food out of dead people's pantries. But nothing was going to give. Nothing was going to change, unless you counted things getting worse as change.

Out in the living room, the walkie-talkie crackled to life. "We've got hostiles north of Route Nine, between Chester and Fifty-Four, heading south-southwest toward Elberton. Repeat, hostiles north of—"

I sprinted for the exit, ending up right on Uncle Joey's heels with Mom and Marie right behind me.

As soon as I was outside I could hear them. It was the high-pitched buzzing of their vegetation teeth, not the lower drone of their meat-eating teeth, but they could switch them out in the time it took me to kiss my ass goodbye.

We'd backed the SUV right up to the house and left the doors open. I scrambled through my assigned door—rear right—and dove into the far back as the SUV roared to life. We peeled across the lawn, thumped over the curb and swung left, away from the sound of the buzztops.

Out the back window, I could see the leaves on a big oak tree quiver like it was being pushed by a bulldozer. Suddenly it slammed to the ground like the bulldozer had found the sweet spot and flattened it.

I caught a glimpse of the termite that had taken it down—black and gold, its skin like mottled stone—before we screeched around the corner.

I had constant nightmares about their mouths, if you could call them that, sliding along the ground at the end of tube-shaped snouts, row after row of shiny silver-gray teeth disappearing into the darkness of their throats.

Eight or nine buzztops chased our SUV, no two shaped quite the same. As we accelerated, the buzztops fell behind.

Were they disappointed when people got away? Were they even *alive*? Or were they machines? Even after dissecting a few the government hadn't been able to say for sure. They were like fat snouted logs with teeth running on a hundred tiny legs, swallowing every twig, every bug, every blade of grass, leaving nothing but concrete and dirt.

"Oh, *shit*!" Joey shouted, making me jump. I spun to face front just as Joey hit the brakes.

More buzztops, coming from the opposite direction.

Joey turned down a driveway, went around the side of the house and into the back yard, which was fenced in.

"Goddamn." Joey crashed right through the fence, sending splintered wood flying.

"*Watch out!*" Mom screamed. We were headed right for an in-ground pool filled with green water.

Joey yanked the wheel; the SUV fishtailed violently, then straightened. Out the side window I caught a glimpse of four buzztops pushing through the gap in the fence. They ignored the trees and grass. Meat always took priority.

"No, no, no," Joey cried. The space between this house and the next was filled by a huge eucalyptus tree, its branches all the way to the ground. Joey swung the SUV right, between the pool and the house.

One of the buzztops glided over the pool, mouth open wide, bearing down as we cut left, around the house. Smaller ones—the ones that swarmed into houses and cars and other cramped places to chew you up—poured out of its mouth as it tried to cut us off. They scurried after us, as Uncle Joey plowed over a bicycle lying beside the house before cutting across the front lawn to avoid a white van blocking the driveway. The little rats fell behind, and suddenly I felt bad for thinking about how sick I was of my relatives, because if one of those rats had gotten on the SUV it would have broken through the window and gone right to work chewing up whoever was closest.

* * *

We flew down the road, the land outside a desert—nothing but collapsed buildings and dirt, chewed-up telephone lines laying in tangles along the side of the road because telephone poles are made of wood, and buzztops eat wood.

"Jesus. Did they do that on purpose, sending two swarms from opposite directions?" Marie asked.

"Nah," Joey said. "They're dumb bastards. We just got unlucky."

"Maybe they're getting smarter," Marie said.

Joey waved a dismissive hand. "They're not getting smarter."

"How do *you* know?" Marie said.

"Why would they suddenly get smarter? They've been doing the same thing for four months, day and night. Suddenly they're gonna get smarter?"

"Why not?"

As my pulse slowed from heart-attack territory back to its post-invasion racing normal, I turned, slid down my seat in the wayback until I was lying down, and propped one foot on the window. The three of them used to bicker about how much salt to put in the spaghetti sauce; now they bickered about which way to go to avoid being eaten.

I reached out, touched the photo of my late best friend Rachel that was taped to the seat back, along with a dozen other photos and a small mirror. I missed Rachel. I missed having in-jokes with someone, missed being in constant phone contact. I missed my room. Even with all of my most important shit laid out and taped up around me, the back of an SUV wasn't much of a substitute for a room.

I sat up and looked out the window. The stripped landscape went on and on as far as I could see. There wasn't much left for them to eat. Would the buzztops leave when they were finished gobbling up everything that wasn't able to run, or would they stay until they'd hunted down every last scrap of fleeing meat? Nobody knew. Not that it mattered. If they took everything, we'd all starve to death after they left anyway. We were probably a month or two away from that.

All we could do was keep driving and hope we didn't run into too many cloudy days in a row, so the SUV's solar battery stayed charged. We always had a destination in mind, were always chasing some new rumor of a place the buzztops couldn't reach that would accept refugees. It was all a pipe dream, though. The few safe places were barricaded, not just against the buzztops but to avoid being overrun by refugees. The rest of the places weren't safe. So we kept driving, because you can't outrun buzztops on foot.

And besides, the people locked in those bunkers were going to run out of food eventually anyway. We were all going to die.

Static burst from the walkie talkie, then a male voice. "Anybody out there?"

"Here, I'll take it." I held out my hand, and Mom gave me the walkie. I'd talk to anyone who didn't have the same last name as me. Even a stranger I would never meet.

I held down the reply button. "Hey there, fellow refugee. What's up?"

From the front seat, Joey called, "Follow protocol. You say 'over' when you're done talking—"

"Joey, leave her alone," Mom said.

I pressed the walkie close to my ear, trying to hear over their yakking.

"Who am I talking to?" the voice asked. He sounded young.

"Carrie Sardonopoli. Who are you?"

"Marcus Abreu. Nice to meet you, Carrie. Is that Carrie with a K, or a C?"

"A C," I said. "Why, you planning to write me a letter? Maybe send an email?"

Marcus broke out laughing. "You never know. Where you headed, Carrie?"

"Colorado Springs. There's a huge underground installation there. Steel doors, a food supply. Or so my uncle says."

"Colorado Springs. That's a looong way," Marcus said.

Uncle Joey slowed as they passed a tank in the road, its hatch open.

"Well, we don't have any pressing engagements to get to. My school is on permanent summer break, since all of the teachers were eaten and all."

Marcus laughed again. "Hey, what a coincidence. All of my teachers were eaten, too."

"How old are you?" I pulled the lipstick from my pocket, twisted the cap with one hand.

"Sixteen. What about you?"

"Hey, major coincidence. Same here. In fact, today's my birthday."

Marcus sang Happy Birthday while Mom laughed, and Joey complained that we were running down the batteries. Not that we didn't have a crate of replacements in the back, more than enough to last until the end of the world.

When Marcus finished, he said, "That's a terrible song."

"Isn't it? I was just thinking that."

Marcus was with his sister and a friend. They'd been out of town at a swim meet the day the invaders came. As far as they knew, their parents were dead. They were heading toward the Pacific, to see if they could locate a boat that had been overlooked that was fast enough to outrun buzztops. They were dreaming.

They were also headed in the opposite direction from me. My spirits plunged; talking to Marcus was the best time I'd had in months. Evidently Marcus was enjoying it as well, because we went on talking as the signal weakened.

"At least my mom got forty-six years of a normal life," I said softly, hoping Mom couldn't hear. "We got sixteen. Now I get to spend the time I have left stuffed in the back of an SUV, listening to my relatives argue. I may never sleep in a bed again."

"Life is screwing us over. Sometimes when I'm at my darkest, I wonder if I'd be better off if the termite—" Marcus's voice faded into static.

"What was that? I didn't hear the end."

"I can—" his voice faded out, then returned. "—you, either."

"Shit," I said under my breath. I'd give anything to be able to go on talking to him, even for just another hour. I pressed the reply button. "Good luck. I wish we'd had a chance to meet."

"—too. Happy—" I only caught a snippet, but I got the gist. *Me too. Happy Birthday.*

"Bye." I set the walkie talkie on the seat beside me and tried not to cry. If I'd been alone I would have, but the last thing I needed was my uncle mocking me, or worse yet, attempting to console me.

How could you have any sort of life if you could never stop anywhere for more than a few minutes?

"Man, what I wouldn't give for a hamburger right now," Uncle Joey said. "Medium rare, mustard and mayo. A thick slice of onion on top."

"Don't talk about food," Mom said.

"Hey, I don't get to eat any good food any more. Don't tell me I can't talk about it, either. This ain't Russia."

I closed my eyes, stuck my fingers in my ears and tried to go to sleep. But I couldn't. I kept thinking about Marcus. What did he look like? Actually, I didn't even care that much what he looked like.

"What kind of name is Abreu?" I called, interrupting the argument.

"Hispanic," Uncle Joey said. "There was a ballplayer named Bobby Abreu. Good player. He skin was medium-well. South American or something."

Medium-well. Lovely. He was going to talk about food one way or another.

I wondered if we were better off heading back toward the coast as well. It was sunny on the coast, so less risk of a string of cloudy days depleting the SUV's solar battery. When you got down to it, though, fast ships weren't much safer than cars. You could see buzztops coming, and they couldn't corner you on some dead end, but if your ship broke down, you couldn't just run to find a replacement. You were a sitting duck if you couldn't get the boat running again.

Those were the only real options: ship, car, steel bunker. Even if you stayed close to your vehicle, staying still out in the world was not an option. You didn't always get a warning that buzztops were headed your way.

* * *

I woke as the SUV slowed. It was dark out.

"I almost hit him," Joey said, rolling down his window.

A guy in military fatigues bent to talk to Uncle Joey through the window. "Man, am I glad to see you. I broke down. Can you take me somewhere I can find a replacement?"

"You got it." Joey gestured toward the back door.

The guy climbed in. His name was Tyler. Mid-thirties, heavy reddish beard, wide, beefy face. After introductions he asked the standard question. "Where you headed?"

"Colorado Springs," Aunt Marie said. She always sounded kind of angry, even when she was saying the most mundane thing. "We heard there's a secure installation there, with—" she trailed off, because Tyler was shaking his head.

"Don't bother. Cheyenne Mountain is sealed tight. Half the politicians in the country are holed up there. The ones who survived the first days, anyway. Unless you're all related to the President, they'll shoot you before they let you inside."

"You military?" Uncle Joey asked. I could see his dark, deep-set eyes in the rear-view mirror.

"Ex. Marines. But my rank's nowhere near high enough to get me into Cheyenne."

"You tried?" Mom asked.

Tyler nodded. "Hard."

"You know any more about what's going on than what we got on the news, before communication went dark?" Joey asked.

Tyler grinned. "I might." He unzipped a pouch on his pack, pulled out a phone pad. "And seeing as how you were kind enough to save my ass, I'm willing to share. Not that it'll help you stay alive, but it's damned interesting." He called up a video, handed the player up to Marie. She held it so Joey could see as well. All I could see from where I was sitting was that the video was shot outdoors in the daytime, and was shaky and amateurish.

"What is this?" Uncle Joey asked.

Tyler waited a beat before answering. "That's what's on the other side of the portals."

I just about crawled over the seat, trying to see the screen as people shouted in surprise. "Let me see. Pass it back here." My heart was thudding. Someone had seen the other side, where the buzztops, and the gigantic whale-things that carried the buzztops, came from? It must be a horror show, something out of my nightmares. I wanted to see.

"That was filmed from this side," Tyler said as Aunt Marie and Uncle Joey watched, with Mom looking over their shoulders. "You can't take a camera through." I was just about to climb over the seat when Aunt Marie finally passed the pad back to Tyler. He re-queued the video and handed it to me.

The video was looking down from a height, onto a huge city winding along a river. The buildings were ink-black, hundreds of stories tall, and were connected to each other so they look like one huge, twisting maze. It reminded me of an endless factory. Either there were no windows, or it was all windows. It was hard to say which. Silver lines that looked like mercury rising and falling in old-fashioned thermometers snaked in all directions, moving around and through the buildings. They must be how the aliens moved around.

The city was surrounded on three sides by wilderness. There was an uninterrupted mat of tightly-woven green and black vegetation, and jutting out of it were trees topped with black and purple canopies as big as hot-air balloons. It was terrifying, and beautiful. My throat clenched as I tried to swallow.

"This was made by a special forces platoon that eventually went through. They were hoping to send a nuke through, but they couldn't even bring their rifles," Tyler said as I rewatched the video. "You can't get anything metal or plastic through. It's like they've got a one-way filter to protect them from just the sort of attack we were contemplating."

I couldn't take my eyes off the screen. A river passed through the city under arches, the water blue-green like the sky on one side, but where it flowed out, where it was wider, it ran red. I thought I saw the tiniest of specks moving around, but it may have been my imagination; and if not the footage was shot at too far a distance to make them out.

"Who lives there? The buzztops?" I asked.

Tyler shook his head. "The buzztops just transport materials through the portals—the things in charge walk on two legs. Based on what our analysts saw, their best guess is they import food and raw materials from the outside so they can keep their world pristine."

The SUV slowed. "I guess we're not going to Colorado Springs. So where are we headed?" When no one answered, Joey glanced back at Tyler. "Where are *you* headed?"

"To find my family. Then, I'm not sure. I'm thinking of going the cave route."

I'd never liked the thought of hiding in a cave. You had to go deep, with ropes and flashlights, because the buzztops swept caves and subway tunnels close to the surface. While you were on your way down you just had to pray no buzztops showed up. Plus it was cold down there, and there was no food except what you brought down with you. Unless you wanted to eat bats. Definitely not my thing. Not that driving around trying to outrun them forever was my thing.

I cleared my throat. "We should head for the coast." One direction was as good as another; why not head in the same direction as Marcus?

"We tried that," Marie shot back.

"You have a better idea?" I asked.

Marie twisted in her seat to glare at me. "Sweetie, you can have a vote when you're eighteen."

"Hey," Mom said to Marie. "Don't talk to her like that. She has just as much right to an opinion as you."

While Tyler sat looking out the window, the other three supposed adults in the SUV argued about whether I was a full voting member of the vehicle. The argument then drifted into where we should go. In the end we dropped Tyler off at a house with a working SUV, then headed back toward the coast, because just as I'd suspected, no one had a better plan.

* * *

"Anyone out there? Marcus, can you hear me?" I let go of the *talk* button and waited. Nothing.

Before the invasion, it hadn't bothered me that I was still a virgin. A lot of my friends weren't. Rachel wasn't, after her family took a month-long trip to London and Rachel met a Dutch guy named Henrich there. But I hadn't been eager to rush into the world of birth control and hoping my period came. School and swimming and life in general had seemed stressful enough. Not that, in retrospect, any of those things seemed even mildly stressful now. Now, though, I wondered how I would ever conceivably have sex. Getting naked in a bed in a house would be suicidal. The alternative was to have sex with someone in a moving vehicle, while a third person drove said vehicle. That was out of the question. There was also the question of how I might meet and get to know this guy who would be my first. How many guys around my age were even still alive?

Which got me thinking about Marcus. He might well be my last chance; the last kind, funny, interesting guy I'd meet before the buzztops got me. Or him.

I tried the walkie again. "Can anyone hear me? Marcus?"

The walkie crackled to life. "Carrie! Carrie, Carrie, Carrie!" It was Marcus. "Hey everyone, Carrie's back!" I heard his friends cheering in the background, which made me feel incredibly good.

"I thought you were headed for Colorado."

"We talked to someone who'd been there. Dead end."

"I'm sorry. But honestly, also kind of glad. It's good to hear your voice again."

"Yours, too!" I said.

"I wish I could see you. Hey, what road are you on?"

I looked for signs out the window. I never paid attention to what road we were on. We stayed off the Interstates. When you ran into buzztops, the more directions you had to flee in, the better. "What road are we on?" I called.

"Route Twenty," Joey said. "We just passed the turnoff for Route Seventy-Five."

When I relayed this to Marcus, he whooped into the phone. "You're fifteen miles behind us! We'll slow down. See if you can get your uncle to speed up."

"Uncle Joey?" I called.

"I heard him." The SUV picked up speed.

I ducked below seat level, into my "room" and checked my face in the mirror taped to the seat back. I definitely needed work. I brushed my hair, reapplied the lipstick from my back pocket, my palms sweaty.

It was silly for me to be nervous. All I was going to be able to do was wave to him. Still, it was the closest thing to a date I was probably ever going to manage.

* * *

"White Lincoln Sunburst," Uncle Joey called.

I leaped up, peered out the windshield. There it was, disappearing around a curve in the road, a few hundred yards ahead.

I grabbed the walkie. "I see you."

"I see you, too." The Sunburst eased partway onto the shoulder. "Pull up beside us?"

"When we catch up, pull up beside them," I called to Uncle Joey.

"Yeah, yeah."

My heart was in my throat as we closed ground, which was stupid, but I couldn't help it. We pulled beside the Sunburst.

A guy with a broad face, Asian-looking eyes and the cutest smile waved from the rear window, a walkie-talkie in his hand. He brought the walkie to his face.

"Can you tell from over there that I'm gawking at you like a moron? I'm hoping you can't."

I grinned like an idiot, unable to think of a reply. Up front, Joey muttered something about guys and their corny lines. If I hadn't currently been using the walkie I would have thrown it at his head.

I pressed the reply button. "You gonna ask me to the prom now, or what?"

He raised his free hand where I could see it and snapped his fingers. "I forgot my tux. How about a walk on the beach?"

Uncle Joey sped up, tucked their SUV in front of the Sunburst. "Okay, that's enough. Last thing we need is to get in a head-on collision because you want to flirt."

I could feel myself turning red from a mix of embarrassment and rage. "I'm not *flirting*." This was hell, having my relatives hear every word I spoke. It was impossible to have even one normal moment.

"Sounds good to me," I said to Marcus. "I could use a little time away from this clown car."

"Hey," Marie turned in her seat. "Joey's the one busting your chops. Don't blame it on me."

"I'm not busting her chops," Joey said. "I'm just saying I don't want to get us all killed."

"It's a date, then," Marcus said over the walkie. I could just barely see his profile through the reflections of trees and buildings on the glass of the Sunburst.

I released the button and handed the walkie up to the front. "We pass a car once a *day*, if that. You could have driven beside them for an hour and we wouldn't have risked an accident."

"We're not going to the beach," Joey said. "Being at the beach is like backing ourselves against a wall."

"You can drop me off and drive. I'm going."

The thought of taking a walk on the beach with a guy my age, listening to the ocean surf and seagull cries … it was worth risking what was left of my highly abbreviated life. I couldn't wait, and there was no way anyone was going to stop me.

Mom was contemplating telling me I couldn't do it. I could see it in her eyes, in the way she was chewing her lower lip.

"You don't even know this guy," Uncle Joey said.

"I don't know *anyone*." I pounded the seat back.

The walkie talkie crackled. "Carrie? You still there?"

Mom handed the walkie back to me. "I'm here."

"So seriously, we're gonna do this?"

I looked right at my mom. "Yeah. We're going to the beach. Maybe we'll even take a swim." Mom had a deep frown line between her eyebrows, but she didn't say anything. She could sense how much this meant to me.

"Awesome." He sounded as excited as I was.

"So what do you like to do when you're not running from aliens?" Marcus asked.

I settled back against the door, pulled my green and gold (school colors) blanket to my waist and settled in for the ride.

We talked for hours. We used our otherwise useless phones to play our favorite songs for each other. I actually laughed a few times. My laugh sounded weird to me, probably because I hadn't heard it in so long.

* * *

Marcus was an inch shorter than me, which seemed the perfect height for him to be. He introduced me to his sister Jerilea and his friend Porter, I introduced him to my family, then we set off down the beach.

As soon as we were out of sight he reached out and took my hand. It was crazy, what we were doing. Completely insane. The odds that buzztops showed up on that stretch of beach on that afternoon weren't too high, but if they *did* show up, we would die. For me that risk only added to the magic of walking in the surf, my fingers laced with Marcus's, our shoes and socks waiting in the sand by the parking lot.

"I'm gonna think about this every day, for as many days as I have left." Foamy sea water washed up Marcus's ankles, wetting the ends of his rolled up pants.

"Me, too." I squeezed his hand. A seagull cried out, gliding on the breeze. The buzztops couldn't catch them. You found dead, emaciated birds on the ground the buzztops had stripped, because they couldn't find anything to eat, but the buzztops couldn't catch them.

Marcus slowed. "I hate to say it, but we better turn around."

I sighed. "Yeah."

We headed back, not saying much, just drinking it in. Marcus's friends were splashing around in the water, laughing, screaming, while my family leaned up against our SUV and watched.

"I wish I was in your car."

Marcus shrugged. "We've got room."

I laughed at the idea of it. "I couldn't leave my mom. She'd be devastated." So would I.

Marcus went on holding my hand as we approached. It felt good that he didn't let go as soon as we were in sight of his people.

"What if we went on caravanning for a while, and I rode with you?" I asked.

Marcus grinned. "That would be fantastic."

"Your friends would be okay with that?"

"They'd be thrilled. We're kind of sick of each other—they'd love to hear a new voice for a change."

"You know this for a fact?"

"I'll have to ask them, but they'll say yes."

"I don't know if my mother will."

He looked toward the SUV. "That, I can't help you with."

As we walked, I tried to think of a way to ask. She had to let me do this.

No. I shouldn't ask, I should tell her. Back when you could count on having another seventy years of life once you turned eighteen, you could tolerate being told what to do until then. But there was no way I was going to make it to eighteen.

They were standing around the SUV, Uncle Joey with his arms folded like he had some important meeting I was keeping him from. As I approached he rolled off the bumper and headed for the door. "Let's go."

"Hang on." I swallowed. "I'm going to ride with them for a while. We'll stick close."

Mom's eyes got huge. "What? No. Absolutely not." She studied my face, like I had a smudge on it or something.

"We're family. We stick together." She pointed at Marcus, who was huddled close to his shivering friends, talking. "Would they die for you? Anyone in this vehicle would die for you like that." She snapped her fingers.

"I don't know if they'd die for me. Right now I'm not thinking about dying, for the first time in four months. I'm thinking about living for a change."

His head down, Uncle Joey came over to me. He grabbed my elbow. "Let's go. Get in."

I yanked my arm free. "*No.*"

Suddenly Mom was beside me. She locked both hands around my arm. Aunt Marie grabbed the back of my sweatshirt and pulled.

I struggled as Uncle Joey opened the back door. "Let *go.*"

Marcus ran to block the door, his friends right behind him. "Hey. Let her go." Uncle Joey tried to shove Marcus out of the way.

"Get off me." Marcus shoved Joey right back, hard, making him backpedal a few steps.

"Stay out of this," Mom said. "It's none of your business."

"If you're dragging her into your car against her will, it is our business," a woman said, probably Marcus's big sister.

A second guy sidled up to Marcus, forming a wall in front of the door.

Marcus looked at me. "It's your decision. If you want to go with them, I'll move."

"No. I want to ride with you for a while." I looked to Mom. She was crying quietly, her whole face shaking. "It's no big deal. I have a chance to make some friends. Maybe my last chance. We'll stay right with you, and I'll switch back in a couple of days."

"Swear to me you will," Mom said.

"I swear." Is that what she was afraid of? That I'd like my new friends so much I'd just drive off and never see her again? "Mom, I wouldn't just leave you."

She didn't say anything, just stared at me, head tilted, like I was someone she'd met a long time ago, and she was trying to remember who I was.

"One day. You come back at dusk," she finally said. "After that, we'll see how it goes."

I hugged her fiercely. We both knew she wasn't so much giving me permission as accepting what I'd already decided, but I was glad to be leaving with things less ugly than they'd been a minute before. I took Marcus's hand and ran to his vehicle, my hair blowing in the sea breeze.

Pork Belly came blaring out of the stereo as Marcus's sister started up the Sunburst. The wheels kicked up sand as we followed my family's SUV.

With Marcus's arm across my shoulders I lowered the window and whooped at the blue sky. The rest of them whooped in reply as we fishtailed onto the main drag, the ocean at our backs.

Marcus handed me a travel cup, and before I even brought it to my lips I knew it wouldn't be fruit juice. Rum flavored with a splash of Coke burned its way to my stomach. I leaned over and kissed Marcus, surprising him, but after a second he wrapped his arms around me and kissed me back.

In the rear view I could see Jerilea watching us, grinning, no doubt happy to see Marcus find a little joy in this fucked up world.

"Hey, I'm sixteen," I said to Jerilea. "Can you teach me how to drive?"

Marcus took the travel cup from me. "None of this if you're gonna drive." As he set the cup in a holder, my last doubt about Marcus and his friends vanished. It wasn't just luck that they were still alive. They were smart, and careful.

* * *

I needed both of my hands, but Marcus kept one of his on my knee. We'd been connected by touch almost continuously from the moment I jumped into their SUV. I think we both recognized that we didn't have time to take it slow.

"So Carrie, what did you want to be when you grew up?" Marcus asked.

"No talking to the student driver. She needs to concentrate," Jerilea said. It wasn't that hard; all I had to do was follow the bumper of my family's SUV.

"A film director. You?"

"Psychologist."

"Five more minutes, then we'll switch out," Jerilea said. "Nice first lesson, Carrie. You earned a second." She lifted the walkie talkie, to tell my mom we were going to pull over and do another quick switch.

There was a bright flash ahead of us and to our left. I jolted. The SUV swiveled, but I straightened it out.

Suddenly everyone was shouting at once.

"Go."

"Turn around. Fast as you can."

"Turn. Turn."

It filled the landscape, crushing buildings as it surged toward us like an ocean liner, huge, gunmetal gray. A whale. A gate had opened right on top of us.

As I turned around, I saw Uncle Joey trying to do the same, only the buzztops were already on top of them. I bumped over the curb as Mom came on the walkie talkie.

"Run, Carrie. Run. I love you. Love you so much." In the background, Uncle Joey was screaming.

"I love you too, Mom," I cried. "So much."

The walkie cut out as I floored the SUV.

"*Look out*," Marcus shouted.

I jerked us hard left as buzztops surged out from behind a strip mall to the right. They'd gotten in front of us in the time it took to turn around.

Only, there was no road going left, only entrances to parking lots. I made a U-turn, hoping we'd hit a crossing street before we reached the oncoming buzztops, but there was no way that was going to work. Everyone was screaming. I'd imagined this moment so many times.

The whale thundered by, not a hundred yards away, spitting buzztops. It would go back through the gate once it had discharged its cargo, back to that strange and beautiful world with its endless forest.

That world where there were no marauding buzztops, where a few people just might be lucky enough to disappear into the forest without being seen.

I jerked the wheel to the left and headed right at the whale.

"*What are you doing?*" Marcus screamed.

We bounced over the curb, into the parking lot of a Wendy's. Buzztops closed from both sides, releasing smaller ones to come inside and get us. We flew over another curb, crashed through the wooden fence surrounding the Wendy's, went up an incline, over railroad tracks, back down and into the wake of the whale. I turned right, away from the whale, and floored it as Jerilea screamed, as Porter screamed, as Marcus screamed and buzztops closed from all sides. We were in a shopping center parking lot, heading right for the side of a supermarket, but the wall was hazy, like there was something between us and it.

There was a blinding flash, and suddenly I was hurtling through the air. My ears popped as the air went from warm to cool, the sky from powder blue to turquoise.

I hit the ground, landed hard, bounced and rolled across vegetation. When I finally came to a stop, I was sure I'd broken every bone in my body. I couldn't breathe.

My lungs relaxed all at once, and I inhaled a rush of weird, mint, and pepper-scented air.

I struggled to my hands and knees. There was no one around except us, although the vegetation was dead and flattened as if this was a high-activity area. The air was cool, the sky blue-green and brilliantly clear. The SUV was gone. Of course it was: no metal or plastic could get through the gate.

My family was gone as well. I heard their screams, squeezed my eyes shut. Mom was gone. I'd lost so many people, but I'd never expected to lose her. I always figured we die together.

Marcus was lying ten feet away in thick black-purple weeds.

I struggled to my feet, relieved to discover none of my bones were broken. We were in a clearing, the black city maybe a quarter mile away, the seamless buildings towering high overhead. The din of an army of whales and buzztops was just a few hundred yards to our right. My arms and legs were scraped and bleeding, my side throbbing, blood seeping through my t-shirt.

"We have to go," I said. "This must be the exit; sooner or later the ones that went in are going to come back out.

The sound of my voice snapped the others out of their stupor. Marcus crawled to his feet. Jerilea must have landed head-first, because she had a bad cut on her scalp and looked woozy.

We limp-ran over a rise into the strangest fucking forest there ever was. The vegetation formed a roof ten feet off the ground; below that was bare ground broken up by the boughs of trees and plants. As we headed under the canopy, the ground was mottled sunlight and darkness, and splattered with animal droppings large and small.

We kept going until Jerilea collapsed, then huddled together in animal shit, our eyes big, as living things made chittering and groaning and popping sounds all around us.

I'd only known Marcus and his people for two days, and suddenly in this place I felt like I was sitting with three strangers. I wanted my mom. I wanted my people. I kept hearing Uncle Joey's scream in my head. I couldn't make it stop. I'd been so tired of being treated like a kid, now the only thing I wanted was to be a kid just a little longer.

"How are we going to get back home?" Porter asked.

"We're not," Jerilea said. "Why would we go back? There's nothing there for us."

I nodded, too exhausted, too devastated to speak. Of course we were staying. There were no buzztops chewing up this world.

Porter looked mortified by the idea of spending his life here, however long that turned out to be. I didn't blame him. "How are we going to know what's safe to eat? What if there are wild animals?"

"We'll figure it out," Marcus said.

"Or we'll die," I heard myself say. "But at least dying's not guaranteed."

Marcus reached out and touched my knee. "We'd all be dead already if it wasn't for you."

"We would," Jerilea said. "Thank you, Carrie."

The tightness in my chest eased a little. I still missed my people badly, but suddenly I didn't feel surrounded by strangers.

* * *

Something round and purple dropped from above. I stopped walking as it bounced twice and rolled to a stop at my feet.

I picked it up. It was spongy, sort of hairy. I dug my fingernails into it and broke it open, praying it wasn't filled with flesh-eating bugs.

It wasn't. The center was purplish liquid; the meat looked suspiciously like fruit. I lifted one half to my nose. It smelled vaguely like chocolate, or coffee.

"Hang on," I called to the others, who were walking ahead of me. Someone was going to have to be the guinea pig, and if it was going to be me, I wanted them to know what I died of.

I took a bite. It was surprisingly chewy, more fruit roll-up than fruit, but it was indeed vaguely chocolaty. I swallowed.

Everyone stood perfectly still, watching me.

As the minutes stretched out, the silence started getting weird.

"You know what?" I said. "I don't think I'm going to die."

Marcus held out a hand. "Let me try it."

I drew it away. "We should wait a few hours, in case it's slow acting."

Three more purple balls dropped through the canopy. Not two, not four, but three. I looked up. A yellow eye was peering down at me through a gap.

I jumped back and shrieked, and the eye disappeared.

"What?" Jerilea was looking up at the canopy. "What did you see?"

"Something was watching us."

Part of me didn't want to know what was attached to that eye, but I still wasn't dying from eating the purple fruit, so whatever it was, it must have helped us. Either that or it was trying to lure us to our deaths, but we were four unarmed people, alone on this world. If something wanted to kill us it didn't need to be sneaky about it.

We decided we had to go up there.

One by one, we shimmied up the bough of one of the big trees and squeezed through the gap between the tree and black vegetation. When I popped free, I found myself on a trampoline of vines, underneath an enormous black-boughed tree that had one blood-red, parachute-shaped leaf ringing the top. Hundreds of fat, snakelike things were crawling up and down the bough, covering it, somehow not falling. Then I realized they were connected—they were like hands with four or five long, fat fingers. There were smaller trees overhead as well, some of them covered in yellow berries instead of leaves. One was dotted with the purple fruit. I moved closer to it, stepping awkwardly on the springy surface.

I caught movement out of the corner of my eye, spun to find a creature standing beside a cluster of fluffy shrubs. It had more limbs than I could count, a wide body that seemed all head. I couldn't see any eyes, just a gaping mouth round.

The thing tore off a piece of the shrub and ate it, chewing slowly, its mouth opening and closing, like it wanted to make sure we could see it was eating. Or maybe that was just the way it ate.

"Could it be one of the aliens who live in that black city?" Marcus asked.

"The soldier we picked up said they walked on two legs." This thing walked on fifty legs. It turned, headed off at a slow pace.

"Should we follow it?" Marcus asked.

We followed it to a copse of trees with wide black leaves that reminded me of the outside of an artichoke. It picked a fallen leaf off the ground and took a bite.

"I think it's showing us what's edible," Jerilea said.

I clapped my hands together and laughed. It was. Like a neighbor welcoming us to the neighborhood with a covered dish.

As we watched it, it pointed at the sky.

I looked up. Was it pointing at those parachute trees? Maybe to tell us they were edible, too? It lowered its limb, then pointed up again. There was nothing up there but blue-green sky.

My head exploded. "Holy shit. 'I'm from the sky.' Is that what it's trying to say?" I pointed to the sky as well, then I pointed at myself.

It repeated the gesture, took a step forward.

I took a step forward. "We're from the sky, too." I pointed to myself, then at the sky. I was crying.

Marcus was beside me, grinning. He pointed at himself, at the sky.

We weren't the first to think of escaping through the gate. Why would we be? Maybe there were others as well.

The creature suddenly took off, moving incredibly fast. It went about fifty feet, then dropped through the web of vines and out of sight.

Jerilea shrieked. She was staring behind us, wide-eyed. Dozens of snake things were slithering silently toward us.

"We gotta get down. *Down*." Marcus grabbed my arm, pulled me toward the spot where the alien had gone. We reached a ragged hole in the canopy; I scrambled through it, hung from the edge for a second before dropping to the ground.

The alien was waiting close by. It watched as Porter, Jerilea, and Marcus dropped through the hole, one after another. Then it turned and skittered off, heading away from the city.

"I guess we should follow it," I said.

We let the creature put some distance between us, then we set off after it. Not taking his eyes off the creature, Marcus patted my shoulder. "I think maybe we're gonna be okay, Carrie with a C."

ABOUT WILL MCINTOSH

Will McIntosh is a Hugo award winner and finalist for the Nebula and twelve other SF/F awards. His most recent books are *Unbreakable*, a dystopian novel with a twist you will not see coming; *Faller*, published by Tor Books; and a middle grade book (ages 9 and up) titled *Watchdog*, which is being developed as an animated TV series by the creators of the *How to Train Your Dragon* TV series, *Dragons: Race to the Edge*. His previous book *Defenders* (Orbit Books) was optioned by Warner Brothers for a feature film, while *Love Minus Eighty* was named the best science fiction book of 2013 by the American Library Association-RUSA, and has also been optioned for a TV series. Will was a psychology professor before turning to writing full-time, and still occasionally teaches Introductory Psychology at the College of William and Mary. He lives in Williamsburg with his wife and their twins. You can follow him on Twitter @willmcintoshSF, or on his website: http://www.willmcintosh.net.

WATER BABIES

by Maya Kaathryn Bohnhoff

OMAR NAVARRO ADJUSTED THE SONAR ARRAY AND TOOK A second look at the infrared imaging. He could've sworn he'd seen a sudden, large flash of ambient heat about 100 yards off the port bow of the submersible. It was in an odd place, though—a relatively narrow dead end canyon at the end of a shallow trench. As he attempted to relocate it, it returned as a sustained event of obviously variable temperatures.

"Hey, Professor," he said, "you might want to take a look at this."

Professor Corwin "Win" Lerner, head researcher at the International Cetacean Institute, turned from his study of his laptop screen to Omar's infrared display.

"Now that's something," the professor said, adjusting his glasses on the bridge of his nose.

"What though? I mean, it looks like a—a fumarole."

Lerner gave the younger man a sidewise glance. "Since your last posting was a geological survey, I suppose that makes sense." The professor peered at the eddying heat signature. "Recalibrate, Omar. Then assess."

"Well, possibly a large, closely grouped cluster of aquatic mammals. Dolphins most likely."

Win Lerner grinned. "Shall we go see?"

This was exactly the sort of thing they'd hoped to encounter on the new submersible's shakedown cruise. ICI-2 (aka, Icky the Second) was less than a week old and just now getting a full test of her equipment and systems. Omar piloted the submersible into the mouth of the little canyon, carefully avoiding the walls. They had just tucked into the narrow cut when the heat signature altered, seeming to break apart into separate entities.

Definitely dolphins.

The walls of the box canyon opened out a bit as they motored into visual range, Icky's headlamps reaching into the swirling gloom like the hands of an inquisitive toddler. They picked out the shapes of six individuals, all with the elegant shape of the short-beaked common dolphin, *delphinus delphis*. It took Omar a moment to realize the coloring was wrong. These dolphins were more distinctly two-toned, and the colors were reversed; they had a dark ventral area topped with a gleaming silver dorsal region.

"Professor, their coloring…"

"Yes, I see." Win's voice was musing. "Could we be looking at a new species?"

Omar cut the thrust of the submersible, letting it drift slowly up to the animals, which reacted with benign interest. One of them—a smaller specimen—even swam up to the little submarine as if to examine it. The others hung back. Omar expected that sort of behavior from dolphins. What he had not expected was the startling morphology.

"It has a *neck*," he murmured. "Professor, am I imagining—?"

"No. No, you're not. Are the cameras rolling?"

"Yessir."

The animal now regarding them through the transparent cowling at the bow of the submersible apparently determined that they were no threat, and turned to swim back to its fellows. In silhouette, the strangeness was emphatic. The rounded head with its tapered beak was set on a short, thick neck that joined the body just forward of a pair of long, narrow fins, flowing into the torso via sloping shoulders. Omar knew without a doubt that this was a species no one had seen before.

What was it doing in a relatively shallow trench off the coast of Gibraltar?

* * *

They deployed both of the institute's smallest submersibles to capture the animals. The dolphins followed Icky II back to the ICI base in Rosia Harbour, so it was a relatively simple combination of luring and herding.

The six abnormal dolphins were of different sizes, though none seemed to be immature. Up close, their coloration was even more striking. There were subtle nuances to both the light and dark colors of their gleaming skin, and the patterns of light and dark on their beaks was highly individualized. Their behavior was typical of dolphins; they were curious to a fault, poking into every nook and cranny of their new habitat.

It was an enormous tank—both deep and wide—and stocked with marine animals and plants common to the waters around Gibraltar. They made themselves comfortable almost immediately, surprising everyone by eating the kelp in the tank while ignoring the fish.

They also seemed affably interested in the humans, which Omar found odd. If they were a species that had never interacted with humans before, why were they so friendly? He raised that with Professor Lerner when the staff gathered to get their first look at the newcomers.

"It may be an instinctive behavior, rather than learned," Win Lerner told him. "I can't imagine that humans have had contact with these creatures before, or they'd exist in our records."

"Maybe they do," said Song Park, the newest of the ICI's research assistants. "They remind me of Inuit and Salish depictions I've seen of dolphins. Maybe ancient aboriginal societies came across them."

Dr. Lerner smiled at her observation.

"Not a bad theory, Song."

While the research team weighed their new acquisitions and took DNA samples, Dr. Lerner alerted the media, offering video and high-res still photos to media outlets and other research organizations. The creatures were calm throughout, only becoming agitated when the team attempted to tag them. It took an hour to insert subcutaneous chips in the left fins of each dolphin to enable tracking when they were later released back into the Alboran Sea.

The team set up to observe the new species in a scale model of their familiar habitat. Omar—who worked the night shift monitoring the institute's specimens—wondered what they thought of their new environment. It was much like the canyon they'd occupied previously in that it formed a rocky cul-de-sac on three sides, but unlike it in that it had a thick sheet of transparent Plexiglas on the fourth side. This fronted onto a gallery from which a number of habitats could be observed.

Omar watched the new arrivals press their beaks against the Plexi-panel repeatedly, and daydreamed about what they made of the human observers on the opposite side, busy tapping away on their iPads. It was a funny sight—one that had Omar picking up his own iPad to sketch a cartoon of the scene. He was infamous at ICI for his comic depictions of the staff and specimens. Everyone enjoyed it except for Felix Berrocal.

He was a post-grad from the Universitat de Barcelona—a tall, statuesque fellow with sleek black hair and a distinctly Moorish angularity of feature. He was scathing of Omar's depictions of him as a romance novel hero, typically striking poses before a bevy of stunned high school girls while delivering soliloquies on the mating habits of sea cucumbers.

Felix accused Omar of rank envy. There was a grain of truth to that, Omar had to admit. Omar was half a head shorter than the Spaniard, and his profusion of unruly hair and raw sienna skin hinted at a heritage that was more Incan than Iberian. Then there was the fact that Felix had shown an immediate and obvious attraction to Song from his first day on staff. Omar had been mesmerized by the petite Korean from the moment he saw her, but had quietly given up on any idea of asking her out.

Song was among the group of studious dolphin watchers he was now sketching. He was especially careful with her likeness. Perhaps out of spite, he drew Felix behind her, looming like a vampire or a vulture. He did quick renderings of the several other scientists in the group, made two vertical slashes to represent the thick wall of the habitat, then began to sketch the dolphins. They bobbed in a ragged line right up against the Plexiglas, watching the humans as intently as the humans were watching them.

As Omar finished the cartoon, two of the animals swam away and disappeared into a stand of kelp. Chuckling, he sketched the two dolphins leaving the pod, and dashed in a caption of one saying to the other, with an oblique backward glance at the humans, "I don't know, Agnes. I think that has got to be the most boring species in the aquarium. They never *do* anything."

Omar heard a decidedly female giggle in his left ear and felt hair brush his cheek. He nearly jumped out of his skin and swiveled his chair. Song stood behind him, trying to cover her laughter with one elegant hand.

"Omar, that is so funny," she said in delicately accented English. "Can I see?"

He allowed her to pluck the pad from his unresisting fingers.

Still laughing, she studied the drawing. "Oh, I see Dr. Win. And there's Nate, and Cecily—oh—that is so very Felix." She met his gaze over the top of the pad. "Is that me?"

Omar shrugged. "It's not a very good likeness. I'm a total amateur."

"I think you're very good. But, you made me so pretty."

"You *are* pretty … *I* think." He cleared his throat. She blushed. "What's so Felix?" he asked, desperate to change the subject.

She handed the iPad back and struck a predatory pose with her hands forming claws. "Like that. Like a—a—"

"Vampire?"

Her laughter was like the peal of silver bells. "Yes. Funny. Does that make me a blood donor?"

While Omar tried to decide what to make of that remark, Song glanced up at the monitors and said, "Oh, look. The dolphins are all leaving. I guess they *do* think we're boring."

Omar had to wonder if they still thought that after the team snatched two of them—a male and a female—for more detailed analysis. The animals were tranquilized and carefully relocated to shallow examination tubs where they could be X-rayed and subjected to a variety of other imaging techniques.

Win Lerner led the examination team, which included Felix and Song, while Omar held down the fort in the observation center, watching the other dolphins react to the absence of their comrades. They were agitated. Extremely so.

They scoured the habitat for the missing animals, even resorting to piercing vocalizations. Omar had to leap to turn down the audio gain on the mics in the habitat, they got so loud. Up until then, the creatures' vocal output had been entirely beyond the range of human hearing, and Omar had been recording it using what amounted to a recalibrated seismic array. Now, the animals went through a series of clicks, burst pulses, and whistles, all the while zipping around the tank and bumping their beaks on the Plexi-panel.

The dolphins seemed so distraught, Omar grew anxious by association. When they swam to the surface and launched into a chorus of what sounded like soprano and alto whale songs, he thought his heart would break. He remembered a female short-beak they'd brought in earlier that year whose calf had become entangled in a discarded parasail. Watching them reunite was one of the most emotional things Omar had ever witnessed.

The memory made him wish he could somehow calm these animals—assure them that their missing companions were okay. On impulse, he got up and slipped out of the observation room into the gallery, which was a short walk down a broad, sloping corridor. He hurried, though he knew Lerner and the team would be at their task for at least another half hour.

He went to the center of the dolphins' aquarium window and looked up at them. The moment they saw him, they swam down. The female who came closest to the window greeted him with a whistle and a series of clicks and pulses. He moved right up to the Plexiglas and pressed a hand to it, willing the creatures to know that the two missing dolphins weren't lost. That they were simply being examined, and would be back soon, healthy and whole.

The female brought her face level with Omar's and touched her beak to the Plexiglas. He tried his best to meet her gaze—impossible, really, because of the placement of her eyes—but in a moment, she stopped vocalizing and floated back to her fellows. They seemed calmer now—less agitated.

Omar heard voices at the top of the corridor and bolted back to his lair. Win came in a moment later, trailed by Song, Felix, and Cecily. They were still comparing notes about the results of their imaging session, which had apparently shown that the dolphins' internal physiology was almost as unusual as the exterior.

"I suspect," said Cecily, who was Win's wife and research partner, "that we're looking at a species that has been separated from the larger populations of dolphins for millennia. In much the same way that Australian species of land mammals became separated from kindred species."

"Yes," said Felix, "but we are talking about marine life forms. How does one separate populations of marine life to that extent, given that the world's oceans are contiguous?"

Win moved to stand behind Omar's chair. "There are a handful of bodies of salt water in the world that are cut off from the oceans. Is it possible that one of these might have suffered a breach?"

The dialogue suddenly ceased. Omar registered that, but was busy watching the dolphins circling their habitat like anxious fathers-to-be in a maternity ward.

"Omar?" prompted Win.

"*Dios mio*, Navarro," said Felix. "Must you always be daydreaming?"

Omar swung away from the displays. "I wasn't daydreaming. I was observing the dolphins, Berrocal. I'm sorry, doctor, I didn't realize you were talking to me."

"You're the geology expert, yes?" said Felix.

Omar shot a dagger-sharp glance at him, but nodded. "The only body of salt water I can think of that might have the right conditions would be the Black Sea. It's possible, I suppose, that some widening or deepening or current outflow in the Bosphorus might have allowed them to slip through, but ... I mean, wouldn't they have been noticed before? The Black Sea's not that large."

"Yes, but who would expect to find a species of dolphin there?" Song asked quietly.

"Nobody. But last year a geological survey group began mapping the sea floor."

Song's eyes lit up. "Perhaps this prompted the dolphins to flee."

Omar had to admit there was a logic to that. Certainly, the dolphins—which Felix the suck-up had already begun to call "Lerner's Dolphins"—must have originated somewhere secluded and recently been forced or enticed into leaving. The Black Sea made the most sense.

"I think it would be fascinating," said Cecily, "to do some sleuthing in the area to see if there are any local legends about large creatures in the Black Sea. I believe I'll contact that survey team, too. See if they've observed these creatures during their mapping project." She pivoted on one heel and strode briskly from the room.

Her husband shot her retreating form a look of affectionate approval, then turned to peer at the monitors. "Interesting," Win said. "They seem to be quite placid. I'd have expected them to be agitated over the disappearance of their fellows."

"Oh, they were," said Omar. "They were all over the tank searching for them. They started vocalizing."

"Really? Would you locate that and replay it, please?"

The group in the observation center watched the recording as the dolphins' agitation reached a fever pitch, then calmed once the Alpha female paid a visit to the viewing gallery.

"Look at that," murmured Win. "They just calmed right down. I wonder what caused it? What were they looking at through the Plexi-panel? Any ideas, Omar?"

Omar flushed. He knew exactly what they'd been looking at. "Uh, they were looking at me."

He felt the three pairs of eyes on him and quailed. "I—ah—I could feel how distressed they were. I thought maybe I could calm them down. So, I went out into the gallery and put my hand on the window and … that." He pointed to the playback, in which the boldest of the dolphins had swum forward to put her beak against the Plexiglas.

"That's it?" asked Felix. "You just put your hand on the glass and she came and kissed it?"

"I don't know what she did. I just thought at them that their friends would be back and they'd be okay."

"You *thought* at them," repeated Win. "What made you do that?"

"Yes," said Felix, slanting a mocking smile at Omar, "are you now Navarro, Dolphin Whisperer?"

Omar ignored the Spaniard and considered the professor's question. "I just felt like … if I could feel their unease so strongly, maybe they could feel my calm."

"Extraordinary," said Win.

"Extraordinary," echoed Song. The admiration in her eyes made Omar's heart skip a beat.

"Well," Win said brusquely. "This bears looking into. I'd like your written observations, if you please, Mr. Navarro. By tomorrow afternoon?"

Omar nodded, not missing the rapier-sharp glance he got from Felix. He'd come up in the world; he was Mr. Navarro now.

Lerner turned and exited the room, waving for Felix to follow. "Felix, let's go grab a couple of the interns and get the Beta male and female back into the tank, shall we? It will be interesting to see how the others react to having them reintroduced to the habitat."

The moment they were gone, Song crossed to Omar's chair, put her hand on his arm and said, "You have a most wonderful gift, Omar. The gift of empathy."

He felt heat creep up his neck. "Oh, no, I ... you know, I probably imagined that whole..." He gestured at the monitors.

"No. The video clearly shows you didn't imagine it. Something you did calmed those animals down. I think Felix is, perhaps, right. You are a Dolphin Whisperer." She smiled and squeezed his arm, then turned and disappeared into the corridor.

* * *

The reintroduction of the Beta male and female was interesting. After an initial burst of whistles, the other dolphins gathered around them, silently, and nosed them, giving Omar the sense of eavesdropping on a conversation. Then, instead of going back to their normal routine of eating and swimming and playing, they seemed to enter a high state of agitation again, swimming in tight circles and pausing to confront each other. When a couple of the staff scientists approached the gallery window, all six of the animals disappeared into the kelp.

Felix, Nate, and the Lerners were mildly bemused. Song was frowning. Omar's stomach tied itself in knots. That same rush of distress he'd felt earlier when the dolphins reacted to the disappearance of their comrades returned. He vaguely registered that the others had left the monitoring room, and contemplated going into the gallery to see if he could do some more dolphin whispering. He almost leapt out of his skin at a gentle touch on his arm.

"What is it, Omar?" Song asked. "What do you feel?"

He ought to be embarrassed, he told himself, but couldn't muster the macho for that. "They're really in distress, Song," he said. "Just like they were before. I don't know why. I mean, they got their friends back and Wiyu checked them both over."

"Wiyu?"

Now he really was embarrassed. "It's the noise she made when she vocalized earlier. The Alpha female, I mean. I find it hard to think of them as letters of the Greek alphabet."

Song put her hands over her mouth and sank into the chair next to his. "Do you think they thought their friends were hurt by what we did to them? They must have been terrified. Pulled out of the water, restrained, and tranquilized … I know I would have been terrified if someone did that to me."

Omar nodded. "I had surgery when I was a kid. My appendix. I remember waking up in the recovery room. I was really scared because I couldn't remember why I was there and I didn't know anybody. And *these* poor guys never had any idea why we brought them here in the first place."

"Maybe you should tell Dr. Lerner."

Omar reluctantly agreed. The conversation didn't go as poorly as he'd feared. Win Lerner seemed to take him seriously, and requested that he be especially attentive to their guests tonight. He also wanted to see Omar attempt to communicate with them again.

To that end, Omar found himself standing in front of the Plexi-panel stretching his senses out toward the dolphins. He brought the one he called Wiyu to mind and tried to think beckoning thoughts at her.

His efforts were met with some measure of success. Wiyu peeked through the curtain of kelp and regarded him steadily for about twenty seconds before disappearing again.

He went up to the exterior surface of the tank and grabbed some of the seaweed treats they fed to other specimens they were studying. He fluttered the water with his hand and floated a couple of the pellets atop the water. He thought friendly, concerned thoughts. Nothing happened for several long minutes, then Wiyu poked her head above the surface. He extended one hand, palm forward, fingers slightly bent.

The dolphin hesitated, then floated toward him until her forehead rested beneath his palm. He heard Song gasp behind him, and heard Dr. Lerner's bemused hum. What Omar felt, however, was far from bemusement. He felt fear, claustrophobia, and a longing to return to a familiar place—to go home. He had a sudden, vivid impression of water lit by trailing banners of sunlight, of waving kelp, sea ferns, and other aquatic plants. Of cool, azure shadows and silk soft sands.

The dolphin suddenly swam away and sank back into the pool, but not before capturing several of the seaweed treats in her mouth and taking them with her. She didn't eat them, Omar noticed, but simply held them between her small, sharp teeth.

He rose and wiped his hands on his jeans. He had a vivid imagination, but not that vivid. Somehow, Wiyu had shown him that peaceful place. "They want to go home," he said. "They want us to let them go. They're frightened. They don't understand what's happening to them."

"Well, of course," said Win. "That's perfectly natural. And we may well let them go once we've concluded our study of them. They're unique, Omar. The length of time they've spent secluded from the environment shared by other dolphin species has led to some fascinating adaptations." The older man, sensing Omar's unease, put a hand on his shoulder. "They'll be fine once they've acclimated to their new habitat. Maybe we'll move them to one of the larger tanks. They might be happier there."

Omar hesitated momentarily before nodded his agreement, but he knew that was wrong. *They won't be happy,* he thought, *until we let them go home.*

* * *

Omar wasn't, strictly speaking, required to spend every moment in the observation center watching the monitors, but he did tonight. He was worried about Lerner's Dolphins. They'd been hanging back in the kelp most of the day.

He was worried enough that he considered putting on a wetsuit and venturing into the tank. But if he went in without asking permission, he'd be in a world of trouble, and if he asked permission, he'd have to wake the Doctors Lerner up. In the end, he made a pot of strong coffee and camped out in the most comfortable chair in the room.

Of course, he fell asleep at some point, waking suddenly when he realized the dolphin vocalizing he'd been dreaming about wasn't a dream. He checked the monitors quickly, one by one. The disturbance was definitely coming from the new animals. They were rowdy, bleating and whistling. The streamers of kelp in the rear of the tank were writhing, and bubbles escaped the thick tangle of vegetation, but there were no dolphins in sight.

As Omar watched, the chaos slowly calmed until there was no noise, no motion among the kelp, and no bubbles.

He waited. When nothing more happened, he breathed a sigh of relief. But his relief didn't last long. The habitat seemed *too* quiet. As if …

He got up from his chair and went out into the gallery to peer into the tank through the big Plexi-panel. There was nothing. He leaned against the glass and gazed up through the fronds of kelp toward where the surface lights held vigil around the other habitat pools. Slivers of undisturbed light shone down through the kelp.

A shaft of cold penetrated Omar's heart and froze his brain. Without thinking about what he was doing, he launched himself up the stairs to the outdoor decks. When he reached the rim of the dolphins' pool, he peered down through the kelp. If they were so well hidden that they couldn't be seen from below, then they must be visible from up here. But they weren't.

He went to the nearest equipment rack and grabbed a long-handled net. He thrust it into the kelp thicket and shifted aside a cluster of bulbs and leaves. That gave him a clear, momentary view of the gallery floor.

There were no dolphins in the habitat. He pulled out his cell phone and called Corwin Lerner's number. He barely remembered what he said to his boss only moments after he said it, then hung up, heart thumping, eyes seeking some sort of clue. He found one. The decking between this tank and the next was unusually wet.

Omar followed the watery track to the next tank. *Had the dolphins somehow crossed the decking to get into the tank next door?* If they had, they didn't appear to be there now.

He circled the tank—one that was supposed to hold sea turtles—and found that the deck had been soaked on the other side as well. And on the far side of the sea turtle habitat lay Rosia Harbour.

"Omar!"

He turned to see the Lerners emerge from the stairwell. He beckoned to them, wondering how he could possibly explain this.

* * *

In the end, neither Lerner blamed him for losing track of the dolphins.

"Who would've even thought they could escape a tank at the surface level?" Cecily asked as they hurried to retrieve the animals.

They took out both submersibles and followed the pings from the animals' tracking devices to the canyon where they'd first discovered them.

That puzzled Win Lerner. "Dolphins are intelligent animals. You'd think they'd avoid the place we found them initially."

They hadn't, and in the end, a combination of tranquilizer darts and 'gentle netting' allowed the scientists to return the dolphins to the institute. This time they were ensconced in the largest tank the facility possessed—one disconnected from the other habitats and linked to Rosia Harbour by a pair of marine locks that had housed submarines in wartime. Omar had always thought of that particular habitat as Solitary Confinement. They dropped the water level four feet below the rim of the tank to ensure the dolphins couldn't escape again and installed netting over the top.

Omar felt like a torture-monger. When he finally slept in the wee hours of the morning, he dreamed. He dreamed of ocean depths—dark, comforting, and familiar, and of the shallows—sunlit, warm, and colorful. The dream was one of contentment until it changed in the twinkling of an eye to a dream of grand adventure, then just as swiftly to a nightmare in which little was familiar, and the familiar was deceptively so.

He remembered the last time he'd been home—over a year ago, now—and realized how many people he'd left behind when he'd come here. Parents, siblings, friends. For all that Gibraltar life was interesting and the society friendly, he was intensely aware of what he had lost. And he might be forever cut off from it.

He woke suddenly, eyes grainy with lack of sleep, head muddled. Forever cut off from his parents? From Jo and Marin? No. He was a plane flight away and FaceTimed them at least once a week.

It dawned on him, then: these losses were not his.

He sat up and swung his feet to the floor. He could feel the anxiety as if it were a tangible mist, and knew it had to be the dolphins. He dressed, grabbed a cup of coffee and a bagel from the institute kitchen, and made his way to the deck surrounding the dolphins' tank. Two of them bobbed on the surface of the tank four feet below where he stood, as if waiting for him. Wiyu, he recognized immediately by her size and the pattern of gray and charcoal striping around her beak. The other was the one they'd identified as the Alpha male.

"Hey, guys," he said, downing the last of his coffee.

He knelt at the edge of the tank and extended a hand toward them. Wiyu tried to reach him, but she seemed unable to push herself that high out of the water, even with the other dolphin pushing from below.

Omar was suddenly desperate to touch her, to communicate with her. He leaned further forward, hand outstretched. He was almost touching her beak when he heard a gasp from behind him.

"Omar! What are you doing?"

Song's voice completely short-circuited him. He tried to pull up, but succeeded only in throwing himself off balance. He toppled headfirst into the tank.

The dolphins flocked to him and, for a split second, he was terrified. But as soon as they touched him, buoying him up toward the surface, he knew they would do him no harm.

His head broke the surface, and he shook strands of wet hair out of his eyes. Song stood above him on the deck, holding a long-handled cleaning net. Her eyes grew wide when she saw his escort—dolphins under each arm, a third beneath him pushing him upward—but she thrust the net at him and he grasped it with both hands. She threw her whole weight into the pull and, with a shove from the dolphins, Omar all but catapulted onto the edge of the deck. Song grabbed his belt and helped him the rest of the way.

She knelt beside him, her eyes bright with concern. "Are you all right? What were you trying to do?"

"I was trying to—to communicate with them," he stammered. "When I touched Wiyu—I mean, the Alph—"

"Wiyu," said Song, firmly.

"When I touched her before, I felt how much they wanted to go home. I saw their home. They think they'll die here."

"But we would never harm them—" She cut off. "They have no way to know that with certainty."

Omar looked down into the habitat. Wiyu and the alpha male—Omar decided his name was Owu—were still bobbing at the surface, watching the two humans. "But it's not just that. It's like … they're afraid of being cut off from their families and friends. Like …" He thought back to the tide of impressions that had raged through him at the animals' touch. "For us, it would be as if there were suddenly no airplanes, no ships, no way to get home."

"That's what you felt. That's why you came here." Those weren't questions.

"Why did you?" he asked.

She moved closer to him, until their noses were almost touching. "I felt … sadness. Loneliness."

Omar swallowed. "Are we crazy?"

"I don't think so."

Omar got to his feet. "Then we need to convince the Lerners to let them go."

* * *

"I don't feel anything like that," said Cecily. She sat across from Omar and Song in the office she shared with her husband. "I mean, yes, I pick up on their fear, but any intelligent creature responds to the unknown with trepidation. We're the unknown, Omar. They'll acclimate."

"No, Professor," said Omar. "I don't think they will. This isn't just fear of the unknown. For some reason, they're certain that if they stay here much longer, they won't get home. They left people behind and—"

"Do you hear yourself?" asked Win. He was half-sitting in a window embrasure behind his wife's desk. "They left *people* behind. You've come to identify too much with these animals, Omar. Be honest, are you thinking of the people *you* left behind? Gibraltar can seem pretty remote…"

Omar flushed and glanced at Song. "I admit, I dreamed about leaving my family behind—but I realized that wasn't the same thing, because I can always catch a plane to San Francisco. It wasn't my home I was dreaming about, it was theirs. And when I touched them, it was really clear what they felt. I can't explain it. I just know that it is. Song feels it too, don't you?"

She nodded. "Not as much as Omar does. But I, too, woke and felt compelled to help them."

Win spread his hands in a gesture of frustration. "I don't know what I can do. I can't just let them go—"

"Why not?" Omar challenged him. "We have MRIs, sonograms, DNA, video. Why not let them go back to their canyon? We could even visit them there, or anywhere else they go. They've got tracking devices, after all."

The Lerners traded glances, then Cecily said, "I'm sorry, but we just can't let such scientifically valuable specimens out of our hands until we've studied them thoroughly. Look, you two must be exhausted. Why don't you take the day off? Do something relaxing."

* * *

After a morning spent fretting over the dolphins, Omar and Song finally took Cecily's advice and ended up at a gelato stand on the wharf. They sat in the sun at one of the small, wrought-iron tables littered about, and ate chocolate gelato so dark it was almost black. They spoke little, at first, preferring to salve their bruised consciences with sugar.

Then Song sighed and said, "Is that it, then, Omar? Is there nothing else we can do?"

"Nothing that won't get us fired and maybe even arrested. And it's on me, Song. I'm the one who started this."

"That's silly," she said. "*They* started it—the dolphins—by reaching out to you. You're only responding to their cries for help. I've only just started feeling them, myself. Which makes me wonder why no one else feels them."

"I'm not sure. I've been thinking about it. Maybe it's an age thing. We're the youngest people on staff."

"What about Felix? He can't be more than a few years older than we are."

Omar snorted. "Felix is a jerk. He's too into himself to notice somebody else's discomfort."

"You don't like Felix," she observed.

"Do you?"

She gazed down into her gelato. "He makes me want to punch him."

"Well, that doesn't mean you don't, y'know, *like* him. You can be attracted to people you don't like."

"I can't." She looked up and speared him with her dark, shining gaze. "I am only attracted to people I *like*." As if to underscore her words, she reached out and lightly touched the back of Omar's hand.

He felt a ripple of heat run from his head all the way down to his extremities. Song smiled impishly, as if she knew exactly what he was feeling. He let his spirits be lifted by her gesture all the way back to ICI. But the moment he stepped through the institute's doors he was immersed in the dolphins' anguish.

It was time to plot a more permanent escape for them.

* * *

By mid-morning the next day, the dolphins' distress was so palpable, Omar found it difficult to believe that only he and Song could sense it. He arrived at the observation room early, surprising the intern, Shelley, who was nearing the end of her shift. He gave her his most winsome smile and offered to relieve her. She gratefully disappeared, which gave Omar the opportunity to sit down at one of the computers and pull up the schematics for the habitat systems.

If the dolphins were going to make a break for it, he realized, it would have to be through the seagate that connected their tank to the old submarine pen. The seagate was old and had two modes of opening and closing. It could be triggered to open by a motor controlled from a panel that was physically in the pen, or operated manually via the archaic latch mechanism itself, either from within the pen or the habitat.

The gate's motor was noisy as hell. Getting into the tank unnoticed was unlikely, which left manually opening the seagate from inside the old sub pen.

Omar's plotting was interrupted by a brouhaha on one of the decks. He closed the schematics and scanned the displays dedicated to the surfaces of the habitat tanks. There was a blur of motion in a frame to the upper right—Solitary. Omar zoomed in on it to find Nate chasing the industrial cart he used to deliver food to the habitats. It careened across the cement deck toward the big tank that held Lerner's Dolphins. Before Nate could catch it, it plunged into the water.

Adrenaline pumping, Omar leapt to his feet and charged out of the observation center, across the gallery, and up to the isolation area. Several other staffers—two interns and the junior marine veterinarian—had arrived to help with retrieval. The pieces of fish floating to the water's surface were easy scoop up with nets, but the cart itself had plunged to the bottom of the habitat.

"We'll have to dive for the rest of it," said Nate. "D'you think it's safe?"

"Yeah, sure," Omar said, already thinking of ways he could use the retrieval as a means of furthering the dolphin's Great Escape. "We can use a crane to hoist the cart out." He pointed overhead to one of the cranes they used to remove animals from the habitat that needed to be relocated or taken in for examination. "In fact, why don't I go into the tank, while you position the crane and send down a cable. I'll attach it to the cart, then signal you when it's ready to haul up."

Nate seemed relieved. He wasn't as good a diver as Omar, and swimming with anything the size of dolphins would spook any amateur.

Omar got suited up in his scuba gear, then lowered himself down into the tank, guiding a cable from the overhead crane. The dolphins were at the bottom of the tank near the seagate. So was the cart, which was odd because there was no way it could have floated there. Long scrapes in the sandy bottom of the tank hinted that the dolphins had pushed it. Why?

They eyed him apathetically as he approached, then swam away as if bored with the cart. Wiyu, however, wandered quite close to him, giving him a look he would've taken as a grin in a human being. He swam the remainder of the way to the food cart and was surprised to find that it was missing some parts. Specifically, the rear axle and both wheels.

Omar looked around for the missing parts, but the rock and sand around the cart were clear of debris. He had the eerie sensation that the dolphins had removed the axle for reasons of their own. He couldn't begin to imagine how or why.

"Omar, you okay?" Nate's voice came across his comm.

"Yeah, fine. I'm just looking for the best way to do this."

He fastened the cable around the cart's push bar and told Nate to take it up. Then he swam over to the seagate to get a close-up view of the locking mechanism from this side. It was essentially a wheel valve set on a short axle that ran through the gate, itself, into the old submarine pen. He wondered if there were some way to pre-jimmy it so it would be easier to unlatch from the pen.

Omar put his hands on the wheel—one on the thick spokes and one on the wheel itself—then pulled with one hand while pushing upward with the other. The valve grudgingly moved an inch or two.

Feeling as if he were being watched, Omar glanced back over one shoulder and found Wiyu hovering behind him. For a moment, they just stared at each other, then Nate squawked at him.

"Omar, you okay? You coming up?"

"Yeah, I was just checking the seagate and looking for the missing parts of the cart."

"Missing parts?"

"You'll see when you beach it. I think they've been covered by the sand. I can't find 'em." He gave Wiyu a wave, then launched himself toward the surface.

* * *

"I think they're making a lockpick." Song stared, wide-eyed, at the habitat monitor.

As ridiculous as that sounded, Omar had to agree. They watched as the dolphins nosed the parts they'd "borrowed" out into the sand near the seagate. The axle was steel; the wheels affixed to the ends like something from a super heavy-duty baby stroller. The dolphins were prodding it this way and that as if trying to decide what to do with it.

"What if someone comes in and sees them doing that?" Song asked.

Omar chewed his lower lip. "Well, I've thought about killing the feed and pretending it's malfunctioning, but honestly, I think anyone else would think they were just playing."

As if to prove his point, Felix poked his head into the room. "Hey, Song," he said, "I'm going down to the cantina for some dinner. Join me?" Before she could answer, Felix's attention was captured by the feed from Solitary. He made a chuffing sound. "I guess that explains what happened to Nate's food cart. You better get in there and take the kiddies' toy away from them before they hurt themselves, Dolphin Whisperer."

"Yeah," growled Omar. "I'll get right on that."

Felix fixed his dark eyes on Song once more. "Dinner?"

"No, thanks. I have other plans." Her gaze wandered toward Omar, which had him blushing to the roots of his hair.

Felix's handsome face froze in a rictus of disbelief. He withdrew without further comment.

Eventually, Song went down to the cantina and brought back food for both of them. Though they watched for several hours, the dolphins did no more than poke and prod and examine the cart axle. Eventually, they nudged it back into hiding and lost themselves among the kelp. The quiet nearly put Omar and Song to sleep.

The sun set and shadow fell across the deep pool. Suddenly, there was a flurry of activity. The dolphins reappeared, pushed the axle and wheels out of hiding, and laid them on the floor of their tank near the seagate. The others hung back while Wiyu and Owu approached the device and studied it intently. That was when things got really interesting.

Omar, who'd been nearly napping, was suddenly and completely awake. He rocked forward in his chair and flipped on the camera's night vision filter.

Song gripped his forearm. "What's happening?" she whispered.

He had no words. The solid steel axle, wheels and all, was floating up from the sand and drifting toward the sea-gate. It floated, ultimately, to the manual control for the sea-gate, at which point, the Beta male used his beak to nudge one end of the device through the spokes of the locking valve.

Static chills danced up and down Omar's spine as he watched two of the dolphins use the axle as a jimmy to rotate the valve. Each animal grasped a wheel in its mouth; one pulled up, one pushed down. The wheel turned, the bar pulled back out of its slot, and the seagate opened.

"How did they *do* that?" breathed Song. "How did they know that's how the seagate worked?"

Omar swallowed. "I sort of showed them when I was in the tank today."

She turned to look at him, obviously as stunned as he was. "What do we do?"

Omar answered her by reaching over and switching the tracking program offline. If the dolphins were detected leaving their habitat, it would set off alarms on every connected computer and cell phone.

"What's to do?" he asked, watching the dolphins disappear into the inner lock of the submarine pen. He leaned back in his chair. "Hey, I've got a deck of cards. Want to play Egyptian War?"

* * *

At midnight, long after Song had turned in, Omar reluctantly relinquished his chair to the graveyard operative, Lana. He'd taken the additional precaution of rotating the telltale camera away from the seagate so it was monitoring a stand of kelp. He hoped Lana wouldn't notice right away, nor that the tracking program was off. All operators were supposed to perform a systems check when they came on duty, but even Omar occasionally forgot to.

He headed to his room in staff quarters. He wondered if Song was still up as he passed her room. No light crept beneath the door, though. He had no real romantic intent; he simply doubted he'd be able to sleep—waiting for the axe to fall and all that. He just wanted her company.

The axe fell at 4:23 A.M. Omar's cell phone warned him that tagged animals were not where they were supposed to be. He'd been dozing, fully dressed, atop his comforter and hit the floor running. Song's door flew open as he passed it. She stepped out into the hall and, for a moment, the two stared owlishly at each other. Together, they bolted for the observation center.

They were the first to arrive. Being fully dressed had given them an advantage.

"What's wrong?" Omar asked Lana, as if he didn't already know.

She pointed at the computer. "I ran a system's check about fifteen minutes ago. Did you know the tracking program was shut down?"

Omar and Song exchanged a nervous glance. "Shut down?" he repeated. "You're kidding."

"Not kidding. Worse than that—Lerner's Dolphins are gone."

"Wow, I … I must've glitched and closed the wrong app. I'm … but how did they get away?"

"That, Omar, is an excellent question."

Win Lerner entered the room on a prickly wave of concern that made Omar's nose itch. Win gestured Lana to move over and took her place at the computer. His eyes raked the displays that showed the activity—or lack thereof—in Solitary Confinement.

He frowned. "Didn't we have a camera on the seagate?"

Omar suddenly found it hard to breathe. "Uh, yessir. We did. It seems to have moved."

"Well, reposition it."

Omar was in the process of doing so when Cecily arrived. "Oh, my God," she said. "It's the Lerner's Dolphins again." She made a beeline for the secondary computer station, called up the tracking app, and peered at the desktop display. "And it looks as if they've gone right back to that canyon." She glanced up at her husband. "How did they escape?"

"Apparently through the seagate." Win gestured at the monitor that now displayed the open access between the habitat tank and the lock. The cart axle still hung from the valve's thick spokes. He looked down at Omar. "Did you do that?"

"Me? No. No, sir. I didn't."

"You wanted to let them go."

"Yes. I did."

"*We* did," confessed Song. "But we didn't let them out. They did that themselves."

The room was momentarily still and silent.

"It's true," Omar said, finally. "We have it on video."

"That's impossible," said Win.

Cecily cut him off. "We can deal with that later, Win. Right now, we need to mount a recovery team." She turned her angry gaze to Omar. "You, Mr. Navarro, will pilot one of the subs."

* * *

Omar would love to have done something to slow Icky II down and hinder the recovery effort, but what would be the point? There was no mystery about where the dolphins had gone. They were congregated in the box canyon where they'd been discovered. He had no doubt they'd be recaptured and returned to the habitat. The Lerners would probably have the seagate welded shut. And fire him. Probably Song, too.

The sun had risen by the time they reached the trench, and the water around the submersibles had lightened to a deep aquamarine. Omar's insides felt like lead as he piloted his craft into the mouth of the canyon. Roughly fifty yards from their bow, the six dots of light that represented the dolphins circled in a tight group. At twenty yards, they made visual contact.

The images in the video displays were twilight gray, at first, but they grew clearer and sharper as a shaft of sunlight penetrated the water's surface. Omar wasn't sure when he realized it couldn't be sunlight. That it was too early in the day for it to be that bright or to have that penetrative power—if it ever did in this trench. But there it was—a bright patch of wavering light, right at the end of the canyon.

The dolphins swam toward it.

Professor Lerner opened a channel to the second submersible. "Cec, I'm prepping the tranquilizers. Ready on the nets and have Felix move into flanking position. The sunlight should make targeting easy."

"Uh," Omar said, "Professor, that can't be sunlight. I don't know what that is."

Lerner glanced up at the monitors and froze. The patch of sunlight had grown unbelievably bright; the dolphins swam into it in single file. As they disappeared into the sunny swirl, their tracking beacons blipped out one by one.

Omar's hand was still on the throttle and he couldn't bring himself to move. Icky II was heading right into the heart of the light. Their bow was less than a foot away when the light simply died. Mere yards ahead of them, a wall of solid rock rose out of the sea floor.

"Oh, shit!" Omar yelped, and threw the sub into full reverse. "Back off Icky One! Back off!" In his rear monitors, he saw the older submersible swing hard to port and throttle into reverse.

Disaster averted, the two little vessels hovered side by side, lights trained on the canyon's rocky face.

"Win," said Cecily's voice over the comm, "I've lost all the beacons. Where did they go?"

"I don't know," her husband murmured, his voice hushed. He turned to Omar. "What did we just see? Those weren't … what were those animals?"

Omar had had more time to consider this than his bosses had. He had no answers, per se, just a sneaking suspicion. "I don't think they were animals, sir," he said. "At least, no more or less than we are. I think they were just folks not from around here who needed to catch the last flight home."

ABOUT MAYA KAATHRYN BOHNHOFF

Born in California, raised in Nebraska, Maya's fascination with speculative fiction dates from the night her dad let her stay up late to watch *The Day the Earth Stood Still*. Mom was furious. Dad was unrepentant. Maya slept with a nightlight until she was fifteen and developed a passion for things that came from outer space or went bump in the night.

Maya started her writing career sketching science fiction comic books in the back row of her elementary school classroom. Since, her short fiction has been published in *Analog*, *Amazing Stories*, *Century*, *Realms of Fantasy*, *Interzone*, and *Jim Baen's Universe*, and often anthologized. She's also been a finalist for the John Campbell, BSFA, and Sidewise awards. Her debut novel, *The Meri*, was a *Locus Magazine* Best First Novel. More recently, she penned a series of Star Wars novels with Michael Reaves, including the *New York Times* bestseller, *Star Wars: The Last Jedi*—a Legends novel of the Expanded Universe.

Maya is a founding member of Book View Café and lives in San Jose, where she writes, performs, and records original and parody music with her husband Jeff. The duo have plumbed the depths of absurdity with a series of parody music videos, including the viral "Midichlorian Rhapsody." The song is on their Grated Hits CD. The couple has also produced three musical children: Alex, Kristine, and Amanda.

You can follow Maya on these websites and on Facebook and Twitter: www.mayabohnhoff.com, www.jeffand-maya.com, and www.bookviewcafe.com.

TAKE ONLY MEMORIES, LEAVE ONLY FOOTPRINTS

by David Bruns

There was no section in the Ranger Handbook labeled "grief."

Sure, there were requirements for a complete physical and a mental health recertification following the loss of a familiar—Ziva had completed all that months ago. Since then, she'd been through the handbook cover to cover and there was nothing—*nothing*—to tell her how she should *feel* without her best friend by her side.

So she'd gone back to work. Her hand strayed to the smaller seat next to hers, aching for the feel of his dense fur. Emptiness.

"We are in stable orbit over Ragos, Ziva," said Lola, her ship's computer.

"Acknowledged," Ziva said. Felix's slim figure had barely reached her hip when he stood on his hind legs, but the ship seemed awfully empty without him.

The blue and green planet, so similar to Earth, raised a lump in her throat. It seemed as if everything around her was some sort of emotional trigger now. Maybe she wasn't ready for active duty after all.

The comm panel trilled, indicating an incoming transmission. The green and blue logo for the World Interstellar Park Rangers flashed on the screen.

Ziva squared her shoulders and told Lola to accept the call. Her spine got even more rigid when she saw who was calling. Brigadier General Halsey Taylor had a close-cropped haircut and an even closer smile.

"Sir, I expected Commander Acton," Ziva blurted out. She cursed to herself. She should have changed into a clean uniform and at least bothered to comb her hair.

Despite the light years of separation, Taylor's eyes bored into hers. "I wanted to talk to you myself, Ranger Hansworth." The skin around his eyes softened a fraction. "I know how hard it is to lose a familiar … there're no words. Your partner's name was Felix, right? Venusian sand otter?"

"Yes, sir," Ziva managed to get out.

"My first familiar was a sand otter, too, you know."

"I didn't, sir."

Taylor's eyes drifted off screen and he gave a slight nod. "Look, Ziva, here's the thing. I know you've just returned to active status, but we've got a bit of a situation brewing in your sector."

"I think work is the best thing for me right now, sir."

Taylor's tight smile returned. "I was hoping you'd say that, Ranger." An incoming file opened on the right side of her screen. "Ragos is a habitable planet, pre-industrial technology base. Bio-diversity rating of 6—and falling fast."

Ziva grunted. She'd seen worse, but the trend lines showed a precipitous falloff in the next few decades.

"Why the drop, sir? Natural disaster?"

"I wish. Poachers." Her screen showed a large, four-legged animal with leathery skin and a crown of horns, reminding her of a cross between an old Earth elephant and a triceratops. "The survey bots categorized them as hathosaurs, but the natives call them *broosers*. They hunt them for their horns, if you can believe it. What these natives don't realize is that everything in their ecosystem relies on this creature. From the birds that feed off the insects on its skin to the way it keeps the forests clear of underbrush to the unique bacteria that thrives in its dung, this animal is the glue that holds that region's bio-diversity together."

Taylor's tone had gotten increasingly heated. You didn't get to his rank in the WISPR Corps without a passion for the job. For two centuries, mankind used Earth and its biome as if they had a spare somewhere in the universe. The result was a planet where citizens had to get respiratory enhancements implanted at birth and most of the necessities of life were imported from off-planet. Humans survived, but they also recognized there was a better way.

The WISPR Corps was modeled after the old National Park Service of the United States, an agency with a mission to preserve bio-diversity—hopefully, without interfering with the native humanoid population.

"Anyway," Taylor continued in a calmer voice, "this is a simple, but time-sensitive job." He brought up a topographical map on the adjoining screen. A red circle pulsed like a beacon. "That's the herd we've identified for intervention. The native humanoid population is in the middle of a civil war, making these animals vulnerable to poaching. If you can just move them across this mountain range"—a dotted trail stepped across the map—"they're out of harm's way, at least for now."

"Sounds simple enough," Ziva replied. "Do we have a contact baseline for the hathosaurs?"

Taylor shook his head. "All we have is the original survey from fifty years ago."

Ziva grunted. She understood Taylor's quandary now. A lot could change in fifty years, which was why the handbook specified two rangers for jobs without a recent baseline. With Felix by her side, this assignment would have been a piece of cake. After all, improvised contact was what they'd done best together—and they'd earned a Bio-Diversity Silver Star to prove it. But on her own?

She found her hand straying to the empty chair again. She pulled it back into her lap. It was time to move on.

"I'm in, sir."

* * *

The valley was shaped like an elongated oval nestled up against a steep mountain range. She landed her scout craft in a gully two kilometers downwind of the herd and on the opposite end of the valley from the poacher's camp. The terrain around her—rolling grasslands sprinkled with clumps of trees—provided plenty of cover to approach the herd unseen and make contact.

A quick in and out, she told herself. *Easy peasy.*

Ziva buckled on her ranger belt, settling the heaviness around her hips. It held all the essentials for a three-day excursion: food tablets, water purification, first-aid kit, power pack, and body shield, a sort of cloak that bent light around her form to make her nearly invisible.

She hesitated for a moment, then drew a small energy pistol from the arms locker. Probably overkill for the situation, but Ziva was feeling increasingly stressed about making this approach without Felix. The WISPR Corps motto on the wall said "Take only memories, leave only footprints," but that was more of a guideline. Actual results may vary.

The night air was dry and chill with not a breath of wind. "Comms check, Lola," she whispered, unwilling to disturb the peacefulness of the scene. In response, Lola accessed the implant in her optic nerve, projecting a transparent display across Ziva's field of vision.

The dots on the display representing the herd were already moving in the direction she wanted to send them. Not a panicked stampede, but a slow migration. Ziva let out a sigh of relief. Maybe all she would have to do is follow them over the mountains to complete the assignment.

She set off at a brisk trot, the body shield shimmering slightly with her movement. The shields weren't perfect. To the human eye, she would appear as a ripple in the darkness, a barely there phantom.

As she drew closer to the herd, the synesthetic sensor translated raw emotions from the hathosaur herd into colors on her heads-up display. For cold introductions the synesthetic link was a quick and dirty way to gauge emotional response. Her display showed a grouping of about thirty hathosaurs, all registering a contented blue sprinkled with the green of affection for one another. She slowed to a walk. They were just over the next rise.

A spike of red on her display and the crack of a gunshot occurred at the same time. She powered her way up the slope.

Dots of brightness pierced the darkness like fireflies. *Headlamps*, she realized. *Poachers*.

"Lola, what's going on?"

"It appears interference from the mountain range masked the approach of the poachers. Recommend you fall back, Ranger."

Baaa-waaah! A panicked wail floated through the night from the direction of a cluster of lights. A juvenile hathosaur struggled underneath a heavy net. The poachers were trying to take a small one alive.

An enraged roar shattered the night. More gunshots sounded, and the gaggle of headlamps scattered as a female hathosaur—Ziva could tell by the smooth ripples of her crown—staggered into the circle of light. Blood streamed from the massive animal's side, but she was determined to get to her baby. She seized the netting in her teeth and backed away.

More gunshots. Pools of black blossomed on the creature's hide, and painful red splashed across Ziva's display. The big female stumbled, but held on to the net. The poachers swarmed around her, some wielding clubs and knives.

"Ranger," Lola said, her voice a beacon of calm in the chaos, "fall back."

Ziva stood rooted. No question this was a cut-and-dried first contact situation. If she interfered here, she'd almost certainly be seen by the humanoid population, a serious violation of the Ranger Handbook. The correct move was for her to withdraw, find the rest of the herd, and complete her mission. The mother was dying, the baby captured. There was nothing she could do.

Instead, Ziva's feet took her toward the carnage. Her brain told her she was reacting to the loss of Felix in a way that endangered her and her mission. Ziva's heart didn't care. She was going to save that baby, no matter the cost.

Ziva entered the circle of headlamps as a blur of bent light. One of the poachers looked straight through her, his eyes wide, his mouth wider. She punched him right in the face, feeling a satisfying tremor run up her forearm, a spike of pain in her split knuckles. She swept another's feet from under him. A third yelled something and backed away. The headlamps retreated into the night.

Ziva was alone with the dying hathosaur and her baby.

She whipped out her laser knife and sliced through the net pinning the youngster to the dirt. The baby staggered to its feet and raced to its mother. The elder hathosaur nuzzled her child, licking its face while the little one squealed muted cries of panic. The mother's aura started to fade from Ziva's display.

The beast rolled to her knees and tried to heave herself to her feet. Her hind legs straightened, quivered, then collapsed. Blood frothed at her lips and her nose sank into the dirt. Ziva's vision was crazy with color: the crimson of the mother's pain, the little one's panicked yellow, but also a wave of deep green connection between the two. Ziva swiped at her cheeks.

"Ranger," Lola said in her ear. "You need to clear the area. There's nothing you can do for her."

Ziva ignored the voice. She slipped a painkiller hypo out of her first-aid pack and sidled next to the dying animal. Her fingers slid across the leathery skin, searching behind the lip of her bony crown. The mother's sides, black with steaming blood, heaved against Ziva's torso. A dark eye, as big as a baseball, watched her, frightened by her presence but unable to move.

"It's okay," she crooned. "I'll keep him safe." The mother lowed at her as if the hathosaur understood. Ziva's fingers found the spot behind the crown, a faintly pulsing artery as big as her thumb. She touched it with the tip of the hypo, releasing the maximum dose into the animal's bloodstream. The rumbling breath slowed, then stopped. Ziva rested her forehead against the dead animal's rough skin.

The baby bumped his crown against Ziva's hip, mewling. She slipped her arm around his neck and pulled him close.

"Let's get you back to the herd, little one," she whispered. "I promised your mama."

Her display told her the poachers were gone for now. The hathosaur herd had moved far ahead, a clump of dots traveling fast toward the pass. A silver lining for the mission. She'd return the baby to the herd and get the hell away before the poachers came back.

She urged the youngster to walk faster. His back was elbow-high, a perfect height for her to rest her forearm on as they walked. Her fingers found the life-giving artery behind his soft crown. As a male, he would grow up to have a huge bony headpiece with wicked curving horns, but at this young age, the top of his head was like rubber, warm and elastic to her touch.

They rose through the tree line, breath singing in Ziva's nostrils, the path before them latticed with moonlight filtered by the trees. She realized with an ache that this was the most alive she'd felt since Felix's death. The baby's eye glimmered in the dark as he watched her.

"You would have liked Felix." She patted his back. "He could have ridden right here and talked your ear off the whole way. He was good with languages. The best." The baby purred in reply, but whether his response was for his lost mother or her lost companion, Ziva wasn't sure.

Soon—too soon, she felt—they arrived at the pass, a ten-meter gap in a sheer rock face. Beyond she could see a band of thick forest, and then more rolling grassland dotted with stands of trees. Indistinguishable from the land at her back, but also safer for these magnificent animals.

Ziva drew a deep breath. Being a ranger at a time like this was heady stuff. She was making a difference in the universe, maybe even saving this planet. These were the moments she and Felix had loved.

Suddenly, she was weeping. Uncontrollable, racking sobs that threatened to drive her to her knees. For the first time in her career, she was celebrating a successful mission alone.

A low rumble issued from the shadows, making Ziva's head snap up.

A massive bull hathosaur stalked into the moonlight. The horns of his crown curved out like enormous scimitars, so long the ends almost crossed. Scars on his hide, bleached silver in the moonlight, rippled as he closed the distance between them. Ziva's breath stilled. The crunch of gravel under his massive feet screeched in the stillness of the night.

He stopped, lowering his gaze to her. She sensed intelligence there, understanding.

Another rumble. She felt it resonate in her chest cavity. The youngster replied, his response several octaves higher.

They're talking. Given time, a full suite of instruments, and Felix, and she could have told the patriarch of the herd what had happened. But she had none of these.

The old bull's muzzle lowered to sniff the youngster, and she saw the fine questing nostrils touch the soft crown tenderly, like a kiss. She gulped at the horns hovering over her, so close she could see the fine polish on the ebony shafts, the razor-sharp tips. He raised his head, blasting her still-wet cheeks as he breathed out. She smelled the warm scent of chewed grass, the tang of peppermint leaves, and the musk of river water.

With a final rib-tickling sigh, the big animal wheeled around, lumbering toward the pass. The youngster gave her hip one last nudge, then followed.

Ziva watched them go, feeling more alone than ever.

Mission accomplished, she thought with an edge of bitterness.

She plotted a course back to her ship that would keep her well away from the poachers and started down the slope, letting gravity lengthen her strides. She found a wide game trail and stuck to the center. It was mostly bare except for a broad patch of grass and leaves covering the path. Ziva pushed ahead, eager to be away from this place.

Then the ground opened up and she was falling.

* * *

The wretched smell was so overpowering, it forced her awake. Ziva gasped for a clean breath in the oppressive darkness.

"Lola, where am I?"

"My sensors show you are in the poacher's camp."

Ziva sat up, realizing her ranger belt was gone. Protection, weapons, food … all gone. Her fingers probed the inky space. Smooth wooden bars all around her. She was in a cage.

"Help!" she called out.

There was a shifting in the shadows, and a sliver of light appeared in front of her. Ziva rushed to the side of the cage. "Please, help me."

The crack of light disappeared. She poked at the narrow space between the bars. Rough cloth met her finger tips. She parted the material. "Who's there?" she called.

A gruesome face filled the space. "Shhhh!" it said. Ziva fell back in horror. A flattened nose, a single large brown eye on one side of the face and a livid scar bisecting an empty eye socket on the other side. Her brain tried to process the image.

"Lola," she whispered. "What are the indigenous primate species?" A row of images ran across her vision; her eye selected the closest match. A lascar monkey, the readout said. Also called the singing primate for their love of music. Ten kilos, bipedal, with short russet-colored fur.

Ziva hummed a soft tune—the only one she could think of was *Twinkle, Twinkle, Little Star*—and used her finger to part the cloth covering her cage.

At first, she thought the monkey had fled the room, but then she heard a sound. Someone was humming along … in harmony. Slowly, the primate came into her field of view, the humming getting louder, head bent. Ziva let the song end after the third time through. The monkey clapped his hands and looked up at her.

Ziva kept her face still, despite the revulsion she felt. The lascar monkeys in the data stream had round, soulful faces with features that drooped. This individual had a wicked scar like a lightning bolt of red that ran from the center of its forehead across an eye and slashing through the cheek muscle. A wound from an axe or a knife. He covered the damaged side of his face and hooted softly as if apologizing.

Ziva wormed her hand between the bars, pulling the monkey's palm from its face.

"It's okay—" She stopped in shock.

His touch electrified her, stilled her breath. The ranger name for the feeling was *kinship*, the sensation of mutual awareness with another being. Ziva had felt it before. Once, when she'd met Felix and they'd selected each other as familiars.

The monkey screeched and backpedaled to cower against the far wall. Before Ziva could ease the animal's terror, the door to the room burst open and two men strode in.

They were barely Ziva's height, heavily muscled and dressed in a mixture of roughspun cloth and leather. One unlatched the cage door while the other stood by to grab her. She had hand-to-hand combat skills, but this matchup was not in her favor. Ziva let them bind her hands and drag her out the door.

It was dark outside, save for the flickering light of a roaring campfire. The moon had set, leaving a vast carpet of stars overhead—where she should be right now.

"Lola," she subvocalized, "engage the translation program."

The pair dumped her inside the ring of people gathered around the fire. Half of her face roasted while the cheek facing away from the flame was chilled.

"You." The voice was low and husky, like ice crunching under the heel of a boot. "Who are you?"

Ziva raised her head. The man was taller and leaner than the two who had brought her out, with eyes like shiny black marbles and a shaved head. Despite the chill, he was shirtless. A necklace hung across his bare chest, strung with what looked like dried fruit.

Her eyes shifted past him. Just outside the firelight, she saw the outline of the monkey, watching. The man's eyes followed her gaze. "Gar," he roared. "Get over here!"

The animal slunk forward, his nose practically touching the dirt, holding a carved wooden mug over his head like an offering. The man took the mug and drank. Gar's good eye found Ziva.

Without warning, the man launched a kick that sent the monkey sprawling. He was on the animal in a flash, a long machete gleaming in his hand like a shard of ice. Gar squealed, cowering. He touched the tip of the knife to the monkey's scarred face. "You lookin' at her? Did I say you could look at her?" Gar's head cycled back and forth slowly, wary of the blade against his flesh. "Maybe I should cut the other side of your face, so it's even-like, eh?"

A chorus of laughs sounded around Ziva.

"Or maybe you want a new eye?" The man plucked at the necklace. "I've got dozens right here. Just add water." He gave the monkey a final kick and bawled out a laugh. As Gar scampered away, the man stalked back to Ziva.

"My men say you're a ghost," he said, drinking deeply from his mug.

"You tell her, Max," someone called out.

"Your men are drunk," Ziva shot back in his language.

"Ziva," Lola began, "I think it's best not to—"

The kick made her see stars. She blinked, cursing at herself. The blow had severed her connection to Lola.

Max said something and strutted back to his chair. He waited for Ziva to sit up.

He threw her ranger belt into the dirt. With her connection to Lola gone, she couldn't understand him, but his question was pretty clear.

Ziva eyed the distance to the belt. It was keyed to her DNA, a precaution for exactly this kind of scenario, but she judged it just out of reach. She'd seen Max move and she'd probably lose an arm before she could get out her weapon.

Her brain raced. She could really use Lola right now. "Broosers," she said. That was the only word in their language she could remember.

Silence reigned around the campfire. Then Max laughed, a booming roar that echoed off the shanties of the camp.

It turned out Max didn't really care where she was from or why she was there at all. He was more concerned about making sure he maintained discipline among his men.

"Haji," he roared. A man with a black eye stumbled forward. Ziva thought he might have been the one she'd punched in the face. Max spoke again, and she recognized their word for *ghost*.

Haji shrugged and stared at the ground.

Max spat in the dirt and said something that had the sound of a challenge.

The crowd migrated into a tight ring around her and Haji. Ziva got to her feet. She didn't need Lola to recognize her bad situation had just gotten worse. Max barked out an order, and to her surprise, someone cut her free.

Well, Ziva reflected as she rubbed some circulation back into her wrists, fighting was the best worst option.

* * *

Ziva woke up again in the cage. At least they'd left the tarp off this time so she could breathe.

She tried to sit up and groaned in pain. Bruised ribs, and her face felt like someone had walked on it. Probably had.

Her combat training had gotten her through two contenders and the betting had gotten pretty fierce when the crowd started chanting "Sabo, Sabo, Sabo..."

Sabo turned out to be a squat mound of muscle with a center of gravity like a brick of depleted uranium. He wasn't a boxer, he was a wrestler and once he got hold of her, Ziva knew it was all over. The last thing she remembered was the ground rushing up to meet her face.

The door slid open and Gar entered. He seemed upset, slapping his face with his long fingers and humming *Twinkle, Twinkle, Little Star* in a rushed way, over and over again. Ziva wanted to give him a reassuring smile, but her face felt like it might split open if she tried. She settled for joining him in a group hum.

The monkey shut the door behind him and made his way across the room with a rolling gait. Ziva let him touch her bruised cheek. The animal teared up and made a whimpering sound. He stepped back, shaking his head, slapping his face with both hands.

"It's okay," Ziva mumbled. "It doesn't hurt that much." She stuck her fingers through the bars. "I've had worse."

Slowly, Gar calmed down. He interlaced her fingers with his own. Despite her pain-muddled mind, she felt the kinship connection again. This time, Gar didn't back away. He pursed his lips and started humming again.

Ziva moved close to the bars. "Gar," she whispered, "can you get me out of here?"

She braced herself for the expected frantic outburst. It was obvious the animal had been abused, his spirit broken. She was asking him to go against the man he feared more than anything.

For a long moment, Gar didn't react; he just kept humming. Ziva was tempted to make the request again, when the monkey loped across the room and cracked open the door. Standing stock-still, he pressed his good eye to the slit. Ziva held her breath.

Finally, Gar slid the door shut, scrambled back, and busied himself with the side of her cage. He hooted softly as the door swung open. Ziva climbed out, her limbs bruised and stiff. When she started for the door, Gar gave a little shriek and jumped in her path. Taking her hand, he led her to the back of the room where a pink snake as thick as her thigh was coiled in its cage. The snake's spade-shaped head rose, swaying back and forth, watching them.

Gar ignored the snake and slid its cage aside to reveal a gap between the wall and floor just large enough for Ziva to squeeze through. She knelt down. It smelled like a refuse pile on the other side.

She took the monkey's hand. "Come with me, Gar." The Ranger Handbook forbade removing indigenous life from a planet, but she'd be damned if she'd leave him here. Max would kill him once he'd figured out what Gar had done.

"Please," she tried again.

The monkey stepped back, shaking his head violently. He pointed to the gap and hooted.

"Gar…"

His finger didn't waver.

Ziva wriggled through the gap. She was right about the refuse pile. With filth smeared across the front of her uniform, she stood. The night was silent and cold, but it felt clean after the fetid atmosphere of the kennel. Behind her, she could hear Gar moving the snake's cage back in front of the gap.

She took her bearings from the stars and started walking back to her ship.

* * *

Ziva had stumbled through the grassland for more than an hour. She was safe now. If she stayed on this bearing, she'd find her ship.

Technically, the intervention was a success. Once she got reconnected to Lola, she could send a self-destruct signal to her belt. That would erase any positive proof of her interaction with the natives. The story of the fighting woman in strange clothes would eventually fade into an old man's campfire story.

Try as she might, Ziva could not shake Gar from her thoughts. The disfigured monkey had connected with her in a way she hadn't felt since … Felix. Was it possible? Many rangers who lost their partner never found another familiar. After all these months of living with the loss of Felix, Ziva assumed that was her path as well.

But she had felt the kinship—and Gar had felt it, too. She was sure of it. It had terrified him, but he'd felt it.

She shook her head until her brain hurt, anger and guilt contributing in equal measure to the violent motion. It was over. Whatever connection she thought she'd experienced was behind her. It was time to get the hell off this world.

The ground trembled under her feet, silencing the maelstrom in her mind.

Earthquake?

The flesh of her bruised belly quivered with the vibration filling the air around her.

She knew that sound, that full-body sensation. The giant bull hathosaur loomed in front of her, blotting out the stars. Behind him, she saw many more beasts gathered. His head lowered until his eyes were level with hers, and his heavy breath washed over her aching face. The dark eyeball glimmered with intent.

The hathosaurs had a plan. No translation needed.

He knelt in the dust and turned his horns away from her so she could climb onto his back.

* * *

What had taken her an hour to walk they covered in minutes. The wind whistled in her ears as the herd thundered down the valley toward the poacher's camp.

Ziva saw the flicker of a bonfire on the horizon. Surely the poachers would hear them coming. As if in answer to her thought, she heard the boom of rifles, but the herd did not falter. The mass of bodies swept through the camp like a living wave, smashing buildings, cracking open cages, tossing poachers aside like rag dolls.

Ziva looked for any sign of Gar as they thundered through the camp. Nothing. She pounded on the old bull's crown, tugged on his horns. "Go back," she cried.

Like an ocean liner, the animal steered a wide, looping turn back to the flattened village. The remains of the huts had caught fire, casting the area in flickering yellow.

Not completely flattened, Ziva saw. The back wall of the kennel, including the cage where she'd been imprisoned, was still standing. Max was there, bare-chested with his necklace of withered eyeballs. His machete shone in the firelight as he brandished it over his head.

He held Gar upside down by one foot.

Ziva kicked her heels into the old bull's neck, and she felt him pick up speed. She stood, cupping her hands around her mouth. "Max!" she screamed.

The man's head snapped up, his lips curled into a snarl.

Ziva leapt from the bull's back into open space.

She could read Max's mind—he had time to use the machete on the monkey or on Ziva, but not both. The glowing sword quivered with indecision.

That was when Gar bit him in the leg.

Max screamed, his mind made up. But his split second of indecision was all it took to change the calculus of the fight. Just as the machete started its downward swing toward Gar's head, Ziva's body hit Max square in the chest.

The long blade bit into her back, but the blow had lost much of its power. The momentum of her collision smashed Max back against the heavy cage, and she felt the wind rush out of his lungs. The machete spiraled away. Gar, unharmed, fell to the ground with a squeak.

Ziva pressed her advantage, landing blow after blow on the larger man. Blood covered his stunned face. He managed to jam a knee into Ziva's bruised ribs and she staggered back, clutching her side. Her boot connected with the machete. She picked it up, advancing on Max again.

He was on his hands and knees, lips peeled away from blood-stained teeth. "Do it!" he screamed at her.

Ziva raised the long knife, fully ready to grant the man his wish, when a body bowled her over. She lost her grip on the machete. Gar stood over her, shaking his head violently, slapping his face with both hands. Ziva writhed in the dirt from the fresh wave of pain radiating from her ribs.

A long chuckle danced in the air. Max stood over them, machete in hand, laughing.

Gar stepped in front of her, baring his teeth. The muscles of his shoulders bunched as the monkey prepared to defend her. Max raised the long machete.

In the darkness behind the poacher, a familiar shape loomed. Two enormous ebony horns, so long the ends nearly overlapped, scooped up Max. His screams disappeared into the darkness.

* * *

"Incoming transmission," Lola said.

They were in transit to the nearest ranger station, recalled from the field for a formal inquiry. Ziva made one last check of her immaculate uniform. "Accept the transmission, Lola."

The WISPR logo was replaced by Brigadier General Taylor's square features.

"Good morning, sir," Ziva said. Most of the swelling in her face had gone down so she could speak clearly, but she knew she looked a sight: two black eyes, a split lip, and a brilliant purple-green line along her jaw.

Taylor's eyebrow twitched. "I'd make a lighthearted comment about how the other guy looks, but I know from your report that it's very likely he didn't make it."

Ziva settled for a simple, "Yes, sir."

"There'll be an investigation, of course."

Ziva nodded. First-contact violations with a humanoid population triggered an automatic investigation.

"That said," Taylor continued, "I'm reasonably confident you will be cleared … on *that* charge." His gaze shifted to the seat on Ziva's right. "This is the candidate for your new familiar?" Gar nodded back, his eyes large and solemn.

"His vocal module is not installed yet, sir. But Gar is very pleased to meet you." The monkey nodded again.

"Likewise, Gar." He looked back at Ziva. "I assume you've been candid with him about what he can expect from training?"

Gar hooted a response before Ziva could answer.

The general hesitated. "You know, Ziva, I don't have to tell you that what we do is hard. On every mission, a ranger walks a fine line between serving the greater good and disturbing the natural development of a culture. We make judgment calls and we hope they're right. But we both know it's a lot easier with a trusted partner by your side. I wish you the very best, Ranger Hansworth—and you, too, Gar."

Ziva gripped Gar's hand. "Thank you, sir."

After the call ended, she leaned back in the pilot's chair, watching the stars in silence.

Gar began to hum. Ziva joined in.

ABOUT DAVID BRUNS

David Bruns is a former officer on a nuclear-powered submarine turned high-tech executive turned science fiction writer. He is the creator of the sci-fi/fantasy series, *The Dream Guild Chronicles*, and the bestselling military sci-fi novel *Invincible*, based on Nick Webb's *Legacy Fleet* series. His short fiction has appeared in such speculative fiction anthologies as *The Future Chronicles* and *Beyond the Stars* and well as online magazines like *Compelling Sci-Fi*. David is also a 2017 graduate of the prestigious Clarion West workshop. In his spare time, he co-writes contemporary thrillers with a retired naval intelligence officer. Find out more at www. davidbruns.com.

THIS DECEITFUL STATE OF TRUTH

by Patty Jansen

CLOUD CITY, MELLIVAR.

Outpost of humanity, rough and primitive as the Wild West, and the next dot on the map in my travelling audit show. Just kidding—I'm an auditor with the Solaris Agency and have just arrived on the shuttle for my regular check of the accounts.

Cloud City is as weird and quaint as I remember from my previous visit. The city hangs—quite rightly—in the clouds, suspended by ropes from large, bulbous, semi-transparent balloons.

I make my way down the walkway, carrying my awkward bag over my shoulder, bumping into people coming the other way. It looks like the shuttle is not going to stay here for long. The pilots haven't killed the engines, and their high-pitched screaming sends children running while covering their ears.

For those who, like me, are not used to it, walking is not easy on this wobbly walkway hanging in the clouds. The planks are made from some kind of synth-wood and, while they may not rot in the constant humidity, they're wet and slippery. There is a railing and guy ropes to hang onto, but they're wet, too. Water leaks down the suspension ropes and drips from transparent pink flanges that dangle from the balloons past the walkway. Sometimes they come close enough that I can feel their soft fleshiness brush past me. That gives me the creeps. I look up to their bulbous bodies crowding above, each with their harness holding their part of the city up in the clouds. Against the light of the enormous sun, you can see their widely spaced organs floating inside their inflated bodies. A heart, always beating, and intestines churning and gurgling at whatever it is these things eat. One end has a snout-like protuberance, and the fleshy flanges hang down the back. I cannot make out any eyes, and I'm unsure if they have any. But they're alive. They're constantly moving, vibrating, flapping. One of the things spreads its flanges and sprays a gout of water which twinkles and sparkles on its way down, becoming a fine mist which rains over me.

Not even a minute into my commission and I'm already being pissed on. Great.

* * *

I remember the way to the council building. The whole of Cloud City spans several hubs with walkways in between. Some hold official rooms, others hold apartments, all rooms with windows to the clouds. The walkways along the outside and between the structures bustle with activity: men carrying baskets of fish from the ocean below; women in frilly dresses with stiff bodices, sheltering under umbrellas; men in leather coats and hats wearing goggles; children running and playing. A couple of boys have captured a young balloon on a rope. The creature is barely as wide as the boys are tall, and in its efforts to escape from the net, it inflates and deflates with squeaks and farts that would make a whoopie cushion blush.

It's something out of an ancient play.

I climb the steps into the council meeting hall. The door is open, as usual. Cloud City is not big and everyone knows each other. Citizens are welcome to speak to the councillors at any time.

The hall with the arched windows resembles something out of ancient history. Not the same, though, because the floor moves, and every now and then a rain of spray trails, twinkling, past the window.

There is a long table at the far end of the room, and a group of ancient men sit around it, engrossed in a discussion.

They look up and nod greetings when I come in.

I search the table for a familiar face, and find none. It was three local years ago, to the day, that I was here, and of course things would have changed since then. Heaven knows, any number of men this age could have died, but *all* of them?

"Yes, Lady, can I help you?" says the man at the head of the table.

"I'm Ellinor Darga, auditor for the Solaris Agency."

He nods, and says nothing.

"Is administrator Markan here?" I ask.

"Clarys Markan does not hold the position of administrator anymore. I'm Farber Endovan, his successor."

Oh, well, that's … interesting. One was apparently never too old for political upheaval. "He is all right, though, isn't he?"

I like Clarys. He is entertaining, and jovial and funny, in all the ways these prunes around the table are … not.

There is brief moment of hesitation. "Yes. Of course he is."

I don't like that hesitation, not at all.

* * *

Farber Endovan bids me to sit, and tea appears at the table.

The cup in front of me breathes trails of steam into the air. I pick it up and warm my hands.

"Welcome to Cloud City, auditor," a thin man says. "I think you will be much pleased with our financial situation." He introduces himself as Symen Closki, the accountant.

I don't recall ever being displeased. For a world like Mellivar, an audit is a mere formality. Nobody cares about their accounts, because there is no external money to speak of.

"Today, we talk not of work," Farber Endovan says. "Tea is for enjoyment. Tea and politics don't mix."

There are sage nods all around.

Well, that's different. During both my previous visits, Clarys used to question me to death about developments in the rest of the inhabited galaxy, political or otherwise. He wanted to know about *all* of it.

But as auditor—and I'm a very experienced one at that—my brief is not to rock the boat unless necessary, so I don't press the issue.

We drink tea.

One can talk only so much about the weather—how does "always sunny and humid" sound?—or about an exceedingly boring long-distance trip through the depths of space. I find that I have nothing in common with the wizened, wrinkled men of the latest version of the Mellivar Council, and they seem thoroughly uninterested in life beyond their backwater world.

I tell them—to bored silence—that we have a new Governor and that the extensions to the Solaris Hub are almost finished. But I suspect they have little interest in what goes on at the hub, and they have no idea who the governor is and why they need one.

Or for that matter, what I'm doing here.

To keep the conversation running, I ask them what their news is. "At the hub, we don't exactly get a lot of news from Mellivar." Then I remember a bit of news that scrolled across the screen as I was waiting at Artemis for the shuttle to Mellivar. "I heard some news about a murder."

It is as if I've fired a shot through the room. Eyes widen. Backs straighten.

Farber Endovan says, "It's all solved. This is a peaceful society."

"And we want it to stay like that," adds Symen Closki. "We deal with people who commit crimes." Implying that the Solaris Agency didn't? Or did he mean *deal with* as in: mete out cruel punishment?

He gives me a pointed look from under his white eyebrows, unruly and fashioned into horns.

"I have no interest disturbing your peace," I say. I'm not sure why they're all so defensive all of a sudden. "I just saw it mentioned on the news. But if there is anything you want from the agency regarding justice, I can help."

"We don't want your modern frippery," says Symen. "It drives the young ones to greed."

Whoa.

Farber Endovan shoots him a sharp look across the sweet cakes and empty cups.

"I was a bit surprised, and curious, because I've always been told the crime rate in Mellivar is extremely low."

Symen opens his mouth, but Farber talks over the top of him. "It is extremely low."

Interesting. "Accept my apologies. I was curious, and I'm sorry if it offends you that I mentioned it."

It seems that finally the supply of tea has come to an end, and I'm allowed to leave.

"Jorak will take you to your rooms," Farber says.

Jorak appears to be the young man in uniform who has been standing motionless at the door. He springs to life the moment his name is mentioned. He bows to me and to Farber, who acknowledges him with a wave of his hand.

"He will look after you while you're here."

Great. I'm being guarded.

I get up from the table and gather my bags. I really need to pee after all that tea, and hope the rooms are not too far.

"Have a good rest, auditor," Farber says. "Work starts tomorrow."

* * *

Of course, there is no tomorrow.

On a tidally locked planet, the sun is always in the same position every day, and it stays there for however many hours you put in. Mellivar *has* no days. It has a dayside and a nightside and they never change.

The planet is covered in a thick ice sheet except at the subsolar point, where the sunlight is strong enough to melt the ice and where there is a perfectly circular ocean, most of it shrouded in low cloud. That's where the city floats and life goes on at any time of the endless day.

Fishermen go up and down the ropes in little cages made from fish bones—I hate to think of the size of the fish—using mechanisms that creak.

The live balloons that hold up the city spray their hearts out. Their intakes of breath sound like a coming storm. They spray excess water like rain. Every time one releases surplus helium, it does so with a squeak reminiscent of someone trying and failing to hold in a fart, only a hundred times louder.

People walk past my room talking.

I'm restless. I don't like the new council and their strange attitude. I don't like that I've heard nothing about Clarys.

I hope I won't get caught up in any trouble. I've got a month before the shuttle comes back, and I'd planned to do some stargazing out on the planet's terminator. I've got my final project due for my Astronomy Navigation degree. It's my little secret, my planned career change. But the agency won't be told until I have that qualification.

There is a reason I planned my visit at the exact anniversary of my previous visit. If I'm right, my thesis will knock the Board of Examiners' socks off. I will solve one of the greatest mysteries in all of human space settlement. But first I must arrange this cold and long trip out there. And do the accounts. Yawn.

I lie on my bed, wide awake.

The whole structure of the city is constantly moving and creaking. I stare at the rough synth-wooden ceiling and the gentle dangling of a couple of lengths of leather hanging on a hook on the wall. They look like whips without a handle.

Needless to say, there is no sleep for me.

* * *

I have a reason to want a career change: being an auditor is boring.

I used to like the travel, but having been to all the settled worlds in the corner of the galaxy that is my responsibility, and having been back to each world at least three times, I'm up for something new.

At Mellivar, the only thing you get used to is constantly being wet. When you get up in the morning, the clothes you left on the end of the bed are wet. Your shoes are wet. Everything you touch is wet.

Of course, I was supposed to have covered my belongings with the waxed cloths that lay folded on the table in the corner. There is also a jar with bags of salt to take away the moisture.

But I forgot, so my stuff is wet.

The sun, big and orange and always at the zenith, doesn't give much warmth, and when there is no breeze, the mist sets in. When there is a breeze, it gets *cold.*

After a breakfast of cold smoked fish, I ask Jorak to take me to the council building. He's quiet and obedient and answers most of my questions with a blank stare. I ask him about Clarys—stare. I ask him about the latest news—stare. I even ask him about the murder, but all he can do is stare.

I'm starting to wonder if he even understands me. But the question of whether he can help me arrange travel to the planet's terminator to do my astronomy project yields a response. I know he's seen my telescopes, and I've seen his widened eyes.

"I can help you, but you should know that we don't go down to the surface," he says in a thick accent.

"I know." Many people don't go down at any rate. Obviously people are down there, because I can see the boats and floating crop platforms from here. "But I want to go anyway. The sky in Cloud City is too light for me to study the stars."

"I can arrange it."

* * *

I find that the council's financial books are … interesting, to say the least.

Not that they're messy, but there are unexplained sources of income that I can't seem to trace. As far as I know, Mellivar doesn't export anything.

I sit at the tiny desk in my room trying to decide what to do about the job I've come to do. I've found no records that show that the city is either financially sound or in the red. Ideally, I would evaluate the level of Agency support we'd give, based on the settlement's current status and income. But where does the income come from?

Unless I find out, I'm going to have to put a mark against their name for financial untrustworthiness.

They're not going to be happy with that.

* * *

"I was wondering if you could help me out with something."

Symen Closki looks up from his work. A piece of leather is spread out over the table, and he's using metal tools to emboss it with an intricate patterns of dots.

Being an accountant is obviously not a time-consuming task.

He gestures wordlessly to the chair opposite him. I sit down, one moment before I realise that I'm in the humid breeze that carries balloon piss. Did he do that on purpose?

"Yes," he says. "You wanted…?"

"I have just started on the evaluation of the accounts. I can see that there is quite a bit of unspecified income flowing into Cloud City. I need to know where it comes from before I can approve the accounts."

He gives me a sharp look. "We sell helium to Artemis hub, so that they can sell it on to passing ships."

That almost makes sense, because there is plenty of helium on Mellivar. But there are a few strange discrepancies. "I thought the council had decided against the sale of helium." That's what Clarys told me last time I visited.

"That's why you wouldn't find it identified as such. Some people … find the harvesting of helium from live animals distasteful."

Hell, it *is* distasteful. "Why do it now, when it has never been done before? It's not as if Mellivar is in a difficult position financially."

"Because we want no more of your meddling." He looks me straight in the face when he says that.

"I'm going to have to put this helium export on my report." My heart is hammering.

"Do that. Report us for untrustworthiness. Withdraw your financial support. Don't come back again. By the time your bureaucracy has made their decision, whichever way, we won't need either your money or you."

Well, damn. "Falling under the Solaris Agency is about a lot more than money."

"Yes. It's about meddling."

"It's about providing shuttles, and transport for your citizens."

"Where would they go?" He gives me another penetrating look.

Also true. The rest of the colonised galaxy is just as uninterested in Mellivar as Mellivar is in them. Helium is valuable but not that valuable.

"Is this why Clarys Markan is no longer administrator?"

"One of the reasons."

"Where is he?"

But he says he doesn't know. I don't believe him at all. In a small settlement like Cloud City, everyone knows one another. Which means Clarys is probably down on the surface somewhere. Or he's dead.

I can't say that either of those two prospects fills me with a lot of confidence.

* * *

Jorak has arranged a trip for me, and this takes up most of my time for the next few days. I'm not sure if I should chase up where and how the helium is sourced—I'm not sure I want to know, and I've got most of a month here until the shuttle comes back. I may be pushing my luck a bit far if I press for answers. Obviously the council is able to make a convincing—dare I say threatening—case for a previous administrator to leave the settlement, and I have no illusions that they will be any more prudent with me. They know I carry an emergency beacon that can send out a message to the Agency, but Agency help will not be able to respond quickly, and by the time they're here, I may be nothing more than bones if the council members decide to "accidentally" let me slip off the walkway.

What was that again about a murder?

Even if Jorak, guide and balloon handler, is a silent taciturn type, it's good to be away from Cloud City and working on my thesis. Once we're away from Cloud City and its satellite towns, it's just us and the wind whistling in the ropes and the squeaking and farting of the two balloons and the serene and surreal landscape below. I can see the agricultural platforms floating on the ocean down there. Away from the subsolar point, the temperature drops quickly. The ocean is more like a large lake. The only reason you can't see the other side is because of the mist. The shoreline is quite steep in some places.

I saw a place last time where the ice cliffs are sheer and blocks of ice continuously fall into the ocean. I had hoped to see it again to take some pictures—something I neglected to do last time—but when I ask, Jorak says something about the direction of the wind that he has trouble expressing in words I can understand.

Oh, well. I have enough time to arrange another trip.

We cross a gentler, sloping shoreline and fly over the ice. The balloon has a capsule for the comfort of the passengers, but I need to bring out my winter gear because it gets cold really fast. The balloons compensate for the freezing temperatures by taking on more helium, which the handler has to trick the animals into releasing by tickling them. The resulting farts are something to behold. The animals don't like it, and they become skittish and fly fast. Really fast.

Eventually we come to the point where sunlight no longer hits the ice plain.

The balloons descend to the ice—under protest—and Jorak bids me to be quick because he is not sure how long he can keep the creatures under control. It's much colder here than higher in the atmosphere, and since balloons live off algae that grow in the clouds, there is nothing for them to eat.

It's bitterly cold out here, and dark, but I am prepared and have my instruments ready. I take pictures and measurements and scans. I watch the screen of my PCD as the telescope dumps its data. We're at the right spot—and still the stars are not entirely where I expect them to be. I ball my fist and shake my gloved hand at the sky. Yes!

Jorak gives me a puzzled look.

* * *

On the way back, I work on my data. I calculate and recalculate, and with each round of checking I become more certain.

Back in Cloud City, I book the small lecture theatre in the library. The locals are going to want to hear this.

At Mellivar, any official speech is a major event, especially when given by someone from outside. The lecture theatre is a room with high ceilings and stately fittings. Seating for the audience comprises many tiers of cushioned benches. The citizens file in, men in long leather coats, women in frilly dresses with petticoats and long sleeves. Most of them wear or carry goggles that keep the balloon piss out of one's eyes.

They give me strange looks. I'm wearing my Solaris Agency uniform, sturdy pants and short jacket made from moisture-resistant material. It looks positively futuristic compared to their attire.

On the far wall hangs a large painting of a space ship on the ice. It's far more elegant than any existing ship. I know that with that design, it could never fly, let alone land safely on the surface of Mellivar. The long shadows that fall over the ice suggest that it's close to the terminator. A group of twenty or so people stand next to the ship. They've made a fire and have put up some huts.

The legend of the Starship *Poseidon*. It vanished about three hundred standard years ago, somewhere in this area. The people of Mellivar believe that the ship developed trouble, landed on their world and that they are descended from the passengers. That is what the scene depicts.

But the real *Poseidon* was far too big a ship to land on a world, and any contact between the ship and the ice planet would not have had a happy ending. The *Poseidon* was a deep space vessel without surface landing capability. I've seen the images of the ship and am familiar with the design.

But the myth is an attractive one, taught to all children at Mellivar.

My project will give some real answers about what happened to the ship.

The hall's attendants shut the doors with many people still waiting to get in. The hall is full to overflowing. People are standing at the back and sitting on the steps.

I spot Farber Endovan and his councillors in the audience.

It is time for me to start.

I begin with the explanation that this talk is not in my capacity as auditor, but as student of the university at the Solaris Hub. I tell them that our navigation data of the outer worlds—of which Mellivar is certainly one—are often based on inaccurate measurements, simply because accuracy was not the first priority of the pioneers to this area.

Throughout its settled period, Mellivar has been called a tidally locked world, because it largely behaves as such. But my measurements show that Mellivar is not entirely tidally locked. Although very much in the process of becoming so, it currently has a day of about three hundred and fifty years long. It is why the shores of the ocean are always moving. It is why one shoreline is steep and the others more gentle, and it is also why, back in the time of the *Poseidon*, their instruments might have caused a crash, because the navigation for the system was calibrated based on the assumption of a tidally locked world. And if anyone thought that would not make a difference, Mellivar's moon is tidally locked to the planet, so the ship might well have encountered a moon where the onboard navigation said there wasn't one.

I'm not sure what sort of reaction I expect to get from my speech, but total apathy is not one. During the speech I've noticed that people are glancing at Farber Endovan, especially the councillors, and there are undercurrents and lots of hinting in the audience. Based on that, I expect a heated discussion.

The silence is disturbing.

Eventually, Farber Endovan gets up, bows to me and says, "Thank you, Auditor. Rest assured that the citizens of Mellivar have known this for some time."

And he sweeps out of the room to lukewarm applause.

I guess they did know it, although I'd seen no evidence for this. Still, the reaction is thoroughly odd.

When I leave the hall, people seem to positively avoid me.

At my room, I find that Jorak has obtained a partner.

* * *

My requests to return to the ocean rim and take pictures of the ice cliffs are denied. Well, not in so many words, but my request seems to fall into a black hole.

I can do nothing except the work I've come here to do. But the auditing of the accounts is simple and doesn't take much time—except for that pesky helium export question.

What should I do? The beamsweep is not due for another two weeks and, this far from the hub, its bandwidth is tiny. I want to send the agency the accounts and ask them for advice, but most of the space is prebooked and my allocation leaves me barely enough room to ask a simple question. Not only that—the encryption is nonexistent so everyone will be able to listen in. I might as well not bother.

Anyway, I'm pretty much confined to my room and the area immediately surrounding it.

I lean on the railing to the walkway outside, watching as ground dwellers bring in fish and produce from below, and a steady stream of balloons brings in barrels of what I presume to be helium. I ask Jorak where they harvest it, but he doesn't reply. I ask him if I can see the council to present my audit report, and the question disappears in the—by now—familiar black hole.

I write my thesis.

I sit on my bed, fiddling with the emergency beacon. I can't trigger it, not really, not until I'm physically restrained from boarding the shuttle that is still three weeks off. But I fear that if they are going to keep me here—although the fear seems irrational at times—I can't wait until the next shuttle, because someone will accidentally push me over the side.

Somehow, in some way, speaking about my discovery was stupid, and I just wish I knew why.

* * *

I'm asleep with the curtains drawn to shut out the eternal light when someone enters my room.

I sit up in shock. The intruder is a young man, and he holds his finger to his lips. He's a man unlike the usual citizens of the city. He wears sturdy leather clothing which bears signs of heavy use. His hair is long and tied in a ponytail, and his face and arms are bronzed.

He whispers, "Quick. The guards are gone."

I get out of bed, pull on clothes and the suit he tosses me. It's made of leather and waxed to keep out moisture. It also has a broad belt with metal hoops at the back.

He gestures. "Come."

He precedes me out of the door. It is only then that I see that he's wearing some kind of pack on his back with a harness. My suspicions are confirmed when he tells me to climb onto the walkway's railing.

"Come, quick," he says again.

He pulls a rope from his pack and threads it through the hoops at the back of my belt.

"Do I get a choice in this?" I ask him. I am not keen on heights.

"Not if you want to get out of here."

And with that, he vaults over the railing—and he pulls me down with him. We tumble and tumble on our way to the ocean below. The rush of air is deafening. The cold of it bites my skin.

A sharp jerk stops our fall. He's unfolded a parachute.

Slowly we drift down to the ocean, where a ship is making its way in our direction, sails billowing.

"What's going on?" I yell at him over the sound of the rushing air.

"We're going to meet my father," the young man says.

"Is he going to be able to help me?"

"To get out of here, yes."

We hit the water not much later. It's icy cold and soaks me through the leather suit.

The young man pulls in the parachute while the sailing boat approaches. Someone on board waves at us.

Not much later, a deckhand hauls us in. I lie, shivering, on the deck as the man pulls the leather suit off me and hands me a blanket.

"I didn't think I'd see you again," another man says.

I shouldn't be surprised that it is Clarys Markan. He looks well, strong and bronzed and dressed in the same utilitarian leather outfit as the young man.

I stammer a few words about being grateful, but I doubt they can understand them, because I'm so cold.

"We'll go straight home, and talk there," Clarys says.

Home turns out to be an agricultural village floating on a giant platform. There are about ten or so dwellings, surrounded by large floating fields of green.

A boy rushes to catch the rope the deckhand throws to the jetty. He ties the boat up and helps the deckhand unload boxes of fish that Clarys has evidently caught.

I stumble onto the shore, my legs stiff from the cold.

Clarys shows me the way to his home, a modest two-room house where a gas burner spreads welcome warmth.

"You're lucky," he says, when we sit at the table, clutching warm cups of tea. "Lucky that my son's friends had a fish delivery due and he could slip in as a crew member."

I look at the young man who sits at the end of the table. Yes, now that he mentions it, I do see similarities between the two.

"What's going on?" I ask.

Clarys starts his story. "You are right about the world not being tidally locked and the cause of the *Poseidon*'s disappearance. What is more, after some manoeuvres to avoid the moon, the ship took damage, either because they collided with unexpected asteroids or because too much strain damaged the ship, and they attempted to land or crashed on Mellivar."

"So the legend is right."

"That much of the legend is right. Everything else is wrong. The state of the wreckage shows that there is very little chance that anyone survived."

"Wait—state of the wreckage? You found it?" I'm thinking about the revolutionary engines.

"It's more like it found us, and to be honest it would have been better to have remained hidden."

I'm puzzled now.

He pours more tea and continues. "I suspected that the planet is not tidally locked long ago, but we lived in Cloud City, where that sort of thing doesn't matter. But the constantly moving ocean and the constant breaking up of the ice shelf on one side of the ocean reveals unexpected secrets."

I think I understand. "The wreckage came out of the ice?"

He nods. "The first thing we knew about it was when a fisherman brought us the body of a woman."

"You were still administrator then?"

"Yes. The young man said he'd found her floating in the water and thought she must have fallen off the platform. But I took one look at the body—wearing a full vacuum protection suit and helmet—and I knew that this was a very old corpse. The young man said he had taken her to Cloud City where he could perhaps sell her suit or get a reward for finding a missing person. But the badge on her suit said *Poseidon*. I was astonished and needed time to prepare a reaction. I'm sure that you're aware of the origin story that all children in Cloud City are told. This was going to upset a lot of people."

He sips from his tea. "Overnight, the badge disappeared off her clothes. I was left with no proof. And what was more, a couple of influential people were saying that the young man who brought the body must have murdered her. I told them that it was a ridiculous proposition, and then I found that my support in the council fell away. They said that if people in Solaris found out that the *Poseidon* had been found, we would be overrun with people from outside, and control of the city, and of the origin story and the way of life on Mellivar, would be taken away from us. I said that the Solaris Hub could easily withdraw funds, and they said that we don't need much anyway, just to buy a few things from Artemis, like some medicines, and we could easily make that money by selling helium to them. And the next thing, they're threatening me. So I came here with my son." He gestures at the young man who had no doubt listened to this story many times.

All of a sudden everything makes sense to me. The Cloud City council is trying to protect their way of life and protect the myth that they have told their citizens from the moment they were old enough to hear it.

They live by the myth, but they don't want to know the facts associated with the ship. And by giving that talk, I put my foot right into it.

Then a boy runs in, speaking a rapid dialect that I can't follow. Clarys gets up from the table and pulls on a jacket. He tosses me one as well. "Come."

"Where are we going?" I ask him, while running to keep up with him over the floating walkway. For his age, he is surprisingly fit.

"The boy says a group of balloons have left Cloud City. We must protect the wreckage, because they will try to destroy it."

On a platform at the edge of the village sits a flyer. It's an old, beaten-up model that went out of fashion over ten years ago.

We're going in that thing?

Clarys must see my incredulous reaction. "I know it doesn't look much, but it works."

I notice that it has been modified with skis so it can land on snow and water.

And we are indeed getting in. Clarys opens the door. There are four seats. Clarys' son gets in the back, leaving me to sit next to the pilot's seat. Oh, joy.

The thing is noisy as hell.

While we rise over the misty water, I wonder what one flyer can do against an army of balloons. I wonder if it is my fight to fight. Certainly, the wrongful punishment of people for crimes they didn't commit is wrong, but will the Solaris Hub appreciate information about the *Poseidon* more than the people at Mellivar appreciate their quiet way of life? Because the discovery *will* bring a lot of people here, that part is true.

* * *

We can see the army of balloons long before we reach the ice cliffs. There are more than a dozen, and they carry between them something black in a box.

We wonder what it is.

"Do they have weapons?" I ask.

"Other than knives and pellet guns, no."

Yet the thing dangling up there looks ominous.

We fly underneath them to have a look, but something clangs off the top of the flyer. They're throwing objects at us.

We reach the ice cliff first. I can see the remains of the ship from a distance.

"Even more of it has come out since last time," Clarys says.

The wreckage is huge, warped and twisted. Metal bent in all kinds of ways you would never think metal could bend. I agree, not many people would have made it alive out of that twisted, melted, charred heap of junk. It's a wonder that the dead woman's body survived at all.

I take pictures from all angles.

The flyer glides back and forth over the water to get the best view.

Then Clarys' son says, "Dad, watch it."

I look out the side window. The balloons are here.

Clarys' son opens a sliding door in the roof of the cabin. Ice-cold air streams in. He climbs on the seat and, leaning against the rim of the hatch, balances himself. He carries a plasma gun, the old-fashioned model that the Solaris troops no longer use because it "overcharges the target," meaning it causes far more destruction than necessary. He turns it on and fires at the balloons—once, twice. He's a decent shot. When stricken, the creatures deflate with a soulful whine while tumbling aimlessly into the freezing water below. If the cabins are not on fire, they sink quickly.

I feel sick. I want to tell Clarys to put down and rescue the people flailing in the water, I want to tell him to stop this. No legend or ancient artefact is worth this much death. Surely an agreement about the wreckage can be worked out in favour of the citizens of Mellivar?

Clarys' son fires and fires, stopping only to reload the weapon. Each time a balloon goes down, he gives a whoop of triumph.

Then there is one balloon left. It hovers over the cliff, struggling to stay up while carrying the black thing by itself. It swings back and forth.

Clarys' son aims.

I tell him, "Stop, enough! They've learned their lesson." Whatever lesson there was to learn.

Clarys says, "They never showed us any compassion. They pushed me out based on lies, they killed a man for a murder he didn't commit, and they were going to kill you for speaking the truth. I have no mercy."

His son fires. A hot bream sizzles through the air, hitting the balloon. The poor thing explodes.

Clarys' son whoops. "We got all the bastards."

Clarys balls his fist.

But the black thing is falling, and falling.

As it comes closer, Clarys gasps. "It's a gas tank."

His son shouts, "Get out of here, Dad! Get out!"

Clarys pushes the throttle of the engine right back. The flyer jerks forward, skimming over the water. It pulls up sharply, narrowly missing the cliff face.

A giant explosion rocks the air. Slowly, as in slow motion, the entire side of the cliff starts to crumble. Chunks of ice tumble down faster and faster. The full wreckage of the ship is exposed. I keep taking pictures as much as I can while being pushed in my seat as the flyer climbs.

Then the giant, twisted shape breaks loose from the ice and slides into the water. Waves lash at the bottom of the cliffs, breaking off avalanches of ice. The sea churns.

Then the water calms. There is no evidence that the ship was ever there.

"We lost it," Clarys says. His voice sounds dejected.

"I've got evidence," I say.

The Solaris Agency will have plenty of equipment to retrieve the ship. The ocean under the ice is deep, but there are many ways to go down there.

He shakes his head. "There is no point now, because Farber Endovan will deny entry to anyone who comes to investigate. We lost."

* * *

Later, in his hut, I finally activate the emergency beacon. I can't go back up to Cloud City and there is no way to get off the planet from down here.

I end up writing two reports. One is for the Agency to investigate the recent murder. An investigator will probably conclude that the council has no provable fault, since they've destroyed all the evidence that this woman—and her ship—ever existed.

The second report includes all my footage of the wreckage.

I don't know what to do. I have the only evidence that the *Poseidon* was found, and I'm the only one from outside Mellivar who knows where it is. On one hand, the world deserves to know; on the other, how many more lives will need to be destroyed over this?

I watch Clarys and his son get on with their lives. They catch fish, they grow crops on the platforms, they sail the ocean. And they watch the skies for an inevitable retaliation.

Help is despatched from Artemis and arrives a few days later. The shuttle is small, and comes directly to the agricultural island. As I watch Mellivar recede in the viewport of the shuttle, I weigh all the options.

Now that I'm back in familiar comfort and technology, I can't imagine that the people down there want to keep living their primitive, restrictive lives. The adults, maybe, but I think of the children. They deserve the truth. They deserve to be part of humanity.

I press *send* on the second report.

ABOUT PATTY JANSEN

Patty Jansen lives in Sydney, Australia. After having worked as a research scientist and non-fiction bookseller, she decided to try her hand at fiction.

She is most known for her Ambassador series (space opera thriller) and Icefire and Moonfire Trilogies (dark fantasy), although she also writes historical fantasy and hard science fiction.

She has written short stories for genre magazines, such as *Analog Science Fiction and Fact.* "This Deceitful State of Truth" is a second story in the Solaris Agency world. The first story, "This Peaceful State of War," won the Writers Of The Future contest in 2010.

You can find out more about Patty on her website: http://pattyjansen.com.

AFTERWORD

I think in today's age of technology, people tend to accidentally take books and shows and all manner of storytelling for granted. Collecting this many stories from so many great authors is incredibly difficult, so here at the end, I'd like to thank everyone who had a part in crafting Bridge Across the Stars.

First, my co-founders of Sci-Fi Bridge: Jason Anspach, Chris Pourteau, and I had an idea about a year ago to create a web service completely focused on Science Fiction. We wanted to do something that would set us apart from other, similar endeavors aimed at marketing Sci-Fi stories to readers. Our goals were twofold: to offer free promotions to independent and traditionally published authors like ourselves (so we wouldn't have to depend on a paid service to shill our works for us) and, secondly, to offer readers a great opportunity to find new favorite authors who write innovative, though-provoking Sci-Fi stories. The undertaking has gone better than we ever could have expected. I still remember the first email we got from a subscriber saying how much they appreciate our suggestions and promotions. It's an incredible feeling (and responsibility) to know there's a group of readers looking to us for reading recommendations.

I have to give a special shout out to Chris Pourteau, however, for editing a ton of the collection. Without him serving as my co-pilot, this whole thing would be a mess. I'd also like to thank Steve Beaulieu for not only submitting a story to this, but also helping to design the front cover (using the amazing art provided by Elias Stern) and for beautifully formatting the entire book for production.

I want to thank all the other authors for working with us on this: Daniel Arenson, Lucas Bale, Maya K. Bohnhoff, David Bruns, Lindsay Buroker, Ann Christy, Chris Dietzel, Patty Jansen, Will McIntosh, Craig Martelle, Josi Russell, Felix R. Savage, and David VanDyke. They went above and beyond to deliver great stories as quickly as they possibly could. I'd especially like to thank Kevin J Anderson for writing a truly wonderful Foreword. It was immensely satisfying (and truly humbling) to have an author of his stature getting behind our little collection.

We also appreciate our advance-review copy (ARC) readers, who took on the responsibility of reading the anthology (under a tight deadline) and helped us launch with enough reviews to make a splash. Without them, we'd just be one more lonely e-book drowning in the crowded sea that is today's publishing marketplace. I'd especially like to thank Debby Stapleton, our warp-speed ARC reader, who proofed the collection for us.

And last—but certainly not least—thank you, dear reader, for spending your time reading the stories in this collection. Few things are as precious a gift as another person's time, and we at Sci-Fi Bridge appreciate your sharing yours with us. We hope you enjoyed the stories. Could we ask you for one small favor before you go?

Reviews are a key factor in promoting a work's visibility—to other readers, of course, but also to critics and booksellers, who use reviews to determine, for example, what books to feature in promotions. As our readers, you're both our market and our marketing force. So please, if you have a few moments, review this collection at the venue where you purchased it (as well as on Goodreads if you're a member).

Thank you again for reading *Bridge Across the Stars*. We'll see you again for Volume 2!

Rhett C. Bruno
Author, Editor, and Co-Producer
Bridge Across the Stars

THANKS FOR READING

CPSIA information can be obtained
at www.ICGtesting.com
Printed in the USA
LVHW041519220219
608472LV00013B/546/P